本书是国家社科基金项目"二十世纪非裔美国文学中的种族政治研究"（14BWW073）的阶段性成果和浙江省哲学社会科学基金项目"美国黑人作家作品中体现的多种族文化民主理念研究"（11JCWY19YB）的结题成果

族裔 文学与文化研究系列丛书

莫里森小说中的创伤与身份建构

李美芹
姜志强 著

浙江工商大學出版社 | 杭州
ZHEJIANG GONGSHANG UNIVERSITY PRESS

图书在版编目（CIP）数据

莫里森小说中的创伤与身份建构 ＝ Trauma and
Identity Construction in Toni Morrison's Novels：
英文 / 李美芹，姜志强著． — 杭州：浙江工商大学出
版社，2019.4
　　ISBN 978-7-5178-2514-2

　　Ⅰ．①莫… Ⅱ．①李… ②姜… Ⅲ．①托妮·莫里森
—小说研究—英文 Ⅳ．① I712.074

中国版本图书馆 CIP 数据核字（2017）第 307738 号

莫里森小说中的创伤与身份建构
MOLISEN XIAOSHUOZHONG DE CHUANGSHANG YU SHENFEN JIANGOU

李美芹　姜志强 著

责任编辑	王　英	
封面设计	林朦朦	
责任印制	包建辉	
出版发行	浙江工商大学出版社	
	（杭州市教工路 198 号　邮政编码 310012）	
	（E-mail：zjgsupress@163.com）	
	（网址：http://www.zjgsupress.com）	
	电话：0571-88904980，88831806（传真）	
排　　版	庆春籍研室	
印　　刷	杭州高腾印务有限公司	
开　　本	710mm×1000mm　1/16	
印　　张	16.25	
字　　数	285 千	
版 印 次	2019 年 4 月第 1 版　2019 年 4 月第 1 次印刷	
书　　号	ISBN 978-7-5178-2514-2	
定　　价	50.00 元	

心怀桃花源，放歌沧桑间

  喜欢莫里森，也喜欢评论莫里森的作品。不仅因为她是获诺贝尔文学奖后仍笔耕不辍的黑人女作家，还因为她所描写的生命中的厚重感。在她的笔下，生命或是一株压抑了生命活力的金盏花（《最蓝的眼睛》），或是一场精神顿悟的认祖苦旅（《所罗门之歌》），或是一树花开（《宠儿》）……这些生命或安静或热烈，或卑微或璀璨，或跃动或沉思……经年过往，生命的年轮或深或浅，仿佛刻着一笺烟雨，半帘幽梦。

  凡尘喧嚣，莫里森笔下的非裔美国人，更是在累日灵魂的挣扎中寻找着适合自己的地方，用来安放灵魂。他们需要的也许是一座安静的灵魂宅院（在莫里森大多数作品中，似乎实现了这一愿望），也许是一本无字经书，也许是一条迷津尽开的小路，心之所往的尽头，是可供心灵休憩的驿站。再次起程时，没有了迷惘，更没有了彷徨……

  沧桑阡陌中，没有人改变得了纵横交错的奴隶制和种族歧视的曾经。只是，在渐行渐远的回望里，那些伤过的、痛过的、失落过的、挣扎过的、哭泣过的，都演绎成了坚强；那些无法遗忘的、刻骨铭心的、耿耿于怀的、念念不忘的，都风干成了风景。于是，莫里森小说中的人物，一路放歌，一路纵情，一路相互扶持，一路相互伤害，山一程，水一程，趟过红尘、沧桑、流年、清欢，站在岁月之巅放眼，躺在心灵谷底放牧。回望时，月光如流，蹉跎芳华者有之，奋起抗争者有之，狂野嚎哭者有之……愈是艰难处，愈是修心时。经年流转，踏浪生活之洋，云帆尽头，回眸处，斑斑点点，是愈合的疤痕，还有透过枝叶的明媚。

在莫里森的笔端，流露着沧桑经年中的期盼：怒放的生命需要微笑的理由。生命是一场负重修行，但心灵需要减压；即使雪压青松，也要给自己寻找一种取暖的方式。以夸父的执念求索，以女娲的姿态重塑生命，以普罗米修斯的胸怀盗火，以浮士德的决绝告别庸碌，向往美好……沧海巫山过后，峰回路转处，或许，最美的风景都在路上。

心若浮沉，浅笑安然。童年的疤痕，可以有一生那么长，也可以心怀桃花源，放歌沧桑间！

感谢国家社科基金和浙江省哲学社会科学基金的立项，使我有勇气在书山电脑前拨开思维的迷雾，坚持着自己的求索。感谢浙江工商大学外国语学院领导和同事们的激励，使我有信心砥砺前行。感谢姜志强教授的宽容和携手，使我有恒心以梦为马，虽韶华不再，却不敢负少女初心；而且他亲力亲为，为全书谋篇布局，并撰写了第四章关于黑人文化意识构建和文化杂糅的部分内容。感谢我的双胞胎儿女给我的生命带来的丰盈和美好，他们懂感恩，肯奋发，使本就为母则强的我获得了更强大的慰藉，切身体会到"在爱你当中，我遇到了最好的自己；在爱你当中，我的生命成了恢弘的庙宇"。感谢我生命中的摆渡人，他们默默的支持是我奋发前行的精神支柱，也助我开启了思维的点点曦光。成稿后的审校和协调过程中，浙江工商大学出版社的编辑王英女士做了大量有效工作。在此，作者表示衷心感谢！

李美芹

2018 年 9 月于杭州金沙学府

Contents

Introduction

Toni Morrison, one of the foremost writers in American history, editor, and professor, the first African American Nobel Prize laureate in literature, is considered one of the foremost figures in contemporary American fiction. The prize marks "not only a personal triumph, but also the recognition of the artistry of African American fiction and the validity of the black woman's voice" (Taylor-Guthrie, 1994: vii). She made her debut as a novelist in 1970, soon gaining the attention of both critics and a wider audience for her inventive blend of realism and fantasy, unsparing social analysis, passionate philosophical concerns and her poetically-charged and richly-expressive depiction of Black America. Up to now, Morrison has published eleven novels, two plays, a short story, a collection of critical essays, and several edited volumes.[1] The combination of social observation with broadening and

---

[1] The eleven novels mentioned here are *The Bluest Eye* (1970), *Sula* (1973), *Song of Solomon* (1977), *Tar Baby* (1981), *Beloved* (1987), *Jazz* (1992), *Paradise* (1997), *Love* (2003) , *A Mercy* (2008), *Home* (2012) and *God Help the Child* (2015). Morrison's only short story is *Recitatif* (1983). Other influential works and edited books include two plays—*Dreaming Emmett* (performed in 1986) and *Desdemona* (first performed on 15 May 2011 in Vienna), Children's literature (with her son Slade Morrison)—*The Big Box* (1999), *The Book of Mean People* (2002), *Peeny Butter Fudge* (2009), A libretti—*Margaret Garner* (first performed in May 2005); An important critical work—*Playing in the Dark: Whiteness and the Literary Imagination* (1992); Nonfiction—*Remember: The Journey to School Integration* (April 2004), *What Moves at the Margin: Selected Nonfiction* (edited by Carolyn C. Denard, April 2008). In addition, Morrison edited *The Black Book* (1974), *Re-raciing Justice, En-gendering Power: Essays on Anita Hill, Clarence Thomas, and the Construction of Social Reality* (1992), *Birth of a Nation'hood: Gaze, Script, and Spectacle in the O. J. Simpson Case* (co-editor) (1997), *Burn This Book: Essay Anthology* (2009).

allusive commentary gives her fictions the symbolic quality of myth, and earns her a number of literary distinctions.[1] In 1993, Morrison was honored with the Nobel Prize in Literature for her giving "life to an essential aspect of American reality" in novels "characterized by visionary force and poetic import" (Frangsmyr: 135). Nevertheless, the most important contribution Morrison makes for American and world literature, as is maintained by Tao Ming, is that "she has fictionalized—thus culturally carved out—a territory in which black people are not marginal anomalies but a genuine human society" (2002: 338–339). Morrison's novels have been translated into many languages, and a number of scholars and doctoral candidates over the world have criticized and assessed her works, seeking to "unravel the complexity that she prides on" (Samuels & Hudson-Weems, 1990: 142). Her success signals that African American literary canon will sooner or later come to the fore onto the stage of mainstream American and world literature, a development that will make it impossible for future exclusion.

The extent of the critical interest in Morrison's works, which is extraordinary by any standards, is wide and varied. Morrison's novels have invited a number of reviews, essays and book-length studies in different critical methodologies and from various perspectives since the 1970s: feminism, psychoanalysis, post-structuralism, post-modernism, reader-response criticism, post-colonialism and cultural approaches. However, it's difficult to talk about critical responses to her fiction without examining the nature of a black aesthetic and to African-American critical paradigms.

In the Black Aesthetic movement of the 1960s, sociopolitical African-American critical canon dominated African-American critical paradigm. Henry Louis Gates Jr. was among the first of a group of literary scholars to question the predominance of sociological approaches to black literature. In arguing for wider critical paradigms, which as he later said respected the literary text as "a rhetorical structure" with its own "complex set of rules," he unleashed a long-running and

---

[1] Morrison has received honorary degrees from Harvard, the University of Pennsylvania, Yale, Dartmouth, Sarah Lawrence, Spelman, and Oberlin, SUNY Albany and Princeton. *Sula* was nominated for the 1975 National Book Award and in 1978 *Song of Solomon* won the National Book Critics' Circle Award and Institutes of Arts and Letters. *Beloved* won the Anisfeld Wolf Book Award in Race Relations and the Melcher Book Award. It also received the 1988 Pulitzer Prize for fiction.

fierce series of debates, which tolled the knell of sociopolitical canon. Even so, the contested assumptions that black literature has a role in countering negative representations of black people and in promoting black consciousness inform much of the critical writing on Toni Morrison, emphasizing upon the White American cultural domination of African-American communities—arising, of course, from the priority given it in Morrison's *The Bluest Eye* and *Song of Solomon*. Though early in 1974, Barbara Smith discussed Morrison's use of "mascon images" in *Sula* in her essay entitled "Beautiful, Needed, Mysterious," and in 1975 Joan Bischoff read the novels *The Bluest Eye* and *Sula* as having a universal theme— the "thwarted sensitivity" of Pecola and Sula in her essay entitled "The Novels of Toni Morrison: Studies in Thwarted Sensitivity," an editorial in the 1977 summer issue of *First World* called attention to the fact that, despite public acclamation of Toni Morrison's novels, there was little scholarly or critical analysis of her works. In 1977, a criticism based on black culture began to emerge. More importantly, two writers for *First World*, Philip Royster and Odette C. Martin, laid down the groundwork for a criticism that positioned Morrison specifically as an African-American writer.[1] In the same year, a feminist reading of Morrison's novels also began to take shape. Barbara Smith proposed a mode she called "black feminist criticism." Though her reading of *Sula* as a black lesbian text gave rise to many controversies, her article led to a movement of black feminist criticism of Morrison's works and that of many other black writers in the following years. In the 1980s, there have been few attempts to apply a liberal humanist model to Toni Morrison's works or indeed to black literature in general. C. W. Bigsby offers the most interesting reading of African American literature from this perspective, finding in black writers a refreshing moral assuredness which white liberal American writers had rejected in favor of "cosmic conspiracies and fragmented layers of experience" (Peach, 2000: 9). Critics often concerned themselves with Morrison's use of mythic structure and the subject of female self-discovery in her novels. Most notably are Jacqueline de Weever, Cynthia Davis and Jane S. Bakerman.[2] There also appears

---

[1] Sandra Adell. *Literary Masters: Toni Morrison*. Detroit: Thomson Gale, 2002, pp. 113–115.

[2] De Weever. "The Inverted World of Toni Morrison's *The Bluest Eye* and *Sula*." *CLA Journal*, 1979 (22), pp. 402–414. Cynthia Davis. "Self, Society and Myth in Toni Morrison's Fiction." in Linden Peach ed. *Toni Morrison*. New York: St. Martin's Press, 1998, pp. 27–42. Jane S. Bakerman. "Failure of Love, Female Initiation in the Novels of Toni Morrison." *American Literature,* 1981(52), pp. 541–563.

the study of Morrison's novels focusing upon their language and how they are constructed, upon various methods of unlocking their multiple meanings, and upon how other texts impose meanings upon them. It employs a number of perspectives on language, meaning, narrative and history, which are normally placed under the general label of post-structuralism. Psychoanalytic perspectives on Morrison's fiction developed in the mid-1980s, but it is only more recently that critics have pursued their psychoanalytic criticism within a poststructuralist framework.[1] By the end of the 1980s, complex readings of Morrison's novels had begun to appear in a number of important black and ethnic studies venues—*Black American Literature Forum*, *CLA Journal*, *Black Scholar Minority Voices*. The glowing reception of *Song of Solomon* and *Tar Baby* encouraged further development in criticism including a variety of critical approaches.[2] In the 1990s, Marxist perspective found its voice in Morrison's fiction. Doreatha Mbalia traces Morrison's developing class consciousness in *Toni Morrison's Developing Class Consciousness*, discovering in Morrison's works Marxist principles such as humanism, collectivism and imperialism. Morrison has also been compared to Faulkner and Marquez in her use of stream of consciousness and magic realism (Wilentz, 1997: 109). The 1990s and the present century witness a number of the essays drawing on black feminist criticism and anthropological/cultural criticism in tandem with post-colonialism theory, the crux of which consists of seeing literary symbolism in the context of symbolic structures operating in society. Among them, Homi Bhabha expounded the post-colonial theory in *The Location of Culture* by citing examples from Morrison's fiction, while Houston Baker's argument that what Morrison "ultimately seeks in her coding of Afro-American place is a writing of intimate, systematizing, ordering black village values out of a woman's consciousness, a writing conscious always of black woman's self-possession" (1997: 136) echoes Morrison's own elaboration in her "City Limits, Village Values" and "What the Black Women Thinks About

---

[1] See Houston A. Baker, Jr.'s "Knowing Our Place: Psychoanalysis and *Sula*" and Jennifer Fitzgerald's "Selfhood and Community: Psychoanalysis and Discourse in *Beloved*," both in Linden Peach ed., *Toni Morrison*. Another important paper is Ashraf H. A. Rushdy's "'Rememory': Primal Scenes and Constructions in Toni Morrison's Novels," published on *Contemporary Literature* in 1991.

[2] Nancy J. Peterson. *Toni Morrison: Critical and Theoretical Approaches*. Baltimore and London: The Johns Hopkins University Press, 1997, pp. 5–6.

Women's Lib."[1]

As far as macroscopical perspectives are concerned, the published works on Morrison's fiction since the 1980s can be categorized into three perspectives. The first perspective is on Morrison and Womanism, the representatives of which are Babara Hill Rigney's *The Voices of Toni Morrison*, Aoi Mori's *Toni Morrison and Womanist Discourse*, and Michael Awkward's *Inspiriting Influences: Tradition, Revision and Afro-American Women's Novels*. The second perspective is on Morrison and Afro-American literary tradition, the representatives of which are Trudier Harris's *Fiction and Folklore: the Novels of Toni Morrison*, Denisee Heinze's *The Dillema of "Double Consciousness,"* and Philip Page's *Dangerous Freedom: Fusion and Fragmentation in Toni Morrison's Novels*. The third perspective is on Morrison and the white classic writers, which equals Morrison with such white writers as Christina Rossetti, Virginia Woolf, William Faulkner and James Joyce.[2] A number of doctoral candidates in the United States have based their doctoral dissertation on Toni Morrison's fiction. Roughly speaking, their critical focuses are similar to that of the critical works on Toni Morrison.

A distinct phenomenon deserving our notice is that although Morrison herself has not used any theoretical vocabulary in her reviews or essays about her works, most of her non-fictional works concern issues of colonization for African Americans. Early essays such as "What the Black Women Thinks About Women's Lib" and "Behind the Making of *The Black Book*" center on her belief in the importance of black resistance to internalizing white culture and instead, focusing on African American cultural values. Such a concern also appears in her later non-fiction, such as the essay "City Limits, Village Values," thereby indicating the issue of colonization as an on-going thread throughout her works.[3]

---

[1] Calling her work "village literature, fiction that is really for the village, for the tribe" (Thomas Leclair. "The Language Must Not Sweat." *New Republic*, 1981, p. 26.), she believes that good novels ought to "clarify the roles that have become obscured ... and they ought to give nourishment" (pp. 120–121).

[2] Jill Matus. *Toni Morrison*. Manchester and New York: Manchester University Press, 1998, pp. 145–153.

[3] "Behind the Making of *The Black Book*." *Black World*, 1974, pp. 86–90; "City Limits, Village Values: Concepts of Neighborhoods in Black Fiction," in Michael C. Jaye and Ann Chalmers Watts, ed., *Literature and the Urban Experience: Essays on the City and Literature*, New Brunswick: Rulgers UP, 1981, pp. 35–43; "What the Black Woman Thinks about Women's Lib," *New York Times Magazine*, 1971, pp. 14–15, 63–66.

Because she does not make literary concessions to white ignorance of African American language and tradition, Morrison has been accused of a sort of cultural exclusivism. Addressing such comments from white critics, Morrison declares: "I don't know why I should be asked to explain your life to you. We have splendid writers to do that, but I am not one of them. It is that business of being universal, a word hopelessly stripped of meaning for me … If I tried to write a universal novel, it would be water." (LeClair, 1981: 124) Morrison believes that truly good literature always has something meaningful to say about what it is to be human, whether speaking of whites or people of color, and suggests that critical demand for a "universal novel" is often merely a disguised request for literature written from a white point of view. Morrison notes that "[i]nsensitive white people cannot deal with black writing, but then they cannot deal with their own literature either" (Tate, 1989: 160). While the white world that surrounds Morrison's black characters is usually a symbol of violation and oppression, she "rarely depicts white characters, for the brutality here is less a single act than the systematic denial of the reality of black lives" (Davis, 1998: 323). Morrison's writing, then, is an ongoing attempt to reclaim the collective past of African Americans in order to allow the definition and maintenance of a personal and cultural identity.

One controversial aspect of Morrison's work has been her delineation of the heterogeneous nature of the African-American community and her exposure of the violence and sexual abuse which black women and black children have suffered at the hands of some black men, as Calvin Hernton concluded: "Variously she has been accused of 'selling out,' of turning back the clock of racial progress, of being a tool of white feminism, of being a black-man-hater, and of engendering sexual immorality among black women." (1990: 203–204) Some critics caustically counterattack Morrison for polarizing language itself into white discourse and silenced black speech. However, since the record of history under slavery was mostly written by non-slave writers, Morrison must re-write her own people's history. In doing so, it is crucial for her to trace the social and political oppression of African Americans to its origins in slavery. Moreover, her interest is not to accuse whites of enslaving African descendants but to recover the fragmented pieces of the black past. Thus, she does not polarize language but deliberately uses the polarized language of the racialized dominant culture in order to challenge its racist binary effects.

Studies on Morrison's novels from interdisciplinary perspective are few if there are any. Several critics have touched upon the relationship between Morrison's novels and music aesthetics. In "Recovering an Art Form," Aoi Mori argues that oral narrative including music is a matrix for conserving African-American culture. Those of Morrison's characters who are dispossessed of their own "art form" (1999: 89) as a creative outlet for their feelings simultaneously lack the knowledge of their identity and self-worth, while those who are capable of singing are also able to communicate effectively and to foster solidarity.

In addition to the follow-up studies of the earlier research perspectives, many new perspectives, such as narration, psychoanalysis, post-modernity, post-structuralism and post-colonialism, emerge gradually at the same time. Morrison's novels present their unique narrative features, so many researchers interpret them from the perspectives of narrative discourses, strategies, structures and so on. In *Fictions of Authority: Women Writers and Narrative Voice*, Susan S. Lanser puts forward a new narratology which will be "attentive to issues that conventional narratology has devaluated or ignored" (1992: 8). She thinks that conventional narratology has been too concerned with formal structures and has ignored the ideological implications of its narrative procedures. In this book, she defines "three varieties of narrative voice for her study: the authorial, the personal, and the communal" (Ginsburg, 1995: 69). In her opinion, it is these special narrative structures that narrate black women's unspeakable secrets.

There are also essays devoted to Morrison's jazzthetic strategies. Lars Eckstein analyzes Morrison's musicalization of *Beloved*'s words and jazzthetic techniques, and their functions in his "A Love Supreme: Jazzthetic Strategies in Toni Morrison's *Beloved*." Cheryl Hall in "Beyond the 'Literary Habit': Oral Tradition and Jazz in *Beloved*" also probes into the oral tradition and jazzthetic techniques in *Beloved*. In "Kinds of Blue: Toni Morrison, Hans Janowitz, and the Jazz Aesthetic," Jürgen E. Grandt argues that the aesthetic gesture in Morrison's novels is explicitly inventive, just as African American jazz has always been. Barbara Williams Lewis probes into the function of jazz in Morrison's fiction, especially in her novel *Jazz*, arguing that Morrison's stylistic approach is also jazzy, while Paula Gallant Eckard claims that jazz is the essential narrator of the novel *Jazz* in "The Interplay of Music, Language, and Narrative in Toni Morrison's *Jazz*." Many critics such as Anthony

J. Berret, Rinaldo Walcott and Nicholas F. Pici have pointed out Morrison's fiction is also jazzy on the level of language itself. However, to study systematically how Morrison's music aesthetics influence her motifs and her philosophy, or rather to say, how these qualities interact with one another to form her soul-liberating texts rests with this dissertation.

The study of Morrison abroad starts earlier than domestic study, so the research results are more fruitful and the research perspectives are more various. Compared with the study of Morrison abroad, China's Morrison study starts later and is not so good in research quality. It begins from late 1980s, there are many research results during the short development time. There are many repeated researches, especially in research perspectives and methods.

In China, the critical efforts paid to Morrison appear to be interestingly dramatic. Before she won the Nobel Prize for Literature, Chinese scholars paid little attention to her and her writings, and there were altogether only 7 articles criticizing directly her fiction in Chinese academic journals. After she won the Nobel Prize in October 1993, she has become more and more popular among Chinese scholars and media. The number of essays on Toni Morrison are increasing, most of which focus on the analysis of one single book of hers. Critical methodologies such as feminism, psychoanalysis, post-colonialism, eco-feminist and anthropological approach are employed to analyze her fiction from different perspectives. Domestic study of Morrison has reached two climaxes. The first one is after 1993 when Morrison was awarded the Nobel Prize for Literature; another is after the 21st century. In 1993, the winning of the Nobel Prize for Literature attracts numerous domestic scholars' attention to Morrison's works. Domestic Morrison study is still rising in recent years, the study of Morrison has become a significant study, and Morrison herself has become well known in academic circles. Du Zhiqing divides domestic Morrison study into two stages: " (1) The initial stage (from middle 1980s to 1993) … (2) The developmental and in-depth stage (after 1994)." [1] (2007: 122) At the initial stage, scholars pay more attention to the translation and introduction of Morrison's works, so the academic research results are limited. After 1993, the study of Morrison gives priority to academic researches. Research results at this stage include interviews of

---

[1] All the cited Chinese literature in this paper is translated by the author.

Morrison, introductions to Morrison's awards, discussions of themes of Morrison's works, and explorations of her narrative features. The study of Morrison's works can be roughly divided into the following two categories. The first category is the study of themes of Morrison's works. For example, in 1994, Wang Shouren wrote in *Foreign Literature Review* that "racial problem in America hasn't been resolved because people all avoid talking about the dark slavery history to some extent" (41). In the same year, Hu Quansheng proposes in *Contemporary Foreign Literature* that narrative structures and plot lines of novels advance the development of stories, and shows to readers the slavery experience's deep influence on the blacks after the collapse of the slavery. The second category is the study of artistic features, such as narrative features, structure features and magic realism features, in Morrison's works. For example, Li Guicang writes in *Journal of Northwest University* that "it's Morrison's innovative and unique writing techniques that deeply revealed the possibility of 'psychological reality'" (1994: 27). By the tentative analysis of narrative techniques in *Beloved*, Li discusses some narrative techniques to show that Morrison uses these techniques to represent a common theme in modern western literature—the absurdity and perplexity of people's living. All these research results have broadened the horizon of China's Morrison study, thus have promoted the development of China's Morrison research.

Since 1999, China's Morrison study continues to develop. This period is marked as the third period. It indicated that China's Morrison study is developing and maturing. The outstanding features of this period are plentiful research results, wide criticism perspectives and deep analysis. The first Morrison study monograph in China, *Gender, Race and Culture: Toni Morrison and the 20th Century Afro-American Literature*, was published in 1999. In this monograph, Wang Shouren and Wu Xinyun explore Morrison's writing thoughts and artistic features, and deeply analyze Morrison's first seven novels from the perspective of gender, race and culture. In 2004, they changed the title of this book to "Gender, Race and Culture: On Toni Morrison's Novel-Writing" and also added the analysis of Morrison's eighth novel *Love* in it. Thus this book becomes more comprehensive and more systematic, and has a milestone significance on China's Morrison study since it has illuminated other Chinese scholars and induced their interest.

Later, Chinese scholars have published more than 20 monographs relating to Morrison study. In 2004, Hu Xiaoying wrote the first book in domestic which concentrates on Morrison's single novel *Beloved*, and titled it as "Unforgettable Stories: On the Art World of Toni Morrison's Beloved." Based on the narrative theory of French literary theorist Gerard Genette, Hu analyzes *Beloved* from the perspective of narrative discourse. Through the study of narrative discourse, indirect narrative discourse and dramatized narrative discourse in *Beloved*, Hu finds that Morrison's handling of narrative discourse is quite ingenious. The varied narrative discourses expand and deepen the theme of this novel. In the same year, Zhu Rongjie published *Pain and Healing: A Study of Maternal Love in Toni Morrison's Fiction* which elaborates the special meaning that Morrison endows to maternal love by using feminism and post-colonialism theories. This is the first English monograph in China. Zhu points out that Morrison resists the hegemony of mainstream culture, gender discrimination and class oppression within a race through the reconstruction of black women's history and culture. Some other monographs discuss themes and narrative techniques in Morrison's novels from different perspectives such as feminist, spatial politics, psychoanalysis and trauma theory. For example, Zhao Lihua's *Spatial Politics: On Toni Morrison's Novels* (2011), Hu Ni's *On the Study of Spatial Narrative in Toni Morrison's Novels* (2012), Tian Yaman's *A Collage of Black Glass: A Study of Morrison's Novels Under the Perspective of Freud's Psychoanalysis Theory* (2012), Xiu Shuxin's *A Study of Toni Morrison's Novels from the Perspective of Ethical Literary Criticism* (2015). Although these works have different research perspectives, they still have a big gap in both quantity and quality if compared them with Morrison study abroad. This phenomenon is mainly due to the fact that scholars in China only focus on the interpretation of Morrison's works, but ignore the research of Morrison's literary thoughts. Till now, comparative study between Morrison's works and other writers' is still a blank. This shows that Morrison study is still worth to further explore. The year 2007 has witnessed altogether five articles talking respectively about Morrison's music aesthetics in *The Bluest Eye*, *Beloved*, and *Jazz*,[1] while before

---

[1] The five articles are "On the Esthetic Beauty in *Beloved*: Musical Language" by Li Min, "Singing Out the Miseries: The Blues Characteristics in *The Bluest Eye*" by Meng Ping, "The Blues Aesthetics in Toni Morrison's Novel *The Bluest Eye*" by Du Xiaohui, "Playing the Melody in the Deep Heart: On the musical Narratives in Toni Morrison's Fiction" by Ha Xuxian, and "Playing Literary Jazz: on Toni Morrison's *Jazz*" by Zhang Qingfang.

this year, few scholars in China have paid any attention to the music aesthetics in Toni Morrison's fiction.

Trauma theory originated from 1990s in America to seek for detailed interpretation to cultural and ethical connotations of trauma. It is widely applied in the interpretation of literary texts centered on the themes of wars, Jewish literature, minority women literature and so on. The study of Toni Morrison in the light of trauma becomes a hot issue in literary studies in recent years.

The study of Morrison's works from the perspective of trauma started at the beginning of the 21st century. The most iconic work is *Quiet as It's Kept: Shame, Trauma, and Race in the Novels of Toni Morrison* written by J. Brooks Bouson in 2000. This book is the pioneer one to interpret Morrison's seven novels under trauma theory. However, its "potential contribution to new scholarship on Toni Morrison remains limited" (Cutter, 2001: 671). Although it provides an important reference for the following trauma studies, Bouson gives more emphasis on analyzing embodiment and causes of African-Americans' race shame instead of applying trauma theory in her analysis. Like Cutter criticizes in her review,

> Critics such as Claudia Tate and Jean Wyatt have successfully employed psychoanalytic and psychological approaches to African American texts in ways that open up new avenues of inquiry. But Bouson's methodology seems to allow her to repeat—with some degree of elaboration but little innovation—what many other critics have said previously. (2001: 671)

Although Bouson proposes that making white men ashamed is an important way to help black men avoid self-ashamed when she interprets *The Bluest Eye* and *Beloved*, her point is not comprehensive enough. If she pays more attention to the analysis of how black men get rid of shame and heal their trauma, instead of repeatedly interpreting the embodiment of shame in each novel and emphasizing each character's feeling of shame, her book will be more valuable for the further study of Toni Morrison and her novels.

Another book which also interprets Morrison's works from the perspective of trauma was Evelyn Jaffe Schreiber's *Race, Trauma, and Home in the Novels of Toni Morrison* published in 2010. In this book, Schreiber "examines all the novels with a clear and focused textual analysis joined together with insights drawn from the disciplines of psychoanalysis and neurocognitive science" (2010: 469). By using Lacan's mirror theory, attachment theory and psychoanalysis theory, she analyzes the relationship among trauma, memory and the construction of individual's subject identity, and the important role a home plays in black men's construction of subject identity and trauma healing. In Schreiber's opinion, home is a physical place which could provide living space for black men from generation to generation. What's more, it is also a mental place which could relieve and cure black men from the trauma of the slavery. This book is a successful work which concretely interprets the theme of trauma in Morrison's novels. However, it has some defects at the same time. For example, Schreiber analyzes the slavery history's traumatic influences on black men in different times. Her research only focuses on this single perspective, so it is not comprehensive enough.

Besides these books, there are several doctoral theses about trauma study in Morrison's novels, such as *Literary Witnessing: Working Through Trauma in Toni Morrison, Nuruddin Farah, Wilson Harris, and Chang-Rae Lee* (2005) written by Matthew L. Miller and *The Things We Carry: Trauma and the Aesthetic in the Contemporary United States Novel* (2005) written by Kathleen L. Macarthur. Those doctoral theses put Morrison's fifth novel *Beloved* and some other kinds of literature, such as post-modern literature, post-colonial literature, African-American literature, ethnic American literature, together to do some comparative studies around the theme of trauma. Obviously, they haven't emphasized on the discussion of trauma in Morrison's novels. All studies are concentrated on the slavery trauma in one novel *Beloved*, but Morrison's traumatic writing features are not presented well.

In recent years, there are several doctoral dissertations which have paid their attention to *Paradise, Sula, A Mercy, Song of Solomon* and *The Bluest Eye*. However, these researches just make some comparisons between Morrison's novels and other writers' to analyze cultural trauma, incest trauma between father and daughter, and traumatic realism. In 2009, Kristy A. Bryant-Berg analyzes cultural trauma and traumatic realism by comparing the novels of Toni Morrison and Louise Erdrich. Her analysis of Morrison's and Erdrich's narratives of cultural trauma reveals "the complex intersections between communal trauma and personal trauma," "historical trauma and trans-historical trauma," "the cyclical nature of collective trauma," as well as "evidence that the continuing consequences of colonization like chronic poverty, cultural dislocation and racism are forms of trauma" (Bryant-Berg, 2009: iv). In her opinion, it is the persistence of the pressure and inequality from racism society that made people unable to get rid of the shadow of trauma. This opinion denies the possibility that one can recover from individual trauma. Although the blacks' racial trauma cannot be cured in a short time, individual trauma can be cured through treatment.

In Christine Grogan's doctoral dissertation, she addresses "literary representations of father-daughter incest and the complex trauma associated with it" (2011: iii). She shows how six works of modern American literature, including Morrison's *The Bluest Eye*, "compel us to confront the traumatogenic nature of social oppression, especially that which is endemic to the structure of the heteropatriarchal family and American racism and classism" (iii). Grogan analyzes in very great detail the trauma of father-daughter incest by using feminism and trauma theory. However, she only discusses the trauma to female caused by incest, but ignores the analysis of other aspects of female trauma and how to cure female trauma. What's more, using narrative theory to analyze how Morrison switches her narrative perspectives to show trauma stories is a way to interpret trauma in Morrison's works. Her research only involves one aspect of women's individual trauma; it hasn't summarized the root causes, different symptoms and treatments of female trauma.

These doctoral dissertations which interpret the theme of trauma in Morrison's novels from different perspectives enriched the results of trauma study in Morrison's works. However, these dissertations only interpret one or two of Morrison's works in a comparative way. They are not systematic enough to interpret Morrison's overall writing features of trauma, or to summarize the characteristics of black women's individual trauma and collective trauma. In addition, these studies' research perspectives are limited. Most of them pay attention to the slavery trauma in *Beloved* while some of them analyze the blacks' collective trauma from the perspective of racism. Compared with these doctoral dissertations, papers published in academic journals have more research perspectives and innovative views.

For instance, Florian Bast puts forward an idea that Morrison uses "red" as a metaphor to show the slavery trauma in *Beloved*. He proposes that " 'red' symbolizes slavery and concepts associated with it, such as racist violence after the Civil War. This is evident in the fact that the color appears when characters face their memories of slavery and the horrific wounds it has caused them" (Bast, 2011: 1071). In his opinion, "red" not only has a very close relationship with trauma, but also reflects the deep influence of trauma on the characters. First of all, "red" arouses the characters' traumatic memories and makes them silent. Secondly, "red" is internalized by the characters to show their inner depression caused by trauma. In the novel, "red" appears as some specific items, such as blood and comb, as well as metaphor images to symbolize the terrible influence of slavery. Therefore, he believes that "red" highlights and strengthens the effects of the blacks' trauma caused by slavery in *Beloved*. Bast extends from the using of "red" to the theme of trauma in the whole novel; his unique opinion and careful analysis have great academic value in Morrison study.

Study of Morrison's works from the perspective of trauma has been not since the 21st century. Although there are a number of research results, the breadth and depth of these researches still remain to be expanded. Firstly, a lot of studies discuss trauma from a single perspective of racism. Secondly, most studies concentrate on the slavery trauma in *Beloved*. In addition, the study of individual trauma and how to recover from trauma is obviously insufficient because only a few papers mention these themes. Therefore, there still has a great space as well as important academic value to comprehensively and systematically interpret Morrison's works from the perspective of trauma.

In recent years, there appears a small amount of papers in China which interpret Morrison's works by using trauma theory, but the research range is narrow. The earliest relative study is Chen Jie's "The Aftermath of Slavery System and the Healing of Historical Trauma: A Brief Analysis of *Beloved* by Toni Morrison" (2004). In Chen's opinion, what Morrison wants to express in *Beloved* is that "the black people are able to get rid of the influence of the slavery system and heroically stride toward a new life, and that realization of all these depend on the joint effort of the blacks themselves" (2004: 106). Although "the healing of historical trauma" is used in the title, Chen actually doesn't pay her attention to explore trauma issues in the novel. What she does in the paper is discussing the ways the blacks get rid of the oppression of racism by revealing the impacts of slavery on individuals, families and the black community. In fact, this paper is a study of racism instead of trauma in *Beloved*.

Zhao Qingling (2008) discusses collective trauma and female traumatic experiences reflected in both *Beloved* and *Paradise* in her thesis. In her opinion, what brings trauma to the blacks in *Paradise* is the historical memory which is repeatedly emphasized from generation to generation. Black men carry the trauma of collective memory, while black women have no rights to speak. Zhao notes that female characters in *Beloved* carry enormous individual trauma, but she turns her attention to the function of narrative techniques in revealing trauma in this part; it seems somewhat stray from the point.

With reference to Chinese classical literature, Chen Ping's thesis "Traumatic Feeling, Historical Narrative and Lyrical Representation: A New Interpretation of Toni Morrison's *Beloved*" discusses "the novel's traumatic theme (content) and 'poetic-picturesque text' (form)" (2010: 104) in *Beloved* based on trauma theory. He points out that Morrison employs "'poetic-picturesque text' to fully express the traumatic experiences and feelings of fictional characters in specific historical circumstances" (104) and analyzes the relationships between the expression of traumatic theme and black music, stream of consciousness, modernist writing patterns and application of colors in the novel. He pays much attention to the analysis of the artistic features of the novel. This kind of analysis is distinctive in the traumatic study of Morrison's works.

In "The Unbearable Agony in Life: A Study of the Black Transgenerational Trauma in Toni Morrison's Novel *Beloved*," Huang Lijuan and Tao Jiajun analyze "the traumatic agony caused by maternal love, heterosexual love and sisterly love" (2011: 100) in *Beloved* from the perspective of transgenerational phantom trauma. In their opinion, Morrison reveals African-American novels' homogeneous intertextual connection with the blacks' traumatic history, spiritual autobiographies and historical questionings, and *Beloved* has its unique function and value in working through the blacks' transgenerational trauma. This thesis is a good example which combines trauma theory and text analysis very well. It makes a detailed analysis of the blacks' individual trauma caused by the slavery, but it ignored to summarize the ways to cure individual trauma and repair interpersonal relationships.

Shang Biwu analyzes the characters' individual psychological trauma from the perspective of trauma theory in "Trauma, Memory and Narrative Therapy: On Morrison's *A Mercy*." He believes that "in building up the identity of the traumatized and in reprojecting the traumatizing events in the characters' mental worlds, memory displays its cruelty" (2011: 93). Different from Morrison's other novels, *A Mercy* shows individual trauma under the perspective of micro-narration. Memories of traumatic events will arouse reappearing of those events, and then increase the pain. After experiencing a variety of trauma, different people will choose different ways to cure trauma. But Shang points out that only by narration the trauma can be cured finally— "the character narrators not only survive to tell the tale of trauma but also tell the tale of trauma to survive" (93). This thesis is the first one which analyzes *A Mercy* from trauma, memory and recovery three overall angles in detail. It inspires a lot of further studies.

Yang Shaoliang and Liu Xiamin (2012) analyzes *A Mercy* from the perspective of traumatic memory in an essay published on the *Journal of Tianjin Foreign Studies University*. They notes that almost all the characters in this novel are more or less traumatized either physically or psychologically to become "the other" in their society. They believes that "the haunting memory not only aggravates their trauma, but renders their morbid identity construction, and it is the reason why they fail to construct their identity" (65). Following in Shang Biwu's study, this is the second thesis which analyzes the traumatic theme in *A Mercy*. Although they share some similar views toward traumatic memory in two theses, this thesis creatively analyzes the novel based on the relationship of traumatic memory and identity construction. In the same year, Xue Yuxiu analyzes black female in *A Mercy* from the perspective of cultural trauma. She puts forward that cultural trauma results in black female's loss of self-identities. The key for them to get rid of cultural trauma is the awakening of their social subjective consciousness and self-affirmation of their values. Although Xue writes that she will discuss the issues of women's identity construction from the perspective of cultural trauma, she doesn't even illuminate the basic definition of cultural trauma. Actually she confuses the interpretation of slavery trauma with cultural trauma to some extent.

Based on the above reviews both in China and overseas, it is easy to find out that traumatic study of Morrison's works is relatively a new research perspective in recent years. It is a hot study now, but obviously the breadth and depth of the research are quite insufficient. Books which interpret her works from the perspective of trauma are limited, and the research objects are so concentrated that the research results are unsystematic. Most of these studies focus on *Beloved* or *A Mercy*; the other novels still need further exploration, especially the latest novel *God Help the Child*. What's more, most scholars only pay their attention to the theme of racism; that's why we need to interpret those works from more and much broader perspectives.

However, few efforts are devoted to the comprehensive study of all her fiction from interdisciplinary perspective to probe into the trauma and identity construction, which is where this monograph found its voice.

Chapter 1

Healing Trauma Through Music:
Aesthetic Sensitivity and Cultural Conservation

Morrison's eleven novels reflect African-Americans' traumatic experiences from different perspectives, and also reproduces both physical trauma and psychological trauma to African-Americans caused by the slavery, racial discrimination, white supremacy, patriarchal society and so on. Those traumas didn't disappear along with the abolition of the slavery. On the contrary, they sealed into African-Americans' deep hearts and became painful memories lingering in their minds. These memories afflicted their lives after they were freed and influenced their next generation's fate. In addition to depicting African-Americans' trauma in her novels, Morrison also probes deeply into the way to help them forget their traumatic history and escape from trauma. Black music becomes an effective expression for African-Americans to express their traumatic experiences and for Morrison to build her narrative structure and to provide healing and therapeutic power as well as survival technique to black people suffering from various setbacks.

1.1 Trauma and Black Musical Expression

In all Morrison's works, she pays a lot of attention to cultural trauma, psychological trauma, race trauma, collective trauma and individual trauma. The depiction of trauma reflects African-Americans' traumatic experiences throughout American history. As an African-American female writer, Morrison is more concerned with black women's miserable fate under the oppression of racism, male chauvinism and living predicament than other writers. Among all her novels, there are eight which set female as protagonist. "Her writing perspective turns from black women's cultural trauma to psychological trauma, and finally to race trauma, from their individual trauma to collective trauma." (Wang, 2014: 4) Black women suffer not only the influences of the dominant culture of the whites, but also discrimination and oppression from patriarchal society which put them in the bottom and to the margin of the society. After exploring cultural trauma and psychological trauma of individual black women, Morrison turns her writing perspective into the root of black female's trauma, race trauma and collective trauma caused by the slavery. She profoundly reveals the trauma of African-American women caused by the slavery in *Beloved* which was published in 1987.

After more than two decades, Morrison wrote a sad story in her ninth novel *A Mercy* that a mother is forced to abandon her daughter under the oppression of the slavery. This novel not only describes the slavery trauma to the blacks, but also reveals that "all kinds of people are carrying their shackles of body and soul, and their path to liberation" (Wang & Wu, 2009: 43). Both *Beloved* and *A Mercy* strongly criticize the darkness and cruelty of the slavery.

Morrison also pays her attention to the traumatic experiences of black men and the whole black community in her works while focusing on the trauma of black women. Her third novel *Song of Solomon* concerns about black men's stories of self-pursuing and self-growth. In this novel, Morrison skillfully combined modernism with realism, wonderful stories with serious themes. The publication of this novel has drawn a heated discussion among readers and literary critics. Taking the fate of black people over one hundred years, particularly the difficult position of black women in the whole society, as her main concerns, Morrison tells us black people's, especially black women's, misfortune in American society which still exists racism in all her works. Using her outstanding creative talent, Morrison depicts a historical picture for black people, including many female characters that experience countless obstacles and seek hardly for their self-identities, and a lot of male characters who suffer from miserable slavery and wars.

The word "trauma" comes from Greek which originally refers to an injury inflicted on a body. Then its meaning extends to medical circle, psychological treatment and some other fields. In its later usage, particularly in the medical and psychiatric literature, and most centrally in Freud's text, the term "trauma" is understood as a wound inflicted not upon the body but upon the mind. His psychoanalytic theory and his view of trauma are the source of trauma theory. But what seems to be suggested by Freud in *Beyond the Pleasure Principle* is that the wound of the mind—the breach in the mind's experience of time, self, and the world—is not, like the wound of the body, a simple and healable event, but rather an event that is experienced too soon, too unexpectedly, to be fully known and is therefore not available to consciousness until it imposes itself again, repeatedly, in the nightmares and repetitive actions of the survivor. That is to say, psychological trauma events usually repeat in individual's psyche in replay, dreams, hallucinations and other uncontrollable ways. Therefore, trauma is not locatable in the simple violent or original event in an individual's past, but rather in the way that its unassimilated nature returns to haunt the survivor later on. Freud's interpretation of psychological trauma from the perspective of psychoanalytic theory is groundbreaking, and it lays the foundation for contemporary trauma research.

Trauma theory originates from Victorian England in the 19th century. It relates to clinical medicine of industrial accident trauma and the late 19th century's modern psychology. This theory especially has a close relationship with Freud's psychoanalytic theory, and gradually penetrates into literature, philosophy, history, cultural studies, anthropology, sociology and many other fields. In 1980, American Psychiatric Association (APA) listed post-traumatic stress disorder (PTSD) into diagnosis range of U.S. medicine and psychoanalysis for the first time, which marks the beginning of the research of contemporary trauma theory.

Since the mid-1990s, the research of trauma theory was going into climax. Some excellent works include *Testimony: Crises of Witnessing in Literature, Psychoanalysis and History* which is written by famous contemporary trauma theorists Shoshana Felman and Dori Laub in 1992, *Trauma: Explorations in Memory* and *Unclaimed Experience: Trauma, Narrative, and History* which are written by Cathy Caruth in 1995 and 1996 respectively. As the names of these books show, the study of trauma theory embodies its interdisciplinary characteristic from the very beginning. In recent years, the literary studies which based on trauma theory and chose existence, history, memory, testimony, and witness narrative to interpret have become more and more common. Trauma theorists who emerge in the 1990s, especially the Yale School, pay more attention to the traumatized people's unbearable and unspeakable psychological trauma caused by the Nazi in World War II.

Among the Yale School's trauma studies, Shoshana Felman and Cathy Caruth are the greatest contributors who promote the development of the study of relationships between trauma and literary criticism. Their works reveal close relationship between trauma theory and literary criticism, and imply that trauma theory intrinsically linked with literature. For example, in *Testimony: Crises of Witnessing in Literature, Psychoanalysis and History*, Felman and Laub discusses the relations between literature and testimony, narrative and history. Felman's study clarifies the relationship among history, witness and literature. Through this book, literary criticism redraws its borders, identifies its functions and constructs its, as well as traumatic study's, interpretation patterns, based on the rethinking and criticism to historical and cultural events.

In recent years, the study of trauma theory has not only limited to the medical field, but also gradually penetrated into culture, history, literature and many other fields. Trauma theory has become the inspiration for writers. For example, many overseas Chinese female writers and African-American female writers have described marginalized women's traumatic experiences and miserable fate in their novels. In addition, war trauma and disaster trauma are also important writing materials for writers. For literary criticism, trauma theory provides a new research perspective and innovative method to literary text interpretation, as well as better reveals the themes and narratives in the novels.

Black characters in Morrison's novels suffer incurable psychological trauma caused by the slavery. After the abolition of slavery, they keep living in the shadow of slavery trauma. What's more, white-dominated culture gradually destroys their spiritual beliefs. They lose themselves, psychologically confused or become crazy when they try to find out a way to get rid of white-dominated culture's damage. In addition to suffering the trauma caused by history and culture, these people who are at the lowest level of society also suffer severe emotional trauma. These traumatic experiences left painful scars in their memories when they were children, and damaged their self-consciousness. These negative effects not only affect their emotional and mental health, but also have negative impacts to the growth of the blacks' next generation. Therefore, using the basic concepts of trauma theory and trauma healing methods to analyze the characters' childhood trauma in Morrison's fiction is conducive to revealing African-Americans' traumatic history, interpreting Morrison's traumatic writing arts, and broadening the research perspectives of trauma theory. Morrison not only concerns about the fate of unfortunate black individuals, but also concerns about the historical development of the black nation. Black children's growth and survival problems are Morrison's writing focuses. She portrays many black characters who suffer severe historical trauma, cultural trauma and social trauma. Her works reflect that, as the heirs of the blacks' history and culture, black people suffer multiple traumas and bitter ordeals. Her fiction bears the inescapable burden to help black people to face their traumatic experiences and to get rid of pains through a variety of narrative means. Among these narrative means, black music is the most constructive way to help to describe the painful experiences black people suffer and to help the black people with the way they express their trauma and release their pains, as music is not only a healing and therapeutic power, but also an effective survival technique to them.

According to Stephen Henderson, literature is the "verbal organization of experience into beautiful forms" (1973: 4), but what is meant by "beautiful" and by "forms" is to a significant degree dependent upon a people's way of life, their needs, their aspirations, their history—in short, their culture. Because of the unique experiences of African-Americans, their culture is largely dependent on their double consciousness as both African descendents and American citizens, which find their best expression in Afro-American songs.

Black music as art is one of the black traditions that have been transmitted to provide a safe location where black people have come to voice. "Art is special because of its ability to influence feelings as well as knowledge," suggests Angela Davis, "black people were able to create with their music an aesthetic community of active struggle for freedom." (1990: 201) In Africa, songs served the dual purpose of not only preserving communal values and solidarity but also providing occasions for people to symbolically express deeply held feelings which ordinarily could not be verbalized because of the inevitable restriction of their environment and society. Since blacks were sold to be slaves, their songs have always been heard on the American continent. The whites can define the blacks' physical body, but they cannot prohibit their music, for music can be heard and spread without permission. Since it's of absolute necessity for all communities struggling for self-repossession, one of the major steps is the ability to recover a voice for oneself, to become the speaker again, to become the teller of one's own " (hi)story."[1] The African American communities started telling their own " (hi)story" and appropriating the "I," the language, the voice out of the mouth of the other, through music, since any other kind of self-expression was forbidden under slavery. Black music unites the joy and the sorrow, the love and the hate, the hope and the despair of black people. The blacks sing everything in music when spoken language fails to communicate since music provides the African Americans with the adequate expression for the deepest and most complex spiritual and emotional realities. Music is not only a healing and therapeutic power, but also an effective survival technique to them, which can be found in jazz and the blues. In *The Souls of Black Folks*, W. E. B. Du Bois tells of how slaves were able to turn the words of their oppressors' own songs against them with "veiled and half-articulate messages" (1990: 57). According to David L. Middleton, in Spirituals like "Swing Low Sweet Chariot," it would be clear to the slaves that the "home" to which the chariot carries the listener is not the tranquil green pastures of the twenty-third psalm, but instead the original home of the slaves—Africa and "the promise of freedom" (1997: 97) which that continent has held for generations of black Americans. Bearing an essential expressive potential of traumatic experience, at first sight, they seem to be "preoccupied with love and survival rather than death" (Eckstein, 2006: 279). Some people claim that there's something about music that is so penetrating that one's soul gets the message. No matter what trouble comes to a person, music can help him face it. So music plays an important role in the former slaves' lives, and such role can also be found till now in blacks' lives. Slaves cannot speak freely to one another; the shout and the song must carry all of the expressive needs of the moment. In slaves' lives, music and song at that time act not only as a way of communication, but also as a way temporarily forgetting the terrible situation and being like a free man. Therefore, the remembrance of personal or collective traumata, of what Gilroy calls the "condition of pain" (1993: 200) is inherent in black music.

---

[1] (hi) story means both history and story.

Many African-American writers have employed music in their literary medium and state with remarkable pride that their work is definitely informed by African-American music since in an act of transcendence, song can record the terrible price of slavery while sustaining a spirit that might otherwise, and sometimes does, break. "The songs of the slave represent the sorrows of his heart; and he is relieved by them, only as an aching heart is relieved by its tears." (Douglass, 1960: 22) Tones of joy and sadness are thought by Douglass to form the core elements of slave song. In explanation of the fusion of the two, he notes, "such is the confusion of the human mind, that, when pressed to extremes, it often avails itself of the most opposite methods. Extremes meet in mind as in matter" (Douglass, 1994: 185). He writes of being "broken in body, soul, and spirit," of being "crushed," of "the dark night of slavery" closing in, of "sinking down" and mourning over his condition (1994: 58, 59). Ellison believes that basically his "instinctive approach to writing is through sound" (1997: 278). James Baldwin declares in a sermonic, authoritative tone: "It is only in music, which Americans are able to admire because a protective sentimentality limits their understanding of it, that the Negro in America has been able to tell his story." (1985: 65) Du Bois holds that the souls of black folk are revealed in the sorrow songs. To Du Bois, the song of the black slave is "the most beautiful expression of the human experience born this side of the seas." He believes that the songs indicate the deepest sadness and highest joy of a slave:

> (The songs) tell of death and suffering and unvoiced longing toward a truer world, of misty wandering and hidden ways ... Through all the Sorrow Songs there breathes a hope—a faith in the ultimate justice of things. The minor cadence of despair changes often to triumph and calm confidence. Sometimes it is a faith in life, sometimes a faith in death, sometimes the assurance of boundless justice in some fair world beyond. But whichever it is, the meaning is always clear: that sometime somewhere, men will judge men by their souls not by their skins. (1990: 188)

Indeed, this is also true of Morrison's message conveyed through her fiction.

To adequately describe how the conventions of specific forms of black music influence Morrison's motifs and narratives, a literary aesthetic derived from those conventions must grow out of an awareness of the cultural, social, economic, and, above all, historic forces that shaped them.

1.2 Black Music as a Historic Process of Acculturation and Cultural Identification

The development of black slave songs can be divided into three stages: The first stage is African music; the second is Afro-American music; and the third stage is the mixture of Afro-American music and the music that Afro-Americans hear on the American continent, which distinctly maintains the original features of Afro-American music. This process of development points to the fact that black music is also a historic process of acculturation and cultural identification.

The first musical form they employed to express their longing is black Spirituals, which grew out of the black experience with human enslavement and were adapted from music they brought from their African home. Religious and psalmodical, it's a collective expression of the black slaves.

Spirituals were often expressions of religious faith, although they may also have served as socio-political protests veiled as assimilation to white, American culture. They were originated by enslaved African-Americans in the United States. During slavery in the United States, there were systematic efforts to de-Africanize the captive black workforce. Enslaved people were forbidden from speaking their native languages. Because they were unable to express themselves freely in ways that were spiritually meaningful to them, enslaved Africans often held secret religious services. During these "bush meetings," worshippers were free to engage in African religious rituals such as spiritual possession, speaking in tongues and shuffling in counterclockwise ring shouts to communal shouts and chants. It was there also that enslaved Africans further crafted the impromptu musical expression of field songs into the so-called "line signing" and intricate, multi-part harmonies of struggle and overcoming, faith, forbearance and hope that have come to be known as "Negro Spirituals." While slave owners used Christianity to teach enslaved Africans to be long-suffering, forgiving and obedient to their masters, as practiced by the enslaved, it became a kind of liberation theology. The story of Moses and The Exodus of the "children of Israel" and the idea of an Old Testament God who struck down the enemies of His "chosen people" resonated deeply with the enslaved

("He's a battleaxe in time of war and a shelter in a time of storm"). In Black hands and hearts, Christian theology became an instrument of liberation. So, too, in many instances did the Spirituals themselves. Spirituals sometimes provided comfort and eased the boredom of daily tasks, but above all, they were an expression of spiritual devotion and a yearning for freedom from bondage.

The blues, "a communal expression of black experience," and the "complex interweaving of the general and the specifics and of individual and group experience" (Carby, 1986: 232), is one of the derivative forms of Spiritual (the other one is Gospel music), which gained prominence after Emancipation and is considered as a kind of improvised lyric.

With African American Spirituals and work songs as stylistic origins and West African music, brought by slaves to southern United States, especially the Mississippi Delta as its cultural origins, the blues is a vocal and instrumental form of music based on the use of the blue notes and a repetitive pattern that most often follows a twelve-bar structure. It emerged in African-American communities of the United States from Spirituals, praise songs, field hollers, rhymed Scots-Irish narrative ballads, shouts, and chants. The use of blue notes and the prominence of call-and-response patterns in the music and lyrics are indicative of the blues' West African pedigree. The blues influenced later American and Western popular music, as it became part of the genres of ragtime, jazz, bluegrass, rhythm and blues, rock and roll, hip-hop, and pop songs.

Albert Murray explains clearly that the blues was:

> a statement about confronting the complexities inherent in the human situation and about improvising or experiencing ... such possibilities as are also inherent in the obstacles, the disjunctures, and the jeopardy. It is also a statement about perseverance ... resilience ... the maintenance of equilibrium despite precarious circumstances and about achieving elegance in th[at] very process ... It is thus the musical equivalent of the epic .... (1976, 250–251)

Jazz, born of the blues, is the urban version of those statements. With the blues and other African American folk music, ragtime, West African music, European brass bands, 1910s New Orleans as its stylistic origins, jazz is the polyrhythmic music characterized by its extensive use of improvisation, blue notes, swing, syncopation, and call-and-response patterns in connection with audience participation. It blends West African musical styles with Western music technique and theory. Therefore, jazz is rooted in the blues, the folk music of former enslaved Africans in the U.S. South and their descendants, which is influenced by West African cultural and musical traditions that evolved as black musicians migrated to the cities. Jazz was the result of the confluence of two distinct musical traditions: the gentrified concert and dance music of professional black theater and vaudeville orchestras in the North that strove to imitate white bands for economic and social reasons, on the one hand, and the predominantly rural and Southern tradition of the blues that the migrating workers brought North, on the other (Schuller, 1969: 67, 70, 77–79; Jones, 1963: 104–112). No one is exactly certain how the word "jazz" originated. Emerging sometime around 1910, the term is usually associated with the folk mores of black men, and therefore its roots have been linked to Africa. Eileen Southern, author of *The Music of Black Americans*, suggests that jazz may have derived from an itinerant black musician named Jazbo Brown whose appreciative audience chanted, "More, Jazbo! More, Jaz, more!" (362) Jazz musician Wynton Marsalis states that "Jazz is something Negroes invented … the nobility of the race put into sound … jazz has all the elements, from the spare and penetrating to the complex and enveloping." Travis Jackson also defines jazz in a broader way by stating that it is music that includes qualities such as "'swinging,' improvising, group interaction, developing an 'individual voice,' and being 'open' to different musical possibilities."

Furthermore, Amiri Baraka explains: "Jazz incorporates blues … as cultural insistence, a feeling-matrix … So at its strongest and most intense and indeed most advanced, jazz expresses the highest consciousness of that people [the African American nation] itself, combining its own history, as folk form and expression, with its more highly developed industrial environment." (1987: 263–264) Hence, jazz is well adapted to the claiming of the narrative "I," i.e., to stand as the teller of the African American (hi)story. Besides, Jazz has never hesitated in appropriating and integrating elements from Western classical music.

Jazz is the music that designates the division/zone of interpenetration between African music and European music, for it is a hybrid form that has maintained the polyrhythm as well as certain melodic and harmonic qualities of African music, while at the same time appropriating European musical features and instruments. Furthermore, jazz pieces more often than not are comprised of appropriating revisions of well-known tunes from classical and popular music, or even from other jazz pieces. In this way, jazz stands for the sign of the letter, i.e., for the expression of the texture of the African Americans' experiences in individualistic, materialist and racially prejudiced cities. It speaks of their struggle to appropriate their own spaces, literally and figuratively—housing, jobs, educational and social opportunities, civil rights.

Born in an urban environment, jazz became "the first form of aesthetic statement" (Foner, 1988: 171–175, 231) in African-American culture to offer common emotional ground for the entire community beyond the class differences and prejudices that had developed among African-Americans in the wake of Reconstruction. Those differences had only intensified and deepened with the influx of unskilled agricultural laborers into the Northern cities during the successive waves of migration since the end of the 19th century.

According to L. Jones, the jazz player could come from any part of the social spectrum, but if he were to play a really moving kind of jazz, he had to reflect almost all of the musical spectrum, or at least combine sufficiently the older autonomous blues tradition with the musical traditions of the Creoles or the ragtime orchestras of the North. And thus, jazz could not help but "reflect the entire black society" (1963: 140).

In short, the development of jazz ran parallel to significant economic and social changes that affected a considerable part of the African-American community. Music, like any other form of social statement and organization, is a culturally specific response to particular environmental conditions, both natural and social. As the new music of the 1920s, jazz incorporated and expressed in its various elements a new and greater sense of individual and communal freedom and achievement.[1]

---

[1] Leroi Jones has made that connection between music and general culture in the socio-anthropological sense of the term succinctly clear in much greater detail. Aesthetic statement in its different forms is, just as any other aspect of a given culture, indeed, as culture itself, the product of learned social behavior, subject to specific patterns of retention and reinterpretation (1963: 25, 152). Melville J. Herskovits, whose findings, it seems, have yet to penetrate the public consciousness, initiated the study of those patterns in African-American culture based on such an understanding of culture with his groundbreaking work *The Myth of the Negro Past*.

As the most prolific, accomplished, and emotionally satisfying contemporary aesthetic response to the world in African-American culture, this music became nearly synonymous with the culture from which it had sprung, transcending boundaries of class and gender. As one form of black secular music, jazz stood in a continuum of tradition with earlier black sacral music, in which the fusion of the material and spiritual world characteristic of African aesthetics and religions had been preserved. For the black culture, particularly during times of great cultural oppression, it was an act of physical, emotional, and social commitment. Black music was a direct reflection of the combined experiences of many individuals, all of them grounded in reality. The communal nature of black music never lost its impact, as the integration of the individual into the society is one of the primary functions of oral modes.

At the same time, the economic advances of members of the lower classes within the African-American community created a market for black music that the young recording industry rushed to tap, beginning with Mamie Smith's recording of "Crazy Blues" in 1921. Black music was a readily and publicly available cultural artifact in the city. Records also provided a strong impetus for standardization of musical concepts simply because those concepts were available for examination and imitation; musicians would routinely play along with records to learn new songs and copy solos off records to hone their own skills at improvisation based on the models that the recordings offered them. For the first time in history, improvised music existed beyond the moment of its creation. It could be analyzed and recreated by others; it could also be changed into something new and personal. This standardization of black musical forms based on the imitation of spontaneous musical traditions that went with it established black music as "the definitive statement of contemporary African-American culture" (Sidran, 1983: 17).[1]

Yet even though the basic form was relatively rigid, the element of improvisation gave the performer much greater latitude for a personal interpretation of the musical material than the musicians in, a French military band had ever known. The music of the Creole Jazz Band was the result of a well-established pattern

---

[1] W. E. B. Du Bois had said as much in 1904 in *The Souls of Black Folk*. Also see Lawrence W. Levine's *Black Consciousness: Afro-American Folk Thought from Slavery to Freedom*, which is published in 1980.

of adaptation: In short, African-American culture routinely assimilates elements of "white" culture "by accepting its forms while drastically altering its content" (Sidran, 1983: 25).

One of the defining features of jazz has been its role as a progenitor of new forms, an inventor of new languages, and a creator of new ways to express meaning. The relationship between language and jazz, black music, is described by John Gennari as follows: "The blues notes, microtones, polyrhythms, and extended harmonies of jazz constitute a musical vocabulary and grammar that cannot be accurately represented by the standard notational systems of Western music. Likewise, scat singing dissents from the logocentric tyranny of Standard English, eschews referential lyrics in favor of vocalized sounds … whose meaning is their own sound." (1991: 449–450)

Nina Simone also considers that "the Negro in America is jazz. Everything he does—the slang he uses, the way he talks, his jargon, the new inventive phrases we make up to describe things—all that to me is jazz as much as the music we play" (156). Accordingly, it's safe to conclude that jazz is not just music. It's the definition of the Afro-American black. It's a way of life, a way of being, and a way of thinking.

1.3 Morrison's Music Aesthetics

Music has occupied a special place in black people's expression of their self-definitions. In Morrison's fiction, jazz and the blues, presence and influence are constantly felt, some way or other. When presenting an important warning to critics who view Toni Morrison's work as a response to, or derivative of, academic postmodernism, Anthony Hilfer argues that "Morrison derives her indeterminacies not from French postmodernism nor from the new, oddly dematerialized forms of Marxism but from the center of African American culture … Jazz" (1991: 93).

As the voice of the griot, the storyteller of the African diaspora, whose function is to act as a skilled mediator of his/her community's (hi)story, as the voice of the blues men and women or of the jazz horn players, Morrison's voice is that of the whole African American community. Realizing the importance of music to African-American people by stating that "music was everywhere and all around" (Taylor-Guthrie, 1994: 28), Morrison has many times articulated her awareness of the significance of black music for the African American community; she has also expressed that the African American novel has to take over the functions of the music that no longer belongs exclusively to the blacks. This conviction seems to owe something to Albert Murray's claims that fiction at its best "can also function as activating force which at times may be capable of even greater range and infinitely more evocative precision than music. In truth, it is literature, in the primordial sense, which establishes the context for social and political action in the first place" (1973: 10).

Black Americans were sustained and healed and nurtured by the translation of their experience into art above all in the music. In an interview highlighting the importance of African American music to her political aesthetics, Morrison herself suggests her music aesthetics: "That was functional … Music makes you hungry for more of it. It never really gives you the whole number. It slaps and it embraces; it slaps and it embraces. The literature ought to do the same thing. I've been very deliberate about that … " (Gilroy, 1994: 181) She has always wanted to develop a way of writing that was irrevocably black. Although she doesn't have the resources of a musician, she thinks that if it is truly black literature it will not be black because she is, and it will not even be black because of its subject matter. It will be something intrinsic, indigenous, something in the way it was put together— the sentences, the structure, texture and tone—so that anyone who reads it would realize. She uses the analogy of the music because it's still black ranging all over the world. She "appropriates" the blues, Spirituals or jazz and tries to reconstruct the texture of it in her writing with its profound simplicity.

In an interview with Nellie McKay, Morrison remarked, "Classical music satisfies and closes. Black music does not do that. Jazz always keeps you on the edge. There is no final chord. And it agitates you … I want my books to be like that." (429) It is significant that there are some shared conditions of urbanity and the chaos of modern life in Morrison's fiction and jazz. Of the intersection of jazz music, history, and the erotic, Toni Morrison has talked about the very limiting environment the ex-slaves were in when they were moving into the city, running away from something that was constricting and killing them and dispossessing them over and over again:

But when you listen to their music—the beginnings of jazz—You realize that they are talking about something else. They are talking about love, about loss. But there is such grandeur, such satisfaction in those lyrics ... They're never happy—somebody's always leaving somebody, risking love, risking emotion, risking sensuality, and then losing it. All didn't matter, since it was their choice. Exercising choice in who you love was a major, major thing. And the music reinforced the idea of love as a space where one could negotiate freedom .... (Schappell & Brodsky, 1998: 365)

For some black people jazz means claiming their own bodies. It can be imagined what that must have meant for people whose bodies had been owned, who had been slaves as children, or who remembered their parents' being slaves. The blues and jazz represent ownership of one's own emotions.

The artistic goals informing Toni Morrison's fiction have been amply described by her in numerous works. She claims that black music is an important part of the cultural framework that significantly shapes her own aesthetic production. "The sound of the novel, sometimes cacophonous, sometimes harmonious ... [becomes] an inner ear sound or a sound just beyond hearing, infusing the text with a musical emphasis that words can do sometimes even better than music can." (1989: 28, 31–32)

Morrison means to faithfully reflect the aesthetic tradition of Afro-American culture, to make conscious use of the characteristics of its art forms and translate them into print: antiphony, the group nature of art, its functionality, its improvisational nature, its relationship to audience performance, the critical voice which upholds tradition and communal values and which also provides occasion for an individual to transcend and/or defy group restriction. Discussing her relationship with her audience, Morrison explains: "Working within those rules, the text, if it is to take improvisation and audience participation into account, cannot be the authority—it should be the map. It should make a way for the reader (audience) to participate in the tale." (1984: 388)

It was above all black music that, in her view, exemplified better than any other form the communal nature of black art; Morrison saw her own work as an attempt to recreate and supplant the music's power to forge a distinct group identity based on a common cultural tradition. As Morrison attempts to appropriate the novel as a Western literary form from an African-American perspective, the musical conventions in jazz of the 1920s and beyond provide an adequate structural metaphor to resolve these questions. Such a perspective is informed by a distinct and in many ways different cultural tradition, in which language and music are correlating aspects of a "total vision of life, in which music, unlike the 'art music' of Europe, is not a separate, autonomous social domain" (Schuller, 1969: 4). In West African cultures one is indeed conceived of in terms of the other: Music is a derivation of the spoken word in its representation of basic vocalizations, and musical improvisation is a derivative of the practice of circumlocution that demonstrates the mastry of language. "In language, the African tradition aims at circumlocution rather than definition. The direct statement is considered crude and unimaginative; the veiling of all contents in ever-changing paraphrase is considered the criterion of intelligence and personality." (Sidran, 1983: 6) Through her writing, Morrison tactfully realizes this mastery of language.

In "Rootedness: The Ancestor as Foundation," Morrison identifies the function that these aesthetic characteristics serve in advancing her goal to draft the reader into the role of collaborator in the creation of the text. She explains, "To have the reader work with the author in the construction of the book—is what's important. What is left out is as important as what is there." (1984: 341) According to Morrison, the goal and the aesthetic characteristics that assist it are both native to African diaspora oral traditions that generate a performance dynamic that assigns creative agency to the teller and the listener by deliberately positioning the latter as participant, not outside observer. This performance dynamic is commonly referred to as call-and-response. Call-and-response structures, inherent in Spirituals, the blues, sermons, folktales, and so on, anticipate and require a response that may extend, challenge, revise, clarify, or transform any previous utterance, and they outline a generative sequence in which the response becomes the new call, and this is also Morrison's goal in writing her fiction: to deconstruct the master language and to affirm the black meanings in a black text.

1.3.1 Aesthetic Sensitivity and Identity

In Morrison's work, the Black community and the musical narrative are described as a matrix of conservation for African-American culture and one of the methods to heal the wound. The aesthetic sensitivity as represented most of time by musical sensitivity is closely related to the conservation of culture and community value. Any lack of musical expression seems to have a serious effect on Morrison's characters, preventing them from developing an identity and cultivating a communal relationship with other people, while those who are capable of expressing themselves through music and other art forms can also form reciprocal relationships with their ethnicity and their community, as Ralph Ellison suggests in characterizing the effect of the blues as being able to appeal emotionally to a black audience without relying on language.[1]

Knowing the important role of music in blacks' lives, past and present, Morrison describes in her works the close relationship between the alienation of African Americans from aesthetic sensitivity and their oppressed identities as well as their displacement from a supportive community. Those of Morrison's characters who are dispossessed of their own "art form" as a creative outlet for their feelings simultaneously lack the knowledge of their identity and self worth. Singing, in the literal sense, significantly enables Morrison's characters to express their emotions and links them to the community, the reservoir of collective knowledge and the source of caring, while an inability to sing frequently coincides with isolation from the community and destructive displacement caused by unvented feelings.

The MacTeers and the Breedloves

In *The Bluest Eye*, the MacTeers and the Breedloves form a clear contrast either in the emotional sense or in the communal sense. The MacTeers embody the communal resiliency at the heart of black culture. They are spiritually strong partly because they can remember the healing and restorative black songs when the poverty and oppression silence many people, and partly because of the fact that they survive with a sense of self and culture. Singing serves as a collective, communal act to defy oppression and to survive difficulties. By singing they

---

[1] In his article, "Richard Wright's Blues," Ellison points out the healing and transcending power of the blues: "The blues is an impulse to keep the painful details and episodes of a brutal experience alive in one's aching consciousness, to finger its jagged grain, and to transcend it, not by the consolation of philosophy but by squeezing from it a near-tragic, near-comic lyricism."

express their thoughts unreservedly and virtually direct the spirit of their feelings from confinement toward release, toward free movement. Thus music saves them from despair, and is a source of pride and happiness. The Breedloves perish because they can not find in black songs the emotional support and outlet which is necessary for their survival in a society full of frustrations and setbacks, which stands in striking oppositions to the black community.

Mrs. MacTeer conserves the wisdom of her foremothers who have sought survival communally no matter how oppressed their situation might have been. The warmth of her tone and the importance of her conversation with her friends in the community function as a vital emotional outlet, like an open circle vigorously being transformed into a spiral. Claudia recalls the constructive and healing potency of the blues which her mother hums or chants: "If my mother was in a singing mood, it wasn't so bad. She would sing about hard times, bad times, and somebody-done-gone-and-left-me-times." (Morrison, 1970: 25) Her mother's music is so sweet that Claudia understands the significance of the blues, which contain the female sexual politics of black women. More important, the blues transform the pain, sorrow and suffering of African-American experiences into a source of lyric energy for living so as to make children like Claudia understand that "pain was not only endurable, it was sweet" (26).

In contrast, the Breedloves' lack of musical expressions prevents them from developing wholesome identities and cultivating communal relationships with other people, causing tragedies to the people concerned. Cholly represses his frustrated feelings, which could otherwise be creatively expressed if he were allowed to be a musician. Morrison explicitly implies that a musical sensitivity could convey his distorted and damaged sensitivities: "Only a musician would sense, know, without even knowing that he knew, that Cholly was free. Dangerously free. Free to feel whatever he felt—fear, guilt, shame, love, grief, pity. Free to be tender or violent, to whistle or weep." (125)

The appealing contradiction of his life could find expression only in black music. His lack of talent as a musician significantly suggests his restricted selfhood and fettered emotional life. As Melvin Dixon comments: "Without music, Cholly's freedom has no voice, no meaningful or cohering performance to tie together the loose tangling strands of his life thus far." (121) After his mother's abandonment and his father's rejection, Cholly has little to lose, and his behavior is disdainful of consequences. Without an appropriate emotional outlet like music to make his shattered life coherent, he perversely displays his love toward his daughter, Pecola, by sexually assaulting her, mixing his affection with sexual desire and confusing his daughter with his remembrance of his wife when she was about Pecola's age. Obviously, his lack of creative outlet is congruent with his failure of emotional articulation. His brutal expression of love toward his daughter reflects the otherwise unexpressed devastation of his own life. In the end, his family reject him, and he dies a lonely death in jail without any dignity or compassion.

Pauline's inability to sing displays her inner isolation from the community. Unlike Mrs. MacTeer, Pauline never sings the blues. Unable to sing, she cannot share the collective suffering of African Americans, and lacks the integral strength of her people. Without any knowledge of how to connect herself, not only to her community but also to her own daughter, Pecola, it is inevitable that Pauline will fail to provide Pecola with the love, advice and cautions crucial to the daughter's survival in a hostile society.

Similarly, Pecola's unexpressed misery, frustration and unhappiness accumulate little by little until her life is irreparable. Deprived of a nurturing mother-daughter relationship, she does not have any role model to follow in order to avoid her own isolation and victimization. Finally, overwhelmed by the unbearable burden of her incestuous pregnancy, she confines herself to an insanity that isolates her completely from the destructive outer world. Her tragedy is induced because "Pecola is unable to articulate the pain she feels or channel it through the form of the blues," as Trudier Harris (1988: 75) remarks. Thus, Pecola indeed becomes "the bluest I," a pun on the title of the book, which connects the story to the blues tradition. The Bluest Eye, then is a blues moan in that it describes the pain of blacks in America and their attempts to grapple with the pain which cripples both their lives and the lives of their children. But while the narrative is a "blues" moan, Pecola herself does not have a voice to sing her blues, which suggests that her total isolation in derangement emphasizes the destructive result of unexpressed feelings. Pecola, who does not have the ability to sing, similarly lacks a community where they can discover support and strength. At the end of The Bluest Eye, Pecola is geographically driven to the periphery of her neighborhood, "on the edge of town"

(Morrison, 1970: 159). Her displacement from the black community underlines her total isolation and decimated identity.

Sula Peace and Nel Wright

The destructive displacement caused by unvented feelings can find its best expressions in *Sula*, while dissolution of identity crisis through music also finds its expression in Nel, Sula's best friend.

Although Sula Peace fearlessly wages a battle against the conventional place allotted to women and feminine and "sex roles," she suffers from both the absence of an artistic outlet and displacement from the community: " Had she [Sula] paints, or clay, or knew the discipline of the dance, or strings; had she anything to engage her tremendous curiosity and her gift for metaphor, she might have exchanged the restless and preoccupation with whim for an activity that provided her with all she yearned for. And like any artist with no art form, she became dangerous." (Morrison, 1973: 121)

Despite Sula's potential artistic talent, society deprives her of the freedom of expression which is granted to more fortunate artists who creatively transform their feelings into artistic form. Unfortunately, Sula has no access to art, no way to use her talent positively. Therefore, she has to direct her fruitless struggle to find an outlet of self-expression towards empty affairs with men, because each momentary relationship with a man is one of amorality rather than immorality and one of narcissistic indifference. When she has an affair with the husband of her best girlfriend, Nel, Sula only wishes to discover a confidant with whom she can share her private thoughts which have been frustratingly suppressed rather than hurting her friend. What she wishes to obtain is a channel for her feelings, not a lover. Unaware of a proper, constructive way to express her feelings and thereby to liberate herself, Sula mistakenly replaces her search for freedom with a series of superficial love affairs which never fulfill her unsatisfied desire. Both Cholly and Sula, overwhelmed by their unvented feelings, destroy themselves through their inability to have reciprocal relationships.

As a result, her decline in health and spirit are apparent when she realizes that she is no longer able to find, metaphorically speaking, a new song to sing. "There aren't any more new songs and I have sung all the ones there are. I have sung them all. I have sung all the songs there are." (Morrison, 1973: 137) Without a song to express her feelings, her exploration of freedom and identity ends because she is now literally confined to her deathbed. The absence of new songs implies the lack of new experiences which she can feel with her curiosity and evidently foreshadows the failure of discovering freedom and any outlet for her feelings. Her refusal of support and caring from the community inevitably accelerates her loneliness. Her limits as a "singer" indicate the boundary imposed on her life.

In contrast, Nel's restlessness and identity crisis dissolve through the effects of music when she discovers the importance of her friendship with Sula other than self-possession. The moment occurs when she is walking in the cemetery and finds the engraving on Sula's family's tombstone which "read like a chant: Peace 1895–1921, Peace 1890–1923, Peace 1910–1940, Peace 1895–1959" (171). In Nel's mind, the visual image of the engraving changes to the aural effect of a chant, drawing forth Nel's repressed feelings and finally liberating her. Because of her realization of the sound, Nel joins the matriarchal line of the Peace family. Her awakening to the importance of the female alliance is related to her ability to distinguish the ancestral force of Sula Peace's lineage that the chant represents, a force accommodating and waiting for acknowledgement since Sula's death.

Jadine and Ondine Childs

In *Tar Baby*, alienation from African culture and art forms fails Ondine in her attempts to guide Jadine and renders Jadine uproot from her origins.

Jadine's access to an art form is also diverted from its original purpose of free expression and sharing. Despite her prestigious art degree at the Sorbonne and her love for painting, Jadine regretfully denies her talent as an artist and instead considers herself as an art historian. She assumes that she lacks the artistic gift, concluding that "still she was lucky to know it, to know the difference between the fine and the mediocre, so she'd put that instinct to work and studied art history— there she was never wrong" (Morrison, 1981: 181–182). She fails to understand that the demarcation between the fine and the mediocre solely reflects the Western aesthetics, depreciating her own original expressive art form. Her knowledge of Western aesthetics rather makes her despise African art and her original art expression, convincing herself: "Picasso is better than an Itumba mask." (74)

Without pride in her African origins and songs to explicate her feelings, connecting her to her people, Jadine dismisses African art which is never discussed in her Euro-centric art class. Having cultivated her sense of aesthetics in dualistic Western formal education, Jadine denies African heritage and thereby withdraws herself from African-American autonomy, uprooting herself from her origins.

Jadine is also separated from the traditional notion of the community and ignorant of her own culture and values. Her aunt, Ondine, fails in her attempts to explain to her niece the values of African-American womanhood and the importance of taking care of elderly women. Ondine's failure derives from the fact that she is also alienated from the community. It is her displacement from her original place that stifles her qualities as a nurturing woman. Living on an island without any close neighbors, friends and relatives, Ondine, who, like her niece, is without the ability to sing, forgets how the community functions. Without this memory, Ondine is unable to guide Jadine toward any kind of self-sustaining integration into the black community.

Baby Suggs, Paul D. and the Slaves

In the African-American tradition, singing has functioned as an important means to communicate and to foster solidarity. In slavery, which silenced speech and dehumanized the victims, music and song were not only a way of communication and temporarily forgetting the terrible situation and being like a free man, but also the African-American secret code which expressed the unspeakable experiences which slave holders persisted in repressing. *Beloved* seems just like a necklace chained by the most informative and beautiful blacks' mundane ballads. In *Beloved*, music hovers the life of the main characters: Sethe and Paul D. When they cannot read or write or even talk about the brutality they experience as slaves, they associate songs with their life and use it as a shield against indignity and despair. Song offers them the opportunity to express their personal emotions and defend their personhood. Songs are imperative to their survival. Sethe composes and sings her own song to her children; when Beloved hums this song, she knows for certain that the girl is the daughter she has killed. Morrison establishes the ability to sing as the barest and most rudimentary essentials of human existence early in the novel.

Baby Suggs, Sethe's mother in law, in turn, clearly evokes the Afro-Christian tradition of sermonizing and singing. Her "call" in the Clearing adheres to the typical features of antiphonic sermonizing. "Love it. Love it hard. Yonder they do not love your flesh. They despise it. They don't love your eyes; they'd just as soon pick them out. No more do they love the skin on your back. Yonder they flay it. And O my people they do not love your hands." (Morrison, 1987: 88) At the end of her call, in a sudden turn to music and dance typical of the sermonizing tradition, Baby Suggs "stood up then and danced with her twisted hip the rest of what her heart had to say while the others opened their mouths and gave her the music" (89). In this way, Afro-Christian styles such as the Spiritual and gospel are also associated with the character—vocal forms that are partly based on the harmonic material of Western hymns, yet have come to be typically "black" forms of expression through their adaptation to the specific patterns of interaction and intonation typical of the African American vocal arts (Eckstein, 2006: 275).

If Baby Suggs thus represents an Afro-Christian musical tradition, Paul D. clearly embodies the secular tradition of the blues. Paul D., a "singing man," is a blues character, steeped in southern or country blues. Not only do his experiences of slavery in the Deep South, of the chain gang, and of his restless wandering take recourse to typical blues topoi, *Beloved*, moreover, directly quotes from the blues repertoire in Paul D.'s tunes. It is indeed only in his blues that Paul D. is able to express his traumatic past. When Sethe asks for his story, he replies, "I don't know. I never have talked about it. Not to a soul. Sang it sometimes, but I never told a soul." (Morrison, 1987: 71) At the house on Bluestone Road, if Paul D. could "walk, eat, sleep, (and) sing," he could survive and "asked for no more" (41). Paul D. also sings while he mends "things he had broken the day before" (40) in an effort to reconstruct his life after physical and emotional trials have shattered his identity at prison camp in Alfred, Georgia. Empowered by these songs, Paul D. is able to bear eighty-six days of pounding rock and eighty-six nights while "reaching for air" (110). He never told another human being about the Schoolteacher experience but sang it sometimes—the significance of music lies in the fact that Paul D. cannot afford to tell another person his traumatic event, but singing empowers him to confront his horrific past and make meaning of his dehumanizing experiences and that song not only mends broken things, but also gives him the entrance to survive.

During Paul D.'s devastating and horrible ordeal after experiencing the worst and most dehumanizing despair where his dignity is aggressively violated on the chain gang in Georgia, the only possible way for the oppressed to express their feelings is to sing: "They sang it out and beat it up, garbling the words so they could not be understood; tricking the words so their syllables yielded up other meanings." (108) As Paul and other prisoners "dance two-step to the music of hand-forged iron" (108), they sang to affirm their humanity while being oppressed and tied like animals: "They sang the women they knew; the children they had been; the animals they had tamed themselves or seen others tame. They sang of bosses and masters and misses; of mules and dogs and the shamelessness of life. They sang lovingly of graveyards and sisters long gone. Of pork in the woods; meal in the pan; fish on the line; cane, rain and rocking chairs." (108)

The singing assert their humanity and an effort to defend against the atrocities of the camp, and it is consolation for these black slaves to tolerate their inhuman life and also the only mode for them to cherish their memory that the whites want to remove from their brains.

Their songs, indecipherable to the white overseers, do not rely on words but on the shared experience of affliction threaded into the style of the music, a coded mode of expression, which connects each member of the chain gang and sustains the unity of the group. Later, the solidarity fostered by singing together with the encoded songs of sorrow, pain and rage enables the imprisoned slaves to successfully execute the mass escape from the prison camp. Their survival of the chain-gang experience would have been impossible without the cooperation promoted by a shared singing fraught with a spirit of resistance. "With a sledge hammer in his hands and Hi Man's lead, the men got through. They sang it out and beat it up, garbling the words so they could not be understood; tricking the words so their syllables yielded up other meanings." (Morrison, 1987: 108) As David Lawrence states, "the human voice in song is a potent material force" (197). Song which secretly reveals the oppressed feelings of African Americans enables them to develop the will to survive, relieving pain and sorrow. Pushing against the pressures of a virulently oppressive system, Paul D. and the other men create their own codes, their own poetry. Ultimately it is this code that frees them, as in the midst of a flood, they talk through that chain that binds all forty-six together, wordlessly coordinating a group escape.

1.3.2 Collective Community Expression

As observed in antiphonal patterns in music, like call-and-response patterns which require both the preacher and the congregation to participate in the sermon, African-American music has been characterized by reciprocal participation, communal support and healing potency. Morrison explains the function of call and response in relation to the community: "It is a very personal grief and a personal statement done among people you trust. Done within the context of the community, therefore safe. And while the shouter is performing some rite that is extremely subjective, the other people are performing as a community in protecting that person." (1984: 339) African-American music involves such collective participation as encourages individual and personal expressiveness while it nourishes interactions among people. Thus, the absence of music indicates isolation from a community, a lack of nurturing, caring and support that gradually undermines the solidarity of African Americans.

In Morrison's works, the community is presented as the source of racial empowerment, and gatherings of the characters are employed in much the same manner as the chorus in a Greek drama. Kathleen O'Shaughnessy explains the values and roles of Morrison's community as a chorus: "The community as a formal chorus is an important element in Toni Morrison's fiction ... As in ancient Greek drama, the effect is one of heightened audience or reader participation." (1998: 125) Both for the readers and for Morrison's characters, the encouragement of participation is indispensable since the community or the chorus is the source of knowledge and of the wisdom of survival. Morrison argues that in the black community "there was this life-giving, very, very strong sustenance that people got from the neighborhood" (1979: 214). In other words, alienation from the community inevitably means a lack of communal support and understanding, which is deleterious for the healthy formation of individual identity. In her fiction, as an important medium by which Morrison's characters can reclaim their identities, and an essential aspect of the recovery of the black community and strong maternal figures (which, meddling as they may be, is a particularly important task if the subjectivities of African Americans are to be recovered), music is closely related to the conservation of community and the retrieval of the silenced voice. By revealing the forces behind and the process of the unraveling of selves, bodies, and communities, Morrison uncovers what is fundamental to the creation of personal and communal identities: the freedom to desire, to imagine, and to live narratives not of coherence, necessarily, but of continuity.

The Dead and Their Genealogy

The blues constitute the black sociohistorical matrix in *Song of Solomon*. "The middle-class Negroes had gotten 'free' of all the blues tradition," as Leroi Jones wryly documents in his history of black music. Morrison interprets this "freedom" as cultural deprivation, vividly pictured in the scene where Macon Dead stands in the shadows outside his sister Pilate's window, listening to her sing with her daughter and granddaughter while brewing the wine they bootlegged. Macon "knew it was not food she was stirring … They ate what they had or came across or had a craving for." Her singing, however, is soul food: Macon "felt the irritability of the day drain from him and relished the effortless beauty of the women singing in the candlelight" . His position as an outsider to this spiritually sustaining world is a reminder of the price of middle-class respectability. Against "the persistent calls to oblivion made by the mainstream of the society," the blues constitutes, according to Leroi Jones, "the peculiar social, cultural, economic, and emotional experience of a black man in America". For Milkman, then, initiation into the blues is "a kind of ethno-historic rite as basic as blood" (Davis, 1990: 6). Angela Davis further points out that in the postslavery years African American women musicians would impart through music "a collective consciousness and a very specific communal yearning for freedom" (10). Morrison admits that she hopes to have her fiction do "what the music did for blacks." *Song of Solomon* intends to save or keep alive by inscribing in print the unifying force of aural/oral forms such as music and storytelling. The blues song Pilate sings and its referent, the historic/mythic flying African, lead Milkman to search for his identity and his family history. His self-centeredness begins to dissolve when he approaches Shalimar, his place of ancestral origins, sharpening his senses, including his aural perception. He listens to what existed "before things were written down." He hears Shalimar people's communication in terms of black music: "All those shrieks, those rapid tumbling barks, the long sustained yells, the tuba sounds, the drumbeat sounds, the low liquid *howm howm*, the reedy whistles, the thin *eeee*'s of a cornet, the *unh unh unh* bass chords. It was all language." (Morrison, 1977: 281) Milkman is able to recognize the song of children in Shalimar which deciphers the enigma of his genealogy. Although Milkman's first impulse is to write down the song, "he had no pencil to write with, and his pen was in his suit, he would just have to listen and memorize it" (306). By memorizing it in the manner of the oral folk tradition out of which the song is collectively created, Milkman is able to reconstitute the history of his family and repossess the African-American oral tradition, drawing him into the integral African-American community. Forced to use his ear and the incorporating power of memory instead of the silent and visual mode of the written word, Milkman becomes an active participant in the African-American oral tradition. Although based around the material hunt of Milkman Dead for his gold, Milkman's journey to the South turns out to be his spiritual quest for his root, a search for spiritual values and the black ancestry in which he had previously shown no interest and which had been denied also by his father. With the help of the black mythologies and the blues sung by his aunt Pilate and the children in Shalimar, the birthplace of his ancestry, he is able to find out his real family name Solomon. In recovering his genealogy, he also discovers his native American heritage.

Moreover, at Pilate's death, Milkman, who has never sung before, inherits her song and turns to the blues matrix from which he was disconnected, and further improvises a new female version of the flying song, "sugargirl" for her. His song not only expresses his love and his desire to comfort his dying aunt, but represents Milkman's first creative participation and active extension of the very cultural tradition of his own origins. His maturation as a compassionate person, as a man capable of nurturing in the spirit of Pilate, is closely related to his receptivity to the identity-shaping music, which links him to the source of African-American wisdom and culture. In the "blood oozing from [Pilate's] neck into his cupped hand," in the "darkness staining his hand" (Morrison, 1977: 340), there is a cultural transfusion and transference, a culture's insurance against death.

Sethe and the Clearing People

In *Beloved*, Morrison shows that to claim one's self comes not merely through one orator's rhetoric, but also through communal movement and music. By having Baby Suggs dance "with her twisted hip the rest of what her heart had to say" to music that the community provides her, Morrison achieves several goals at once: She notes the limitations of even her own language, points us toward a notion of orality that includes the corporeal and the musical, and represents a community with its own particular codes. When Sethe is taken back to the Clearing by the women's song in her yard, it is a sign of both personal and community redemption; the community has returned finally not only to loving themselves but also to feeling compassion for those who have died. Led by church women, Sethe's contrite neighbors and the reformed community acknowledge their complicity in Sethe's plight and, after eighteen years, make amends. In the yard of 124 when the women found "the sound that broke the backs of words", "It was a wave of sound wide enough to sound deep water and knock the pods off chestnut trees. It broke over Sethe and she trembled like the baptized in its wash." (Morrison, 1987: 261)

This passage points to the significance of music, not only in the context of *Beloved*, but also with regard to the predicament of the black diaspora at large. The women's song was powerful enough to break "the backs of words"—words used to define African Americans, such as "animal", "breeding stock" and "slaves." It baptizes and restores Sethe into a new life of wholeness, into a radical spiritual transformation. And there is a redemptive potential: Sethe and Denver are eventually redeemed of Beloved—who embodies a part of Sethe's unresolved and repressive past—by the sheer force of sound relying on the polyphony of a collective layering of "voice upon voice upon voice." It is in the tension between the individual voice and a collective chorus that the "condition of pain" involved in the Black Atlantic experience can be fully expressed; it is in a culture of antiphony, *Beloved* teaches us, that memory is not self-destructive, and that trauma can be overcome whole (Eckstein, 2006: 280).

Alice Manfred, Joe and Violet

Jazz depicted a most prominent "resting place" in music. Like their ancestors who constructed a mode of analysis and articulation first, in the Spirituals, and later, in the blues, survivors in the city have created a "resting place" in jazz. The sounds of saxophone, drums, clarinet, guitars and songs on the streets in Harlem reverberate throughout *Jazz*. Morrison shows not only how damaging it is to renounce music but also the restorative potency of jazz which encourages interaction between listeners and performers and "nourishes personal wholeness and group togetherness" (1997: 270), as Anthony J. Berret notes. Moreover, improvised jazz represents the repressed voices of African Americans without narrowly relying on authoritative and conventional rules of classical written composition.[1] The flexibility of jazz in escaping traditional musical rules underlines the unyielding and vigorous voice of African Americans against a mainstream cultural hegemony which tries to suppress their voices and feelings. Repossessing jazz, which can accommodate a collective African-American identity, is essential for the survival of African Americans because the music functions as a communal repository, preserving and conveying identity-shaping truths. Describing the "tide of cold black faces" marching down the Fifth Avenue following the Chicago riots in which hundreds of Black people were killed, the narrator states "what they meant to say but did not trust themselves to say the drums for them, and what they had seen with their eyes and through the eyes of others the drums described to a T" (Morrison, 1993: 54). For Alice Manfred, the drums help to put in focus the connection between her own grief and that of the people with "frozen black faces." While she is able to decipher in the drums an articulation of "fellowship, discipline and transcendence" (60), she is unable—and perhaps unwilling—to interpret the full complexity of its message. Deciphering the music's full message would require her to confront the one emotion to which she feels unentitled—anger. She blames the music, which she believes was the cause of the riot, for the loss of her sister and brother-in-law. Without her knowledge, the dominant society suppresses her anger and manipulatively replaces it with her hatred for the music and the drums that accompanied the silent participants of the riots and voiced their resentment, despair and frustration. Her suppression of this emotion leads to a futile struggle to keep "the Fifth Avenue drums separate from the belt-buckle tunes vibrating from pianos and spinning on every Victrola" (59).

Alice refuses to acknowledge African-American music as a positive repository of strength. Her negative perception of "race" music as nasty and lowdown makes her insensitive not only to the power of music nurtured by the community but to the community itself. She does not consider the community as having indispensable

---

[1] Shelley Wong explains the flexibility of jazz as follows: "Jazz articulates meaning through attention to the particulars of the moment, to the work under hand, rather than through any strict adherence to received, and preconceived, notions of the bar or the line." (1990: 475)

integrity, nor does she see it as the source of information. Unwilling to attend to the other statements in the music, Alice Manfred is unable to move beyond the crisis in her own life and in Dorcas's life; she is unable as well to help Dorcas to negotiate the destructive and creative potentials in this new environment.

Although Alice tries to suppress her origins, she is finally able to realize the important function of the community as the source for the survival of African Americans and is thus not far away from an awakening to a true racial identity. Exposed to jazz in her daily life, Alice cannot help feeling its embracing and healing power. One day the drums she hears on the street appeal to her like "a rope cast for rescue, the drums spanned the distance, gathering them all up and connected them: Alice, Dorcas, her sister and her brother-in-law, the Boy Scouts and the frozen black faces, the watchers on the pavement and those in the windows above" (58). It is not possible for her to repress an intuitive recognition of her own culture's sustaining musical expression. Violet's appearance in her life is a symbolic entry of that mediational and liberating capacity of the music.

Violet and Joe, the devastating characters at the beginning of *Jazz*, gradually recuperate from loneliness and oppression through music and try to gather their shattered lives together. Music fills the empty, silent spaces between them, functioning as an activator and facilitating their communication. Their conversation stimulates their alienated consciousness, and they agree that music is important for them to compensate for their distorted life: "Violet decided, and Joe agreed, nothing was left to love or need but music." (224) Their recognition of music promotes their contact with the community and its people. The community's music is necessary for them to break the shell of their loneliness. The broken beats of the blues, Spirituals, and jazz that the novel takes up are so firmly rooted in the African diaspora that they establish a secure foundation for the exploration of suffering and pain. James Baldwin argues that "[m]usic is our witness and our ally. The beat is the confession which recognizes changes and conquers time. Then, history becomes a garment we can wear and share, and not a cloak in which to hide, and time becomes a friend" (Morrison, 1996: 330).

In the expressive tradition of African American music, in the security of its off-beat phrasings, history becomes concrete without being destructive, and its stories can be told. Morrison attempts to revitalize the community with jazz that shakes the mind of the audience with its powerful beat as if it intended to break imposed conventions and oppression.

Chapter 2

Morrison's Spirituals: Traumatic Loss of Identity

When talking about the origins of slave music, W. E. B. Du Bois argues: "Sprung from the African forests, where its counterpart can still be heard, it was adapted, changed, and intensified by the tragic soul-life of the slave, until, under the stress of law and whip, it became the one true expression of a people's sorrow, despair nad hope." (1990: 134) It seems to be the very description of the Black Spirituals. As an important music form born in African continent, the Spirituals occupy an important position in American music. In essence, Spirituals are inseparable with the blacks' past in their African tribes. From the very beginning, the Spirituals are carriers for their love and longing for their homeland, but once rooted in an isolated world, the Spirituals have become a balm for them to forget all the tribulations they are facing and the last connection they can still keep to approach their ancestors. In their onerous daily work, they sing to reduce their hardship and at the same time express their protest against the inhuman slavery. Of course, with their white masters listening to their exotic singing, they cannot make any immediate expressions about their real feelings. That's why the Spirituals have a unique charm of deep connotation, unaffected emotion, healthy themes and poem-like language.

Having grown out of the black experience with human enslavement, the black Spirituals or "sorrow songs," said by Southern to have begun evolving from about the 1820s, are strikingly similar to the spirit of the Old Testament literature. Indeed, according to Nathan Wright Jr., the literature of the Spirituals may be said to be—and perhaps in due time will be officially or generally recognized to be—a kind of Third Testament, adding a new dimension of hope to the insightful "God encounters" in the present Old and New Testaments (2001: 87). They are contemporary encounters of a people with a contemporary culture which has made its mark on the entire world. Therefore, African American Spirituals are historic songs of "protest and defiance, based on the passion and eventual triumphs of the Hebrew slaves of Egypt" (Bennet, 1984: 103). As James Cone observes, "We are told that the people of Israel could not sing the Lord's song in a strange land. But, for blacks, their being depended upon a song."

2.1 Cultural Trauma and the Loss of Cultural Identity

Musicologist Eileen Southern points out: "Many Spirituals convey to listeners the same feeling of rootlessness and misery as do the blues." Continuing with these distinctions, she notes that the "Spiritual is religious … rather than worldly and tends to be more generalized than direct, and more expressive of group feelings than individual ones" (1983: 331).

Morrison's novels are concerned with people who in terms of their ancestry are displaced, dispossessed and separated from their identity and history. In most of Morrison's works, the United States is initially a site of exile for most Afro-Americans. What defines this as a site of exile is the psychological condition of the arrivants—their longing for a resting place, their need to release painful memories, and, most importantly, their lack of self recognition. Like their ancestors dispersed by the forces of Slavery, the entire "wave of black people running from want and violence" (Morrison, 1993: 33), is part of a continuing cycle of dispersion that began—but did not end!—with the Middle Passage. As Morrison notes, "the music kept us alive, but it's not enough anymore." The implication is that the younger generation growing up in the urban industrial cities of the North, in a culture of mass commodification, is not able to withstand alienation. Like a singer of Black Spirituals, Morrison writes with her word-song about the feelings of rootlessness and misery suffered by the Black people.

Morrison poses people the questions that have plagued African Americans since emancipation—African Americans' place in American society. In Morrison's novels, the theme of exile/homelessness corresponds with Spirituals in its emphasis on the needs for a home, a resting place in the wilderness. The cultural beliefs that inform the storytelling in some of her novels are manifested in a reversal of cultural health for black people. Morrison creates an environment and a landscape in which infertility is the norm, where values with the potential to sustain have been reversed or perverted, and where few individuals have the key for transcending their inertia. Many of her characters live on the periphery of society. They treat each other savagely, partly because a hideous aspect of the legacy of slavery is that its victims perpetuate the violence they have managed to survive and partly because they writhe with frustration. Excluded from even the most meager possibilities associated with contemporary America, they are virtually consigned to a life wherein ordeal follows ordeal. They feel that they want a way out of their misery. Throughout her writings, Toni Morrison suggests that living with unexamined roots as much as living with no roots creates a stunted and deformed tree, and she has clearly taken this lesson to heart in the creation of her own storytelling style by probing into gender and racial "identity," which is a rather up-to-date issue. In *The Bluest Eye*, for example, her depiction of the cycle of seasons without growth, from autumn to summer, evokes, in their mythological implications, comparisons to the world T. S. Eliot creates in *The Waste Land*. Her novels embody ritualized explorations of the dissolution of culture and the need for an attendant rite of affirmation. She poses such questions as how society can be saved from itself, and what hero, heroine, or heroic change of mind will effect its repair. But she also accomplishes more than these surface comparisons; by setting her novel in a black community, she emphasizes even more the need for rites of renewal, for rebirth from within the community as well as outside of it. The strands of tradition that she fuses in the novel enable Morrison to enrich her story line, to show the peculiarities of her characters, and to connect them to the larger human community.

In Eliot's wasteland, people engage in sex without sharing, indeed without even a minimal concern for their partners; money is valued above all else; there is a meaninglessness in human interactions; and a general malaise exists in which abortions are preferable to delivery, infidelity is common, and culture has collapsed into bar hopping. In Morrison's spiritual wilderness, marriage becomes, for most of the characters, an escape from their humdrum previous existences; sex is economic (for the prostitutes), pristine (for the likes of Geraldine and Soaphead Church), or degenerative (for Pauline); change, though constant, does not bring the improvement in people's life; and potentially sustaining values (love, morality, belief in God) have been destroyed by the very institutions that should perpetuate them (church and family). Though Claudia's family provides an oasis in the desert of mythological infertility in *The Bluest Eye*, Morrison's world is primarily one in which stagnation is the norm, and where the pursuit of values alien to one's culture ultimately leads to destruction. The seasons of infertility become a metaphor for a larger condition that wears away at the very foundation of the society.

All of Morrison's characters exist in a world defined by its blackness and by the surrounding white society that both violates and denies it. The destructive effect of the society can take the form of outright physical violence, but oppression in Morrison's world is more often psychic violence. In view of subject matter, she does not follow the predominant tendency in Afro-American literature of directing the struggle solely toward the external white racist world; instead, she examines the problems within the black community, revealing the serious existence of sexism that has, in collaboration with racism, destroyed many black men and women. She rarely depicts white characters, for the brutality here is less a single act than the systematic denial of the reality of black lives. In fact, Morrison's works do not only focus on black experience of white racism. There is a recurring interest in black people who have acquired social status through accommodating themselves to white society and by appropriating white values. The theme of "invisibility" is, of course, a common one in black person "invisible" in white life (Ellison's *Invisible Man* trying to confront passerby). She doesn't just focus on conflict between blacks and whites, instead, she concentrates on the black experience and in the black community; she does provide a broader social context to make the white society's ignorance of that concrete, vivid, and diverse world even more striking.

But it does reflect a distortion. Blacks are visible to white culture only insofar as they fit its frame of reference and serve its needs. Thus they are constantly reduced and reified, losing their independent reality.

By displaying the collective crisis of motherlessness/fatherlessness (orphanhood) and homelessness/homesickness (exile), Morrison tries to make people realize how important an established identity (who and what people are) is for the black people and black community in a land that is full of feelings of frustration, alienation and displacement for them. Therefore, throughout Morrison's work, identity is the product of psychic struggle. The whole Afro-American ethnic group, including black women, encounters social constraints that corner the black race and extends the doubled vision of being African by culture and American by instinct for survival. As is argued by Patricia Waugh, "for those marginalized by the dominant culture, a sense of identity as constructed through impersonal and social relations of power (rather than a sense of identity as the reflection of an inner 'essence') has been a major aspect of their self-concept." (1989: 3) Gender and race become issues of identity and difference. Therefore, Blacks have long been suffering from loss of subjectivity and black identity. To reclaim this subjectivity and this identity, it's necessary for them to first realize the folly of losing them. Therefore, Morrison also explores the collective reaction of the black community to the state of being in the spiritual wilderness, thus enabling people to get a glimpse of the folly that is devastating and engulfing by revealing the damages caused by multiple oppressions as well as the hope that is releasing and liberating by presenting the solutions to the problems and by putting forward the method to redefine identity—individual and group identities.

2.1.1 Loss of Subjectivity

Morrison in her novels addresses such issues as black victimization, the emotional and social effects of social and sexual oppression, and the difficulties African Americans face in trying to achieve a sense of identity dominated by white cultural values by analyzing the complexities of class, race, and sex and how they affect black women and the whole Afro-American ethnic group still captive in this present-day life. Due to these sufferings, the blacks suffer constantly from loss of subjectivity. Morrison illuminates the profound nature of each individual and community's struggle to gain a sense of self and identity. She not only pictures problematic black women who gradually achieve individuality but portrays pressurized black men who are in constant struggle for their racial wholeness and sexual supremacy as well. By exploring the histories and memories of numerous characters to show how these women and men come to battle, Morrison exposes racial and sexual prejudices, examines black people's painstaking search for self-definition and inquires into the real quality of the Afro-American identity. Different and oppositional as the black men and black women are, their gender problem is deeply rooted in their loss of identity: "They had a problem about what work to do, when and where to do it, and where to live. Those things hinged on what they felt about who they were, and what their responsibilities were being black. The question for each was whether he or she was really a member of that tribe." (McKay, 1988: 147)

Clearly, there are no "whole truths" or "whole" men and women in Morrison's novels, at least not in any traditional fictional sense, though she writes in *Song of Solomon*: "You have to be a whole man. And if you want to be a whole man, you have to deal with the whole truth." (Morrison, 1977: 70) Just as she challenges the dominant cultural view of language and signification, Morrison also subverts traditional Western notions of identity and wholeness.

2.1.1.1 Loss of Female Subjectivity

African American women's situation is that they are wrongfully and unjustly enslaved. Black women suffer from the triple devaluation of being female, black, and poor. Black female identity, as its name indicates, is by all means a rising by-product of the Afro-American identity, a particular and more marginalized side of the second notion. As a black woman writer, Toni Morrison writes with a doubled consciousness of being both a black and a woman by always emphasizing her self-identity. She expounds in her conversation with Gail Caldwell: " ... I've just insisted—insisted!—upon being called a black woman novelist ... As a black and a woman, I have access to a range of emotions and perceptions that were available to people who were neither." (1985: 243) Here, she urges the importance of two terms, namely black and woman, and stamps herself a racial identity as well as a gender one. Therefore, she queries about the black women's doubled consciousness of being caught in a dilemma. Black women, according to Beauvoir, for one thing, suffer from the social construct that woman "is defined and differentiated with reference to man and not be with her ... He is the subject, he is the Absolute—she is the Other" (1953: 56). Black women in Morrison's fictions discover "that they [are] neither white nor male, and that all freedom and triumph [are] forbidden to them" (1973: 44). Womanhood, like blackness, is "Other" in this society, and the dilemma of woman in a patriarchal society is parallel to that of blacks in a racist one: They are made to feel most real when seen. This sexual inferiority marks women's marginalized status as an "Other"/object and their doubled awareness of the opposition between the two sexes, namely the object against the subject. For another, these African American women, together with their male counterparts, experience their dual African and Euro-American culture. Needless to say, they acquire another doubled understanding of their binary cultural identity and, again with their male halves, strive to survive as a racial whole. In the course of trying to clarify their racial and gender identity, as the black feminists of the Combahee River Collective in their manifesto of April 1977 observed, "they struggled together with Black men against racism, and for another, they strove against Black men about sexism" (Eisenstein, 1979: 275). They had to fight on many fronts: against white patriarchy, against white women's racism, against the sexism of black men because black men, prevented from looking outward at the oppressor, displace blame and humiliation they suffered onto black women, the "Other" who "saw" and who were "owned" by them. In *The Bluest Eye*, Morrison exposes black women's suffering by presenting the sufferings of a group of women:

> Everybody in the world was in a position to give them orders. White women said, "do this," White children said, "Give me that," White men said, "Come here." Black men said, "Lay down." The only people they need not take orders from were black children and each other. But they took all of that and recreated it in their own image. They ran the houses of white people, and knew it. When the white men beat their men, they cleaned up the blood and went home to receive abuse from the victim. (138)

The history of their whole lives is a history of oppression because of race, gender, and class as is recognized by Claudia, the narrator of *The Bluest Eye*: "Being a minority in both caste and class, being poor, black, female, we moved about anyway on the hem of life, struggling to consolidate our weakness and hang on, or to creep singly up into the major folds of the garment." (11) What emerges in this historical consciousness is the stultifying reality of black women's truncated lives. Women's subjection, their lack of dominion over their own lives, is the subtext of Morrison's novels.

However, their response is to recreate lives, grounded in their personal formula.

Toni Morrison not only undertakes the fundamental task of exploring black women's individuality to conceptualize the black female self and to expose patriarchal premises and prejudices, but also, in a broader sense, examines the Afro-American identity. For the most part, Morrison first looks into gender-oriented identity issues such as female subjectivity. She examined the enslaved or imprisoned state of the black women, their doubly "Other" scapegoat position, their suffering from the loss of subjectivity and their craving and searching for a more wholesome individuality. Striving in the spiritual wilderness, some of them adopted some violent methods; still others perished under the duress of the multiple pressures, but most of them survived to achieve wholesome selves.

Women Losing "Me-ness"

One of the reasons for women to lose their subjectivity is their loss of individuality or "me-ness." Morrison deliberately gives an example of a girl named Nel in *Sula*, whose journey from assertion of selfhood to losing it after her marriage and to finally reclaiming it typifies a black woman's growth. Nel's "me-ness" and her assertion of selfhood, whether an indication of false pride or merely an adolescent delusion, end in the reality of her common identity with other women of the community. For Sula, at least, Nel has become one of those unindividuated women: "The narrower their lives, the wider their hips. Those with husbands had folded themselves into starched coffins, their sides bursting with other people's skinned dreams and bony regrets. Those without men were like sour tipped needless featuring one constant empty eye." (Morrison, 1973: 105)

Although at first adopting me-ness as her mantra and gathering power, joy and the "strength to cultivate a friend [Sula] in spite of her mother" (25), Nel's daring is eclipsed, however, by marriage to Jude, as for many other female characters, "female aspiration is a joke. Female rebellion may be perfectly justified, but there is no good universe next door, no way out, young potential revolutionaries can't find their revolution. So they marry in defeat or go mad in a complicated form of triumph, their meanings the inevitability of failure" (Spacks, 1975: 158).

For her mother, marriage is one of the neat conditions of living that defines a woman's place, and Nel accepts a similar arrangement for herself. Nel does not choose Jude; she accepts his choosing her as a way of completing himself. Without

Nel, Jude is an enraged "waiter hanging round a kitchen like a woman" (Morrison, 1973: 71) because bigotry keeps him from doing better. "With her he was head of a household pinned to an unsatisfactory job out of necessity. The two of them together would make one Jude." (71) In marrying Jude, Nel gives up her youthful dreams (before she met Sula) of being "wonderful" and of "trips she would take, alone … to faraway places" (25). In marrying Jude, she gives up her "me-ness."

In Sula's ten-year absence, Nel has developed into the very conventional feminine voice "proclaiming its worth on the basis of the ability to care for and protect others" (Gillingan, 1982: 79) for which her family has trained her. Predicatably, when Jude leaves, after his betrayal with Sula, Nel suffers psychic disintegration with circles of sorrowful torments and begins to rethink of her lost "me-ness." After a necessary recovery, she endures falseness, emptiness and shrinkage of the self. She considers the release that may come with death, but that will have to wait because she has three children to raise. In this condition Nel wraps herself in the conventional mantle of sacrifice and martyrdom and takes her place with the rest of the women in the community. All her life she has practiced an extreme of the repression to preserve a self-image of goodness which has a nasty flavor of complacency. She breaks out of the conventional vision of goodness, which, in its preoccupation with propriety, fails to nurture truthfulness necessary to relationships that clarify the self. Although Nel does not discover it until after Sula's death and she is old, the real loss in her life is that of Sula, whose "me-ness" remains intact, and not Jude. And the real tragedy is that she has allowed herself to become less than herself and has betrayed herself.

Women Suffering from Bad Faith

Morrison's novels are full of characters who try to live up to an external image—Dick and Jane's family, or cosmopolitan society, or big business. They are human beings whose human relations, as Sartre has pointed out, revolve around the experience of "the look," for being "seen" by another both confirms one's reality and threatens one's sense of freedom: "I grasp the Other's look at the very center of my act as the solidification and alienation of my own possibilities." (1966: 239) The Other's look makes "me" see "myself" as an object in another perception. "If I can make the other into an object in my world, I can 'transcend' him: Thus my project of recovering myself is fundamentally a project of absorbing the Other" (Sartre, 1996: 340). The result is a cycle of conflicting and shifting subject-object relationships in which both sides try simultaneously to remain in control of the relationship and to use the Other's look to confirm identity. The difficulty of such an attempt tempts human beings to Bad Faith, "a vacillation between transcendence and facticity which refuses to recognize either one for what it really is or to synthesize them" (547). This conformity is not just a disguise, but an attempt to gain power and control. There is always the hope that if one fits the prescribed pattern, one will be seen as human. Helene Wright puts on her velvet dress in hopes that it, with "her manner and her bearing," will be "protection" against the reductive gaze of the white other (Morrison, 1973: 17). Light-skinned women, already closer to white models, aspire to a genteel ideal: Green-eyed Maureen Peal "enchanted the entire school" (Morrison, 1970: 62), and "sugar-brown Mobile girls" (82) like Geraldine "go to land-grant colleges, normal schools, and learn how to do the white man's work with refinement" (83). The problem with such internalization is not that it is ambitious, but that it is life-denying, eliminating "[t]he dreadful funkiness of the wide range of human emotions" (83). One who really accepts the external definition of the self gives up spontaneous feeling and choice. Such characters can become victimized not only by dependence on one another, but also by internalizing the "look" of the majority culture.

The "look" of white society, supported by all kinds of material domination, not only freezes the black individual but also classifies all blacks as alike, freezing the group. They become a "we-object" before the gaze of a "third":

> It is only when I feel myself become an object along with someone else under the look of such a "third" that I experience my being as a "we-object"; for then, in our mutual interdependency, in our shame and rage, our beings are somehow mingled in the eyes of the onlooker, for whom we are both somehow "the same": two representatives of a class or a species, two anonymous types of something .... (Jameson, 1971: 249)

Again, the basic problem may be ontological, but the institutionalization of the relation, the coercive power of the "third," exacerbates it. This is the reason for all the misnaming: A whole group of people have been denied the right to create a recognizable public self—as individuals or as community. Given that combination of personal and communal vulnerability, it is hardly surprising that many characters choose the way of the least agony and the fewest surprises: They "choose" their status as objects, even fiercely defend it. Helene and Geraldine increasingly become perfect images rather than free selves. In this retreat from life they are abetted by a community so dominated by white society as the "third" that order and stability are its primary values. In *The Bluest Eye*, narrator Claudia comments that the worst fear is of being "outdoors" (Morrison, 1970: 11). Any "excess" that might challenge the powerful look and increase their isolation is terrifying. And so the images that caused the alienation, excluded them from the real world, are paradoxically received and imitated as confirmations of life. Living in a white-male-dominated world where eyes are blinded by racism and male chauvinism, black women are consequently marked down as the Other and objects. This forms the circuit of looking relations between Master and non-white Other in which the Master looks upon the Other and sees an absence of humanity. In turn, the Other looks upon the Master and sees omnipotence and the negation of self.[1] Enveloped in the hierarchy of racism, sexism and classism, the position of black women is doubly difficult because they are neither white nor male. Being non-male and non-white makes them invisible to the hierarchical world and the easiest way to become acceptable by the world is to accept the white-male standardized value system. This is also the case with Pecola in *The Bluest Eye*.

The most powerful illustration of Pecola's ontological problem is her failure to realize the beauty of her black skin when she purchases the Mary Jane candies she loves so much in Mr. Yacobowski's vegetable and meat store. When the black girl looks up, she only finds "the total absence of human recognition—the gazed separateness" in the shop owner's eyes. Identifying Yacobowski's look with one that she sees "in the eyes of all white people," Pecola decides that "the distaste must be for her, her blackness ... And it is the blackness that accounts for, that vacuum

---

[1] John Berger, *Ways of Seeing*. London: Penguin, 1972, p. 96. Also see Judith Williamson's "Woman Is an Island: Feminity and Colonization", in which she notes that "the most likely Other for a white working-class man, is either a woman ... or a foreigner—in particular somebody black. It is not likely to be someone from the class which controls his livelihood" (103).

edged with distaste in white eyes" (Morrison, 1970: 49). For the storekeeper, the racism and sexism are so deeply rooted that he cannot bear to look at Pecola, even to "touch her hand" (49) when he takes her money. The cultural blindness of such people as Yacobowski leads to what Henry Louis Gates theorizes that blackness signifies absence.[1] Pecola cannot be seen by the candy seller "because for him there is nothing to see" (48). She becomes absent. As a matter of fact, she internalizes the western masculine ideas of physical beauty and unconsciously disqualifies her as the professor of her own cultural standards. Pecola's unloving childhood, her repudiation by nearly everyone she encounters, her values dictated by the white mythology, failure to instill a healthy self-perception, the negative examples of parenting and the absence of role models worthy of emulation precipitate her psychic disintegration, leaving her alienated from any sense of an authentic black self, and finally insane. All endure that Pecola cannot depend upon her own family unit as a way out of the stagnated wasteland. No values are passed on to her that would sustain her, and she is too outside the community in her hypersensitivity to have the leisurely occasions on which to draw sustenance from sources beyond her home.

Women Confined

Morrison also cites some examples of women who lost their subjectivities because they were "pressed small" by a society which would not allow them to grow and thus became the slaves and prisoners of middle class ideas. Among them, Ruth in *Song of Solomon* is the typical one.

Born in Foster family, the richest black family in the vicinity, Ruth is an immediate victim of class-consciousness, and material wealth indirectly. To make prominent himself and his family and to differentiate his people from the others, Dr. Foster confines Ruth to the big house, dolls her, and humors her, which shapes her distorted character, and she believed her father to be the only friend that she had (Morrison, 1977: 124). Her husband, taking over the relay stick from his father-in-law, devotes himself to pressing her into "a small package" (137), as she told

---

[1] Henry Louis Gates, Jr. *Black Literature and Literary Theory.* London: Routledge, 1984, p. 7. He has commented on the irony of African-American writers attempting to "posit a 'black self' in the very Western languages in which blackness itself is a figure of absence, a negation."

her son Milkman: "I don't mean little; I mean small, and I'm small because I was pressed small. I lived in a great house that pressed me into a small package. I had no friends, only schoolmates who wanted to touch my dresses and my white stockings. But I didn't think I'd ever need a friend because I had him[her father]. I was small, but he was big. The only person who ever really cared whether I lived or died." (124)

Unfortunately, her father added to her "smallness" and alienation so that her love for him has become distorted with profanity. Ruth suffers under Macon's rule, her creativity stunted, her flowers dying; she is "a beaten-down, faded rose" (Wilentz, 1997: 110). Isolated from her community and culture, Ruth, from the very beginning, is turned into a decoration on man's property and class status, which molds a morbid character that lives on morbid pleasure. Impotent to live safe and sound in the outer world and failing to acquire contentment, she builds up instead in her inner heart an inner world, where she curls and curls up, where she is the only dweller that matters, and where she thinks she can free and protect herself from being disturbed. Being tormented by a strong sense of alienation, from her people as well as from the outside world, Ruth props up and consoles herself by things. She is a person with fierce yet unfulfilled desire for possession, whose growth is in proportion to its unfulfillment. Hers is the possession of affection. With Dr. Foster taking his love for her to his tomb, she, having failed to retrieve tender feelings from Macon, turns to inanimate things in virtue of their "deadness" that makes it impossible for them to betray her or desert her as human beings can. Her father's grave and the ugly spreading watermark left on the dining-room table from a bowl that once held fresh flowers are among her relievers and the only confirmations Ruth can find of her existence is. As so often happens in literature and reality that things remind one of people related, they are infallible witness to past love she once enjoys, from which she draws eagerly a thread of warm feelings, and to which she cannot but hold tightly, just like the fake roses Ruth and her daughter make.

The two daughters, Magdalene called Lena and First Corinthians, pine for lack of love and life, since no man in the community is good enough for Macon Dead's daughters. When Lena eventually wakes to what is happening to her, the outburst recalls Guitar's condemnation of how white people want black people quiet and "dead": "I was the one who started making artificial roses ... I loved to do it. It kept me … quiet. That's why they make those people in the asylum weave baskets and make rag rugs. It keeps them quiet. If they didn't have the baskets they might find out what's really wrong and … do something. Something terrible." (Morrison, 1977: 215) Her hesitation before she can bring herself to say the word "quiet" underscores its significance, for her and her whole family, as well as the pain in the realization. The phrase "something terrible" is set apart and as such highlights the fear whites have of blacks that rise against their confinement. In the description of the suicidal leap at the outset of the novel, roses occur along with wings and song as specific images, each of which eventually provides this multi-layered text with a sense of coherence around the subjects of freedom, spirituality, life-in-death, the value of myth and the role of the ancestors: "The sight of Mr. Smith and his wide blue wings transfixed them for a few seconds, as did the woman's singing and the roses strewn about." (Morrison, 1973: 6)

In *Love*, Morrison describes two other women, May and Heed, who are confined in the patriarchal house. Morrison shows her sympathy with the woman who has slaved for the Patriarch but who has been rewarded with despise by describing May, the devoted daughter-in-law of Bill Cosey. Her whole life was making sure her husband and her father-in-law had what they wanted: the father-in law more than the husband; the father-in-law more than her own daughter. She took to the hotel business like a bee to pollen. Even pregnancy didn't slow her down. She weaned her baby at three months. After the death of her husband Billy Boy, for the next seven years she put all her energy into the hotel's business. But seven years of hard work were rewarded by watching her father-in-law marry her twelve-year-old daughter—Christines's eleven-year-old playmate Heed and put that playmate ahead of everything, including herself, her daughter, and all she worked for. Not only that. She was supposed to teach and train the playmate to take charge of the family affair. Instead of fighting her father-in-law for the unfair treatment, she directed her hatred towards the child bride Heed by verbally abusing and taunting her, who is in essence also the victim of the patriarchal society. When conflicts between her daughter and Heed became hot, instead of fighting her father-in-law for the protection of her own daughter, she sent her daughter away, following Mr. Cosey's self-centered willful decision. When she was afraid of the fire of civil rights, Mr. Cosey despised her dread. When "everyone decided her mother was insane and speculated as to why: widowhood, overwork, no sex, SNCC" (Morrison, 2003: 97), Christine finally understood her mother. The world May knew was always crumbling and her place in it was never secure: "Husband dead; her crumbling hotel ruled by a rabid rat, ignored by the man for whom she had slaved, abandoned by her daughter to strange ideas, a running joke to neighbors—she had no place and nothing to command. So she recognized the war declared on her and fought it alone" (99–100). Her worth dejected by the one patriarch she slaves for, she confines herself in the insane kingdom to fight the war declared on her as she imagined.

After she became Cosey's child bride, Heed was thrust into adulthood. She had no access to education, lost her best friend, suffered the humiliation of Cosey's affairs, and was broken-hearted that a man, for whom she intended to leave Cosey, did not share her affection. Heed's hands, "small, baby-smooth except for one scarred spot, each one curved gently away from its partner—like fins" (28), are deformed, useless, burned, and arthritic. These "fins" are alternately described as "wings" (99) that "fold" (141), which map the pain of the Cosey women's lives and are a testament to her disempowerment. While Heed's marriage to Cosey brought financial and socio-political gain, the uselessness of her hands, which are described through animal imagery, discloses her powerlessness. A Cinderella trapped in marriage, she internalized the oppression from her husband Mr. Cosey willingly even after his death.

Women in War with Each Other

There is still another kind of loss of subjectivity: Black women suffering from the double or triple devaluation of being female, black, and poor fight each other in the process of courting favors from men. Morrison examined this kind of situation in her novel *Love* by describing the intimate relationships that women have and how they can be damaged by the random cruelties of fate, time and man's manipulation. Despite their respective confined position, Christine Cosey, May Cosey and Heed Johnson Cosey, the granddaughter, the daughter-in-law and the child bride of Bill Cosey, the charismatic owner of an ocean-front resort that serves the black elite of the South, fight each other after Heed's marriage to Bill Cosey. Christine and Heed are childhood friends until Cosey takes Heed for a wife after his son and first wife dies and Heed is all of 11 years old. Not realizing their victim position in the patriarchal family, they become bitter enemies occupying the family home on Monarch Street, a house haunted with the spectral presence of Bill Cosey, who is "everywhere [a]nd nowhere" (Morrison, 2003: 189). Their damaged relationship causes the 60-year blood feud they had afterwards.

The three women have not yet understood that they are all the victims of their seemingly great patriarch: The "Papa" that overshadows their lives even after his death. This mystery spawns years of tragic misunderstanding between the women. They vie endlessly for Cosey's love and affection, even after his death, with his visage frozen in a portrait and his spirit roaming the house on Monarch Street. Indeed, death has done very little to stop the Cosey women from having intimate relations with this powerful patriarch. He overshadows their lives, their home, and their relationships with one another. Ultimately they develop a deep and dark hatred for one another, although it's a thin line between love and hate. Eventually after years of seething resentment, the Cosey's conflicts are finally resolved, albeit shockingly, after the truth is finally brought to light through their communication. The war turns out to be meaningless and futile.

Subjectivity Gone Wild

Loss of subjectivity can be found in some other expressions. Among them subjectivity gone wild can be considered a deviation form. In order to retrieve the lost dignity or honour or to redefine themselves, at least seemingly, some black people exert their own power towards their own people, causing great damage to the people concerned. Among them, Eva and Sula are women figures that try to redefine their worth in some wild ways in order to rise against patriarchal society.

As Morrison has said in an interview with Bettye J. Parker, "Eva is a triumphant figure, one-legged or not. She's playing God. She maims people. But she says all of the important things" (1979: 255). Eva certainly starts out as a traditional mother; she tries desperately to keep her family alive after her husband's departure, but her efforts soon become ineffectual. Her redefinition of role begins with her depositing her three children with a neighbor and not returning for eighteen months. She chooses self over sacrifice, borders on immorality, and therefore becomes free. Her separation from people in the community and acting against their norms enable her to develop an ironic posture in relation to them. Her freedom, somehow tied to the loss of her leg, gives her the ability to love, hate, create, conquer, and kill, with responsibility and accountability only to herself. She is free to be moral if she wishes, amoral if it pleases her, and immoral if necessary. Her transformation is like Cholly Breedlove's when he becomes free through killing three white men; he has stretched the bonds of humanity and can now accept or discard them at will. After she is deserted and revisited by her husband BoyBoy, Eva's hatred for her husband strengthens her or protects her "from routine vulnerabilities" (Morrison, 1973: 36). Hatred keeps her "alive and happy" (37). In making hate into a positive and sustaining emotion and motivation, Eva inverts notions of right and wrong, thereby standing morality on its head and identifying with the folkways that defy absoluteness in behavior. She therefore forces other men to worship where her husband has not—literally at her feet. She presents the men who visit her over the years with a tantalizing morsel that they will never have the opportunity to savor. By encouraging their presence and flirting with them, Eva assures herself of the male attention that must unwaveringly atone for Boyboy's desertion. She manifests her hatred and scorn of men in what they see as her attraction for them, her inability to live without their attention.

In a goddess-like way, Eva provides shelters in her home for the three deweys, but by naming them out of a mixture of fun and meanness, she makes them into "grotesques"—"a trinity with a plural name … inseparable, loving nothing and no one but themselves" (38), remaining children into their adult years. She can laugh at them or control them, because she is ultimately disinterested in them; as part of the landscape she has created in that huge house, they have as much or as little claim to belonging as any of other inhabitants. Like a perverted artist, Eva gives them a place in her home as well as a place in the lore of the Bottom; together, they increase Morrison's population of "grotesques," as Darwin T. Turner labels her characters (1984: 38). The denial of individual dewey reality gives way to one of Eva's pastimes: She creates the concept of the deweys for her own amusement. She names them and thereby determines their fate.

In deciding that her drug-addicted son Plum would be better off dead, she burnt him in the mixture of love and revulsion, egotistically and self-centeredly eliminating what offended her.

Sula is another more immoral version of her grandmother Eva. She sees herself as the center of the universe around which other people can revolve or not—as she needs or uses them. Eva's actions have at least been motivated by love for her children and hatred for her husband. Sula simply is—whatever she decides is convenient or desirable or pleasurable. None of her motivations comes from caring about or hating or fearing anyone. She is simply in the community; what it does or how it responds to her is of no consequence to her, the only reactions she has concerning other people are her slight remorse that Nel has responded so unexpectedly to her sleeping with Jude and feeling that she has become possessive enough of Ajax to drive him away.

2.1.1.2 Loss of Male Subjectivity

The historical circumstances of the 19th-century America amplified what European ideology traditionally prized as the essential elements of manhood: autonomy, agency, and power, control over one's self, family, and environment. As E. Anthony Rotundo has noted, freedom from the limitations of European hierarchies and socially defined identities led the 19th-century white American men to believe they possessed a "limitless capacity to invent their selves" (1993: 3–4). America was perceived as a virgin wilderness, ready to be shaped by the untrammeled white male will in a way that enacted white masculinity. Morrison has endorsed this interpretation of American masculinity in *Playing in the Dark*, describing how "the American's new, white and male" was constituted by "autonomy, authority, newness and difference, absolute power" (1992: 43–44). For Morrison, a key element of this new masculinity was the subjugation of African Americans; control over men reduced to objects confirmed the "absolute" masculine power of white men. Being denied all the elements that hegemony deemed essential to manhood was a traumatic, dehumanizing experience for black men, hence, Orlando Patterson's characterization of their experience of slavery as "social death."[1] They could own no property, nor impose their will on any aspect of external reality, not even their own bodies; they were totally unmanned.

---

[1] See Patterson's explanation of how slavery inflicts "social death" by stripping men of agency and honor, based on Frederick Douglass's famous statement: " A man without force is without the essential dignity of humanity." Orlando Patterson. *Slavery and Social Death*. London: Harvard UP, 1982.

Morrison herself had said in an interview: "Every immigrant of America knew he would not come as the very bottom. He had to come above at least one group— and that was us (black people)." (Taylor-Guthrie, 1994: 115) This expounds how deep and large the influence of whites' supremacy and racial discrimination exerts on people. This not only results in black women's suffering from triple oppression, but also causes black men to lose their masculinity and become the childish men. Some of them suffered from emasculation; still others rose to fight this loss. However, their target is not the one that victimizes them, but their sisters who suffer no less than them, and this is another kind of loss of masculinity, and therefore subjectivity.

Men Suffering from Emasculation

Social background where the blacks live is very nasty, where black men are severely discriminated against by the whites. Life of the people in the black community is so hard and humiliating that they scrabble for survival; a passage from *Sula* best illustrates this situation:

> What was taken by outsiders to be slackness, slovenliness or even generosity was in fact a full recognition of the legitimacy of forces other than good ones. They did not believe doctors could heal—for them, none ever had done so. They did not believe death was accidental—life might be, but death was deliberate ... the purpose of evil was to survive it and they determined to survive floods, white people, tuberculosis, famine and ignorance ....
>
> (Morrison, 1973: 90)

This situation destroyed the confidence and sense of dignity of men, rendering some of them free of the necessary responsibility that makes a man, and they become dangerously free. Cholly, Pecola's father in *The Bluest Eye*, is such a victim of the society as well as victimizing his daughter. He is deprived of his dignity and lacks knowledge of how to be a responsible and reliable father. Abandoned on a junk heap by his unmarried mother, his dignity is ignored from his birth. When he begins to experience the possibilities that lie in discovering selfhood, a sensual appreciation of nature, and his nascent manhood, his first sexual experience becomes an ordeal when he and his girlfriend are caught during their lovemaking by white hunters who force them into a humiliating sexual display, publicly mocking Cholly's personal sexuality. Not knowing how to vent his anger, he safely blames his girlfriend instead of the threatening white hunters. This incident illustrates how black behaviors and consciousness are destructively influenced by the whites. In order to preserve his dignity, Cholly must misdirect his anger toward an even more powerless person. He cannot challenge the hunters who brutally intrude into his private space and consciousness. The dominant doctrine of white patriarchy obviously excludes black men's maleness and ignores their identity. "In a society in which patriarchal dominance and the supremacy of the phallus are considered coterminous," as Michele Wallace puts it, "the black man is perpetually denied the authority of the Great White Father" (1990: 232). After becoming "free," as Morrison describes him, Cholly probably sees no great commitment in doing anything: "free" to kill, to nurture, or to contribute to someone else's happiness.

In *Sula*, Morrison writes about a group of characters that are in flight from the responsibilities of adulthood and manhood. For the most part, as is argued by Samuels, the men are superficial (Ajax), immature (Boyboy, Little Chicken), untrustworthy (Jude), and anonymous (deweys) (Morrison, 1973: 46). Eva's husband abandons her and three children, leaving them hardly any chance to survive; her son Plum was forced to leave for wars, devastated and "losing" himself in heroin to seek oblivion and drug-addicted when he came back, which enables him to effect the regression to a comparatively safe childhood he desperately desires, rather than to act responsibly to establish an order and chart a direction for his fragmented life. His infantile behavior is a metaphor for lack of independence. Calling Plum "Sweet Plum," Eva further emasculated and rendered him infantile. Plum has regressed completely; almost entirely passive, he becomes active only to steal from everyone in the house. Eva painfully refused to accept an adult baby by describing him to be "crawlin' back. Being helpless and thinking baby thoughts and dreaming baby dreams and messing up his pants again and smiling all the time" (Morrison, 1973: 62). Eva mourns Plum, however, before she burns him and cuts off his retreat to infancy, grieving that her child's personality has died.

Nel's husband Jude is another case in point. His case is one to illustrate how the masculinity of black men is deprived by the whites. As black people are less educated, they have trouble in finding jobs. Even if they had jobs, the jobs are not their level. Jude acts as a waiter in a hotel, and he is not satisfied with this job. He is trying to find a challenging work. The chance comes—a new road is to be built near his community. He wishes to build that road "not just for the good money, more for the work itself. He wants to swing the pick or kneel down with the string or shovel the gravel … " "I built that road," he could say. However he is not fortunate to get this job and show his masculinity. "He stood in lines for six days running and saw the gang boss pick out thin-armed white boys from the Virginia hills and the bull-necked Greeks and Italians and heard over and over: 'Nothing else today. Come back tomorrow.'" (82) It is more humiliating that they hire three old colored men, "but not for the road work, just to do the picking up, food bringing and other small errands" (81). Jude marries Nel out of his feeling of impotence. As he is precluded from the "masculine" work of building the new road, Jude chooses to release his "rage and determination to take on a man's role" (82) in marriage and seeks to complete himself in obtaining a surrogate mother, which renders him even more childish because Nel's concept of goodness damages her and those she serves. To ensure that her husband remains dependent on her goodness, Nel encourages his worst traits: "[Jude] told them a brief tale of some personal insult done him by a customer and his boss—a whiney tale that peaked somewhere between anger and a lapping desire for comfort. He ended it with the observation that a Negro man had a hard row to hoe in this world. He expected his story to dovetail into milkwarm commiseration … " (88–89) This explains and encourages his later irresponsible desertion of Nel and his children after his affair with Sula is disclosed.

Among Morrison's childish men, the deweys may be the most tragic and most repellent. The deweys' individual identities dissipate completely to merge into one, and they not only stop growing physically but remains boys in mind, "mischievious, cunning, private and completely unhousebroken" (Morrison, 1973: 73). Their abnormal shortness (four feet) mirroring their stunted emotional and intellectual growth, the deweys are the novel's most extreme versions of childish men. Three boys of disparate ages, races, and temperaments under Eva's tutelage gradually merge into one entity. It does not matter that Eva asks for a dewey to perform a chore, for they are all orphans, dependent, easily intimidated, and as strange as their personalities and Eva's house make them. Finally, the name is not even capitalized, and "them deweys" become "a trinity with a plural name ... inseparable, loving nothing and no one but themselves" (38), indistinguishable in their appearance as in their childlike behavior. Made comical by their antics and diminutive size, they remain children into their adult years. Their size, combined with their acquisition of only the basic, functional command of language, gives their mental otherness a physical dimension. Yet they nevertheless figure more frequently as a concept than as separate entities in the novel; the lower-case references to them reinforce this idea. They remain unable to care for themselves for as long as they live, expecting Eva and then Sula to provide their food, shelter, and clothing—to mother them.

Prior to their migration, Morrison's Old Fathers in *Paradise* typify the problematic relation African American men have experienced with hegemonic American ideologies of masculinity. As important officials in reconstruction regimes, the Old Fathers could briefly escape the traumatic objectification and conceive of themselves as men according to hegemonic American ideals of masculinity; men whose wills command respect and authority in the public sphere. But the return of white supremacy to the South strips them of this masculine power, reducing them to a shameful impotence, which they refuse consciously to acknowledge. They fiercely repress the threat to their sense of manhood posed by racist humiliations beneath an increasingly rigid façade of ideal masculinity. Morrison describes them as becoming "stiffer, prouder with each misfortune" (1999: 14). They behave with a "dignified manner" and "studies speech" that other African Americans interpret as "arrogance" (302). Their inability to acknowledge the actual, shaming impotence that racism inflicts is illustrated well by the story of Zechariah Morgan's rejection of his twin brother, Tea, for dancing for drunken white men who threaten otherwise to shoot him. As one character eventually recognized, Zechariah rejected Tea not merely out of disgust at his behavior, but because he feared that seeing his brother would remind him that "the shame" produced by such racist humiliations was also "in himself" (303). Traumatized by experiences of dehumanizing rejection and humiliating impotence inflicted by white racism, they migrated to the Oklahoma Territory, which represents a unique opportunity to escape the dominant power of white racism. However, their migration didn't strengthen their manhood. Instead, they suffer a humiliation that threatens to shatter their already fragile and embattled sense of manhood: the Disallowing by lighter-skinned African Americans as a dehumanizing judgment on their dark skin.

2.1.2 Loss of Black Identity

Although it is defined quite differently, identity at its most basic gives a man a sense of personal location, the stable core to his individuality. Caroline Brown has argued about the complexity and inconsistencies of identity: "Identity is the ultimate structure of improvisation: erratic, ambiguous, artful. It is scrappy, shifting according to necessity, opportunity, and desire. It is as of the self's interaction with its environment, the result of both self-creation and other's convictions." (637)

Vickroy analyzes how the traumatic experience of social powerlessness and devalued racial identity prevent the African American community from joining together and truthfully evaluating the similarity of their circumstances, much less finding ways to oppose dominant forces (Vickroy, 1996: 91). Similarly, Jacqueline de Weever in her essay explores the crisis of black identity when cultural values are defined by a white society in *The Bluest Eye* and *Sula*, and she points out clearly that "the desire to transform one's identity, itself an inverted desire, becomes the desire for blue eyes, and is a symptom of Pecola's instability." "Her two heroines find no help as they grope toward possession of identity," which suggests that "the struggle to establish identity in a world which does not acknowledge one's existence is sometimes lost." (403) As a result, some black people lose their ethnic identity.

2.1.2.1 The Devaluation of the Black Self-image

Unlike white women who are oppressed chiefly by sexism, black women, oppressed not only by sexism, but also by racism and classism, suffer from the triple devaluation of being female, black, and poor. Deborah K. King termed "multiple jeopardy" to show that "racism multiplied by sexism multiplied by classism" (1988:47) results in the black women's subordinate status. Instead of focusing on the direct oppressions on the black women, Morrison attaches great importance to how the intersecting oppressions are internalized in the minds of black women and serve as the destructive forces to damage their identities. Internalizing the multiple oppressions, some black women are unable to realize the beauty of their black images, fail to defend their rights, and finally isolate themselves by breaking off with their families and communities.

Therefore, one of the aspects of the loss of black women's identities caused by the multiple oppressions is the denial of their black images. Failure to realize the beauty of their black skin is one of the reasons for black women to devaluate their black self-images, which results in the intraracial acceptance of the world's denigration of blackness, their marginalized existence and devalued sensitivities. Black people are taught the destructive, devaluing power of white standards of beauty that the blonde hair, blue eyes, and white skins are not only wonderful, but also the surface manifestations of the very best character God and nature ever molded. The oppressive standard of beauty promoted by movies and advertisements deteriorates black self-esteem. Morrison's black characters internalize "the look" of the dominant social order, construct themselves and others through, and in a few instances against, the gaze of the Master—the dominant, hegemonic ideology which devalues black people. They reject their own heritage and assume facades that please dominant white society.

In *The Bluest Eye*, Morrison theorizes how confused, shattered and psychotic self-images come into being for black people:

> You looked at them and wondered why they were so ugly: You looked closely and could not find the source. Then you realized that it came from conviction, their conviction. It was as though some mysterious all-knowing master had given each one a cloak of ugliness to wear, and they had each accepted it without question. The master had said, "you are ugly people." They had looked about themselves and saw nothing to contradict the statement; saw, in fact, support for it leaning at them from every billboard, every movie, every glance. "Yes," they had said, "you are right." And they took the ugliness in their hands, threw it as a mantle over them, and went about the world with it. (1970: 34)

Pecola Breedlove infers from her daily experiences that her distinctive features as a black woman do not fit the standards of the male-dominated ruling class aesthetics, and that her "ugliness" isolates her at school as well as at home. Under the overwhelming power of white culture toward standard of beauty, white baby dolls, little white girls and movie images are constant reminders that blackness is of lesser value. Imputing her gloomy life to her physical appearance, she wishes for blue eyes, which, to her, represent an imagery of the privileges given to the whites. "It had occurred to Pecola some time ago that if her eyes, those eyes that held the pictures, and knew the sights—if those eyes of hers were different, that is to say, beautiful, she herself would be different." (46)

The imposition of white ideology on the black people has distorted the heart of Pecola so deeply that she "each night without fail" prays for blue eyes, believing her ugly reality will be made beautiful through them. She stays with the milk for a long time in order to gaze at the silhouette of Shirley Temple's dimpled face and will take "every opportunity to drink milk out of it just to handle and see sweet Shirley's face" (23). For Pecola, to eat the Mary Jane candy seems to eat the supernatural and magic thing in order to consume its power: "To eat the candy is somehow to eat the eyes, eat Mary Jane. Love Mary Jane. Be Mary Jane." (50) The blue eyes gradually deprive Pecola of her dignity, self-confidence and her identity, because in her insanity she experiences the illusion that blue ones replace her dark eyes. She does not come to possess them as she prays; instead they come to possess her, consuming her mind and destroying her spirit and making her the bluest "I."

In "Behind the Making of *The Black Book*," Morrison makes her point clear as follows:

> When the strength of a race depends on its beauty, when the focus is turned to how one looks as opposed to what one is, we are in dumbest, most pernicious and destructive ideas of the Western world. And we should have nothing to do with it. Physical beauty has nothing to do with our past, present or future. Its absence or presence was only important to them, the white people who used it for anything they wanted. (1974: 89)

Unable to resist the overwhelming influences of the male-dominated white beauty and perceive the beauty of their black skin, some black women model after the whites' dressing up and the way of life, attempting to fit the standard of their esthetics, which further devalues the black women.

The first example is Pecola's mother Pauline, who imitates the white actress' dressing up. When loneliness and boredom drive Pauline to frequent the movies, she allows herself to accept the standards of beauty represented by the Hollywood films. Locating her standards of beauty from the movie world, Pauline fixes her hair up, part on the side, with one little curl on the forehead. Then she sits in the cinema with her hair done up that way and has a good time. The films present her with a romantic world. In that world, money is never a problem. Her appreciation of the ways white men care for their women gives her "*a lot of pleasure, but made coming home hard, and looking at Cholly hard*" (Morrison, 1970: 123; italics in original). She begins to assume the values of people who laugh at her. Her attempt to be incorporated in a cinema world alienates her from reality. It damages her real life which does not match up the commercialized fantasies projected on the screen. She is never able to "look at a face and not assign it some category in the scale of absolute beauty, and the scale was one she absorbed in full from the silver screen" (122). Believing that the cinematic illusions are real, she cannot accept the reality of her unfulfilled life and start to have difficulty in facing her irresponsible black husband, her black children as well as her black image.

Another instance is Geraldine's imitation of whites' way of life. Coming from a black neighbourhood Mobile, Geraldine and her friends are concerned only with the things related to the white (123), and do everything possible to "get rid of the funkiness." "Wherever it erupts, this Funk, they wipe it away; where it crusts, they dissolve it; wherever it drips, flowers, or clings, they find it and fight it until it dies." (83)

What Geraldine is fighting in fact is her blackness, the very conditions of her birth that identify who she is. Instead of nourishing the seed of her being, she attempts to destroy it. In order to distance herself from black community, Geraldine goes to "land-grant colleges, normal schools, and learn how to do the white man's work with refinement: home economics to prepare his food; teacher education to instruct black children in obedience; music to soothe the weary master and entertain his blunted soul" (83). Following the whites' requirements of "thrift, patience, high morals and good manners" (83), Geraldine builds "her nest stick by stick," makes it "her own inviolable world" (84). She decorates her house beautifully with "little lace doilies" everywhere and "potted plants" which charm Pecola who lives in a storefront apartment. Although Geraldine superficially reproduces the domestic lifestyle dictated by the controlling culture, she cannot accommodate her race in it, but only validates by exclusion of others, contributing to reinforcing a racialized hierarchy, which implicitly suggests a displaced isolation from her origins.

Geraldine makes every effort to escape and deny the evidences of her black images. Like Pauline, she straightens hair and parts it on the side. At night she curls it in paper from brown bags, ties a print scarf around her head, and sleeps with hands folded across her stomach. She regards herself as "coloured people" and explains to her son "the difference between colored people and niggers." In her opinion, they are "easily identifiable" because "colored people were neat and quiet; niggers were dirty and loud" (87). She tells Junior to play only with white children and dresses him in white shirts with blue pants. However, Geraldine overlooks the fact that the discrimination directed to "niggers" also applies to herself, which indicates how vain and destructive it is to comply with white standards.

In *Sula*, Helene displays the same negative attitudes toward her own race as does Geraldine. Helene's concern is to assimilate to the white society, negating African-American identities. Her insistence on clothespinning her daughter Nel's nose symbolizes her powerful need to channel her daughter's development in socially acceptable directions. It is ironic, therefore, that Helene, who faithfully observes white middle-class standards, suffers an insult from a white racist conductor who scornfully calls her "gal," and she coquettishly smiles at him. Her fawning not only disgusts other black passengers but also completely undermines her legitimacy with her daughter. Noting that the counterfeit superiority is displayed only toward black people, Nel notices the fraud in her mother's proud self-righteousness.

In *Song of Solomon*, Morrison elucidates the fatal damage of rejecting African-American origins and copying false models. Deserted by her boyfriend, Milkman, Hagar ascribes his rejection of her to not having straight hair and fair skin like a white girl. In order to compensate for this lack, she decides to dress like a white model, believing that with this self-reconstruction she will be able to attract Milkman. She frantically buys cosmetics and clothing, commodities manipulatively produced by the white consumption culture, in order to falsify her appearance. In so doing, Hagar becomes the ultimate victim of commodity consumption. Returning from the desperate shopping, she is caught in a heavy rainstorm which spoils her purchases, arriving at home with "the wet ripped hose, the soiled white dress, the sticky, lumpy face powder, the streaked rouge, and the wild wet shoals of hair"

(Morrison, 1977: 318). Eventually, she dies of fever and, probably, of the despair brought about by her failure to reproduce herself as a fashionable white woman. All the torn outfits and smeared cosmetics with which she pathetically adorns herself symbolize the absurdity and the serious destructive effects of blindly imitating white feminine styles. Internalizing the consumerist values, she conforms herself to standards of the majority culture which so effectively exerts control over the oppressed and fatally destroys their identities.

2.1.2.2 The Absence of Emotional Commitment

The second aspect of the loss of black people's identities caused by the multiple oppressions is the absence of their emotion to their black families. The intersecting oppressions that have created the distorted, alienated and ill feelings to their families and communities are embodied most obviously in the case of Pauline Breedlove, Geraldine Louis, Macon Dead II and the Childs.

Pauline's unlove of her daughter begins with her pregnancy. The experience in the delivery room dehumanizes her. Instead of showing her how to deliver her child, the doctor says to others that "these women you don't have any trouble with. They deliver right away and with no pain. Just like horses" (Morrison, 1970: 125). Pauline has decided to love her baby no matter what it looks like, but this experience humiliates and hurts her. Instead of hating those white doctors, she hates her daughter and decides she is "black and ugly."

As ironically named, Pauline Breedlove is unable to provide the love, identity, socialization and security that are essential to children's healthy growth and development. The emptiness of her life and her negative self-image are particularly hurtful. The perception of themselves as ugly isolates the family from the black community further. Actually, it is not their ugliness, but "their conviction" of their ugliness that makes the difference. Clearly, with such vision, Pauline can only shape a childhood world of alienation, distortion and self-hatred. As a result, Pecola's struggle toward selfhood takes place in infertile soil, leading to a life of sterility. Like the marigolds planted by Claudia, Pecola could not grow.

Pauline's attitude toward her daughter, Pecola, is in contrast with that to her employer's blue-eyed, blond-haired daughter. She treats the little girl better than she treats her own daughter, as Pauline is ashamed of her daughter's blackness.

The level of inauthenticity that she reaches from her distorted life manifests itself in the contempt she shows to Pecola, who accidentally spills a berry cobbler on the Fisher's clean, white kitchen floor. Rather than attending to Pecola's injuries, Pauline scolds her, showing more concern for the little white girl and the clean floor than for her own daughter. She lavishes upon her employer's daughter the love she is unable to give Pecola. This damage is profound and destructive. Through her mother's attitude, Pecola learns that she is ugly, unacceptable, and especially unloved.

To Morrison, the mother/daughter relationship is a fundamental relationship among black women. Patricia Hill Collins points out in *Black Feminist Thought* that "black mothers empower their daughters by passing on the everyday knowledge essential to survival as black women. Black daughters identify the profound influence that their mothers have had upon their lives" (2000: 102). In order to develop the skills in their daughters, "mothers demonstrate varying combinations of behaviors devoted to ensuring their daughters' survival—such as providing them with basic necessities and protecting them in dangerous environments— to help their daughters go further than mothers themselves were allowed to go" (184). But for Pauline, she fails to help her daughter come to understandings of black womanhood. Rather she transfers the self-loathing to her daughter. In her eyes, Pecola is "*ugly. Head full of pretty hair, but lord she was ugly.*" (Morrison, 1970: 126; italics in original) It is no accident that Sammy runs away from home twenty-seven times by the time he is fourteen and that Pecola's only prayer is the never-ending one for blue eyes. Into her son she beats a desire to run away, and into her daughter she beats a "fear of growing up, fear of other people, fear of life" (Morrison, 1970: 128). Pauline obviously has never said directly to her children that they are ugly, that she does not love them, and that they should be white, but she has undoubtedly conveyed those feelings in any number of ways. Pecola, then, has absorbed the hints and is seeking after the formula for understanding them. Apparently, what most wrenches the heart about Pecola is "not the poverty and her madness, but her motherless love" (Rigney, 1991: 13). There is no qualified mother to teach her the feminine language, to help her love herself and her body. Pecola has only "three merry gargoyles" (Morrison, 1970: 55) to sing to her or tell the stories that unmask the lie of the story contained in the Dick and Jane reader, but the prostitutes and their stories cannot save Pecola from going insane eventually.

Pauline's attitude to her husband, Cholly, is another evidence to show her distorted, alienated and ill feelings caused by the intersecting oppressions. Her battles with Cholly involve both physical violence and psychological abuse. On the one hand, Pauline finds zest and passion in her formalized battles with Cholly, while he projects on to her a sense of innate inferiority arising from the way he has been treated by the whites. Husband and wife use sex for ulterior motives, Cholly to retain some control over his wife and Pauline to show how much she suffers as the wife of Cholly Breedlove. They get complete satisfaction and fulfillment from each other only by inflicting pain upon each other, the pain associated with kicking, biting, slapping, and hitting each other with objects such as sticks and frying pans. On the other hand, she needs "Cholly's sin desperately." "She avenges herself or Cholly by forcing him to indulge in the weakness she despised." (126) "Holding Cholly as a model of sin and failure, she bore him like a crown of thorns, and her children like a cross." (127) It seems that "the lower he sank, the wilder and more irresponsible he became, the more splendid she and her task became" (42).

The most ironical thing may be the addressing terms to show the alienation between Pauline and her family. To her husband and children, she is "Mrs. Breeedlove," while to the white family for whom she works, she is "Polly," a nickname Pauline has long aspired after. The name is totally appropriate to her, for Pauline has diminished herself through her obsequious dedication to whiteness just as surely as little Pecola is diminished by her desire for blue eyes. Here it is clear to see that naming has played an important role in judging one's identity. For Pauline, the nickname "Polly" represents her rejection of herself, her race and her black culture.

Pauline's indifference or even hatred to her husband and her children quickens the destruction of Pecola, her daughter.

Women like Geraldine spend their lives getting rid of "the dreadful funkiness of passion, the funkiness of nature, the funkiness of the wide range of human emotions" (64). Incapable of giving genuine affection to another human being, Geraldine's loss of passion for her husband and her son is an indicator of the erosion of her identity. To Geraldine, her husband, Louis, is just like the moving furniture in the room: no sound, no image. She is so indifferent to her son that she even doesn't allow her baby son to cry. She doesn't "talk to him, coo to him, or indulge him in kissing bouts" (86), but always brushes, bathes and oils him in order to maintain the cleanness. Consequently, she forfeits all the joys of life— sex, motherhood, companionship, and ultimately self-expression, and settles for the rather perverse sensations she derives from her blue-eyed black cat "who will love her order, precision, and constancy; who will be as clean and quiet as she is" (85). She places the cat at the center of her affection and attention, to the exclusion of her husband and son, Junior. If a husband is a necessary condition of domestic respectability, she prefers him absent; if she must be a mother, she will unfailingly keep her son clean but will not talk to him.

As a result, her son, Junior, suffocates in this atmosphere. Neglected and maltreated by her mother, Junior loses his innocence and becomes cruel. He kills the cat, and then distorts the facts, accusing Pecola of killing the cat to his mother. Enraged by the injury done to the cat, but more by the presence of a little black girl in her home, Geraldine expels the innocent girl to get out. Geraldine's rejection of Pecola is a total rejection of her black image and the way of life she comes from and is in eternal fear of returning to. Pecola disturbs her because she represents the disorder, dirtiness, and the past she doesn't want to face. In other words, she orders Pecola to get out of her world, out of the vision she unrealistically conjures up before and around her. She automatically negates Pecola, forgetting that she herself is also a black woman like Pecola. She deserts Pecola just as she deserts her black identity that she doesn't want to love, to study, to analyze, and even to face. Although Geraldine superficially reproduces the domestic lifestyle dictated by the controlling culture, she cannot accommodate her own race in it, contributing to reinforcing a racialized hierarchy, which implicitly suggests a displaced isolation from her origins.

Macon Dead II

Macon Dead II in *Song of Solomon* has lost the essential spiritual freedom by trading it for wealth under the mistaken belief that "money is freedom ... The only real freedom there is" (Morrison, 1977: 163). Macon advises his son to "own things. And let things you own other things. Then you'll own yourself and other people too" (55). But despite his thinking so, property does not elevate Macon above other blacks or earn him respect from whites. In truth, blacks do not hold him in high esteem; they merely fear his ruthless exercise of power, and corrupt whites respect not him but his money. A lifetime of acquiring property, collecting rents, and making deals has rendered Macon a greedy, self-absorbed, unforgiving (and unforgiven) man who is incapable of showing love or of receiving it. Proprietorship consumes Macon and alienates him from family and community, leaving no room for spiritual values like love, compassion, kindness, and tolerance. He loves only the keys to buildings that he carries in his pocket and that he fondles often and reassuringly. Morrison offers them as a symbol of his empty victory. During this process, Macon loses himself, loses his original end to fight the whites back with their weapon, loses black heritage, and is captured by the process of accumulation. Owing to the cast-aside of black culture, he becomes rootless. Alienation goes side by side with materialization. A materialized Macon is at the same time an alienated Macon. Hating his wife, Ruth, ignoring his daughters, Lena and First Corinthians, and disowning his sister, Pilate, are the sum of Macon's family connections. Even the one relationship—with Milkman—which promises to humanize him is contaminated by their scheme to steal the gold that he thinks his sister possesses. Family for Macon is just another category of personal wealth. His Sunday drives in the new Packard with Ruth and Milkman in the front seat and Corinthians and Lena in the back are merely parades of possessions. The lifeless metallic form of the Packard, which the people in the community dub "Macon Dead's hearse," is a looming symbol of the dead relationships and feelings of the people inside.

The Childs

While it is true that the ruling class in the United States (all of whom are of European descent) consists of those who own and control the means of production, it is also true that there are those (including Africans) who so ardently wish to belong to this class that they exhibit the same behavioral patterns, dress in the same manner, use the same language patterns, and, most unfortunately, share the same ideology as those of their oppressors. Often referred to as the petty bourgeois, this group of people exist between two worlds, denied entry into the ruling class due to their lack of wealth and/or their skin colour and refusing to identify with the African masses to whom they owe allegiance. Jadine, as well as Sydney and

Ondine in *Tar Baby*, symbolizes this group of the African petty bourgeois.

Called Kingfish and Boulah by Margaret Street, Sydney and Ondine symbolize those unconscious servants who identify more with their employers and their employer's culture than they do with their own people and their own culture. Clothed in somebody else's notion of civilization, Sydney and Ondine have for years been willing to allow their relation to the natural world to be formed by their employer. Unable or unwilling to separate their identity from his, they are just as caught in the unnatural perpetuation of their existence as he is. That unnaturalness toward the organic world is mirrored in the strained relationship between them and Jadine, who can never really conceptualize what it means to be a responsible niece/ daughter/woman. Sydney, in the light of day, proudly refers to himself as "one of those industrious Philadelphia Negroes—the proudest people in the race"— ignorant of the fact that in the dark night his "refreshing" dreams of childhood days in Baltimore are what give him the stamina to cater to Valerian's whims (Morrison, 1981: 51). Ondine, painfully reminiscent of Mrs. Breedlove in *The Bluest Eye*, calls the Streets' kitchen "my Kitchen" and does not want it violated by the African masses. Living a secondhand life, they accordingly have secondhand furniture, secondhand visitors ("No visitors ever came" for them) and a secondhand daughter. Because Jadine was a niece, Ondine's relationship with her "was without the stress of a mother-daughter relationship" (82). It is most significant that they are surnamed Childs, for they are indeed the children of Valerian who do as they are told. Yet, despite the humiliation and degradation of being adults treated as children, they both share the racist, capitalist ideology of their employers. As a consequence, they recognize no bond and make no alliance between themselves and the other African servants such as Thérèse and Gideon who work for the Streets. In fact, Sydney and Ondine are unable to distinguish between them, an unwillingness to recognize "lower class" African as human beings with unique identities: Gideon is referred to as Yardman, and Thérèse is thought to be several different Marys. On the whole and in true capitalist fashion, these Childses respond to the other Africans as if all African people look alike.

Not only do they embrace the same racist stereotypes as do their exploiters, but the Childses use the same negative jargon to refer to people who look just like them! The poor African masses are niggers who steal; in contrast, the Childses are

Negroes, respectable Africans. It is a respectability that prevents them from seeing themselves as a part of the African masses. For instance, in seeking to disassociate himself from Son, Sydney proudly reveals his ignorance of African culture by stating that "I am a Phil-a-delphia Negro mentioned in the book of the very same name. My people owned drugstores and taught school while yours were still cutting their faces open so as to be able to tell one of you from the other" (Morrison, 1981: 140).

Indeed, it is only by understanding Sydney's petty bourgeois mentality that we can account for his reaction to Son's humane and friendly greeting of "Hi," a greeting that at once establishes a bond and equality between the two men. Seemingly, Son's "Hi" strips Sydney of his status as head African, and not until Son begins calling Sydney "Sir" and "Mr. Childs" does the older man begin to communicate with the younger.

An orphan both literally and metaphorically, a Europeanized African, Jadine shows her insensitivity to the people who have nourished her. Her behavioral patterns, dress, language, associations, and ideology are all those of the ruling class. Not surprisingly, her allegiance is more to the Streets, her white patrons, whom she regards "like family, almost," (77) than to Ondine and Sydney, who slave for her. In fact, except for her aunt and uncle, whom she visits only in troubled times, her acquaintances are all Europeans or Europhiliacs like her. Ideologically, she thinks like the European, and like her aunt and uncle; she embraces the stereotypes of the African, calling Son a raggedy nigger and thinking he is about to rape her. Having no connection to her cultural past, Jadine is a cultural orphan. Jadine shows her insensitivity to the people who have nourished her. She allows her aunt and uncle to wait on her; she does not value their opinions, and clearly wants to avoid commitment and responsibility when Ondine declares "Don't you ever leave us, baby. You all we got" (40), and she sees herself as "playing daughter" (68) to Sydney and Ondine instead of being daughter to them.

Without ancestors' guidance, Jadine may never discover the path to black womanhood. When it is too late, Ondine tries to guide Jadine, but all that she is really able to do is to express regrets ignored by Jadine: "Jadine, a girl has got to be a daughter first ... You don't need your own natural mother to be a daughter. All you need is to feel a certain way, a certain careful way about people older than you are … A daughter is a woman that cares about where she comes from and takes care of them that took care of her." (242)

In their own pride and arrogance, Sidney and Ondine have tacitly encouraged their niece's cultural disconnection as a sign of her and their success. They liked her living in Paris; they liked her acceptance by their employer. But they had not heeded the price of such acceptance: someone who prefers Picasso to Etumba masks, a woman who does not know how to be a respectful daughter. Being black, Morrison suggests, is not only a matter of genetics; it's also a matter of culture. Jadine does not choose blackness because, as Ondine knows, she has never learned what it is; she has been acculturated.

Jadine has not learned the things she needs to know to be the "real woman" that Ondine describes. She has never known the "ancient properties" of black womanhood. "She also fears intimacy with her heritage." (Reyes, 1986: 23)

2.1.2.3 The Internalization of the Oppressions

The third aspect of the loss of black people's identities caused by the multiple oppressions is the forsaking of their fighting rights. Confronted with the multiple oppressions, as mentioned above, those black women such as Pauline, Pecola and May simply internalize the oppressions. Instead of fighting courageously, they passively receive the oppressions imposed on them by the white and their people.

In *The Bluest Eye,* Pauline's tragedy lies in that she has regarded the interactive oppression as a matter of course. It never occurs to her that she has the right to complain or even fight against them. Pauline is a typical mammy image that permeates the literature. "By loving, nurturing, and caring for her white children and family better than her own" (Collins, 2000: 71), Pauline is regarded as an ideal servant. She bathes the little white girl, arranges things, cleans the house, and defends the benefits of her white employer, Fisher. More and more she neglects her house, her children, her man—"they were like the afterthoughts one has just before sleep, the early-morning and late-evening edges of her day, the dark edges that made the daily life with the Fishers lighter, more delicate, more lovely" (Morrison, 1970: 127). She no longer belongs to the home in the South where she "cultivated pleasures"; the Fisher house is now the sanctuary where she "could arrange things, clean things, line things up in neat rows," for she could find "beauty, order, cleanliness, and praise" (127).

However, no matter how loved Pauline is by her white employer, she remains poor because she is an economically exploited worker in a capitalist economy. Fisher family maintains their class position because they use black women domestic workers as a source of cheap labor. She cannot earn adequate wage to support her family. It is very natural that she still lives in an abandoned store in which there is no bathroom, no privacy, no dignity. No matter how loyal Pauline is to her employer, she cannot achieve the true equality with her employer and is denied membership because she is a black living in a society dominated by the white. Her black skin makes her feel inferior to the white. What she is ready to do is to hate her blackness and admire the whiteness. No matter how faithful Pauline is to her employer, she remains an ideal servant because she is a black woman who is always degraded by the male-dominated society. Instead of fighting against the intersecting oppressions to obtain the higher salary and true equality, Pauline keeps "this order, this beauty, for herself, a private world, and never introduced it into her storefront or to her children" (128).

Different from her mother, Pecola's tragedy is not that she is unaware of the intersecting oppressions, but that she gives up her right to fight against them. She simply judges herself through the look of other people, fails to achieve the responsibility of defining herself. The following examples will prove that Pecola fails to recognize that she is responsible to arrange life for her self. These are the crucial points that Morrison reveals about Pecola to the readers.

One of the evidences is Pecola's attitude towards Maureen Peal's accusation. Maureen Peal, a light-skinned mulatto, is a new girl in school "with long brown hair braided into two lynch ropes" and dark green eyes. Whilst Pecola is ignored or despised at school as the only member of her class who sits alone at a double desk, classmates and teachers admire Maureen Peal, because her features are lighter than the average black people's. By accusing Pecola of seeing "her old black daddy" naked, she demoralizes her. Towards the charge, Pecola's response is inertly passive. She "tucks her head in—a funny, sad, helpless movement" and seems to "fold into herself, like a pleated wing" (Morrison, 1970: 72–73). Enraged by Pecola's inactivity, Claudia and Frieda want "to open her up, crisp her edges, ram a stick down that hunched and curving spine, force her to stand erect and spit the misery out on the streets" (73). Similarly, when Geraldine yells at Pecola out of her house, Pecola just backs out of the room silently.

Another evidence is Pecola's attitude to her black schoolmates who humiliate her by making fun of her father. They call her name and make fun of her family, "the colour of her skin and speculations on the sleeping habits of an adult" (65). It is their contempt and hatred for their own blackness that forces them to take it out on her. They are subconsciously transferring the pain caused by their blackness onto the vulnerable Pecola and directing their self-hatred onto a communal scapegoat. Like the feather amid wind, helpless and powerless, poor Pecola "edges around the circle crying" (66), dropping her notebook.

The most poignant illustration of Pecola's failure to act occurs in a central scene in the novel, when she enters Yacobowski's store to purchase the Mary Jane candies she loves so much. After she enters the store and meets the "vacuum" in the shop owner's blue eye, Pecola purchases the candy and leaves, embarrassed and overwhelmed by shame. Outside, she equates herself with the dandelion she passes. They are not "pretty" any more: "They are ugly. They are weeds." (50) The total absence of human recognition Pecola sees in Yacobowski's glance corresponds to her own negative self-perception. She can be only thing and object. With this as her central standpoint, Pecola seems able to respond only with shame. This shame ebbs when she leaves the store. "Anger stirs and wakes in her; it opens its mouth, and like a hot-mouthed puppy, laps up the dredges of her shame." (50) Instead of choosing a courageous act to attack back, Pecola is consumed again by shame. She finds that "the anger will not hold; the puppy is too easily surfeited. Its thirst too quickly quenched, it sleeps. The shame wells up again, its muddy rivulets seeping into her eyes. What to do before the tears come? She remembers the Mary Jane." In her state of self-hatred, she resorts to eating the blue eyes of the pictures on her nine "Mary Janes," which brings her "nine lovely orgasms" (50).

Her inability to be incorporated into white standards of beauty destroys her self-confidence, and she attributes herself to the cause of her family problems, poverty, and humiliation, especially her ugliness. To her, the only solution is to escape, to disappear.

2.1.2.4 The Abandonment of Black Culture

Black culture, including black aesthetics, as a branch struggling for room of existence in the crevice of dominant culture, lives in the tension between the force and counterforce of dominant society and African complex. The strength of those two forces, each not willing to give way to the other, rises and ebbs alternately. Those African-Americans who abandon their own history and culture become cultural orphans.

The most obvious example of this kind can be found in Jadine Child in *Tar Baby*. She is trapped between two cultures: black and white, European and African-American. Conditioned by her sophisticated European education, Jadine is detached from her own blackness. By educating her in Europe, the Streets crystallize her status as orphan; the foreign culture makes an impact on the young child at her most transitional and impressionable years. Her behavioural patterns, dress, language, associations, and ideology are all those of the ruling class and as such, demonstrate her hatred of Africa and all that is associated with it. Educated and privileged, Jadine both dissociates herself from her blackness and commodifies it in the fashion worlds of New York and Paris. In fact, except for her aunt and uncle, whom she visits only in troubled times, her acquaintances are all Europeans or Europhiliacs like her. Indeed the best there is, she belittles African art: "Picasso is better than an Itumba mask." (Morrison, 1981: 74) she tells Valerian, and she confesses her embarrassment at attending "ludicrous" art shows put on by pretentious blacks in Europe. She ridicules Michael's attempt to politicize her as to her Africanness: "Actually we didn't talk; we quarreled. About why I was studying art history at that snotty school instead of—I don't know what. Organizing or something. He said I was abandoning my history. My people." (61–62) She had long since moved into a white society where "the black people she knew wanted what she wanted" and where success required her "only to be stunning ... Say the obvious, ask stupid questions, laugh with abandon, look interested, and light up at any display of their humanity if they showed it" (126–127). Although she still remains aware of her cultural orphanage, she has received a cultural makeover.

2.1.2.5 Black Identity Gone Wild

Morrison in her novels also examines the wild racism existing among black people germinating out of their hatred toward the white people whom they consider as having done wrong to them. She provides a broader social context for the coming of age of some characters in her novels to probe into the reasons for the cases of black identity gone wild.

Enraged by such white brutality against blacks as the lynching, the burnings, the murder, Guitar was impelled to join the Seven Days as their Sunday man. The anger inside implodes, and he becomes what he hates—a murderer. Although Guitar is a self-declared avenger of his people, the love of black life is eventually twisted into a love of power. That power gives him, he thinks, authority which he uses to kill indiscriminately—white and black. As a result of his way of black militancy as response to white violence, eventually, the appealing interplay of street wisdom and hard-edged generosity that defines Guitar gives way to brooding paranoia. But stalking Milkman and killing Pilate, whose healing, ancestral guidance he rejects in favor of street justice, place Guitar outside all boundaries of rationality and morality because there can be no moral authority in killing one's racial brother or sister for gold or for pleasure.

The slaughtering of the Convent women carried out by Ruby's men is another case of violent black identity. In order to protect themselves and their descendents from their grandfathers' experience of the racism as exhibited in the action of Disallowing, they release their painful memory in the form of violence against the Convent women who are considered as Other either in race or in gender, which is typical of black identity gone wild.

2.1.3 Loss of Black Communal Identity

At the same time that Morrison does not condemn all whites, neither does she exonerate all blacks. Morrison writes not only about individuals who lost their subjectivity and racial identity, but also about communities that lost their communal identity by exploring the problems within the community. Morrison wonders if economic and social gains are worth the sacrifice of community, because without community the cultural traditions that inform characters are lost to future generations. In Morrison's fiction, identity is always provisional; there can be no isolated ego striving to define itself as separate from community, no matter how tragic or futile the operations of that community might be. Individual characters are inevitably formed by social constructions of both race and gender, and they are inseparable from those origins. The multiple and fragmented selves reflected in her fictions are sometimes undefined, inevitably amorphous, always merging with the identity of a community as a whole or with the very concept of blackness. She talked about her purpose in an interview about *Paradise*: "I think the threat for many of our communities is internecine. By that I mean the enemy is within, as opposed to being on the outside. Quarrelling within the family." (Verdelle, 1998: 56)

What Morrison tries to convey is that black communal identity lies in black people's connectedness based on their family relations or their capacity and willingness to help each other and share secrets. By examining the opposite of maintaining the black communal identity, Morrison tries to enlighten people what follies will be brought by losing them.

Morrison writes about the most illustrious examples of people's denial of their love for their people in *The Bluest Eye*. Overcome by the white-male dominated society, they totally abandon their black identity by building their judgments on the physical features. They laughs at Pauline when she comes to the community because "she did not straighten her hair. When she tried to make up her face as they did, it came off rather badly. Their goading glances and private snickers at her way of talking (saying 'chil'ren') and dressing developed in her desire for new clothes" (Morrison, 1970: 118). Though they belong to the same class and race, those black women make her feel uncomfortable and seem "no better than whites for meanness" (117).

Their attitude to Pecola further illustrates the loss of their identities. When Pecola is raped and impregnated by her father Cholly, these black women are "disgusted, amused, shocked, outraged, or even excited by the story" (Morrison, 1970: 190), but no one shows concern and sympathy to Pecola. On the contrary, Pecola becomes the central scapegoat for the pain and suffering of all black people in community. When standing astride her ugliness, they feel so beautiful. Her simplicity decorates them, her guilt sanctifies them, and even her pain makes them glow with health.

In a biblical reading of *Beloved*, Corey explores how Morrison "calls attention to the collaboration of the black community in Sethe's fate, refusing to represent blacks only as victims" (Corey, 2000: 42). Their betrayal at first may seem merely inadvertent, and thereby blameless, but as Corey argues: "While the [black] community does not directly betray Sethe, as Judas betrayed Jesus, they betray her indirectly, like Peter, in their failure to warn her of the coming danger." (157) Their inaction might easily be interpreted as the opposite of what might be termed "Good Samaritanism"[1] since they should have warned Sethe but elect not to, something which definitely goes against the norm for their otherwise tightly-knit community where mutual aid is essential to survival. This clearly illustrates how Morrison implicates the black community in the evil that arrives at the house on Bluestone road the day after the feast. Terri Otten notes the way in which "[e]vil persists in the 'meanness' of the blacks who refuse to warn Sethe about the white men come to reclaim her ... " (1989: 82) Morrison highlights the extent of divisiveness and "othering" when she shows how Sethe's own community turns its back on her. When the Clearing people betray Baby Suggs and her family by failing to warn of what they instinctively know is trouble when white men come to town asking questions, the community fails its obligation to the individual. Baby Suggs is mortally disillusioned. She abandons her ministry of love and slowly gives up life. "To belong to a community of other free Negroes—to love and be loved by them, to counsel and be counseled, protect and be protected, feed and be fed—and then to have that community step back and hold itself at a distance—well, it could wear out even a Baby Suggs, holy." (Morrison, 1970: 177) Through describing Baby Sugg's feeling, Morrison enunciates her concern with communal disloyalty.

Like the individuals that comprise it, the community is collectively subject to character flaws: Envy of Baby Suggs's generosity and of Sethe's youth and deftness flowers into meanness. After holding themselves at a distance and not warning Sethe, people in the community gather but do not raise their voices in the customary unifying ceremony of song when Sethe is taken to jail. Later they rumor doubts about Sethe's past: Did she really escape from slavery in her condition? Was Baby Suggs's son really the father of her children? Ten years later, after Baby

---

[1] Good Samaritan: (from a story told by Jesus) a person who gives kind and unselfish helps to someone in need. Hence "Good Samaritanism."

Suggs's funeral, they congregate in the yard, eating the food they brought and leaving Sethe's untouched. After that time no one visits 124, and rankled by her independence and self-sufficiency, "just about everybody in town was longing for Sethe to come on difficult times" (Morrison, 1987: 171). For nearly two decades Sethe and Denver (and later Paul D.) are left to themselves, solitary figures living at the edge of the community.

Morrison does not censure or judge the community for its treatment of Sethe. Most crimes in her fictional world are redeemable. Despite its coldness, for example, the community does not entirely expel Sethe, and in the end, when she is haunted by the ghost of her daughter and is no longer self-supporting, it reclaims her as its own.

2.2 A Spiritual Home

It seems that the African Americans are forever in the kind of spiritual wilderness. Without figuring out who they are and where they should locate themselves, they constantly suffer from identity crises, which in turn leads to their longing for and searching after a constant spiritual home in correspondence with the black Spirituals' soul-searching liberation. Therefore, identity formation has always been Morrison's major focus on portrayal of her Afro-American characters who embody Morrison's usual and most striking theme—the quest for freedom, identity and wholeness of their people in a racist, white, patriarchal American social arena that advocates life, liberty, and the pursuit of happiness as rights "unalienable" to all men.

Morrison is not just writing about the situation of African American's being in the spiritual wilderness, but through her writing of their lost black identity, she also embarks on a journey that ends with the soaring affirmation of black selfhood. It is a quest not only to de-center the white logos, but finally to rebuild the center, to discover the powers that lie hidden in the black logos. She writes to rise out of the black hole to create a wholy black text. Toni Morrison consciously uncloses the veil of colonial history by neo-slavery narrative discourse and points out the way of fighting against the marginal social position for the black oppressed deeply through the construction of the black people's subjectivity and identity, from awakening, deepening, developing and finally constructing subjectivity and identity. Therefore, the construction and perfection of subjectivity and identity in Morrison's novels becomes an effective weapon for the black to unite as one to strive for ethnic rights and to improve ethnic position, which deeply influences the movement for the black nowadays.

Like the Spirituals that provide for Blacks true homes, Morrison's fiction is to help the African Americans to look for a right and hopeful spiritual home. Therefore, how to redefine the black's identities, which she considers as a main element to form a spiritual home, is one of Morrison's major concerns. She is more concerned with the ways to preserve black's identity and dignity in face of the multiple oppressions. When talking about black women's identity conformation, Patricia Hill Collins, a black feminist, argues that "black women's efforts to grapple with the effects of domination in everyday life are evident in the creation of safe spaces that enable us to resist oppression, and in our struggles to form fully human love relations with one another" (2000: 274). If this theory is to be applied to the whole ethnicity of black people, loving one's black self, loving one's family, community and culture would be the three important solutions concerning the significance of preserving black's identities, and thus constructing the spiritual home for black people. Morrison sets several examples to the black people for them to realize the importance of a spiritual home. Among them, the MacTeers in *The Bluest Eye*, Pilate in *Song of Solomon*, Violet and Joe in *Jazz*, Consolata and the Convent women in *Paradise* are people who are capable of establishing spiritual homes for themselves and thus setting examples to the whole ethnicity eulogized by Morrison. Through these people and through borrowing motifs from the Spirituals, Morrison tries to show what a spiritual home is like.

When talking about the purpose of writing *The Bluest Eye*, Morrison proclaims that her purpose is to show "how to survive whole in a world where we are all of us, in some measure, victims of something" (Bakerman, 1978: 78). She maintains that it's essential for black people, especially black women to retain their identities by transmitting the traditional values of black culture, consciously or unconsciously and by not following the standard of white aesthetics blindly. Because the MacTeers are not obsessed with the need to be beautiful, wealthy, or white, they concentrate their efforts on family and community. Even though they are tortured by the multiple oppressions, they still love each other. The daughters love their black selves, which is one of the essential ways to preserve black women's identities,[1] and the parents keep their children's spiritual and moral integrity. The mother transmits their black culture through her healing and restorative blues singing, and the father works day and night to keep the family fed, clothed and protected. The family also cares if someone is "put out" or "put outdoors." When Pecola's father burns down the house, putting the family "outdoors," Mrs. MacTeer takes the homeless Pecola. Obviously the MacTeers do not have the time, energy and money to adopt all happiness; it is really a miracle that they still share the responsibilities of their community. It is they convince Morrison that there are no boring black people and interest her in "scratching the surface" to discover the complexity and subtlety in their lives.

Pilate in *Song of Solomon*, Violet and Joe in the end of *Jazz*, Consolata and the Convent Women in *Paradise* also define what the spiritual home is like in their respective ways, which will be detailed in Chapter Four, since musical jazz is also the kind of music evolving from the Spirituals and the blues, which decides that there are some motifs that are common in them.

For the black people whose external life circumstances were dictated, circumscribed and strategically conditioned by the operation of undue power—specifically by the unique power and decision of white America—God the unseen, who was nonetheless an indisputable reality met in daily experience, Black Spirituals are liberating, releasing, redemptive and restorative. So the "spiritual" significance to the Spiritual lies in the fact that it makes "home" an immediately realizable and constantly fulfilled hope. As James Cone has noted, the black Spirituals speak of "dat Rock," the slaves' true home, the Promised Land "down by the riverside," where "in dat great gettin' up mornin' the oppressed of the land (are ever) received into 'New Jerusalem'" (1972: 98).

Morrison's fiction creates a world of the Spiritual. Most of Morrison's black characters are the ones who live in the spiritual wilderness created by either racism or sexism or both, suffering from internal crises of incoherence and

---

[1] Morrison thinks it is dangerous to encourage racial solidarity by denying one's individuality. In one of her articles "Behind the Making of *The Black Book*," Morrison points out "when the strength of a race depends on its beauty, when the focus is turned to how one looks as opposed to what one is, we are in trouble" (1974: 88). To her, considering "[the] concept of physical beauty as a virtue is one of the dumbest, most pernicious and destructive ideas of the western world and we should have nothing to do with it" (89).

instability. Consequently, their experiences are like that of the people who sing the Spiritual: Although suffering from spiritual turbulences, they long for and constantly look for spiritual home and hope, therefore some of them may be relieved by the light of hope. Besides the feelings of sorrow, despair, and pain, her fiction also involves that spiritual element so present in jazz and blues music.

Chapter 3

Morrison's Blues: Trauma and Traumatic Release

Etymologically, the phrase "the blues" is a reference to having a fit of the blue devils, meaning "down" spirits, depression and sadness. Many people, including African Americans, view the blues as an isolating, depressing commentary on the miseries and misfortunes of a few misguided individuals and the singers often voice their personal woes in a world of harsh reality: a lost love, the cruelty of police officers, oppression at the hands of white folk and hard times. While this is partly true, it's also a creative form that is uplifting and that promotes positive messages. According to James Baldwin: "White Americans seem to feel that happy songs are happy and sad songs are sad … In all jazz, and especially in the blues, there is something tart and ironic, authoritative and double-edged." (1963: 60–61)

The aesthetic of the blues shapes tones of deeply felt anger. Since the American dream is not colour blind, but colour conscience, African-Americans endure incredible hardships to sustain relationships. The inconceivable brutality and degradation that they experience fractures their communities and inflicts both physical and perhaps irreparable psychological damage on individuals, which results in blacks' living in spiritual wilderness. The sacred quality of the music lies in the fact that every tone is "a testimony against slavery" and "a prayer to God for deliverance from chains," as Douglass argues. The musical tones tell "a tale of woe," are "loud, long, and deep," and breathe "the prayer and complaint of souls boiling over with bitterest anguish" (1994: 24).

3.1 Traumas and Turmoil in Blacks' Experiences

As a poor race in a land of dollars, black people are at the very bottom of hardships. Morrison, by her acute intuition, senses the many reasons that cause the loss of blacks' identity. Her fiction therefore reverberates the blues motifs of suffering, dislocation and alienation, as the blues is the kind of music with unmistakable roots in slavery and the slave trade: "the first great music of Africa does not sing of a lost or even an unknown paradise, but of a very simple, very ordinary human happiness wrested forever from the unfortunate men who improvised on the banks of the Mississippi ... [I]t is the great lamentation, the eternal voice of affliction which, with its searing originality, entered European music as the blues." (Malraux, 1996: 30) After experiencing the exploitive systems of slavery, colonialism, neocolonialism and domestic colonialism, and after being exposed to the ideologies associated with the teachings of Islam and Christianity, black people's predicament of African American cultural dislocation highlights their traumas and turmoil.

3.1.1 Consequence of Slavery

As Susan Bowers notices, the African Americans are torn from the world of their families, communities, their own spiritual traditions, and language to a world of suffering, death, and alienation. The good life doesn't lie not before them but behind them; yet, every attempt is made to crush their memories of the past. Slaves are isolated from other members of their tribes to keep them from communicating in their own languages and maintaining their own traditions (1997: 211). Morrison also exemplifies her understandings of the way the dominant culture colonizes African-American identity from different perspectives in her fiction.

In *Beloved*, she deals with this kind of traumatic experiences under slavery, an institution that is willingly placed under erasure by what Morrison calls a "national amnesia," and its aftermath:

> I thought this has got to be the least read of all the books I'd written
> because it is about something the characters don't want to remember, I don't
> want to remember, black people don't want to remember, white people don't
> want to remember. But *Beloved* is not about slavery as an institution; it is
> about those *anonymous* people called slaves. (Angelo, 1989: 120)

The slaves such as Sethe suffer not only from physical abuses, but also from psychic violence. Hence, in order not to let her children fall into the hands of the slave-owner Schoolteacher, she kills her little daughter by cutting her throat. The nightmare of history lingers on in her mind until Paul D. and the community help her to drive it out.

3.1.2 Misnaming and Naming as a Manipulative Instrument

The constant censorship of and intrusion on black life from the surrounding society is emphasized not by specific events so much as by a consistent pattern of misnaming. Melville Herskovits, in *The Myth of the Negro Past,* focuses on the importance of naming in African American culture. He associates this naming practice with that of their African forbears and comments: "Names are of great importance in West Africa … That is why, among Africans, a person's name may in so many instances change with time, a new designation being assumed on the occasion of some striking occurrence in his life, or when he goes through one of the rites marking a new stage in his development." (1995: 191)

The significance of names and naming in the novel is the subject for many Afro-American writings, and naming is regarded as a method of resisting the hegemony of white society through African cultural practices. The power of a name is so strong in much of Africa and the Diaspora that often people kept a secret name so that an enemy could not use it for evil intent. In the New World, a name could also be employed in opposition to the oppressor, as slaves were wont to do. Just as the mainstream society created stereotypes in order to restrict African-American behaviors and to discredit their values, it has also manipulated the naming of African Americans, manifesting another form of a power structure of oppression. Knowing one's name has a remarkably significant relation to one's ability to claim his or her identity, while not knowing one's name leaves African-Americans fatally confused about their sense of self and roots. The destruction of African-American values is closely associated with the loss of original African names. In an interview with Thomas LeClair, Morrison discusses the cultural orphanage of African-American people in slavery who were forced to accept the names given to them under circumstances not of their choosing. They were deprived of their names when they were snatched from their homeland, and they also lost their families and their tribes (LeClair,

1981: 28). By severing them from their original names and places, the oppressors destroyed their pride in their race and culture, weakening the solidarity of African Americans. Morrison develops the name theme most extensively in terms of the enforced pseudonymity of the main characters and their families. This psydonymity is a persistent concern for a family that must subsist without an authentic name. Thus the reclamation of original names is regarded as crucial to black people for their true identity as well as their pride in their race and culture.

The world of Morrison's novels is distinguished by the discrepancy between name and reality. Incongruence of name and reality mirrors the ironies imposed on black people and their community as seen in Morrison's choice of the surname Breedlove in *The Bluest Eye*. In Breedlove's household, there is nothing that generates love. Ironically, Cholly's incest with Pecola is the only indication of love. As Thomas H. Fick points out, the rape induced by his disgust and love toward his daughter is an "oxymoron" which cannot be conjoined like his oppositional family name to his perverted behavior (1989: 20). Marginal and despised because of their race and poverty, the Breedloves are not able to claim their essential human right to stay together as a family: Their home and lives paradoxically negate love in contrast to the family name, Breedlove, which connotes a promotion of warm, loving and caring interaction in a family. Eventually, embracing an absence of love, this family is dismembered and destroyed.

Morrison further indicates how contradictory a name can be to reality by naming a black community in *Sula* the Bottom, although it is geographically located in the hills. Morrison tells it as a joke: The hill land is called the Bottom, which is named by a white master who was unwilling to give rich fertile valley land, literally, the bottom, to his slave despite his promise. The master equivocates, "When God looks down, it's the bottom. That's why we call it so. It's the bottom of heaven—best land there is." (Morrison, 1973: 5) Expelled to the hilly land, where rain easily washes away soil and the slopes make their farming laborious, black people have toiled to cultivate the hill land called the Bottom. The naming process displays how deliberately naming is maneuvered by a ruling group of people in order to maintain a hierarchical and social order which preserves their own privileges, exploiting black people and relegating them to everlasting disadvantage and the periphery.

Morrison further emphasizes that African Americans are easily deprived of their original names and misnamed. *Song Of Solomon* is full of characters with ludicrous, multiple, or lost names, like Macon Dead I, whose real name was Jake Solomon and who was accidentally named by a drunken soldier who was processing him after the Civil War. Asking where he was born and who his father was, "the Yankee wrote it all down, but in the wrong spaces" (Morrison, 1977: 53). As a result, Jake Solomon, who said he was born in Macon and that his father was dead, was given a new name, Macon Dead. Although his father did not name him Macon Dead, Jake Solomon could not retain his original name under the racist bureaucracy that negligently perceived him only as object, not subject. Later on, "Macon Dead" has displaced more genuine name. The bogus appellation even hints at its own ultimate effect: it "makes dead."

In *Tar Baby*, Morrison employs a name theme to reveal a class issue in Western hierarchy. In this hierarchy, people of a lower class are deprived of their names by their oppressors. No one at L'Arbe de la Croix knows the real names of the indispensable native servants, Gideon and Thérèse, who are known simply as Yardman and Mary respectively, as if their individual personalities were irrelevant. They are given a label instead of a name, a mask without any substance or truth. Yardman and Mary are invisible to their employers whose most important concern is that the power structure and its benefits are securely preserved without the interference of their subjugated vassals.

In *Beloved*, the name of the plantation, Sweet Home, indicates that white masters have a control over naming, disregarding the lives and identity of slaves. Mr. Garner, the ostensibly benevolent owner, boasts that he treats his slaves as men and never abuses them, allowing them to express their thoughts and to acquire literacy if they wish to. Sweet Home, however, loses its "sweet" aspect after his death: The new master, Schoolteacher, deprives them of all the privileges that Mr. Garner generously gave to them. As Paul D. later realizes, however, the slaves did not possess freedom as human beings even when the former master was alive, because even then their lives were capriciously conditional, depending on Garner, who "called and announced them men—but only on Sweet Home, and by his leave" (220). Establishment of the absolute hierarchical order of slavery at Sweet Home by Schoolteacher brings about abrupt change for the slaves, indicating that slaves' lives are always threatened, no matter how humane and benign their masters are. Sweet Home paradoxically represents the discrepancy of the "sweet" master and precarious and vulnerable lives of slaves in the master's "home."

Under slavery, "the power of naming absolutely remained with the white master," as David Lawrence notes (1997: 191). Baby Suggs has never been called her real name by Mrs. and Mr. Garner, who count on her documented name, Jenny, recorded on her bill of sale which legitimates their ownership of a slave. Her lack of a name—"nothing ... I don't call myself nothing" (Morrison, 1987: 141) —is testament to the "desolated center where the self that was no self made its home" (140). Baby Suggs has no "self" because she has no frame of reference by which to establish one, no family, no children, no context: "Sad as it was that she did not know where her children were buried or what they looked like if alive, fact was she knew more about them than she knew about herself, having never had the map to discover what she was like." (140) Even when she claims her real name at her emancipation, Mr. Garner does not approve of it, because "Mrs. Baby Suggs ain't no name for a freed Negro" (142). For those slaves who are dispersed across the country, a name is an important clue in the identification of their missing family members. Baby is how her husband dearly called her, and Suggs is her husband's name, and it is "all she had left of the 'husband' she claimed" (142). By negating her original name, albeit he has no malicious intention, Mr. Garner deprives her of the possibility that her husband might find her, as he can inquire after her by the only name he knows her to possess. After all, Mr. Garner, who agrees to let Halle purchase the freedom of his mother, Baby Suggs, is less interested in the lives of his slaves than self-satisfied with his own generosity, carrying his dominance and displaying his arrogance by directing the naming of his ex-slaves. Under this manipulated circumstance, however, Baby Suggs retains her original name to keep connected with her husband, even if it does not fit the standards of white naming. Her strong sense of identity as an African-American woman who has survived the ordeal of slavery enables her to preach the importance of love and caring in the community and attracts the townspeople until she thoughtlessly and accidentally insults them by extravagantly showing off her joy at being reunited with her daughter-in-law, Sethe, and grandchildren.

Similarly, Paul D. is one of a series of Pauls, identified alphabetically by some anonymous slaveholder, while Sixo is presumably the sixth of an analogous group.[1] Stamp Paid, born Joshua under slavery, has however, chosen and devised his own symbolic name, which represents a rejection of a tradition of white naming as well as a celebration of freedom. His name is also and more specifically a symbol of freedom from debt; because he suffered under slavery and because he has paid in misery any obligation to humanity, he believes, although his continued activity as a conductor on the Underground Railroad would indicate otherwise. All African-Americans are, in essence, "Stamp Paid," Morrison implies.

In all these cases, the misnaming does not eliminate the reality of the black world; invisibility is not non-existence. But it does reflect a distortion. Blacks are visible to white culture only insofar as they fit its frame of reference and serve its needs. Thus they are constantly reduced and reified, losing their independent reality. Mrs. Breedlove in *The Bluest Eye* has a nickname, "Polly," that only whites use; it reduces her dignity and identifies her as "the ideal servant" (Morrison, 1970: 99). When the elegant Helene Wright becomes just "gal" to a white conductor, she and her daughter Nel feel that she is "flawed," "really custard" under the elegant exterior (Morrison, 1973: 17–19).

3.1.3 Double Consciousness

When referring to the "entombed" souls of African Americans, W. E. B. Du Bois defined African Americans' identity as determined by a sensation of "double-consciousness." According to Du Bois,

> The history of the American Negro is the history of this strife—this longing to attain self-conscious manhood, to merge his double self into a better and truer self. In this merging he wishes neither of the older selves to be lost. He wouldn't Africanize America, for America has too much to teach the world and Africa. He would not bleach his Negro soul in a flood of white Americanism, for he knows that Negro blood has a message for the world. (1990: 215)

---

[1] As Trudier Harris has written in "Reconnecting Fragments: Afro-American Folk Tradition in *The Bluest Eye*," which is in Nellie MaKay's *Critical Essays on Toni Morrison*, "To be called 'out of one's name' … can be just as negatively powerful as a nickname can be positive." (72)

He argued that the spiritual striving of freed people is fraught with perils that recall those of their fathers and mothers, their travail of soul "almost beyond the measure of their strength." Nearly torn apart by doubt and aspiration, African Americans are burdened with "two souls, two thoughts, two unreconciled strivings; two warring ideals in one dark body whose dogged strength alone keeps it from being torn asunder" (Du Bais, 1990: 134). Only the tragic spirit of the blues allows for this almost hopeless depiction of the struggle in the souls of the enslaved. Therefore, what African Americans wish is "to make it possible for a man to be both a Negro and an American" (365). The result has been a paradoxical communal identity which is both American and separate.

From Frederick Douglass and William Brown to Ishmael Reed and Toni Morrison, the African-American literature has been dominated by the struggle for freedom from all forms of oppression and by a personal Odyssey to realize the full potential of one's complex bicultural identity as an African-American. Yet up to the 1960s, black writers had had to constantly struggle with "the theological terror" that James Baldwin elucidates in his discussion of protest literature—to distinguish between presenting black people as Americans saw them and as complex human beings; to decide whether to extol the ethnic culture of Africa or to fit into the Euro-American culture. Frequently, they fell into the trap of overemphasizing one and omitting the other, thus failing in presenting the black man's wholeness and balance as an American citizen of African descent. It was not until the present day that black writers achieve a more comprehensive understanding of the status of African-Americans and was able to explore paths for their survival in a larger realm of reality, among whom is Toni Morrison.

From Du Bois's "double self" to Ralph Ellison's "invisible man," the question of identity in a hostile and antagonistic world has been paramount. Often, this search for identity has led to one of two opposite approaches: mainstream assimilation/ accommodation or racial separatism. Two characters in Song of Solomon illustrate these warring factions: Macon Dead II, Milkman's father (assimilation), and Guitar Bains, Milkman's friend (separatism). Besides, in order to show what authentic black identity means, Morrison gives the examples of two young Americans— Milkman Dead and Jadine Childs—whose identities are, at least at first, fragmented and perplexed. The two characters occupy a debilitating psychic space between the desire to assimilate to the values of the white middle class and the voices that urge a black racial identity.

Jadine's double consciousness exhibits most obviously in her reaction to Alma Estée, a native Western Indian who is consumed by white values. When approached by Alma, Jadine is overwhelmed by the red wig and feels an urge to run away from her without knowing the reason. This suggests that Jadine, who is on the way to Paris, the flourishing center of high fashion and white aesthetics, has mixed feelings that she fails to articulate. On the one hand, she is trying to incorporate Western images and values, denying the presence of the marginalized racial sister and brother such as Alma and Son when he first appears. On the other hand, even as she rejects African-American values, she senses her loss of origins and subconsciously fears the ensuing identity crisis. It is impossible for her to be free from the conflict between Western and ethnic values.

Jadine cannot locate the source of her sense of rootlessness; however, her own confusion is both prompted and signified by Alma's red wig which metaphorically reminds her of the danger and absurdity of assimilation, simultaneously inducing her to consider the cost of blindly accepting Western culture and values. Bereft of parents in early childhood, brought up by her Uncle Sidney and Aunt Ondine and sent to school for a higher and prestigious formal education with money given by their white employer Valerian, Jadine is a cultural orphan without knowledge of her parents, her roots and the past, oscillating restlessly between the African-American and white worlds.

Brought up in a middle class black family whose father assimilated to the values of the white middle class, Milkman Dead is a young black American who sets an example to discarding the already assimilated values of the white middle class in the process of searching for his family genealogy—the black consciousness that enables him to transcend his folly and to love his ethnic brothers and community. He is the one who embodies the hope of African Americans to transcend the double consciousness and therefore fulfill the epiphany from innocence to spiritual transcendence.

3.1.4 Commercial Society

Culture, just like race, has no distinction of being good or bad. When two cultures meet against the same social background, however, owing to the differences of their economy, politics and influence, the dominant culture will strengthen its value system and way of life and transfer them to the weak culture. Gradually it will influence, weaken and devour the weak culture eventually. At the same time, the mass media, as part of the dominant culture and the chief vehicles by which ideology is transmitted through information and images, such as baby dolls, food and movies, play an important role in setting the standards for what defines beauty, and anything straying from these standards is viewed as ugly. The white consumption culture is also one of the elements that fatally destroy the black people's identities. Many of them become the ultimate victim of commodity consumption. The United States is a commercialized society. The consumption culture no doubt brings about an equalization of the races in term of commercialized desire so that black people are urged to purchase the same commodity as whites. Yet it still bars people of color from the dominant modes of manufacturing, excluding them from the engagement in producing goods.[1] According to Aoi Mori, the greatest damage of white capitalism is that the images produced by the commodity culture manipulate both the behavior and mentality of African Americans, as stereotypes do (1999: 37). The development and enlargement of this circle of blacks record the popularization of dominant values.

Hagar in *Song of Solomon* is one of the numerous victims of such brainwash. She, as Barbara Rigney pertinently comments, is destroyed by "the vision of herself as self that the mirror reflects," and "mirrors represent only white standards of beauty" (1998: 52). Assimilating and internalizing the too often promoted white standards of beauty, she takes them as something universal and blames herself for not following them and thus not attractive enough for Milkman. In order to retrieve the lost love, she, on the verge of mental collapse, buys a heap of cosmetics and other commodities in accordance with those standards. Consequently, other than Mr. Milkman Dead, she is given to the hand of Mr. Death.

Pecola in *The Bluest Eye* has undergone the same brainwash before her madness, which has been analyzed in Chapter 2. The tragedies of Hagar and Pecola

---

[1] For a further discussion of commodity culture and its dominance, in Susan Willis' "I Shop Therefore I Am: Is there a place for Afro-American Culture in Commodity Culture."

lie in the fact that they fail to understand that they cannot become incorporated into white standards, instead self-destructively internalizing the pain and anxiety caused by sexism and racism. The new controlling images projected by society and commercialism via modern technology effectively perpetuate and reinforce the older stereotypes that were conveniently employed to manipulate African Americans' behaviors and mentality. Pauline hates her own daughter whose appearance hardly meets the aesthetic expectations of the white cinema industry. Her attempt to be incorporated in a cinema world alienates her from the reality of her unfulfilled life and damages her real life that does not match the commercialized fantasies projected on the screen. Believing that the cinematic illusions are real, she starts to have difficulty in facing her irresponsible husband, her black children and her poverty, and her sense of incompetence and dissatisfaction was heightened by Hollywood representations of happy lives fraught with materialistic affluence and high fashion. She fails to discover the flaw of the chimerical world artificially presented by the commercial industry.

Besides, the mass media plays an important and manipulating role in maintaining a social hierarchy of discrimination as they are the chief vehicles by which ideology is transmitted through information and imagery. The pervasive influence of mass media is closely related to the monopoly of capital that enables those who are in power to control the social norms and values through ownership and financial support. The modern dominant society no longer exerts an explicit human exploitation as it did under slavery; rather, the American consumer culture manipulatively takes over the power of control. Thus, black girls placed in the lowest social stratum such as Pecola and Hagar may finally become normative and be pressured into accepting cultural dominance and controlling images disseminated by the media.

Susan Willis emphasizes the restrictions inflicted on a black girl's autonomy by the forceful and irresistible influence of media: "White cultural domination is far too complex to be addressed only in a retaliatory manner. A simple, straightforward response to cultural domination cannot be mounted, let alone imagined, because domination is bound up with the media and this with commodity gratification." (1989: 175)

The media shrewdly keep their values intact and separate from marginalized groups of people, deliberately excluding the counter influences of African-American cultural heritage in order to avoid that source of positive acculturation. The purpose of having control over media is obviously to keep the oppressed immobilized and to eliminate an attempt by any individual in the marginal groups to retrieve their own identity and autonomy.

In *Tar Baby*, Jadine is a signifier of consumption culture, wearing expensive fashionable clothes and jewelry and succeeding to a degree where Hagar and Pecola had failed. Despite her success, she is objectified without an integral voice to express herself. As Mary Jane Lupton puts it, Jadine is simply "adorned with goods for sale" (1986: 417). Her job as a model indicates that she is serving as a mannequin displaying the clothes that the consumption culture is trying to sell. Just as Michele Wallace notes that "black women are more often visualized in mainstream American culture—most prominently as fashion models or as performers in music videos—than they are allowed to speak their own words, or speak about their own condition as women of color, as novelists" (1990: 3), Jadine intuitively perceives that only her youth and exotic beauty are relevant to holding her job and that aging will soon hinder her from remaining as a popular model. Although she shrouds her apprehensive feelings, Jadine unconsciously understands that the cost of modeling high fashion is the circumscription of her racial identity and sensitivity. From the perspective of Westerners who display their curiosity about objects unfamiliar and unique to their culture, Jadine herself is viewed as an exotic concoction without specific African-American origins. If Jadine were able to articulate a sense of loss relative to her African-American origins, she would become stable and less often apprehensive about her beliefs or behaviors.

Unlike Jadine who has a successful career, the more diminished and unnoticed Alma Estée, a native West Indian, also displays in *Tar Baby* how seriously Western culture negates ethnic values. Just as Hagar represents the ludicrous trial of a black woman immersed in white culture, Alma, who is also consumed by white values, believes that if she wears a red wig, it will improve her appearance. Shocked, Son tries to make her get rid of the artificial wig. While Alma, who has bought the wig with money saved by cleaning the toilets at the airport in Dominique, does not doubt that it will make her look like a white girl, it is evident that the racialized commodity culture completely disgraces her even as it exploits her labor as janitor.

3.1.5 Great Migration and Culture Orphanage

Morrison's novels are said to be about place and displacement, referring to her communities, which are strongly evocative of mood, culture, psychology, and to her characters, who are often alienated from the people and places that give them identity. She prefers a unique depiction of migration that interrogates the destructive and distorting effects of physical and emotional dislocation on culturally mobile blacks.

Beginning with the trans-Atlantic slave trade that "commercially deported" millions of Africans from Central, West, and South-Western Africa to Europe, the Americas, and the Caribbean, the cycle of dispersion includes the flight of refugees via the underground railroad to points "North," the early nineteenth century deportation of free African Americans to Liberia under the aegis of the American Colonization Society; the "Scramble for Africa" that distributed African peoples and lands among European colonizers and fragmented cultural nationalities among different imperialist administrations; the Great Migration in the post-Reconstruction era that took hundreds of thousands of Africans from Louisiana, Mississippi, Georgia, Alabama, the Carolinas and elsewhere, North and West to Ohio, New York, Pennsylvania, Illinois, Kansas and Oklahoma; the internal migration of Africans among the various Caribbean countries in the post-Emancipation period, and to Panama and Costa Rica to work on the construction of the Canal and in the U.S. American-owned fruit-exporting industries; the twentieth-century migrations to European and North American metropolises—Paris, London, Lisbon, New York, Miami, Toronto—from the Carribean, the Americas and Africa; and the continuing migrations from the city, and from the city to the suburbs in pursuit of an ever more hazardous "ascent."[1]

Morrison's novels show in serious ways that ameliorative changes— opportunity, mobility, and "success"—have a counterweight: culture shock.[2] Anthropological studies demonstrate that culture shock—the massive psychic reaction to cultural displacement—ensues when travel or migration require an

---

[1] See Robert Stepto's *From Behind the Veil: A Study of Afro-American Narrative* for a discussion of what Stepto calls the journey of "ascent," promoted by "confining social structures" (67–68).

[2] The term "culture shock" was introduced into the English language in 1954 by Kalervo Oberg, Adrian Furnham, Stephen Bochner. *Culture Shock: Psychological Reactions to Unfamiliar Environments*. London: Mrthuen, 1986.

individual to function in a culture that is vastly different from his or her own. All of Morrison's novels inscribe (some might say, bemoan) the varied maladjustments of blacks who lose contact with or have been denied access to native, enculturating, and authenticating communities. These maladapted blacks become ludicrous, pathetic, and dysfunctional when they abandon traditional cultural values and practices for alien ones. Without a native culture to inform or to mediate their existence, life often becomes alienating, meaningless, and indecipherably "foreign" for cultural itinerants.

The phenomenon of culture shock is well documented throughout Morrison's oeuvre. Morrison portrays culture shock as a traumatic, yet inevitable, consequence for upwardly mobile, migrating, or rootless blacks. For example, in *The Bluest Eye*, before the Breedloves move to Lorain, Pauline loves Cholly very much. Although she has a "crooked, archless foot," Cholly's love makes it seem like "something special and endearing." For the first time, Pauline feels that "her bad foot was an asset" (Morrison, 1970: 116). Under the protection of Cholly, she is "secure and grateful." They go picking berry and enjoy the "streak of green the june bug made" (117). She has "not known there [is] so much laughter in the world" (116). After newlyweds Cholly and Pauline Breedlove leave the backwoods of rural Kentucky to pursue the promises of economic mobility in "urban" Lorain, Ohio—a hostile northern environment that ultimately destroys their love and their lives, everything has changed. Ultimately, neither is able to make the necessary transitions demanded by a migratory experience. Pauline learns immediately that life will be decidedly different from her old Kentucky home. Pauline is placed in an alien, hostile land, where whites are more numerous than blacks and where she is judged, not by the superior quality of her work but by the relative attributes of her external appearance—even by blacks influenced by the values of white society. Her days are no longer filled with domestic tranquility. Pauline looks outside her home for a sense of purpose and identity. Because they are black and, to her, ugly, she has no enthusiasm for treating her husband and bringing the children up. Gradually money becomes the focus of all the quarrels. Unlike the ideal family of Dick and Jane, as described in the primer at the beginning of the novel, the Breedloves' marriage becomes quarrelsome and violent.

In *Sula*, when Sula Peace ends her ten-year sojourn through the world beyond

Medallion, her cultural disorientation is heralded by a prophetic plague of dead robins. She divulges the degree of her estrangement from Bottom culture when she puts her grandmother in an (interracial) old folks home, ruins her best friend's marriage, and reputedly sleeps with white men. Consequently, she dies alone and unloved.

Governed by his greed and a lust for power, Macon Dead II rejects his holistic cultural roots to adopt disabling mainstream ideologies of success in *Song of Solomon*. Psychologically maimed after witnessing the brutal murder of his father by white men, Macon seeks revenge by vowing to master the white man's game. The only white man's game Macon knows or understands, however, is the oppression of black people.

Jadine Childs, *Tar Baby*'s cultural orphan, is perhaps Morrison's most fully developed and, therefore, most pathetic victim of cultural contamination and rootlessness. Notwithstanding her media success and her reputation as a brilliant international beauty, Jadine is condemned to Sisyphean wandering because she is unable to affiliate authentically or meaningfully with any cultural group.

In *Beloved*, Sethe, a slave, matures to selfhood without benefit of an enculturating community. After fleeing Kentucky's slavery for life on the "free side of the Ohio," she enjoys freedom and "kin" for only twenty-eight days before she attempts to kill all of her children rather than see them reclaimed by slave catchers. Sethe's newly adopted community rejects her because she clearly does not share their cultural vision.

As its musical name indicates, the "city blues" *Jazz* recounts the traumatic "blues" of the blacks in the city, the various migration experiences and their consequences. Morrison examines in *Jazz* the displacement and alienation that black people suffered during the period of the Great Migration: The place is in New York City, and Morrison's characters are both seduced and repulsed by it. Joe and Violet moved to New York from the South like many others between the turn of the century and World War I. And like these others they were motivated to move by political and economic hard times in the South and by the hope of better times in the North. They didn't find their mecca in the city. Their plans and dreams there are thwarted, however, when the Traces undergo a series of disabling culture shocks. Without an orienting cultural community to sustain them in the North, Joe and Violet fail to cope with the challenges of city life. During twenty years of keeping the beat of city rhythms, Joe and Violet lose their way. Violet is the first, and then Joe. The once-happy Joe and Violet Trace begin their decent into marital discord after a succession of ameliorative moves that take them further and further from their cultural roots, like so many other real-life (and fictional) African Americans, the Traces reified the ambitions of rural blacks who believed that the urban North was the promised land: the land of opportunity, equality, and plenty. As a result, at fifty, in the city, Violet and her world are incoherent, and Joe becomes the kind of man who "knew wrong wasn't right, and did it anyway" (Morrison, 1992: 74). Consequently, he falls in love with and then kills a girl Dorcas with whom he is paradoxically no longer lonely as well as violating himself.

3.2 Release of Pains

Yet the above mentioned phenomena are not the whole truth of Morrison's fictional purpose. Just as the blues is not just the music that expresses the blue spirit, Morrison's fiction is also full of releasing spirit, although some releases are not very wholesome. The motif of transcendence, of moving through pain and longing to a release, matches the blues impulse that propels the novels in their depiction of human relationships, including the relationship between individuals and their past selves.

3.2.1 Violent Release of Traumas

Suffering from negation, fragmentation, alienation, incoherence, displacement and dislocation, some black people can't find wholesome means to release their pains. In order to vent their anger and express their miserable feelings, they resort to violence, causing pains to the people concerned. Among them, Cholly in *The Bluest Eye*, Shadrack in *Sula*, Guitar and the Seven Days in *Song of Solomon*, Violet and Joe Trace in *Jazz*, Sethe in *Beloved* and Ruby's men in *Paradise* are cases in point.

Cholly Breedlove

Abused and neglected himself as a child, parentless, set adrift by the death of his guardian, taunted and humiliated by white men during his first sexual encounter, Cholly in *The Bluest Eye* manifests his life of distortion in distorted love making, the violence and brutality of his domestic relationship. Morrison describes the danger of the "freedom" brought about by negation and incoherence as follows:

> Cholly was free. Dangerously free. Free to feel whatever he felt ... He was free to live his fantasies, and free even to die, the how and the when of which held no interest for him ... Abandoned in a junk heap by his mother, rejected for a crap game by his father, there was nothing more to lose. He was alone with his own perceptions and appetites, and they alone interested him. (1970: 125–126)

Therefore, when seeing his daughter standing in the kitchen cleaning a frying pan, "her head to one side as though crouching from a permanent and unrelieved blow" (127), he is filled with pity, rage and helplessness. In a drunken, confused state, Cholly gropes for something to give his daughter to demonstrate his love and tenderness and return to himself a sense of self-respect. Remaining mute, helpless, and in turmoil, unable to communicate his changing feelings of tenderness and hatred, he rapes Pecola in part to demonstrate his love and in part driven by an inner force almost against his desires, a force he does not fully comprehend in his drunken, muddled brain to do this "wild and forbidden thing that excited him" (128).

The Seven Days

In *Song of Solomon*, for example, Milkman's belated maturation in 1962 and 1963 is the period of germination for the seeds of both the Civil Rights movement and black militancy. Black leaders invited their followers—and sympathetic whites—to make a choice between nonviolent civil disobedience and an often violent counter-racism.

During the period of this novel's major action, many blacks felt impelled to embrace a tendentious ideology of the type espoused and promulgated by men like Malcolm X and Elijah Muhammad,[1] both mentioned briefly in Morrison's

---

[1] Malcolm X was an intransigent opponent of the U.S. government and its imperialist policies. He has been called many things: Pan-Africanist, father of Black Power, religious fanatic, closet conservative ... Elijah Muhammad (October 7, 1897—February 25, 1975) is notable for his leadership of the Black Muslims and the Nation of Islam from 1934 until his death during their period of greatest growth in the mid-20th century.

novel. Black militancy—and occasionally terrorism—began to manifest itself in organizations like the Black Panthers and in a new generation of leaders that included Huet Newton, Angela Davis, Stokely Carmichael, H. Rap Brown, Bobby Seale, and Eldridge Cleaver. Members of these organizations espoused violence to acquire political power—and sexism to recover or reconstitute black manhood. Ron Karenga, for example, openly preached the idea that black women's role was properly to "complete" or "complement" black men. This notion continues to polarize black men and women, and its presence contributes part of the dramatic tension in Morrison's novel.

Morrison sketches in these currents at their most extreme in her terrorist brotherhood, the Seven Days, who cling too tightly to the past to extricate themselves from hatred for the white. Instead of creating, they destroy.

As Guitar, one of the members of the Seven Days, explains to Milkman, the Seven Days enact an Old Testament, eye-for-an-eye form of justice: "When a Negro child, Negro man is killed by whites and nothing is done about it by their law and their courts, this society selects a similar victim at random, and they execute him or her in a similar manner if they can. If the Negro was hanged, they hang; if a Negro was burnt, they burn; raped and murdered, they rape and murder." (154–155)

The Seven Days' philosophy is predicated on cold, calculated revenge a life for life without benefit of due process or regard to questions of innocence or guilt. They make a clear cut division between blackness and whiteness and think that to attack what is contained in whiteness is to defend blackness.

Whenever some black people are killed, for the Seven Days, "the only thing left to do is to balance it; keep things on an even keel" (170), which means to kill the same number of white people. Apparently, in their eyes, nothing but killing can set things right. They announce that the starting point of their action is love. They intend by knocking off white folks to revenge, to challenge white authority, to warn them against misbehaving towards the black, and to change black slave status. But their efforts end with killing, a manifestation of hatred and morbidity. Contrary to their declaration that they abhor killing, they find beauty in it.

Ostensibly, the members of the Seven Days sacrifice their personal happiness, family and life included, to the course and welfare of their people. They even do not need repayment, gratitude, or acknowledgement from those whom they think they are serving. But Guitar claims that he protects black women because they are his. This assertion clearly states that it is, in the final analysis, the detestation towards failure of possession, not love for the black, which contributes much to stimulating and promoting the bloody attempts.

The Seven Days do not want to be hurt and harmed and think it unnatural for the white to treat them thus. But the whites, in their eyes, well deserve their attacks. They actually are counting on the life of the whites to achieve their own psychological balance, not really to keep the ratio of the killed blacks and whites. As a result, it's susceptible as to whether they have actualized their aim to keep the ratio or bring about any good, not to say rescue the black from their wretched living and working conditions. They doesn't take actively preventive measures but wait for the killing and then try to kill in turn. Their action, far from improving living environment for the black, veils horror and restlessness on them. Racial issues get more acute and the feelings of estrangement and insecurity become more severe, which is against their wishes. It is because of this insecurity that Guitar fires at Milkman, willing to pertain to black heritage but resorting to wrong means. Consequently, Guitar is alienated, contrary to his original intention, from black culture.

Guitar's major premise is that his killing is motivated by the love of African-American people, and Milkman objects to this premise by pointing out that "except for skin colour, I cannot tell the difference between what the white women want from us and what the coloured women want. You say they all want our living life. So if a coloured woman is raped and killed, why do the Days rape and kill a white woman? Why worried about the colored woman at all? " (223). By letting Guitar respond angrily "because she's mine," Morrison enables us to see the issue of race bracketed momentarily and instead discover what is really at issue—male possession of women. Thus the Seven Days "heroic" stance on saving the African-American race parallels the perpetuation of patriarchal authority and black racism—typical of black male identity gone wild.

The Seven Days epitomize patriarchal organization. The group is all male and does not permit its members to marry or to form permanent attachments with women. The very name suggests the originating authority of the monotheistic "God the Father of the West" who created the heavens and earth in six days and rested on the seventh. But there is no rest for the Seven Days (Guitar's day is the Christian Sabbath) in its unarticulated efforts to establish masculinity as violent mastery and manhood as the right to say what one's women do. Thus, the unrecognized mission of the Seven Days seems to be the following: If white male violence works to keep African-American men from white women, African-American men need to organize to insure continued property rights in African American women.

The Seven Days cling too tightly to the past, both racial and personal. They are a group of misled blacks. They are sensitive and easily upset, cloistering themselves in the shadow of the past. Their values, being derailed by their ferocious passion, are distorted. Being addicted to self-pity and morbid lust for revenge while regarding themselves as infallible tradition guardians, they fall into a vicious cycle. Consequently, other than keeping the tradition that advocates a harmonious coexistence between men, they are sailing further and further away from it. The pitiable death of Robert Smith and the crazy shooting of Guitar at Milkman prove the danger of their way. They sacrifice themselves without being able to win welfare for others. Only Porter, when finally falling in love with Corinthians, quits the organization, and starts to lead a normal and fruitful life with a heart brimful of authentic love.

Although she allows the reader to see the reasons behind this organization in the various forms of gratuitous violence visited by whites on blacks, Morrison gradually allows the reader to see also that the violence of the Seven Days merely breeds madness and more violence. Thus in the course of the novel she reveals repeatedly the mental toll of membership in the Days. Henry Porter, for example, puts in his first appearance as a shotgun-brandishing drunk; he evidently manages to restore his equilibrium only by getting out of the terrorist organization and by falling in love with First Corinthians. As for Guitar, he eventually becomes virtually psychotic and, attempting to kill his own racial brother, kills the innocent Pilate instead. Morrison's point is unmistakable: Violence by its own nature fails to discriminate; it rebounds on the heads of the perpetrators and their people. She allows the reader a certain amount of sympathy and even satisfaction at the idea of secret militancy, but gradually she reveals the real cost of such short-term gratification. Only well into the novel does the reader learn that Robert Smith, the crazed insurance salesman who attempts to fly from the roof of Mercy Hospital, was a member of the Days. The account of his death introduces and frames another narrative: The birth of a black man who will learn alternatives to the routes Smith takes to achieve justice.

Joe and Violet Trace

Dispossessed in the Southern plantation, fragmented by outer forces such as the seducing and controlling city, as well as social, political and economic conditions, misled by oppressive forces such as the blighted legacy of slavery, racial violence, discrimination, and segregation, Joe and Violet Trace felt dispossessed, fragmented, split and cracked, which results in the tragedy of Joe's shooting his former lover Dorcas and Violet's stealing other's baby and cutting the already dead Dorcas's face. The pains they suffered again find their releases in the emotional and physical violence that human beings are capable of inflicting upon one another.

The Patriarchal Town of Ruby

In *Paradise*, Morrison examines the consequence of violent release of the pains caused by racism by describing a patriarchal town of Ruby founded on the basis of exceptionalism, racism, conformity, rebellion within an insular community with men against women, old against young, the past against the present. The pure black community of Ruby in *Paradise* emerges out of the doubled insult of class and colorism. The community have been ostracized by whites, migrated from the South to Oklohoma and been denied entry into a community of prosperous, lighter-complexioned African Americans. They pushed on to found the town of Haven and constructed themselves as God's chosen people. After World War II, Haven falls on hard times economically. The sons of Haven's founders move west to form a new town, Ruby, dedicated to the preservation of the same sense of exceptionalism born when their fathers were rejected by the lighter-skinned blacks. For Ruby's men, their exceptionalism and sense of freedom lies in their genetically pure African heritage, unsullied by any drop of white blood. It is described as a "quiet, orderly community, unique and isolated" (Morrison, 1997: 8). Having learned from their grandfathers' experience of Disallowing, Ruby's men interpret their isolation as a way of self-protection. However, isolation implies exclusion of others. As the novel shows, Ruby does not welcome any outsiders. For them, "outsiders and enemies are the same word" (212). Therefore, rather than a perfect paradise, Ruby ends up as a "conservative, patriarchal and thoroughly racialized community" (Dalsgard, 2001: 97). Their intention to protect themselves and their descendents from the racism that their ancestors suffered turns into racial violence against others. The rigid rule of blood in Ruby resulting from racism finally results in racism, exceptionalism and a homogeneous cultural identity, which epitomizes black identity gone wild. As is maintained by Toni Morrison in the transcript of Newshour with Jim Lehrer, "isolation, you know, carries the seeds of its own destruction because as times change, other things seep in, as it did with Ruby," in combating racism, Ruby's men have undergone a process of internalization, relocating themselves into the discursive colonization of racist ideologies and remaining unable to develop an identity of self-determination. They have become the man who in fighting against the devil becomes the devil itself. Understandably, the action of Ruby's men opposes racial oppression, an integral part of the community's history, and they aim to assert a self-determined black identity. Its counter-discursive function is limited by its reaction to a colonizing ideology, however. As is pointed out by Bhabha, "it is always in relation to the place of the Other that colonial desire is articulated: The phantasmic space of oppression that no one subject can singly or fixedly occupy, and therefore permits the dream of the inversion of roles." (1997: 44) According to Bhabha, the colonial subject position is shifting rather than fixed. In the creation of a colonial subjectivity, colonial discourse forms a space in which the positions of master and slave not only define each other, but can shift into an inversion of roles.

The act of Ruby's men demonstrates the inversion of roles. In "Othering" the Convent women, they internalize the colonial forces that defined their ancestors and themselves as the Other on the ground of racial differences, thus taking the role of the master. Their act exemplifies their desire to assert their subjectivity and self-determined identity by a kind of inversion of roles, though they take the Convent women rather than white racists as the Other. Like the ideology of white racism, their construction of the Other is grounded on a set of binary oppositions: normal/abnormal, rational/irrational, healthy/diseased, light/dark, which are violent hierarchies where one of the two terms forcefully govern the other. By revealing the internalizing of racial ideologies and the inversion of roles, Morrison deconstructs the master discourse, suggesting that is inevitably entwined with a violent marginalization of the Other. Consequently, this need for racial purity, of course, explains why the men pay such careful attention to the morality of their women and why a man must own his woman's sexuality, which in turn leads to the slaughtering of the Convent women under the ostensible goal to protect their cult of true black womanhood. While the Convent emerges as the liminal space where the monolithic categories of religion, race, class, and gender converge and make cultural hybridity possible, the men of Ruby perceive hybridity as a disruptive evil that threatens their sense of selfhood and nationhood. Having resolved to defend their view of a homogeneous and hierarchical nation, they decide to destroy difference by attacking the women in the Convent, and thus persecuted nonconformity by excluding from their society all those who might threaten their social order based on isolation and racial purity. However, in so doing, they have conducted the opposite of what their forefathers had tried to protect themselves from—isolating and killing the innocent. What they do actually reveals that they have internalized the racist ideologies embedded in the community's history, targeting them at other groups. Their pursuit of paradise is built upon making those different from them the Other and therefore violates the very principle of a paradisal existence—"variety, comfort and flexibility" (Morrison, 1997: 120). They gather the rumors of the past twenty years into a narrative that makes these women the dangerous Other; unlike their decorous women, the Covent women in these men's eyes are child murderers, lesbians, temptresses, and witches who have turned the former Convent into a coven. What is actually more threatening is that these women have claimed, out of their abuse, the power to name and identify themselves. They also represent the "difference" demanded by the colonial discourse internalized by Ruby's men. This is the unspoken reason for the raid on the Convent. The Convent women's proximity to Ruby means that Ruby's women have an alternative model for conceiving of themselves.

In resorting to murder, these men simply take the logic of *Song of Solomon*'s Seven Days a step further. The men of Ruby construct a narrative in which their protection of their black women authorizes their killing of one white girl and four "bodacious black Eves unredeemed by Mary" who in the moment of the killing run "like panicked does" (Morrison, 1997: 18). The collective male perspective on their task is articulated in the thoughts of one of the men who have invaded the Convent:

Certainly there wasn't a slack or sloven woman anywhere in town and the reasons, he thought, were clear. From the beginning its people were free and protected. A sleepless woman could always rise from her bed, wrap a shawl around her shoulders and sit on the steps in the moonlight. And if she felt like it she could walk out the yard and on down the road. No lamp and no fear. A hiss-crackle from the side of the road would never scare her because whatever it was that made the sound, it wasn't something creeping up on her. Nothing for ninety miles around thought she was prey ... When the baby quieted they could sit together for a spell, gossiping, cluckling low so as not to wake anybody else. (8–9)

In his mind, Ruby represents the best of all possible worlds for women, but clearly Morrison exposes through this character's thoughts the central unacknowledged contradiction of the male communal narrative, the patriarchal hegemonic discourses that authorize the hunting of women in the name of protecting womanhood. The women of Ruby may walk without fear but they also do so without a lamp, and they are, by and large, unenlightened about anything but their domesticity. They walk but do not drive and there is really nowhere to go since the nearest town is ninety miles away. It is a safety based on isolation that approximates the carceral. The safety of the women of Ruby, moreover, depends on the good will of Ruby's men. The women who place their dreams of safety in men are compromised, and only when women give up such dreams can they begin to form their own identities. The women who subscribe to the town's patriarchal ideology do so at the cost of limiting their possible identities to that of the tender of a man's home and nurturer of a man's children. But even this cost may be insufficient to purchase safety, since any woman who ever threatens the male order of things immediately moves from the set of "not prey" to that of "prey"—here lies the essence of male subjectivity gone wild: the patriarchal control of women's life. The fact of independent female subjectivity becomes almost intolerable for these men, who feel a need to control women absolutely to confirm their own masculine status.

Morrison is constantly having her characters spell out the meaning of her story. "They think they have outfoxed the white man when in fact they imitate him," she writes toward the end of the novel. "They think they are protecting their wives and children, when in fact they are maiming them. And when the maimed children ask for help, they look elsewhere for the cause. Born out of an old hatred, one that began when one kind of black man scorned another kind and that kind took the hatred to another level, their selfishness had trashed 200 years of suffering and triumph in a moment of such pomposity and error and callousness it froze the mind." Ruby, she adds, was "a backward noplace ruled by men whose power to control was out of control and who had the nerve to say who could live and who not and where; who had seen in lively, free, unarmed females the mutiny of the mares and so got rid of them" (Morrison, 1997: 306). The attempt to enforce an overly rigid community harmony is not only deadening but can easily disrupt the desired harmony. Unity that is too tight only precipitates the dissolution it is designed to prevent.

Central to this rigid unity is a refusal by the ruling fathers to tolerate divergent interpretations of the town's past. The men seek to preserve the town's identity by freezing its past, allowing only their own official reading of the treks, the Disallowing, and the establishment of the town. As Storace argues, they "claim the perpetual overarching authority of the creator at the moment of creation." In this formulation, creator can be taken in the sense of author as well as divine creator, for the townsmen are convinced that their past and their single interpretation of the past have divine sanction, and, unlike Morrison, they "want to stop the life of their work at the moment of writing" (66).

As a result of such tensions, the town is ripe for a shake-up.

3.2.2 Wholesome Release of Traumas

Morrison's novels not only disclose the negative effects brought about by brutality and degradation Afro-Americans suffered, but also afford wholesome ways to transcend and release their pains by restoring and re-clothing their own wounded psyches. Among the healing and therapeutic ways, music is the crucial one. It can be found in Mrs. MacTeer's emotional outlet of blues in *The Bluest Eye*, Pilate and Shalimar people's history—inducing song, Paul D. and the slaves' releasing and shielding ballads, Joe and Violet's recuperating jazz and L's restorative hum.

Besides, Morrison affords some other ways to heal the wound. For instance, in *Sula*, the community people "leap into the living" by participating in National Suicide Day invented and led by Shadrack. The community is indeed reborn by releasing their painful memory of having been oppressed and degraded.

For the Convent women in *Paradise* who suffered from diverse painful memories, communication is another way to release their pains. Reflecting upon her own experience and the distressing tension in her life between Catholicism and sexuality, Consolata advises the women to "never break them ['body' and 'spirit'] in two. Never put one over the other" (Morrison, 1997: 263). Their healing ritual involves the women telling each other their stories in the form of "loud dreaming," which is described as "no different from a shriek" (264), which becomes cathartic and thus is physically and psychically beneficial. Through "loud dreaming" (264), they heal themselves, achieving individual harmony as they acquire communal harmony. They gain self and community—"They understood and began to begin"—and the changes are soon evident, for they have "a markedly different look," something "sociable and connecting" (265), "an adult manner" (266), a calmness, a lack of being haunted.

Through the active, communal process of negotiating strategic alliances across their differences to heal themselves from the consequences of the injustices they have been made to suffer, the Convent women create a nurturing, dialogic space from which their own refashioned subjectivities emerge, subjectivities that, collectively, can not only survive a racist and sexist culture but work to "resist and redress its injustices" (Hooks, 2000: 13).

The above analysis points to the fact that Morrison's novels conjure slaves back to life in many-dimensional characters with a full range of human emotions, just like the blues that wail through pains and turmoil to a release. They love and hate, sin and forgive; they are heroic and mean, self-sacrificing and demanding. Yet above all, the blues impulse to transcend their pains and incoherence to reconstitute their cultural identity is the basic tone of Morrison's novels.

Chapter 4

Morrison's *Jazz*: Constructing Identity Through Cultural Hybridity

In 1951, James Baldwin wrote: " … it is only in his music … that the Negro of America has been able to tell his story." (2000: 24) Since jazz music is paradoxically a distinctly black American art form as well as a cultural hybrid, Morrison, through her grand, epic sweep interrogating the meanings of history and identity, is trying to achieve "the translation of the world into jazz music" (Janowitz, 1999: 24). As LeRoi Jones explains, "Music, as paradoxical as it might seem, is the result of thought. It is the result of thought perfected at its most empirical, i.e., as attitude or Stance" (1963: 106). Morrison's fiction is also the result of her deep thought concerning the fate of African American as a race. Like the music she models on, she tries to tell the story of the black people's continuous struggle for psychic wholeness through her word-music.

Jazz, the product of slavery, segergation, poverty, and disenfranchisement, is many things: a "complicated anger" (Morrison, 1993: 59); the carefree indulgence of the now; a marginalized population's assertion of selfhood, of cultural vitality and artistic pride; the hope for musical synthesis through conflict. Created in an era of socially sanctioned African-American invisibility and stigmatization, "it's also the affirmation of individual and group worth: the soul's manifestation of its love for its complement, the rejected flesh. A tribute to the soul's resilience, it is ultimately one process through which it may heal itself," as Caroline Brown argues (2002: 629).

What is possibly most characteristic of the jazz process is its mutability, its capacity to incorporate disparate cultural, stylistic, instrumental, and performative elements into its diverse repertoire while still remaining essentially itself. Marked by its syncretism and innovation, it takes the familiar and fixed and makes it novel and distinct. Influenced by African rhythmic complexity and European harmonic structure, arising from varied regional combinations of ragtime and the blues, it is often called America's "classical music" (Brown, 2002: 631). Just as jazz itself was and is a hybrid, drawing on and transforming sources from outside the black American experience, Morrison's literary jazz alerts us to the paradox that jazz music is both: a distinctly black American art form and "world music"; just as jazz music is inextricably grounded in the black experience in America—and yet, at the same time, it challenges the received binary pairs of white and black, the New World and the Old (both Europe and Africa, even Asia), oppression and freedom, "jazz and non-jazz" (Grandt, 2004: 316). Morrison's literary jazz tries to tell the traumatic experiences of black people in America and tries to break the binary boundary of white and black, men and women, individual and community, south and north, countryside and city, past and present. As Nicholas Evans tries to explain the paradox, jazz "always involves race, nationalism, and related concerns because it heightens the audibility, palpability, and even visibility of the cultural sameness and difference of whiteness and blackness" (2000: 18). Morrison has produced the kind of hybrid cultural work that proclaims hybridization through communication between different cultures and genders.

This cross-cultural invocation and generation is clearly described through the "white girl" Amy Denver who massages and encourages Sethe on her flight, and aids her in childbirth. Amy accompanies her "repair work" (Morrison, 1987: 80) with a song, humming three stanzas that are quoted in the narrative framework. The first stanza is as follows:

> When the busy day is done,
> And my weary little one,
> Rocketh gently to and fro;
> When the night winds softly blow,
> And the crickets in the glen,
> Chirp and Chirp and Chirp again;

> Where 'pon the haunted green,
>
> Fairies dance around their queen,
>
> Then from yonder misty skies,
>
> Cometh Lady Button Eyes. (Morrison, 1987: 80–81)

It should be noticed that Amy's tune is not Morrison's own, but literally quotes the first, second, and fourth stanzas of a poem by the white St. Louis poet Eugene Field entitled "Lady Button Eyes" (1989: 61–63). The sheer otherness of Field's poem when compared to Baby Suggs's sermon or Paul D.'s blues is immediately obvious. Eckstein argues that the use of a stylized Standard English "collides" with the Black vernacular English of the blues and the hollers, the strictly trochaic tetrameters "clash" with the polyrhythmic off-beat phrasings of the work songs and sermon chants, the regular 10-line stanzas with a rigid rhyme-scheme "contradict" the continuous play with formal conventions in Spirituals and folk blues (Eckstein, 2006: 275). Morrison does not employ Field's poem to point the oppositional nature of African- and European-based music, however, as the tune is clearly seen as a positive in the cautious intercultural encounter of Amy and Sethe. Jazz, Morrison seems to acknowledge here, is not—even though some critics would like to believe so—an autonomously black form of art. While jazz resists any clear-cut definition, it seems safe to say that it first came into being in the contact zones of the Americas, and developed from certain 18th- and 19th-century forerunners. These precursors certainly are the communal drumming and storytelling sessions in the slave quarters (evoked by *Beloved*), the Afro-Christian traditions of sermonizing and singing (Baby Suggs), and the manifestations of work songs, field hollers, and other blues (Paul D.) (Eckstein, 2006: 275). These traditions, however, were always negotiated with elements of the European musical tradition, its harmonic structure, its instruments, and of course, with the English language.[1] With Amy Denver, Morrison symbolically acknowledges the Western legacy as a legitimate

---

[1] In his seminal study of *Early Jazz*, Schuller shows how African American music initially developed very much in a Creole fashion. The rhythmic complexity of African drumming, for instance, had been dramatically reduced, while accordingly, the European diatonic scales and Western harmonics were reduced to accommodate better the largely pentatonic structure of African melody; see Gunther Schuller. *Early Jazz: Its Roots and Early Development*. Oxford: Oxford UP, 1986, pp. 6–26, 38–54.

predecessor of modern black art. What is at stake is not so much an opposition of Western and African styles, but the integrative power of the black musical culture, which, from its beginnings, adjusted western forms to its own needs. With the character Amy Denver, Morrison indeed symbolically accounts for the essential influences that went into the transcultural making of modern jazz, which also embodies Morrison's acknowledgement of Western influences on African-American culture and identity, which in turn influences Western civilization. In this sense, jazz becomes the framework for Morrison to reconstitute identity through cultural hybridity and communication.

In *The Black Atlantic: Modernity and Double Consciousness*, Gilroy investigates what he refers to as the "ethics of antiphony" (1993: 200) in black music. Beyond the improvisional interaction of groups of musicians, Gilroy argues, black music is also receptive to the input of its audience; it works towards communal identity in a process that is fundamentally rooted in the "experience of performance with which to focus the pivotal ethical relationship between performer and crowd, participant and community" (203). In a similar vein, Ellison writes in "The Charlie Christian Story" that "true jazz is an art of individual assertion within and against the group. Each true jazz moment (as distinct from uninspired commercial performance) springs from a contest in which artist challenges all the rest; each solo flight, or improvisation, represents (like the successive canvases of a painter) a definition of his identity: as individual, as member of the collectivity and as a chain in the link of tradition" (234). Morrison makes use of jazz as the framework to reconstitute identity through cultural hybridity or as the consequence of cultural interaction and assimilation. Therefore, she not only writes about how a sense of self emerges from experiences of exploitation, marginalisation and denial, but also defines what true human beings should be in this multicultural, interactive, transcultural and globalized world. With strong female and ethnic consciousness, she isn't confined to improve the material life and social position, but focuses on solving the blacks' problems from the view of the whole. She hopes to help free the blacks from the cognitive mistake, construct perfect subjectivity, carry forward the spirit of ethnic culture and increase the cohesion of the blacks by the construction of the black people. Furthermore, she wants the blacks and the whites alike to realize that in this world characterized by cultural interaction and cultural assimilation, no race, class or gender is superior or inferior to other ones, and communication and hybridization are the unavoidable ways to solve cultural differences. Thus, Morrison connects her novel creation with the historical mission of ethnic liberation and thoroughly describes the blacks' living situations from which she reveals the damage made by hegemonic culture to the minority culture. Furthermore, she appeals to the black intellectual to turn their steps to the blacks' ethnic culture and reconstruct ethnic consciousness based on the tradition disdained by the mainstream culture. What's more, she calls on the blacks and whites, men and women alike to communicate with each other and to help each other to reconstruct their respective identity. At the same time, being a woman writer, Morrison closely combines the process of the black women's self-seeking with the reconstruction of the black ethnic consciousness, relying on her unique female viewpoint and particular female experience. Her fiction relates to the idea of black strength and resilience while also making strength of song—in this case, the power of jazz and the blues combined with Spirituals, which helps African-Americans to survive and overcome adversity. For her, spiritual independence presupposes intellectual independence and neither is easily achieved, but she achieved both through her fiction.

4.1 Re-inheriting Black Cultural Heritage and Awakening Black Cultural Consciousness

Aiming to express a cultural legacy, Toni Morrison wants her novels to have an oral, effortless quality, evoking the tribal storytelling tradition of the African griot, who recites the legendary events of generations lying in oral texts like Spirituals, the blues, and folktales. Morrison creates a place for African Americans to preserve their oral tradition in writing, or "aural writing," not only depending faithfully on written documentation as a text, but on storytelling and people's discernible capacity to respond to the spoken word.[1] This clearly indicates her challenge to the print-restricted discourse of mainstream literature and history, which have

---

[1] Morrison's article, "Rootedness: the Ancestor as Foundation," shows her literary intention to integrate the African-American tradition of oral narratives into writing: "There are things that I try to incorporate into my fiction that are directly and deliberately related to what I regard as the major characteristics of Black art, wherever it is. One of which is the ability to be both print and oral literature: to combine those aspects so that the stories can be read in silence, of course, but one should be able to hear them as well." (1984: 341)

recorded only their own values and perspectives. Improvising her fictions like jazz and making them fluid with the employment of the African-American oral tradition, Morrison tries to deconstruct the fixed relationship of the signifier and the signified, the definer and the defined, the oppressor and the oppressed. Although she uses orally conditioned language to enter the written discourse, she skillfully revises that orality. She differentiates her own language forms from those of the dominant culture used to reinforce and to prescribe the hierarchical advantage of the ruling group. In so doing, Morrison attempts to expand the boundaries of the American literary canon.

Her characters, too, should have a special essence: They should be ancestral and enduring. In pursuing this personal, artistic vision, Morrison creates extraordinary tales of human experience that a less-independent writer should perhaps not attempt: to enlighten her readers about themselves. Her novels are not just art for art's sake, but they are political as well. In fact, "the best art is political" (Morrison, 1984: 345), she says, not in the pejorative meaning of political as haranguing, but as deliberately provocative. Morrison rejects the dichotomy of art and politics, insisting that art can be "unquestionably political and irrevocably beautiful at the same time" (345). She is careful to say, "I am not interested in indulging myself in some private, closed exercise of my imagination that fulfills only the obligation of my personal dreams." (345) Instead, her novels are instruments for transmitting cultural knowledge, filling a void once occupied by storytelling. They replace "those classical, mythological, archetypal stories that we heard years ago" (340). She believes in the artist's measure of responsibility for engendering cultural coherence and cohesion by receiving and interpreting the past—what she calls "bear[ing] witness" (Thomas LeClair, 1981: 26). That responsibility largely informs her literary aesthetic. She shuns what she labels "the separate, isolated ivory tower voice" (Morrison, 1984: 343) of the artist. The (black) artist, for Morrison, "is not a solitary person who has no responsibility to the community" (Davis, 1981: 418).

She finds her expression in the combination of her fictional world and African-American music. Morrison delineates how impossible it is to silence the music and voices of African Americans, even when censored by the community itself, and her fiction demonstrates both the inevitability and the usefulness of recovering musical and vocal expressions.[1]

4.1.1 Black Women as Culture Bearers

It's evident that the stories of endurance and strength in the face of slavery and oppression, as well as the values of the African communities from whence they came have been encapsulated in the orature of the women—the mothers (grandmother, aunt, older sibling, female ancestor) left behind not only to sing the blues but to sing of home. Within an African context, the role of the woman has been that of educator of the children into the culture. Ada Mere, Igbo sociologist, comments on the role of women as tale tellers and instructors. Women, she writes, "are the most primary and constant agents of child socialization" (1984: 3); furthermore, as agents of this education, women "are the mainstay of the oral tradition" (15). As Filomina Steady and others contend, the black women through Africa and the diaspora "represent the ultimate value in life, namely the continuation of the group" (1981: 32). It can be argued that part of the cultural achievement of Africans in the Americas has come from diaspora women who "mothered" African American culture into being (177). For Morrison and other contemporary black women writers, the attention to the role of women in passing on the traditions comes directly from their African and African American foremothers. Morrison, in her role as storyteller, creates an environment within the context of the novel for the stories of women, especially Pilate's, to be recognized and privileged. They are the "grown people" capable of responding to the characters' need for direction and recognition whom Morrison calls "ancestors." Wise in the ways of life, they transmit that wisdom and knowledge of self to the uninitiated. Extending its theological usage in African religion/culture to designate the community of deceased elders who continue to fulfill sustaining roles in the lives of their descendants, Morrison uses the term "ancestors" to designate living elders with a similar responsibility and capacity. In "City Limits, Village Values: Concepts of Neighborhoods in Black Fiction," Morrison describes them as "advising, benevolent, protective, wise" (1981: 39). In

---

[1] Morrison attempts to employ the sound effect of African-American oral tradition and music, which she calls "aural literature", in order to recover the buried voices. In another interview with McKay, Morrison also emphasizes that "it is important that there is sound in my books—that you can hear it, that I can hear it … What you hear is what you remember" (1983a, p. 427).

that essay, Morrison observes that "the worst thing that can happen in a city is that the ancestor becomes merely a parent or an adult and is thereby seen as a betrayer— one who had abandoned his traditional role of advisor with a strong connection to the past" (40).

In *The Bluest Eye*, Morrison describes a group of women such as Aunt Jimmy and her friends who are keepers of tradition and a morality flexible enough to ensue their survival. These women are identified by their hands and arms, the connectors for them to reach out and bind themselves to the generations following them:

> They beat their children with one hand and stole for them with the other. The hands that felled trees also cut umbilical cords; the hands that wrung the necks of chickens and butchered hogs also nudged African violets into bloom; the arms that loaded sheaves, bales, and sacks rocked babies into sleep. They patted biscuits into flaky ovals of innocence—and shrouded the dead. They plowed all day and came home to nestle like plums under the limbs of their men. (108)

Morrison describes these culture bearers as "free," but the freedom they experience is one wrought in nurturing their children and grandchildren, not in defiance and destruction of them.

The hands that could have saved Cholly, but which he rejects, have their counterpart in the hands of Mrs. MacTeer, similarly gruff and unromantic, but which carry in them the bonds of love. They stroke fevers out of Claudia and encourage her back to health. Although Claudia may have objected to her mother's rough hands rubbing salve on her chest, she rightfully recognizes the act as "a productive and fructifying pain" representative of love "thick and dark as Alaga syrup" (Morrison, 1970: 7). She remembers feet padding into her room and hands that "repined the flannel, readjusted the quilt, and rested a moment" on her forehead. When she remembers autumn, she thinks "of somebody with hands who does not want me to die" (7).

As a woman who works hard to raise her children, Mrs. MacTeer is the model for parenting and caring in Morrison's wasteland. She takes Pecola in when Cholly burns his family out. She presides over Pecola's first menses, hugging her reassuringly (the only hug the adolescent Pecola ever receives; Mrs. Breedlove's hugs and assurances are reserved for the little white Fisher girl). Though her brief encounter with Pecola cannot save the young girl, Mrs. MacTeer still has a very solid place in the novel as the spark of healthy fertility in the world of stagnation and a light in so much spiritual darkness.

In *Song of Solomon*, through the characterization of Pilate, a female ancestor, Morrison emphasizes the dead-end of both mainstream assimilation and radical separatism by offering an alternative—perhaps not a reconciliation but a more clearly articulated dialectic of the double self by the acceptance of one's African values and cultural heritage. Milkman's true inheritance, black cultural identity and ancestry, is provided by the women and particularly his aunt, Pilate—Milkman's spiritual guide throughout his passage. It is Pilate's rendition of their past that helps Milkman grow. Moreover, the stories of his sister Lena, his mother Ruth, and his distant cousin Susan Byrd, along with Pilate, help Milkman learn how to be "a single, separate Afro-American person … While also connected to a family, a community, and a culture" (Skerrett, 1985: 200). Just as the Spirituals transformed the slaves' misery into music, Pilate in *Song of Solomon* and the other women storytellers turn their "plea into a note" (321) and pass on the memory of the names that were stolen and the stories suppressed. Having been called a "primal mother goddess" (347), Pilate is described as a teacher, nurturer, life-saver, the family-preserver, surrogate mother and keeper of the blues tradition who embodies the spiritual and community-orientated griot, the "custodian of the culture" (Arhin, 1983: 92) that transmits cultural legacy to their descendents. Ancestral, mythic, free, Pilate embodies memorable traits of character that give form to the major theme of Morrison's work: spiritual transcendence and messianic. As a prototype of the "Great Mother," "Mother Earth," As William K. Freiert explains, Pilate's "smooth stomach was a sign that she was not born from human woman—in mystical terms, she is Earth, the Mother of all" (1980: 78).

In "Rootedness: the Ancestor as Foundation," Morrison states that Pilate functions as the ancestor for Milkman, and it is under her guidance that he becomes responsible and humane (1984: 343–344). As ancestor Pilate bears a major share of the novel's work in passing on cultural knowledge to Milkman and to the reader. She is one of the timeless people who dispatch their wisdom to others, who consciously or unconsciously initiate others to the ways of African-American culture that give life continuity and intent. Instead of repressing the past, she carries it with her in the form of her songs, her stories and her bag of bones. She believes that one's sense of identity is rooted in the capacity to look back to the past and synthesize it with the present; it is not enough simply to put it behind one and look forward. As she tells Macon: "You can't take a life and walk off and leave it. Life is life. Precious. And the dead you kill is yours. They stay with you anyway, in your mind. So it's a better thing, a more better thing to have the bones right there with you wherever you go. That way it frees up your mind." (Morrison, 1977: 210)

During Milkman's infancy and even before, she shields him from Macon's angry attacks, and later, during Milkman's adolescence, she catalyzes his course of self-discovery. She challenges his indifference and initiates him into the legacy of which black womankind are the guardians, a legacy of wisdom and beliefs. Her stories about her life on the farm, about her father's bravery, about her brother's love, and her refusal to adopt the meaningless rituals that occupy most people— these counter Macon's stories about conquest, ownership, and dominion. Moreover, it is her stories and songs, passed on to unravel his family history that implanted in him the desire to know. She becomes quite literally Milkman's pilot or guiding force, and fulfills her father's prophecy: A tree grounded in her own principles, she thus protectively towers over those about her, not only by her six-foot height but by the ascendancy of her love. In the end, she bequeaths to Milkman not only his birthright but also a legacy that allows him, too, to fly: "She had told him stories, sang him songs, fed him bananas and cornbread, and on the first cold day of the year, hot nut soup." (211) More than the traditional West African peanut soup fed to him, Pilate gives Milkman back his heritage through her African-based orature, although it takes him years to understand the true value of the tales and songs. Most importantly, the children's song, turned into a woman's blues by Pilate, is what leads Milkman to the legacy of his great-grandfather and the Flying Africans.

In the end, Pilate joins the other women in Milkman's life in being made a victim to his health, to his growth into a positive sense of self. A free spirit whose body has never weighed her to the earth, Pilate is triumphant in that, by sacrificing her own life, she will bring to an end the sequence of events, both historical and contemporary, which have divided her family and caused so much grief in it. And by setting in motion the events in which Guitar is ready to die for his cause, she also succeeds in eliminating the driving force behind the hatred practiced by the Seven Days. Her victimization, therefore, might have its worth in the larger picture of familial and communal good. And in the folk patterns that inform the novel, it is frequently a good, much-to-be-missed person whose sacrifice has the power to renew. Not only does she sing the lore of her culture, she lives it as well.

In *Love*, through L, the 97-year-old eloquent cook, Morrison shows the power of folklore by letting L's own griot voice speak. L's is the voice of this narrative. L's status as cook, first at Cosey's Hotel and Resort and later at Maceo's Cafe Ria, signifies a performance of nurturance that is understood as an act of love. Indeed, throughout Morrison's work, hands that cook and offer food to family and community are depicted as healing figures.[1] This loaded act symbolizes L's position in the Cosey family, as that of cook and its concomitant roles of healer, savior, and peacemaker. She took the responsibility of raising Christine when she is only at three months, and every time Christine suffered from setbacks, she would crawl under L's bed to find her shelter. She sympathizes with Heed when Mr. Cosey spanked Heed at Christine's birthday party in public and warns him of her anger. Straightforward, opinionated, and knowledgeable about her community, L, who witnessed Cosey's authentic will, in which he gave all his worldly possessions to Celestial, a "sporting woman" with whom he has been engaged in a lengthy affair, forged the informal will in order to protect the Cosey women. It was an act, L admits, designed to keep the women "connected" (Morrison, 2003: 201).

4.1.2 Black Women as Hope-bringers

In the course of reconstructing racial consciousness, black women did a great job as hope-bringers. In *Beloved*, Morrison gives a perfect example of black female's function on awakening dormant racial consciousness by portraying Baby Suggs. With the blessings of her community, Baby Suggs anoints herself out of her

---

[1] Although there are various characters in Morrison's oeuvre who are connected to food, Pilate in *Song of Solomon* provides a particularly illuminating example of healing through food. Upon meeting her nephew Milkman and his friend Guitar, she offers them a perfect soft-boiled egg and provides an unconventional, but bountiful array of food for Reba and Hagar. Unlike Pilate, Ruth's preparation of unpalatable food—including the "red at the bone" chicken—amplifies her inability to nourish her family.

own experiences of suffering and shame, as well as out of appreciation for the fact that she can now call her body her own. She becomes "Baby Suggs, Holy." The respect given Baby Suggs is not only attested to in the crowds that gather at the Clearing, but in her house being a way station on the Underground Railroad and a general community center. In her interactions with the crowds that gather in the Clearing (on Saturday afternoons, not on Sunday mornings), Baby Suggs draws upon the call-and-response tradition informing almost all of African-American folklore to lead the community in spiritual ceremonies. They cry, dance, and laugh in celebration of the humanity they have bestowed upon themselves (Morrison, 1987: 87–89). Then she would direct them all to love themselves deeply. "Here," she said, "in this here place, we flesh; flesh that weeps, laughs; flesh that dances on bare feet in grass. Love it. Love it hard. Yonder they do not love your flesh." (88)

In telling them that "the only grace they could have was the grace they could imagine" (88), Baby Suggs solidifies the notion that their fate is in their own hands. Like their slave ancestors who took to their feet and the woods, they must carve out for themselves a space and a place to be. In the traditional inspirational guise of the master wordsmith, Baby Suggs blends the best of the sacred and the secular.

Baby Suggs becomes a communal poet/artist, the gatherer of pieces of her neighbors' experiences and the shaper of those experiences into a communal statement. Her role is in many ways like that of a ritual priestess.[1] At appointed times, she summons the group, motivates it to action, and presides over its rites of exorcism; the trauma and grief of slavery are temporarily removed in a communal catharsis. Having given up seven of her eight children to slavery, Baby Suggs knows what it means to have to put the heart back together after it has been torn apart valve by valve. As a medium who gives voice to unvoiced sentiments, Baby Suggs articulates what many of her people cannot. She is therefore participant and observer, the subject and the object of creativity. Transplanted to the soil of Cincinnati, Ohio, in the northward progression typical of blacks, Baby Suggs is the archetype of leadership among those sometimes drifting masses.

Her role in the community, therefore, makes her larger than life. She becomes

---

[1] Samuels and Hudson-Weems also refer to Baby Suggs as a "ritual priestess," which also brings to mind secular rather than Christian connotations; Wilfred D. Samuels, Cleonora Hudson-Weems. *Toni Morrison*. Boston: Twayne, 1990, p. 117.

hope-bringer and visionary, suggesting to her neighbors that the possibilities on the northern side of the Ohio River may indeed be realized. As a holy woman, a sane and articulate Shadrack, an unselfish Eva, Baby Suggs uses her heart to become the heart of the community.

4.2 Fusing African Culture and Western Culture: the Southern Past and the Northern Present

In the process of inscribing the past and in making it connect with the present, Morrison is also revising certain aspects of past and contemporary culture. In her fiction, Morrison tries to find a way to fuse African culture and Western culture through juxtaposing the Southern past and the Northern present. As Renato Constantino observes: "A people's history … must deal with the past with a view to explaining the present … It must deal not only with objective development but also bring the discussion to the realm of value judgements."[1] Referring to the attitude of blacks in the late 1950s and early 1960s, Morrison notes:

> In the legitimate and necessary drive for better jobs and housing, we abandoned the past and a lot of the truth and sustenance that went with it … In trying to cure the cancer of slavery and its consequences, some healthy as well as malignant cells were destroyed … The point is not to soak in some warm bath of nostalgia about the good old days—there were none!—but to recognize and rescue those qualities of resistance, excellence and integrity that were so much a part of our past and so useful to us. (14)

The American South, in spite of its iniquitous history of racial segregation and slavery, has become for many African American writers a source of heritage, one's familial home. As Holt notes, the South "symbolizes the worst that America has offered to blacks—racialism, poverty, and oppression. But it also represents the roots of Black culture, history and 'home.' It is 'down home' to many Blacks not born there; a 'homeplace' for people whose fathers and mothers left decades

---

[1] Renato Constantino, quoted in Roy Armes's *Third World Film Making and the West*. California: University of California Press, 1987, p. vii.

ago" (137–138). This may seem, and perhaps is, ironic, but the fact remains that this is where Afro-America began and where the relationship to one's African roots is the strongest. It is this mecca, so to speak, toward which many African American characters turn in their search for a site that represents a home base seeking grounding and stability. For them, it is already an always originary site of their African Americanness, the place of rootedness and perdurability of the African American spirit. For many African Americans the South remains a place of comfort and contradictions—a place to turn toward and a place to turn from. In Morrison's fiction, the present is the North, whereas the past is the South, and characters' journey from South to North or vice versa are weighed with deep social and psychological significance. The action often takes place in Ohio, because of Ohio's "curious juxtaposition" (Tate, 1989: 119) between North and South and its leading role in the underground railroad.[1] As characters in the North struggle to create healthy identities, they must come to terms with their own or their ancestors' Southern pasts by somehow fusing past and present. The characters must also come to terms with abandoning the trappings of their past. In the North, despite their efforts to discard their slave past, traces—names, language, rituals, and traditions—remain.

The Southern communities in the characters' past however, are remembered with both joy and shame. In his former, ritual, Southern life, Cholly Breedlove had a viable family and community. Despite his lack of parents, he had the comforts of Aunt Jimmy and her friends as well as the surrogate fathering of Blue Jack. Yet, in that same peaceful locale, he is abandoned by his mother, father, and—through death—his aunt; and it is there that he learns alienation and self hate. For Nel, the past is in New Orleans where she briefly finds her extended family and a sense of her identity, but that past is also marred by her great grandmother's death and her mother's shame. Similarly, Shalimar provides Milkman with a sense of belonging, but it is also where he suffers his most severe trials and where Pilate dies. Eloe is Son's only community. Yet it is where he causes his wife's death and where his displacement begins. For Sethe and Paul D., Sweet Home is the ultimate

---

[1] Both Dixon and Rigney comment on the symbolic significance of Ohio in Morrison's geography.

bittersweet—a memory which almost destroys them. Vesper County, despite the violence of dispossession and other acts of blatant discrimination, remains the place where Joe and Violet were happy and strong. For the founders of Ruby Oklahoma, the South is where they find the strength to band together as an extended family, but also where they are exiled and forced to travel West.

The dialectic between present North (or West) and past South provides meaning and structure to Morrison's novels. Characters must negotiate between the poles, but the gaps are frightening. They must "make a place for fear as a way of controlling it" (Morrison, 1973: 14). In some cases, this mediation involves physical journeys from South to North or vice versa, journeys that become "defining moments" (Nel, Golden Gray), "mythic quests" (Milkman, Pilate), "failed returns" (Son, Jadine), or heroic accomplishments (Sethe) (Atkinson & Page, 1998: 97).

For the African American community in the twentieth century, however, Morrison suggests that the isolating individualism that erases the memory of the South destroys spiritual and moral identity. Thus, the trip to the South is central to Morrison's subversion of the classic American initiation story. Morrison invents characters whose lives begin in the rural South or Northern characters whose experiences take them to the South, understanding the past as an indispensable reservoir of knowledge and culture necessary for the survival of African Americans.

Morrison's protagonists either find "source" or heal themselves of their displacement and alienation, being aware of their heritage in Southern coastal regions. Therefore, movement south reaffirms a connection to the African diaspora.

In *Song of Solomon*, Milkman's journey south is a learning experience for him as he pieces together the different stories and lore of his family. There are aspects of his culture of which he, from an isolated, assimilated family, knows nothing. Milkman's "backward" trip to the South finally leads him to an understanding of himself, his family, and his culture. His journey into an African American South strips him one by one off superficial external moorings that signal modern civilization and submerges him in the communal and spiritual culture of his larger family. Picking up throngs of old acquaintances of his elders, Milkman discovers the original names of his grandparents, cultivates a sense of community, and obtains ancestry wisdom as well. After retrieving names that belong to his family, Byrd and Solomon, he realizes his dreams to fly like a bird (Byrd) all his life. The discovery of this coincidence is the clarion of triumph for the reunion with black heritage and the union of Western and black cultures. Interestingly, when Milkman is surnamed Dead, what he has is more than a dead past but also a lifeless present. No sooner than the unearthing of his original names, he excavates the ability to fly and achieve a consummate state of being. With his initiation, Milkman moves from a passive, irresponsible ignorance to an active, authentic, and liberating participation in the corporate life of black community. In Pennsylvania, as he hears stories about his family heritage, he realizes certain strength in his culture that he had paid little attention to in the past: "It was a good feeling to come into a strange town and find a stranger who knew your people. All his life he'd heard the tremor in the word … But he hadn't known what it means: links." (Morrison, 1977: 231) Milkman's appreciation that people may be more important than material goods, that family and community are strengths, and that knowing one's heritage is a power separate from the power of money affects him in both conscious and subconscious ways. His awareness of the community, the culture, and the natural world around him leads him to reassess his family as well as his own selfishness. He sees all of his extended family in a different light and is sympathetic to both his father's distorted ambition and his mother's pathetic helplessness. Central to both his maturation and his healing is Milkman's recognition that the cultural past of the African American South continues to create his twentieth-century present in ways that are not constraining but liberating. So Milkman's final ability to fly, other than that of Solomon, great grandfather of Milkman, is one firmly grounded in his connection with people, in black community, in black culture, and, most of all, in a strong sense of responsibility.

"The conflicts between black culture and white society have resulted in creative as well as destructive tensions in black people and their communities." (Bell, 1987: 9) In these conflicts, neither money-thirst Macon, who clutches at a thought-to-be promising future and throws away black tradition, nor hatred-sucking Guitar, who is pinned down to the past by hatred, can be immune from uprootedness and the sense of insecurity. Contrary to their wishes, they both lose the support as well as the protection of tradition and finally are caught in present-day dilemma. Both the practices of clinging too tightly to the past and forgetting it are uprooting. They therefore must be delicately neutralized. Only in this way can one obtain the secret of flying. Milkman, with the help of his trip to the South, is able to put his past into his present and by standing firmly on the ground of ancestry, which is the fountainhead of a sense of responsibility and black culture, acquires therewith the ability to fly without ever leaving the ground, just like Pilate. But for taking ancestry in their hearts with them, Milkman and Pilate could seldom escape the imprisonment of the past. But for taking ancestry with them, it would be hard for them to have a clear understanding of the present. But for taking ancestry with them, it would be difficult to transcend racism. But for taking ancestry with them, it would be impossible to survive whole in society or to attain spiritual freedom. That is to say, but for taking ancestry with them, they could never reach that consummate state of being: to fly without ever leaving the ground.

In *Jazz*, Morrison tells the story of culture shock that happens to the cultural sojourners when they abandon what they know. This time Morrison does not conclude the story (as she does in her other novels) with a relocated family's destruction, dislocation, or despair. She moves beyond the nadir of Joe and Violet Trace's sensational post-migratory crisis—when they each attempt to murder Joe's young mistress, Dorcas—to chronicle their eventual healing, that is, their adjustment to and commensalisms with their new environment and each other.[1] Hence, it is important to note that Joe and Violet are not ruined by culture shock. After many years of attempting to meet the demands of city living, they discover they cannot solve their adaptive dilemma by abandoning their southern roots and traditions for northern ones. In order to recover their personal and social equilibrium, they find, instead, they must reinterpret and tailor mutable native culturalisms to fit their new environment and evolving needs. Upon doing so, they reestablish community and with it a concomitant sense of identity. In the Morrisonian tradition, the Traces retreat to and find rootedness in (re)memories of their individual and communal pasts. Their (re)memories—historically enacted cultural perceptions and interpretations of reality—help them to deconstruct and to negotiate the present. As Joe's and Violet's stories show, one's native culture is ever and always present, even when it is repressed, displaced, or obscured. Thus, in *Jazz*, Morrison not only maps the psychic path of culture shock but also chronicles the

---

[1] Commensalism, a holistic perspective, dictates that constituent elements of an environment exist in harmony with or at least without detriment to each other.

diasporizing of African American culturalisms from the South to the North (and to the Midwest) during the Great Migration. This is Morrison's prescriptive power for contemporary cultural sojourners.

However, eschewing simple binarism, Morrison also points out that a return to a past way of life is impractical by depicting the essential conflict between primitivity and civilization, the rural and the urban in *Tar Baby*. By displaying the follies of Son's attempt to return to a previous black purity and Jadine's total acceptance of Eurocentric lifestyle and culture, Morrison enables people to realize that after experiencing the exploitive systems of slavery, colonialism, neocolonialism, and domestic colonialism, and after being exposed to the ideologies associated with the teachings of Islam and Christianity, neither Son, Jadine, nor African people in general can return to the past, highly romanticized way of life represented by Eloe, the backwoodsy, largely illiterate and certainly economically underdeveloped community.[1] In the words of Aimé Césaire, "If the African … were merely to copy his past, failure would be the inevitable result." [2] The Southern Eloe, with all of its positive elements—humanism, collectivism, and egalitarianism—has its negative characteristics: It is a poor, underdeveloped, uneducated community. Referring to *Tar Baby*, Byerman writes that both Jadine and Son "in effect denie[sic] history: Son by believing in the possibility of returning to a previous black purity and Jadine by assuming that blackness was merely an aberration from the truth of Eurocentric Progress" (Byerman, 1985: 215). Morrison seems to tell people that instead of a return to woebegone days, Son and Jadine in particular and all African people in general must extract the positive from traditional Africa and modern capitalism with Africa as the center in order to forge a new society.

4.3 Creating Future Out of Shadows of History: New Cultural Identity and Traumatized Black Identity

The shadows of the former slaves' history and the traumatized black identity

---

[1] Discussing the significance of collectivism to the Eloe community, Morrison states: "I don't think two parents can raise a child. You really need the whole village. And if you don't have it, you'd better make it." This statement is testament to Morrison's knowledge of and appreciation for the traditional African way of life.

[2] Césaire's comment was quoted in Chinweizu's *The West* and *The Rest of Us*. More likely, as editor of *The West*, Morrison was aware of this quote.

make Morrison's black characters have difficulties in accommodating with their present, creating their future or finding their new cultural identities when they are severed from the past. In Morrison's novels, the past refers to the black characters' personal experiences set against the background of the greater history of slavery and racial violence. The past continues to traumatize black people despite the end of slavery system, while the ideologies of slavery and racism rule out the possibility of having a self-empowered identity. Just freed from the slave system, the former slaves have a problem in identifying themselves. They are torn by the consciousness to disremember the past so as to avoid its traumatic effects, and the unconsciousness to revisit to find an identity for the present and future development. In *Beloved*, Morrison describes the reluctance of black people who had immediate experience with slavery to revisit memories of the past and the painful experiences to live in fear of the ghost of the past permeated with racial violence, both physical and psychological, which hampers the decolonization process. In *Jazz*, Morrison probes into the problem of the generation who moves to the North to escape racial hatred and whose inability to touch the Southern past results in a psychological void that perpetually propels them to fill in the gap. In *Paradise*, she explores the problem of a group of people who suffer a history of being excluded and diminished by racism and racial hatred, and therefore insists that they shall be preserved in a state of fixation to protect the community from any further impairment. The past, however, is malleable and open. It cannot be simply repeated, but rather, it shall be remade for their psychological well-being. The past has to be revised. The way one thinks about things has to change. Otherwise, they will remain in its colonization and an identity of self-empowerment will not be obtained.

Therefore, in these three novels, identity is closely related to the past. Under the slavery and racist ideologies, Black identity is either absent or inscribed with the quality of the Other. To claim an identity of subjectivity and self-determination, black people need to revisit, interrogate and remake the past. Establishing a healthy connection with the past is absolutely necessary for claiming black identities, for, as Stuart Hall has theorized, "identities are the ways we give to the different ways we are positioned by, and position ourselves within, the narratives of the past." (1990: 225) Morrison's trilogy offers certain ways for black people who suffers a lot in the past shadows of slavery, racism and sexism to go out of their traumatic experiences and reclaim black identities through remembering, inventing and interrogating the past in the contemporary society where racism still lingers on. Devoted to demonstrating how attempts fail when the past is disremembered (as in *Beloved* and *Jazz*) or immobilized (as in *Paradise*), Her texts argue that a connection with the past is absolutely necessary for the psychological well-being of African-Americans. This is quite correspondent with what Hall holds that "cultural identities are rooted in histories. To find one's identity, therefore, it is essential to look back to the past. Otherwise, one's identity in the post-colonial era is problematic—either incomplete or falsely conceived." Hall goes on to argue that cultural identities are not "fixed in some essentialised past." Instead, "they are subject to the 'play' of history, culture and power. Far from being grounded in a mere 'recovery' of the past" (225). Not coincidentally, Homi Bhabha discusses the importance of memory to identity in Part 2 "Interrogating Identity" of *The Location of Culture*: "Remembering is never a quiet act of introspection or retrospection. It is a painful re-remembering, a putting together of the disremembered past to make sense of the trauma of the present." (1994: 63) Remembering the past, then, is vital for former slaves to claim "the self that is no self " (Morrison, 1987: 140) — identity denied under the slavery system and yet to be claimed in the post-slavery era. The past cannot be regarded as static and unchangeable, but instead, it shall be open to interrogation, reconstruction and re-reading so that African-Americans may decolonize themselves from ideologies of slavery.

In *Beloved*, Sethe was mercilessly consumed by the slavery past. She has not found a language to effectively counteract the intolerance and violation traced by other discourses. Despite her best efforts to respond to a hopeless situation, despite her attempts to assert agency by becoming a speaking subject, Sethe finds herself subject to the tyranny of history. In fact, the memory of slavery is carried by all the characters in *Beloved* who have suffered under the system. Understandably, they prefer not to bear this memory due to the pain it involves. Instead they would like to get away from the past and live in the present. Paul D. keeps his past in his tobacco tin so tightly shut that "nothing in this world could pry it open" (Morrison, 1987: 73); Sethe tries by every means to avoid the memories of her experiences under the slavery institution: her life as a slave at Sweet Home, stories of escape, as well as the killing of her child when Schoolteacher, the second master of Sweet

Home came to capture her. By refusing to remember the past, Sethe hopes to surpass the uncomfortable realities of the colonial/slavery encounter and to seek emancipation from it, to seek a life at present and future without the pain of such memories. But "the past, until you confront it, until you live through it, keeps coming back in other forms" (239). By telling people "freeing yourself was one thing; claiming ownership of that freed self was another" (95), Morrison poses the difference between physical freedom and psychological/mental freedom.

Only when characters can recover the past do they begin to imagine future. In *Beloved*, Morrison presents the struggle of its characters to confront the effects of the brutality and to recover their human dignity, their selves "dirtied" by white oppression—to transform their experiences into knowledge. *Beloved* combines the personal quest theme with the collective memory of racial brutality, featuring the destiny of the individual and personal as well as communal salvation. Paul D. tries to move Sethe away from the destructive past towards a new beginning by telling Sethe, "me and you, we got more yesterday than anybody. We need some kind of tomorrow" (273). Paul D. realizes the need to rename and re-identify what their past was and, as a result, what their future may be, suggesting a movement beyond the structures of patriarchy and the violence of slavery. He wants to put his story next to hers, to rewrite and to reroute the course of their narrative. In remembering the life under Schoolteacher's rule, both of them revisit the traumatic past and develop a complete picture of what happened during their escape and life thereafter; both of them view a complete picture of the past, which remained fragmented and incomplete before their bilateral remembering; both of them develop some new understandings of slavery and its destructiveness; both of them now show interrogation on even Mr. Garner's benevolence—the privileges which was decided by and therefore totally dependent on Mr. Garner's preference. These understandings and interrogation of their past pave the way for seeking a new cultural identity and are essential for them to claim "ownership of that freed self" (95). Therefore, memories of slavery are "constructive rather than destructive" (Laurence, 1997: 243) to former slaves to develop a sense of subjectivities. In her memories of the past, Sethe has also developed her own discourse about what actually happened, which, in its negotiation with the master discourse, enables Sethe to develop subjectivity and finally leads to the formation of a black identity that incorporates self-determination.

From the very beginning, Sethe, in fact, struggles for autonomy, and does to some degree achieve it. At least, she manages to acquire for herself the capacity to deliberate about her situation in a way that better reflects her real interests. Her deciding to try to kill her children stands out in the novel, not as a decision to deprive her children of the minimal conditions for life accorded them under slavery, but rather as an attempt to claim for herself something of which, under slavery, she ought not even to have been able to dream. When Paul D. insists: "You your best thing, Sethe, Sethe. You are." Sethe's closing response—"Me? Me?"—seems to imply that she may in time come to recognize and claim her own subjectivity.

Denver stands for what Morrison asserts an expansive female character and the site of hope in Morrison's novels. She is the daughter of history, yet she takes lessons of the past and looks forward to the future. Unlike Pecola, who is driven insane by her surroundings, Denver buds forth with the potential for health, and that potential warrants viewing her in a different light. Almost none of the female characters that suffer assaults upon their minds and /or bodies in Morrison's novels survive those assaults. Pecola is insane, Sula and Hagar die, and Baby Suggs wills herself to death. But Denver survives the silence into which she is driven when she learns of Sethe's deed; she survives being ostracized from the neighbors; and she survives her mother's temporary breakdown. In fact, witnessing what happens to Sethe during Beloved's takeover is the impetus for Denver's growth. When neither Sethe nor Beloved seems to care what the next day brings, "Denver knew it was on her. She would have to leave the yard; step off the edge of the world" (Morrison, 1987: 243) and find help. The independence and subjectivity that she firmly claims and asserts by leaving the porch to seek help from the neighbors, her renewing her acquaintance with Nelson Lord, and her newfound voice in strongly articulating her own view of the situation instead of accepting Paul D.'s, all portend possibility for her. And that possibility is more than Morrison leaves most of her female characters. Denver not only represents the future; she brings it into being. Her efforts lead to everyone's salvation: the reunion of the community. It begins with gifts of food accompanied by the giver's names but culminates in the women coming to the yard of 124 to exorcise Beloved.

In *Jazz*, it's also suggested that in the city African-Americans' psychological well-being is achieved only when they have established certain connections with the past and evolve their new cultural identity. Violet does not recover until she comes to terms with Dorcas' aunt Alice Manfred, a parent figure. Joe does not show any sign of recovery until Felice tells him that when Dorcas was dying she was thinking of him. In the final image that the narrator presents, Felice, Joe and Violet are seen together, and the impression given by the narrator is that Felice is Dorcas: "I saw the three of them, Felice, Joe and Violet, and they looked to me like a mirror image of Dorcas, Joe and Violet." (Morrison, 1993: 221) Such an image indicates that finally Joe reconciles with his surrogate mother, thus finding a connection with the past. Having murdered his teenaged mistress, he must atone psychologically, working through his guilt, and accepting responsibility for his actions. He must also identify the conflicted maternal longing for the woman who initially rejected him— his cave-dwelling, feral mother, whom his tortured consciousness finally confuses with the equally rejecting Dorcas. The jazz idiom of Morrison's novel is thus central to the recovery of the past, both personal and historic, and a reenvisioning of the future. It's then that he decides to live a new life, and it's also then that he forms the new cultural identity out of the fragmented past self.

In *Paradise*, Morrison carefully delineates the history of the town Ruby as one created by former slave men who had been discriminated against not only by whites but also by "Negro towns" (Morrison, 1997: 13) and who in response chose a separatism that became discrimination against all others. The freedmen became a tight band of wayfarers bound by the enormity of what had happened to them. The nightmare of their traumatized history, their horror of whites and their hatred for the light-skinned who disallowed them propelled them to found their own "all-black" (5) town, Haven (and later Ruby, after Haven withers), grounded in dogmatic racist and patriarchal terms that simply reverse the hierarchy of the racism they themselves suffered by excluding all who are not so dark as themselves. As Pat Best recognizes, "people get chosen and ranked" based upon "skin color" in Ruby. For example, the community forces Menus to "return the woman he brought home to marry. The pretty sandy-haired girl from Virginia" (195) and marginalizes Roger Best's wife (Delia), daughter (Pat), and granddaughter (Billie Delia) for their "sunlight skin" (196), which marks them as others. Marginalization functions as a form of violence when Delia dies because no one will get her the medical help she needs. The "fastest girl in town" (59) label accentuates and casts a deprecatory shadow onto Billie Delia's racial otherness, and she eventually leaves Ruby.

Eventually, Ruby's patriarchs resort to fascist mechanisms of consolidation as the only means of ensuring its identity: They attacked the Convent women in order to consolidate their rule of skin color. By committing the murder, Ruby's men finally betray the past and violate the very principle of a paradise.

In contrast, the Convent community accepts a more fluid notion of identity that enables ongoing, accommodative coalition work. The Convent women's open attitude to the outside people in spite of their own traumatic past and their capability to look forward to the bright future shows Morrison's attitude towards the solution to the new cultural identity.

Besides, Morrison also indicates her assertion of the openness in the end of *Paradise* by having Lone DuPres, whose intuitive knowledge is repeatedly privileged, say that "God had given Ruby a second chance" (297). The pattern of loss and recovery is suggested earlier in the novel by three passages presumably taken from hymnals: "Something within me that banishes pain; something within me I cannot explain" (211), "I once was lost but now am found" (12), and then "[w] as blind but now I see" (213).

The potentially positive changes in the town are figured in the effects of the raid on Deacon Morgan. Before the tragedy he is the kind of man who would rather open his bank on time than help Sweetie Fleetwood as she wanders down the street barefoot and undressed, and he and his twin Steward epitomizes the rigidly controlling ideology of the town. But after the raid he is the barefoot one, trying for the first time in his life to have an intimate conversation with a man, as he vaguely confesses to Richard Misner about his affair with Connie. He has become what his value system is built to defend against: "His long remorse was at having become what the Old Fathers cursed: the kind of man who set himself up to judge, rout and even destroy the needy, the defenseless, the different." (Morrison, 1999: 302) Deacon is now for the first time on his own, fully separate from his twin. The near-oneness of Deacon and Steward, like the tight harmony of the town, has once been useful but has become too binding. Deacon's need to grow on his own beyond his bond with Steward symbolizes the town's need to grow beyond its confining bond with its own legend. Deacon alludes to this need when he tells Misner, "I got a long way to go, Reverend" (303), with the emphasis on "I" and with the implication that his life's journey is far from complete, and far from being confined in the past or in one ideological position. Like the town, Deacon moves from a restrictive fusion to a liberating fragmentation. Through Deacon, Morrison conveys that if black people are to escape the cycles of trauma and violence that plague their communities, they have to get rid of this traumatic memory of past and violence and be constructively open to the "Other," and to understand the meaning of the "door" or "window" which is open to the future. To achieve psychic wholeness, each character must come to accept his or her memories.

Later in Ruby, the "future painted its gate" (306). Roads connecting the outside are constructed, a gas station is built, and outsiders will come and go. The picture shows that Ruby has a new future, but the future lies in its open attitudes towards the past and building connections with the outside world. Only by breaking up its self-isolation and obsession with the past does Ruby begin to enjoy a prosperous future and an earthly paradise.

Unveiling these interior lives of her characters carries with it titanic responsibility for Morrison. She is continuing an unfinished script of slavery which has begun over two centuries ago by the first slave narrative, and she must do it truthfully and with integrity. Morrison's characters stand in for all those slaves and former slaves who were "unceremoniously buried" without tribute or recognition. She feels chosen by them to attend to their burial "properly, artistically." It is an act of recovering the past in narrative, to "insert this memory that was unbearable and unspeakable into the literature" (Carabi, 1994: 88). Only then is it possible, Morrison believes, for black people, for society, to move on. The shadow of history threatens peace of mind and must be resisted. Only by remembering the past and recreating the future out of the shadow can there be liberation from its burden.

Though violent and traumatic, it is the process former slaves must go through to live a psychologically healthy life at a time when slavery ends materially but persists ideologically and to form new cultural identity in the condition of hybridization of African culture and American culture. This is largely in correspondence with Hutcheon's opinion: "The past is not something to be escaped, avoided, or controlled … The past is something with which we must come to terms and such a confrontation involves an acknowledgement of limitation as well as power."

(1988: 58) In the modern era, it seems inadequate only to remember and repeat the past. It shall be made and remade to be suitable for the modern times. The past is malleable, open to different interpretations. African-Americans' future lies in their right interpretations of their past and their ability to go out of the shadow of the history to create new cultural identity and an earthly paradise based on their own culture.

4.4 Participating in Communications and Bonds: Sisterhood, Community and Fraternity

Jazz is a blend of interacting voices. Just as Eckhard argues:

> Paradoxically, the jazz narrator reflects both a single entity and multiple ones. It speaks in varying tones and rhythms that convey the presence of different voices in much the same way that a jazz performance is rendered through multiple instruments. The voices play off one another, and individual differences are sometimes apparent. At the same time, the voices are blended within the text to give the impression of a single entity. (1994: 13)

Just as the goal of jazz is to merge individuality and community in ways exemplified by the aesthetic of group improvisation, Morrison's goal to write her fiction is also to assert the group function and tolerance of different genders, various races and cultures as exemplified in her writing about sisterhood, communal healing and fraternity. Morrison's narrative strives to accomplish the transformation through integration in a hybrid, common cultural tradition.

4.4.1 Sisterhood

Sisterhood between women is taken by feminists as one of the most important means by which women can comfort, support each other and unify together against the patriarchal society. When women unite together, they have power. This theme has been widely discussed in women's literature, especially in black literature. As a black woman writer, Toni Morrison is clearly aware of the significance of sisterhood for women, especially for black women. In her works, Morrison largely probes sisterhood between women including that between black women and that between black women and their white counterpart. Due to the historical reason, sisterhood is much more helpful for black women. Black women usually get more help and strength from their female friends, instead of male, even less from their husbands. In *Song of Solomon*, Pilate managed to protect her sister-in-law Ruth and helped her to be pregnant even when Macon refused to sleep together with her. In *Beloved*, by portraying a white girl character Amy who helped Sethe, Morrison discusses another kind of sisterhood—sisterhood beyond ethnicity or between races. In spite of area, race, age and skin-colour, the women around the world should and are able to conjoin their strength and strive for their future together. In *Jazz*, Dorcas's aunt Alice Manfred helped Violet Trace to recover from her fragmented self and to love life and herself again. In its depiction of Violet's and Alice's journeying to the "site of memory," a resting place in which the two women recall and remake an enabling identity and purpose, the novel suggests that the re-construction of home, identity, and purpose are complementary acts and needs cooperation between women. Thus, sisterhood becomes a valuable experience and identifiable literary tradition for black women writers. Morrison said in an interview: "When I wrote *Sula* I knew I was going to write a book about good and evil and about friendship. Friendship between women is special, different." (1983: 157) In Morrison's view, men tend to get desire for competition and benefits from their friendship, while women's relationship tends more pure, endurable and supportive.

In *The Bluest Eye*, Morrison tells about the friendship between Pecola, Claudia and Frieda. As little children, Claudia and her elder sister Frieda are not old enough to be consciously aware of the reason why they can selflessly help the mentally weak Pecola in spite of the negative attitude of the adult world towards her; they sympathize and like the homeless girl instinctively and are among the few who love, help and protect her firmly no matter what happens to her. They try to protect Pecola's self-esteem from their mother's unmalicious nagging, and manage to protect her from being harassed by a group of black boys. When Pecola is raped by her father and gives birth to a baby, Claudia plants marigold seeds, praying that the health of the seeds will assure the health of the baby, which for her, represents the collective survival of her race.

In *Sula*, Sula and Nel's friendship enables them to get warmth and strength outside their respective households in which they are both denied a necessary aspect of childhood—affection. Sula cut the tip of her finger to defend Nel against boys' attack while Nel kept the secret of the reason of Chicken Little's death, which was accidentally caused by Sula. It is also the sisterhood between them that enables them to face the danger from the outside and protect themselves from being hurt. They used to have a shared ideal, i.e., to be "wonderful." Although after Nel's marriage, marriage and husband have long replaced sisterhood in Nel's eyes, she still laughs to her heart's content for the first time in her marriage life after Sula's return. After ten years of floating from one city to another, Sula comes back to the Bottom partially for missing the sisterhood established between her and Nel when they were children. Sisterhood between them begins to crack when Nel sees Sula sleeping with Jude, her husband. For some years, Nel never talks to Sula. Though, when Sula lies in the bed dying, Nel goes to see her and helps her fetch the medicine, Nel doesn't forgive her at the bottom of her heart.

Until years after Sula's death, Nel comes to this realization at her friend's grave that the real loss in her life is that of Sula and not Jude. And the real tragedy is that she has allowed herself to reduce to a self-lost woman.

Nel, with her understanding of what Morrison celebrates as "tar quality" (Morrison, 1981: 35) alone can finish Sula's incompleteness, Sula's independent and imaginative spirit, on the other hand, can emancipate Nel from the strain of her morally correct but sterile life. The coming of a complete new black womanhood is only possible when Nel and Sula's friendship maintain intact. It is their togetherness—their friendship together—that leads them to self-wholeness. That is also the reason why their sisterhood is so lasting, charming and irreplaceable.

In *Paradise*, the Convent women not only heal themselves through the sisterly help of Consolata and each other, but also extend their help to Ruby's women who suffer from various pains. Over the course of "more than twenty years," "crying women, staring women, scowling, lip-biting women or women just plain lost" made the trek "back and forth" between Ruby and the Convent (Morrison, 1997: 270); "early reports were of kindness and very good food" (11). " … revolted by the work of her womb," Arnette seeks shelter there to deliver the baby that she has been unable to abort with a "mop handle" (250) and that dies shortly after birth. Soane Morgan depends on a "tonic … one of Connie's [Consolata's] preparations" to help her keep at bay the depression, the "thinning" air, that began when both her sons were killed in Vietnam (100). After a fight with her mother, Billie Delia seeks refuge at the Convent. While the women treat her physical injuries with practical remedies, they also offer her a caring, loving, non-intrusive, inclusive environment based on mutual respect.

The women who find their ways to the Convent for stays of varying lengths find renewal through being cared for and caring for other women in a nonjudgmental, non-hierarchical, non-patriarchal atmosphere. They are included in the community and have a voice in how they will participate in it. Billie Delia describes the Convent community as "a place where you can stay for a while. No questions" and where "you can collect yourself there, think things through, with nothing or nobody bothering you all the time. They'll take care of you or leave you alone"—whichever way you want it" (Morrison, 1997: 175–176). Across their overt differences with respect to age, class, race, and past experiences, nurturing coalition work takes place on the basis of a matrix of historically specific, intersecting subject positions connected to pain endured within a male-dominated culture. The women's healing is made possible in great part by the "blessed malelessness" of the house, "like a protected domain, free of hunters" (177) —at least temporarily. Given that the dominant American culture and the nearby town of Ruby are heavily male-centered and that both envision and enact power over women, the malelessness of the house makes possible the reconceptualization of power in more collective and just terms (10). Moreover, this maleless community allows the women not only to work through their pain but also to begin (re)constructing non-subjugated identities for themselves.

In *Love*, the friendship between Heed and Christine entertains their girlhood, while the breakup of their relationship makes them miserable. While the love of and for a dead man haunts the novel, it is the depth of female friendship that substantiates love. L's menu did indeed suture the Cosey women's lives. Sworn enemies nurture and ear for one another until the time of their deaths. Heed, though verbally abused and taunted by May, physically tends to her. In the last scene, although Heed's trip to the memorial site—Cosey's Resort and Hotel, would end with her death, Christine and Heed, former best friends, after confronting the ghosts of their pasts through communication, review and restart their love, and become strong again spiritually.

4.4.2 Community and Communal Healing

Just as Morrison says in "The Pain of Being Black," "you need a whole community—everybody—to raise a child." (Taylor-Guthrie, 1994: 260) Community in Morrison's novels is a place to nurture, to heal one's pain, to find one's family genealogy and to find source of strength.

When talking about *Paradise* in an interview with A. J.Verdelle, Toni Morrison has talked about the importance of community:

> What was paramount for me was the community, the town and their connections. It is easily the most obvious thing about us [as African-Americans]: the connectedness, the family relations, the history of personal relations, people's attitudes toward one another based on anecdotes and legends about them that you may not have even known. How all of that mixes and becomes a community. All their secrets. All their confrontations. All their reconciliation. The hierarchy within. (1998: 56)

In *The Bluest Eye*, she writes about the ritual of initiation where Mrs. MacTeer joins Pecola, Frieda, and Claudia after the onset of homeless Pecola's menstrual cycle in which there is a demonstrating of nurturing that does not extend consistently throughout the novel; while Pauline Breedlove, displaced from Alabama, lacks communal support system and devaluates black identity in Lorain, Ohio. In *Song of Solomon*, the Southern community in Shalimar provides Milkman with a sense of belonging, their help enabling him to find his family genealogy, while Hagar is lost in the materialism and cultural displacement in the North because she lacks a communal support system in spite of her Grandmother Pilate's rootedness and love. In *Beloved*, it is gifts of food accompanied by the community giver's names that save Sethe from starvation. Most important of all, it is through the collective will and action of the people that Beloved, who stands for the haunting legacy of slavery, disappears. Organized as a whole and led by Ella, the thirty women of the community come to 124 to exorcize Beloved. Correspondingly, the successful exorcism of Beloved provides a catharsis for the town's entire population as well as for Sethe. In *Paradise*, communal healing finds its expression in the Convent women led by Consolata, who takes the spiritualized healing art to another level.

The Convent is a community characterized by openness, tolerance and diversity. It is open to all. It takes in seven women who have sought escape for a variety of reasons from the dominant patriarchal and materialist culture and have found refuge in the Convent, and all of them find comfort in it. In addition, they often offer help to people in Ruby who have troubles. Residents of Convent are free to come and go.

Though at first some of the women are in conflict with each other, they gradually learn to coexist. Casting aside the conventional Western split between mind and body, the Convent offers a space that recognizes the interconnections of physical and psychic pains or imbalances and that allows experiments in ways to face up to and move past these pains or imbalances. Through caring and accepting each other's differences, by willingly sharing and experiencing each other's painful stories, histories, and dreams with their bodies and psyches simultaneously, the Convent women provide for each other unmatched nurturing support. On an immediate material level, the Convent community offers food, shelter, and/or herbal remedies to the women who find their way there; however, the physical healing remains interconnected to psychic healing. Antagonisms and hierarchies rather than differences dissipate through the process of caring for their bodies and psyches communally. Healthy, nourished bodies have a better shot at survival; and carefully, lovingly prepared food satisfies not only physical needs but also psychic ones. Even Ruby's women seek out the Convent women for the specialty foods they produce, the herbal remedies they prepare, and the loving kindness they dispense indiscriminately—which highlights the cracks in Ruby's identity as separatist and self-sustaining. In contrast to the closed community of Ruby, the Convent invites all to join in continuously (re)creating its dynamic, diverse community. The patient, unconditional, loving attention the Convent women show demonstrates their warm empathy for other women hurt by a cruel world, an "empathy" that can "serve as a base for solidarity and coalition" (Hooks, 2000: 27).

To crystallize the dire necessity of collective action and community to the survival of African American people, Morrison juxtaposes isolated struggle with collective struggle and selfish individualism with individualism conditioned by social responsibility. In her fiction, most forms of isolation are genocidal for the race. Sula's individual struggle in the Bottom, Guitar and the Seven Days' isolated revenge, Denver's isolation in life, 124's isolation in the community, Beloved's isolation in death and Ruby's isolated "Paradise" all serve to further divide the African American community and, as a consequence, leave it vulnerable to the oppression and exploitation of the slave society.

4.4.3 Fraternity

The interaction between black women and black men as well as blacks born in Africa and those born in America is that they work in harmonious accord in creating the major artistic forms of the slave community. Similarly, it is the cooperation and cultural interaction between the African-Americans and the white Americans that have produced jazz. Similar to the production of jazz, Morrison is also trying to assert an organic link between black and white souls, the latter in its smug indifference and arrogance largely responsible for anguish in the former. Morrison conveys the important messages of the importance of communication, self-esteem, education, soul-searching, relationships and human nature, which are universal and timeless, transcending gender and race. She not only probes into the significance of sisterhood and community, but also explores communications and bonds between black women and black men, black people and white people—fraternity in essence. Throughout her fiction, Morrison presents healers who accept others and reach beyond self. These healers include not only black people but also white people who participate in the process of black people's reconstruction of their identity.

African-American women who strive to survive the same ordeal inflicted on men established a strong autonomy and a collaborational relationship with men, which can be best exemplified in *Beloved*. In Sethe and Paul D.'s case, they unite because they have to overcome the same sensation of being suffering from the memory of slavery and in the course of gaining autonomy, they put their stories next to each other and thus establish a collaborational relationship with each other.[1]

In Violet and Joe's case, they are both victims of history and migration who victimize others, but who eventually get to understand and love each other through communication and with the help of music. The bond between this couple enables

---

[1] The language of Paul D.'s desire is suggestive: He wants "to put his story next to hers." "Next to" speaks of equality—Sethe's story is as important as his.

them to come to terms with reality and live happily again with each other.

In *Love*, thanks to Romen's grandparents, Sandler and Vida Gibbons, for guiding his decent behavior through communication, Romen becomes a true and upright soul, as evidenced throughout the novel, particularly at the beginning, when in a miraculous turn of events, he saves a girl during a disturbing gang rape. In the end, Romen demonstrates kindness again as he attempts to rescue Heed and Christine from Cosey's old hotel and, though too late to save Heed, he carries both women in the car with ultimate care and compassion. Romen becomes an example of fraternity in which despite the opposite sex, black men can take into consideration of black women's suffering and thus carry out their act of compassion.

Tendency to interracial fraternity can be found in Pilate in *Song of Solomon* and Amy in *Beloved*. Pilate, one of Morrison's most humane characters, has always placed value on altruistic human relationships. She gives voice to the value of human connectedness. She not only loves and helps her own kin and community, but also extends this love to the human beings she meets with. Although rejected by most people because of her lack of a navel, she is still capable of showing her love to the people she has met by collecting stones from every place she has been to. Her will to build a human community in spite of her father's being killed by the whites is manifested in her preventing her brother from killing a white man in the cave and in her burdening herself with the bones which she mistook as was left by the white man that had been killed by her brother, although it turns out that the bones are her father's. Morrison amplifies this spiritual transcendence by adding the significance of a "willingness to love" to her formula (Morrison, 1987: 226) as she exclaims upon her death: "I wish I'd a known more people. I would a loved more." (Morrison, 1987: 340)

Among healers who participate in the process of black people's reconstruction of their identity, Amy Denver in *Beloved* is employed as the bridge to understanding and the promise to bridge the gulf of racism that still exists between blacks and whites. In a novel about the evils of slavery where it would seem easy enough—and perhaps entirely logical—to draw a line of demarcation between black and white as between protagonist and antagonist, Morrison's artistic hands expand the boundaries of the traditional slave narrative to explore not only the far-reaching damage of the institution of slavery but also the promise of acceptance and healing, and thus again transcend binary thinking patterns. As an indentured servant, a prophetic healer, and a compassionate white woman, Amy Denver functions as a bridge between black and white, racism and understanding, destruction and renewal. As she reaches out to Sethe with love and compassion, Sethe survives. Amy reaches out her helpful hands to Sethe by massaging and encouraging Sethe on her flight (which symbolizes the transition from death to survival), and aids her in childbirth, accompanying her "repair work" (80) with a song. Amy and Sethe attract each other heartedly and instinctively in spite of their substantial differences in experiences and racial background. Certainly, raised in the white dominated society, Amy inevitably holds bias toward the black people, especially the black slaves. However, through the seemingly meaningless chat, Amy is deeply moved by Sethe's courage and bravery. Their sisterhood is unconsciously established on the chats. For fear that Sethe is bit by snakes, Amy suggests that Sethe should go to the nearby house to spend her night. Under her encouragement and company, Sethe begins her crawling towards the house, to safety. The path to the house symbolizes a road leading to freedom, on which a white girl and a black pregnant woman support each other against hardships.

It is the grace of Amy, the white girl who helps Sethe deliver a baby with her "good hands" (Morrison, 1987: 77) in water that offers hope not only to Sethe in her own wretched suffering, but, more importantly, to the reader. Page sees this hope directly in Amy, whom he describes as "another healer who despite her own mistreatment and vulnerability, provides physical and spiritual salvation for Sethe" (146). Amy not only treats Sethe lovingly, but, through her words, Sethe finds, at least temporarily, comforts and hope in God's redemptive love. Her transformative powers can heal "the pain and humiliation of slavery." As racism pits the whites and blacks against one another, Amy and Sethe illustrate the possibility of reconciliation through love. Amy helps Sethe provide that bridge.

By abetting an escaped slave, Amy places herself in danger of serious punishment, including imprisonment, under the "Fugitive Slave Law of 1850." Except for her own "fugitive" status as a runaway indentured servant who is in violation of a legally binding contract, she has the opportunity to turn Sethe in to receive a reward. Though she could join the ranks of whites who profit from the slave trade, the fact remains that she does not; rather, she saves Sethe.

If Amy functions as a bridge through her role as a foil to Sethe, it can be concluded that, as Harding and Martin note, "The double of kindred spirit relationship … is an occasion for [Morrison's] characters to practice the absolute imperative never to choose and thus never to exclude, which means once again 'seeing' unity in multiplicity and the possibility of 'identity' in otherness" (1994: 41–42). If the white community cannot accept "otherness," as Amy does when she overlooks racial differences to save Sethe, few hopes exist either to subvert racist notions in Africa or approach any sort of healing, painful as that healing may be. Through Amy and Sethe's encounter, Morrison hopes to show the possibility of mutual understanding and love. Through Amy's example, Morrison pushes readers to examine their own lives, in hopes that if placed in similar circumstances, they would possess the same kind heart and open spirit as Amy to jeopardize the success of their own quest for freedom and safety to aid another human being in need.

And later in memory of Amy, Sethe names the baby girl after her family name—Denver. Like the bluefern spore, Denver holds within her the promise of her people's future. Critic Ashraf H. A. Rushdy notes that "In *Beloved*, Denver becomes the daughter of hope" (1999: 126). The significance of Denver's birth and survival magnifies the importance of Amy's hand in the events, their interconnectedness, since Amy directly ensures that survival and thus the safeguard that Denver's fate will come to fruition. Hope is passed from Amy to Denver in both spirit and name through Denver's very existence. Marc C. Conner notes that, "Like her 'namesake' Amy, Denver provides a link to the white community and a sign of potential interracial healing." (2000: 45) Finally, because Amy is a compassionate white woman, Morrison presents her as a bridge to white society.

4.5 Reconstructing Identity Through Transcending Given Names

In African American literature, naming has always held a special and "double" significance because of its dual cultural heritage. Dropping one's slave name and renaming oneself to begin life anew as a free person was often "the first act of a former slave" (Hayes, 2004: 675). According to Perez-Torrez, "the power to rename represents a reclamation of agency when many other venues are closed that would help the characters establish a sense of subjectivity." (1977; 99) Accordingly, power for Morrison is largely the power to name, to define reality and perception. A name theme is employed to retell the history of recovery in Morrison's works. She uses naming as the epitome of the continuing and haunting presence of the past. Morrison has said in an interview with Thomas LeClair: "If you come from Africa, your name is gone. It is particularly problematic because it is not just your name but your family, your tribe. When you die, how can you connect with your ancestors if you have lost your name? That's a huge psychological scar." (1981: 21) Since a name has the power to define and to possess that which it identifies, the recovery of the past and of true names evidently serves as the antidote to the loss of names and identities. Thus transcending imposed names and acknowledging the meaning of given African-American names are crucial for survival. Naming is considered as a method of resisting the hegemony of white society through African cultural practices. The power of a name is so strong in much of Africa and the diaspora that often people kept a secret name so that an enemy could not use it for evil intent. In the New World, a name could also be employed in opposition to the oppressor, as slaves were wont to do. The biblical names used in Morrison's fiction present a "secret" name since they rarely fit the person named, thus transforming the Old Testament (Pilate, of course, is the most obvious example). Morrison comments: "I used the biblical names to show the impact of the Bible on the lives of black people; their awe and respect for it coupled with their ability to distort it for their own purposes." (1981: 28) It's evident that naming can be a method of regaining control over one's life.

The loss of names and naming process represents a system of burial and recovery that is significant to African-American identity. To counter imposed and narrow restriction, Morrison examines the broader cultural genealogy in order to search for African-American roots, for it were not for the knowledge of a past that transcends Christian history, it would be extremely difficult for an African American to know why he or she exists and who he or she is. Naming in Morrison's novels is an important indication of the effort to claim their own identities. By rejecting the names given by slave owners and usurping the power to name themselves, former slaves initiate a conscious struggle to claim their own identities.

Several compelling examples of the significance that black tradition attaches to the process of naming can be found in the first pages of *Song of Solomon*. Milkman is born at Mercy Hospital, called "No Mercy" by the African Americans who were previously denied admittance to its birthing wards, in a neighborhood referred to by residents as the Blood Bank "because blood flowed so freely there" (Morrison, 1977: 32). After Doctor Foster, the first black doctor in the city, established his office on Mains Avenue, the street was popularly renamed "Doctor Street" until the white city legislators posted notices in business reminding residents of the avenue's official name and declaring the invalidity of that name as a mailing address. Following this official pronouncement, residents promptly, deliberately and unceremoniously changed the name to "Not Doctor Street", a name that signaled their inventive resistance to any oppression.

The connection between a name and history as a source of identity and the vital importance of transcending a given name in African American culture are clearly illustrated throughout the epiphany of Milkman Dead from innocence to maturity. He embodies Morrison's image of a person who comes to possess a balanced knowledge of the past and future, of men and women. Because he lacks knowledge of the past and his ancestors, Milkman is cut off from the townspeople at the beginning, and he must somehow regain "the name that was real" in order to become undead. Milkman's family name Dead is significant in more than one: Firstly, because it falsifies their origins as well as the identities thrust upon them by a federal agent, the name is a living testimony to the dominant culture's disregard of any history or identity other than its own; secondly, it signifies the attitude of the black middle class toward the slave past: they would rather consign it to oblivion than let it persist as a humiliating reminder. Milkman's grandfather accepts a name that would "wipe out the past" (Morrison, 1977: 54) and give him a clean start; in doing so Milkman becomes heir to a historical amnesia that is culturally and psychically debilitating—if not lethal. Milkman's journey South leads him to discard his ancestors' pseudonyms and recover their authentic names. The retrieval of original names assuredly enables African Americans to recognize their roots, retrieve their history, shape their identities and reclaim their own values. True names are indispensable to the sense of identity, and great goal of all who have been denied their humanity must struggle for a sense of their own value as human beings. To know one's real worth, one needs to know one's name. By transcending the given name Dead, which signifies the oppression and negligence of the whites towards the black people, Milkman acquires both his lost identity and his spiritual freedom, enlarging his horizon and sharpening his perception. At the same time, he renounces his narcissistic concerns and learns to develop a sense of responsibility both for his family members and his black community.

Through her fiction, Morrison tries to preach that the discovery of one's own name is essential to the discovery of identity; names and naming function in the development of awareness of one's embodied self and his/her relation to the past. The act of naming and the repossession of original names are a refusal to be controlled by the images and concepts inflicted by the dominating group; and by these means African Americans are able to obtain their identities and history. Therefore, Stamp Paid in *Beloved* renames himself even before freedom, as a repudiation of slavery and a means of claiming subjectivity. When she is freed, Baby Suggs rejects the slave name "Jenny Whitlow"—a name no one but white people have ever called her—and continues to call herself "Baby Suggs."

In fact, the blacks as a race have been over the centuries trying to attain self-recognition and emotional and psychological maturity in American society, which becomes an old-age theme in Black literature. Morrison pays close attention to the question of redefining the blacks' identities and attempts to find ways out for those black people who are suffering from the identity crisis. Just as jazz leads people to a new recognition, Morrison's literary jazz also leads people to the realization of transformation, reconstitution and resurrection through self-analysis, self-understanding, and self-correction.

Chapter 5

Trauma and the Identity Construction in *A Mercy*

Identity construction has come to be one of the recurring themes in contemporary literature, especially in ethnic and diaspora writings. So is Toni Morrison. Her citation reads: "[Toni Morrison] who in novels characterized by visionary force and poetic import, gives life to an essential aspect of American reality." Here, "an essential aspect of American reality" actually refers to the unique life experiences of the marginalized African Americans in the United States. As a black woman writer with a strong black consciousness, Morrison has been focusing on the miserable sufferings of Afro-Americans, especially African American women who are under intersecting oppressions of racism, sexism, and classism.

A Mercy (2008) is Morrison's ninth novel which continues her concern with black women. What is more, this time she extends her focus to ethnic females' existence during pre-slavery period under multiple exploitations of racism, sexism and classism. In view of this, this thesis employs black feminist literary criticism which combines the three factors mentioned above together with a close reading of the text, aiming to explore how the ethnic females in the novel lose their identities under a hostile environment characterized by racism, sexism and classism; then how they negotiate and eventually achieve identity reconstruction by various means.

Through depicting how intersectional oppressions of racism, sexism, and classism affect ethnic female characters, Morrison protests against a flawed social system. Yet this does not mean that she intends to reverse the existing system.

Adopting an open standpoint, Morrison embraces an equal and united world; despite the setbacks facing the ethnic females, they never surrender. Instead, they fight against the multiple oppressions in their own way and finally achieve personal empowerment. By portraying these females' struggle, Morrison brings a marginal group to center and proposes a viable way out. This solution is not only enlightening for ethnic minorities in America but also for all the people who remain invisible throughout the world, which reflects humanitarian brilliancy in her works.

In her more than four decades of literary creation, Morrison constantly explores the struggle of black community against racism, especially African American women. "In addition to foregrounding race and racism, she emphasizes the construction of identity and how identity is not only racialized but gendered as well." (Raynor & Butler, 2007: 175–176)

5.1 Morrison's Black Female Consciousness

As a black and a woman, I have access to a range of emotions and perceptions that were unavailable to people who were neither.

—Toni Morrison (Caldwell, 1994)

There were no books about me, I didn't exist in all the literature I had read ... this person, this female, this black did not exist center-self.

—Toni Morrison (Matus, 1998)

When Morrison was awarded the Nobel Prize in 1993, her citation read: Toni Morrison, "who in novels characterized by visionary force and poetic import, gives life to an essential aspect of American reality."[1] Here "an essential aspect of American reality" refers to the unique and complex life experience of African Americans, African American women in particular, which is well supported by her literary canon, especially her many novels.

In almost all of Morrison's novels, females (notably black females) are major

---

[1] "The Nobel Prize in Literature in 1993." http://www.nobelprize.org/nobel_prizes/literature/laureates/1993/morrison.html.

characters. As a marginal group, they suffer multiple oppressions because of their color (black), gender (female) and class (inferior). Being a black woman herself, Morrison naturally concentrates on this vulnerable group in her writing. This obvious and enduring concern clearly reflects her black female consciousness, which is echoed by her own remarks: "As a black and a woman, I have access to a range of emotions and perceptions that were unavailable to people who were neither." Morrison's identity as a black woman writer equips her with "some special knowledge about certain things" (Lester, 1988: 54). Then why does Morrison constantly explore black females' miserable life and their complex inner world in a hostile world? Or how does her black female consciousness come into being? The answer is related to her family and education background.

Toni Morrison was born Chloe Anthony Wofford on February 18, 1931 in Lorain, Ohio, a small industrial town heavily populated with migrants from Europe, Mexico, and the American South. She is the second of four children of George Wofford, a shipyard welder and Ramah Willis Wofford, a church-going woman. Morrison's family had moved to the North from deep South during the Great Migration, hoping to escape racism and gain increased employment opportunities in the industrial cities and a better education. Though both of Morrison's parents were from the South, they had diametrically opposite opinions of it. While George considered his hometown Georgia as the most racist state in the country and did not believe that such a situation would ever change, he often went back to visit his family. Ramah, by contrast, remembered the South fondly but never returned. Besides, while George harbored a fierce suspicion of white people, Ramah "believed in them—their possibilities" (Morrison, 2008: 7). As Li observes: "These paradoxical attitudes strongly influenced Morrison, who grew up without a singular conception of the South as either wholly violent or as romantically idyllic." (2010: 2) More importantly, the Woffords family's emphasis on their cultural heritage contributed to Morrison's later literary creation. At home, Morrison heard many songs, myths and tales that had been an important part of Southern black culture for centuries. Throughout her childhood, little Morrison absorbed these valuable cultural heritage which became source of inspiration in her subsequent novels.

Generally speaking, Morrison grew up in a liberal family where family members enjoyed an equal and unitary relationship. Morrison's grandmother, Ardelia

Willis, who played a role as ancestor, made a profound impact on her during her childhood. And Ramah, Morrison's mother, inherited Ardelia's hope for achieving racial harmony and instilled in her children values of self-reliance, community, and family. She expected her daughters to be strong and aggressive, like the elder women in the family, women who took on both work and family responsibilities without complaint. As an adult, Morrison came to realize that such behavior could be considered "feminist," but in her family it was simply the fulfillment of one's basic duties to others. (Li, 2010: 4)

Such kind of domestic education not only shapes Morrison into an independent and strong woman, but also has a far-reaching effect on her novel composition. Apart from this aspect in Morrison's family life, the harmonious and unitary atmosphere should be highlighted as well. Recalling the gender relationship in her family during an interview conducted by Mckay, Morrison said:

> There was a comradeship between men and women in the marriages of my grandparents, and of my mother and father. The business of story-telling was a shared activity between them, and people of both genders participated in it ... This was true with my grandfather and grandmother, as well as my father and mother, and with my uncles and aunts. There were no conflicts of gender in that area, at the level at which such are in vogue these days. My mother and father did not fight about who was to do what. Each confronted whatever crisis there was. (1994: 141)

This type of gender relationship ensured a healthy personality of the children who felt "as though there were these rather extraordinary deserving people with us" (Dreifus, 1994: 73). More importantly, it influenced the formation of her writing philosophy.

After graduation from high school with honors, Morrison attended the prestigious Howard University in Washington, D. C. in 1949, where she joined the Howard University Players. On her travels with the theater group, she visited the South for the first time. The natural environment of the South, the black custom and culture and numerous folklores had a deep impression on Morrison. Four years later, after completing her B. A. degree, she went on to study English at postgraduate level at Cornell University. After graduation, Morrison was offered a job at Texas Southern University in Houston (1955–1957), then returned to Howard to teach English. During this period Morrison met Harold Morrison and married him in 1958 but divorced six years later. From 1965 until 1983, Morrison worked as an editor at Random House where she fostered the careers of several young black women writers, including Gayl Jones, who published her first two novels, *Corregidora* (1975) and *Eva's Man* (1976), and a collection of short stories, *White Rat* (1977). Besides, Toni Cade Bambara's short story collection *The Seabirds Are Still Alive* (1974) and novel *The Salt Eaters* (1980) were also published under Morrison's editorship. This early career also gave Morrison an opportunity to read historical data and get to know the miserable history of the blacks, especially the black women, which became important inspiration source of her later creative works. Meanwhile, her unsuccessful marriage forced Morrison to reflect on how a black woman can keep her selfhood in a racist and sexist world. Gradually Morrison desired to write stories about and for women, notably black women, expressing their experiences and feelings openly.

Under such circumstance, Morrison began to produce novels continuously. From *The Bluest Eye* to *God Help the Child*, almost all the novels are woven around black female characters. Based on black women's special and complex life experiences that are different from white females, Morrison is committed to break the stereotypes of black female characters in literary canon and instead depicts a range of vivid and impressive images with complexity and subtlety, demonstrating their struggle against racism, sexism and classism. It must be also noted that different from the traditional black feminist practice of revealing political and economic oppression imposed on black women, Morrison often focuses on their inner world, voicing their needs, emotions and thoughts. This is reflected throughout her novels. For example, in *The Bluest Eye*, Pecola, a traumatized black girl with much self-hatred, craves for a pair of blue eyes which leads to destruction eventually. Of course, as a black woman novelist with a strong sense of ethnic responsibility, Morrison does not just stop here. She also expresses her concern with restoring identity of these black women, who are neglected or forgotten purposely. Furthermore, unlike the radical feminist, Morrison does not take a binary opposition. That is, she does not try to substitute patriarchy with matriarchy. Therefore, besides black women,

Morrison also depicts black men and explores the relationship between black men and black women in her novels. Undoubtedly this aspect is enlightening to other black women writers and enriches black feminist criticism.

In a word, due to her family and education background, Morrison, as a black woman novelist, is concerned with women's (mostly black women) survival and inner world in a white-and-male dominated society throughout her novels. Her occupation has been to give a voice to and establish subjectivity for the marginalized black women, which clearly displays her strong black female consciousness.

5.2 Black Feminist Literary Criticism

First formally put forward in the late 1960s, black feminist literary criticism argues that sexism, class oppression, and racism are inextricably bound together. The way these relate to each other is called intersectionality. Believing "black women are inherently valuable" (James & Sharpley-Whiting, 2000: 264), black feminist critics examine the works of black female writers within the context of African American experience, history, and literary tradition, aiming to explore a black women's aesthetics and language and establish common positive images of black women. By doing this, the black feminists "have laid a vital analytical foundation for a distinctive standpoint on self, community, and society" (Collins, 2000: 5).

From the above analysis, it is evident that black feminism is different from traditional western feminism. Though both challenge a sexist ideology and call for freedom and equal rights, black feminist criticism believes gender is not the only cause that leads to black women's subordinated role in society. For the first time, it introduces the element of race to feminist literary criticism. Then, we may ask, how did this development occur?

Like its counterpart, western feminism, black feminism have to deal with sexual oppression and it is even more prevalent with black males. But it must be noted that black women experience a more intense kind of oppression from that of white women. Bell Hooks points out,

> Black men may be victimized by racism, but sexism allows them to act
> as exploiters and oppressors of women: White women may be victimized

by sexism, but racism enables them to act as exploiters and oppressors of black people. Black women have no institutionalized "other" to discriminate against, exploit, or oppress. They have a lived experience that directly challenges the prevailing classiest, sexist, racist, social structure and its concomitant ideology. (2000b: 16)

In a white/male dominated society, black women are not only oppressed by black males but also scapegoated by white women, as in the history of plantation the white mistress's "true womanhood"—piety, purity, submissiveness and domesticity (Carby, 1987: 23) is often contrasted with black women who are believed to be physically strong and sexually active. Ironically, though black women "have a keener sense of gender, as well as racial inequality" (Ducille, 2006: 30), they are often excluded from the feminist movement and the civil rights movement of the 1960s and 1970s. Neither movement confronted the issues that concerned black women specifically. Because of their intersectional position, black women were being systematically ignored by both movements. "All the Women are White, All the Blacks are Men but Some of Us are Brave," as titled a 1982 book by Gloria Hull, Patricia Bell Scott and Barbara Smith. Black women began creating theory and developing a new movement which spoke to the combination of problems they were battling, including sexism, racism, and classism.

With the development of black feminist movement, significant changes occur in literary area. With the works of black women writers having been excluded from both critical works by white women scholars on the female tradition and those on the African American literary tradition by black male scholars, black women scholars start to establish a specific feminist literary theory that gives a proper treatment to black women and their works. As Deborah E. McDowell concludes in her *New Directions for Black Feminist Criticism*: "The recognition among black female critics and writers that white women, white men, and black men consider their experiences as normative and black women's experiences as deviant has given rise to black feminist criticism." (1985: 187)

The prominent theorists of black feminist literary criticism include Barbara Christian, Deborah E. McDowell, and Barbara Smith. They address various issues in the field of black feminist study.

Barbara Christian championed a black feminist criticism rooted in practice instead of employment of race for theory. In *Black Feminist Criticism*: *Perspectives on Black Women Writers*, Barbara Christian focused on evaluating the contributions of individual black woman writer. By performing extended close readings of major novels, Christian examined the development of themes, characters, and structures in individual works: "In-depth critical analysis of Afro-American women writers is for me the very foundation of the body of criticism we are developing." (1985: 149) Christian's most important contribution is to provide detailed studies of landmark texts hence producing a broadened conception of black women's literary tradition.

In "New Directions for Black Feminist Criticism," Deborah E. McDowell was critical of white feminist racism and male sexism in books on black literature. Like Barbara Christian, McDowell insists black feminist criticism should focus on a rigorous textual analysis. For her, a precise textual analysis is essential for formulating the details of specific black women writers' aesthetics and their characters, languages, and themes must be clearly and convincingly distinguished from those of black men.

As a forerunner in the field of black feminist criticism, Barbara Smith names black feminist criticism and paves a way for its development in her landmark essay "Toward a Black Feminist Criticism" in 1977 which is generally believed to play a significant role in engendering black feminist criticism, and more specifically, as a tool for literary analysis. In her essay, Smith powerfully attacked both black male intellectuals for sexism and white feminists for racism and heterosexism. With regard to black women's literature, Smith rejected employment of white male critical ideas and called for the establishment of an original and specific black feminist modes of analysis: "A Black feminist approach to literature that embodies the realization that the politics of sex as well as the politics of race and class are crucially interlocking factors in the works of Black women writers is an absolute necessity." (1979: 170) To further elaborate on her literary ideas, Smith stipulated two main principles for black feminist criticism.

Firstly, Smith pointed out,

> Beginning with a primary commitment to exploring how both sexual
> and racial politics and black and female identity are inextricable elements

in black women's writings, she [a black feminist] would also work from the assumption that black women writers constitute an identifiable literary tradition. (1979: 174)

Secondly, she proposed,

> Another principle which grows out of the concept of a tradition and which would also help to strengthen this tradition would be for the critics to look first for precedents and insights in interpretation within works of other black women. In other words she would think and write out of her own identity and not tries to graft the ideas or methodology of white male literary thought upon the precious materials of black women's art. Black feminist criticism would be innovative, embodying the daring spirit of the works themselves. The Black feminist critic would be constantly aware of the political implications of her work and would assert the connections between it and the political situation of all black women. (1979: 175)

Humm summarized the two principles as following: "The first is that feminist criticism must recognize the long-term literary history of Black women. Second, criticism must make an ideologically inspired reading of difference." (1994: 174–175).

Briefly, black feminist literary criticism stemmed from Black women's discontent with negative images applied to them in literary and critical works and black women writers' marginal position in literary circle because they are excluded from both female literary tradition and African American literary tradition by white female scholars and black male scholars respectively. Both of the groups view black women's experience as deviant. Claiming that "the politics of sex as well as the politics of race and class are crucially interlocking factors in the works of black women writers," black feminist literary critics hold that there exists a literary tradition of black women. They make a distinctive reading of black women writers' works which is rooted in black women's unique and complex experiences. By adding a new element—race, to its theoretical body and arguing sexism, racism and classism are intersectional in black women's lives and works, black feminist literary criticism becomes the first signs of identity critique. Besides, it also extends the concerns of feminist literary theory and offers a new perspective to women's studies. Last but not least, though black feminist literary criticism was put forward by and stands for the interests of Black women, it does not confine itself to issues confronting black women only. Rather it is of universal implication for women of color and ethnicities throughout the world. Many African American women intellectuals have proposed that Black women's struggles are part of a wider struggle for human dignity, empowerment, and social justice. In her speech to women, Anna Julia Cooper powerfully expressed this view:

> We take our stand on the solidarity of humanity, the oneness of life, and the unnaturalness and injustice of all special favoritism, whether of sex, race, country, or condition ... The colored woman feels that woman's cause is one and universal; and that ... not till race, color, sex and condition are seen as accidents, and not the substance of life; not till the universal title of humanity to life, liberty, and the pursuit of happiness is connected to be inalienable to all; not till then is woman's lesson taught and woman's cause won—not the white woman's nor the black woman's, not the red woman's but the cause of every man and of every woman who has writhed silently under a mighty wrong. (Loewenberg & Bogin, 1976: 330–331)

Linking itself to other projects for social justice, Black feminist literary criticism transcends the either/or mindset or binary thinking, hence showing a humanist orientation.

5.3 Loss of Identity Under Intersecting Oppressions of Race, Gender, Sexuality, and Class

Identity may be defined as a person's conception and expression of their individuality or group affiliations (such as national identity and cultural identity). Weinreich and Saunderson (2003: 54–61) point out the formation of one's identity occurs through one's identifications with significant others, primarily with parents and other individuals during one's biographical experiences, and also with "groups" as they are perceived. In *A Mercy*, the ethnic women, including Florens and her mother, Lina, and Sorrow are all separated from their families and tribes at an early age, which makes it difficult for them to develop a proper identity. On the other hand, they serve as slaves in the late 17th century in America. Under the intersecting oppressions of race, gender, sexuality, and class, these female slaves are relegated to animals. As a result, deprived of all human rights and feelings, including the possibility of experiencing normal girlhood and motherhood, these ethnic females question their worth and are unable to claim ownership of the self. Cote and Levine argue that,

> The development of a strong ego identity (sometimes identified simply as "the self"), along with the proper integration into a stable society and culture, lead to a stronger sense of identity in general. Accordingly, a deficiency in either of these factors may increase the chance of an identity crisis or confusion. (2002: 22)

The victimization of racism, sexism, and classism imposed on the four ethnic female characters in *A Mercy*, namely, Florens and her mother, Lina, and Sorrow, leads to their respective identity crisis. During the pre-slavery period, these females as slaves have to endure not only hard work on the plantation but also sexual harassment that may happen anytime. Apart from physical exploitation, they also endure psychological suffering: All the four females are separated from their families and tribes; more importantly, they are treated as commodities that can be traded and taught to hate themselves. As a result, deprived of everything, including the possibility to experience a normal girlhood and motherhood, these females are unable to claim ownership of the self, hence losing their identities. For Florens and her mother, Lina and Sorrow, inability to claim the self plus being torn apart from their families and tribes at an early age lead them to lose their identities.

5.3.1 Florens's Mother: Distorted Womanhood and Motherhood

In *A Mercy*, Florens's mother is an anonymous salve woman who is forced into slavery after a war destroys her home and community in Africa. Since then she is treated as a commodity rather than a full human being and is constantly traded. What is more, she is raped repeatedly. After experiencing all these miseries, the woman understands that "to be female in this place is to be an open wound that cannot heal" (Morrison, 2008: 163). So when Vaark whom she considers as kind appears in her master's plantation, she determines to give her daughter, Florens away to him to settle her owner's debt. Till here, Florens's mother is deprived of everything, including the ability to love her daughter, hence losing her identity.

5.3.1.1 Distorted Womanhood: Objectified, Commodified, and Raped

A Mercy is set during a time in American history when slavery have not yet been fully formulated. At that time the vast majority of African-American women were brought to America to work as slaves in a situation of oppression, among which race, class, gender, sexuality, nation, age, and ethnicity constitute major forms of oppression. However, the intersecting oppressions of race, gender, and class characteristic of American slavery shape all subsequent relationships that women of African descent have. "Intersecting" means it is hard to separate race from sex and from class oppression because "they are most often experience simultaneously" (James & Sharpley-Whiting, 2000: 264). Such intersecting oppressions are ideologically justified by maintaining images of black women as the "Other." This touches upon one important idea, namely, binary thinking which "categorizes people, things, and ideas in terms of their difference from one another" (Collins, 2000: 77). For instance, each term in the binaries white/black, male/female gain meaning only in relation to its counterpart. What is more, in binary thinking, "one part is not simply different from its counterpart; it is inherently opposed to its 'Other' " (Collins, 2000: 77). So whites and blacks, males and females are not complementary but fundamentally different entities related only through their definition as opposites. In this process of oppositional difference objectification plays a key role. Therefore, in binary thinking imbalance of power or relationships of superiority and inferiority inevitably occurs—one element is objectified as the Other that can be controlled.

In the case of Florens's mother, a black slave woman, due to her blackness which is opposed to whiteness, she is objectified as the Other and viewed as wholly inferior in a white-dominated world. And objectifying her body turns her into a commodity from which her slave holder can profit under U.S. capitalist relations. As a result, she and other black women are constantly traded by Europeans.

During the first passage destined for Barbados she suffers unbearable inhuman treatment and tries many times to commit suicide but fails because she is valued as a piece of property possessed by the white traders, as she says, "whatever the mind plans, the body has other interests" (Morrison, 2008: 165). When they arrive, Florens's mother only stays there for a short period of time and is then purchased by D'Ortega, a Portuguese slave owner. Till now the woman realizes how race becomes the primary determinant of her identity:

> It was there I learned how I was not a person from my country, nor from
> my families. I was negrita. Everything. Language, dress, gods, dance, habits,
> decoration, song—all of it cooked together in the color of my skin. So it was
> as a black that I was purchased by Senhor. (2008: 165)

Florens's mother is thus irrevocably linked to bondage because of her blackness. This also becomes an inheritance for her two children.

"Challenging the pervasiveness of Black women's rape and sexual extortion by White men has long formed a prominent theme in Black women's writings." (Collins, 2000: 158) During the first passage to Barbados, Florens's mother endures numerous rapes. Here her objectified body has been exploited by the white men for pleasure. More importantly, these rapes are designed to strip black women like Florens's mother of their resolution to resist and make them passive and submissive to the will of the rapists. As Angela Davis points out, "rape was a weapon of domination, a weapon of repression, whose covert goal was to extinguish slave women's will to resist." (1981: 23) It is also noteworthy that such victimization is ideologically justified by controlling images applied to black women that depict them as sexually active. At the same time this controlling image is also used to reflect the purity of white womanhood.

5.3.1.2 Distorted Motherhood: Forced to Abandon Florens

After Florens's mother is purchased by D'Ortega and works as a cook on his plantation, she still cannot escape from being raped. She recalls,

> I don't know who is you father. It was too dark to see any of them. They

came at night and took we three including Bess to a curing shed. Shadows of men sat on barrels, then stood. They said they were told to break we in. There is no protection. To be female in this place is to be an open wound that can not heal. Even if scars form, the festering is ever below. (Morrison, 2008: 163)

As a Black slave woman, Florens's mother is deprived of the right to control her sexuality. Besides, the rapists are told to break Florens's mother and other Black women in, which shows that the slave master, D'Ortega, is purposefully intervening in their fertility. D'Ortega's controlling the sexuality and fertility of Florens's mother objectifies the latter as less human and is crucial in perpetuating the intersecting oppressions of race, gender, and class in three ways.

First, motherhood and racism are intertwined. The biological notion of race which underpins slavery requires the so-called racial purity. As children follow the condition of mothers, children born of enslaved black women remain to be slaves. No matter who Florens's father is, be it white or black, she is born as a slave who is bartered first by D'Ortega and is to be sold by Rebekka in the end of the novel. Second, motherhood as an institution plays an important role in passing on values. If presumably Florens's mother instills inferiority feeling into Florens, she can become a willing participant in fostering oppression. Of course, we know the woman wishes Florens to develop self-definition through her narrative, as is illustrated by her confession in the end, "to be given dominion over another is a hard thing; to wrest dominion over another is a wrong thing; to give dominion of yourself to another is a wicked thing" (167). Third, controlling Florens's mother's fertility is key to the maintenance of capitalist class relations. As a slave holder, D'Ortega benefits from exploiting black slaves. He can either trade these commodified bodies or exploit their labor. Therefore, every slave child born represents a valuable unit of property, another unit of labor, and, if female, the prospects for more slaves. By controlling reproduction of Florens's mother and other Black women, D'Ortega aims to increase the number of children and property indirectly.

Not only is Florens's mother forced to enter motherhood, she is also deprived of love of Florens. After suffering rape repeatedly she realizes that "to be female in this place is to be an open wound that cannot heal. Even if scars form, the festering is ever below." For Florens's mother, to be a woman, especially a black woman is extremely vulnerable to sexual assault. There is no protection for them. On the other hand, as Florens grows into a budding girl her mother becomes increasingly worried about Florens's growing breasts, which threaten to attract the attention of D'Ortega and his sons: "I know their tastes. Breasts provide the pleasure more than simpler things. Yours are rising too soon and are becoming irritated by the cloth covering your little girl chest. And they see and I see them see." (Morrison, 2008: 162) What is worse, in spite of the potential dangers confronting her, Florens remains unaware. She even wants shoes of a lose woman, which is an extremely dangerous act because it has caught D'Ortega's eye. Under such circumstance, Florens's mother understands that one more second's stay in D'Ortega's house increases the danger facing Florens and determines to prevent bitter sexual assault visited on her from victimizing her daughter ever again. So when Vaark, whom Florens's mother considers as kind because "there was no animal in his heart. He never looked at me the way Senhor does" and most importantly when gazing at Florens he "see[s] you as a human child, not pieces of eight" (163, 166), insists her bartering for the debt D'Ortega owed him, she decides to offer Florens instead of herself. Though her incredible act astounds both her master D'Ortega and Vaark, at last they agree to the deal.

From the above analysis we can see it is out of protection and deep love that Florens's mother gives away Florens. Given the impending sexual assault to be inflicted on her daughter, the desperate woman has no other choices. Though abandoning Florens is brutal and risky, it is "one chance" (166), there is a faint possibility that Florens will be treated decently and distanced from sexual assault she has experienced personally. Florens's mother can only love and protect her daughter by casting her. This paradox indicates a distortion of the Black woman's love of her daughter. As Collins suggests, "corrupting and distorting basic feelings [especially love] human beings have for one another lies at the heart of multiple systems of oppression," because "love is active, dynamic, and determined and generates the motive and drive for justice" (2000: 185–186). By distorting Florens' mother's ability to love Florens properly, slavery jeopardizes potential sources of power in her.

In short, objectified as "Other," Florens's mother is commodified and exploited (both her labor and sexuality). By controlling her sexuality and fertility and denying her marriage, citizenship, and even humanity, dominant group including D'Ortega deprives her of a normal womanhood and motherhood. She is simply relegated to sex object and breeder woman.

5.3.2 Florens: Disturbed Girlhood

In Florens's memory, she is abandoned by her mother and she attributes this to the latter's preference for her younger brother. This idea deeply scars her and hinders her capacity to love others properly. As a result, she is haunted by this forever and harbors hatred of her brother and baby boys. Apart from inability to love others properly, Florens even can not love herself. Under the intersecting oppression she is objectified as the "Other," commodified and constantly traded. Besides, because of her Blackness, Florens is denied full humanity. What is worse, she internalizes this racial oppression, hence having difficulty asserting her self-worth.

5.3.2.1 Deprived of Maternal Love—"Abandoned by Her Mother"

Several factors contribute to Florens's disturbed girlhood. First and foremost, she is torn apart from her mother. The perplexing scene where her mother offers her to a stranger, Vaark, hurts Florens badly for the rest of her life. Being cast from her mother in an act that she can only understand as rejection, Florens is permanently deprived of a nurturing family life. In Black women's lives, mother-daughter relationship is of fundamental significance because this relationship can serve as a private sphere where a black mother protects her daughter from dangers as much as possible and teaches the small girl the importance of self-definition that can be used to resist oppression. Consequently, lack of maternal love seriously hampers her growth as a strong, self-confident human being. More importantly, Florens is traumatized by this event. As a result, she keeps recalling her mother holding her brother's hand and saying something she can not hear, whether in reality or in her dreams. For instance,

> Lina says Sir has a clever way of getting without giving. I know it is true because I see it forever and ever. Me watching, my mother listening, her baby boy on her lip. Senhor is not paying the whole amount he owes to Sir. Sir saying he will take instead the woman and the girl, not the baby boy and the

debt is gone. A minha mae begs no. Her baby boy is still at her breast. Take the girl, she says, my daughter, she says. Me. Me. Sir agrees and changes the balance due. (Morrison, 2008: 7)

"Forever and ever" implies Florens is deeply scarred and haunted by her abandonment. Besides, she keeps calling her little brother " (her) baby boy," indicating her indifference to him because she surmises it is her mother's preference for her brother that results in her abandonment. It is also noteworthy that, different from reality, Florens's memory is fictional. As in actuality, Vaark intends to take Florens's mother. By emphasizing "Sir saying he will take instead the woman and the girl, not the baby boy," Florens wants to devalue her brother only to find her mother abandons her. Her astonishment and desperation is evident in "Take the girl, she says, my daughter, she says. Me. Me." Deep in Florens's heart, she attributes her unexpected rejection by her mother to the latter's preference for her younger brother. Hence, she bears hostility to him and even all baby boys. This can be seen in her reaction after learning Sorrow is pregnant again:

But I have a worry. Not because our work is more, but because mothers nursing greedy babies scare me. I know how their eyes go when they choose. How they raise them to look at me hard, saying something I can not hear. Saying something important to me, but holding the little boy's hand. (2008: 8)

Besides, Florens even associates her abandonment with ordinary scenes: "If a pea hen refuses to brood I read it quickly and, sure enough, that night I see a minha mae standing hand in hand with her little boy." (3) At a tender age, Florens is supposed to live in her parents' nurturing. However, the reality is that she is abandoned by her mother. As a result, she is traumatized by this and cannot show sympathy for the weak baby boys (including her younger brother) who she thinks grabs maternal love from mothers.

5.3.2.2 Enslavement

The second factor concerns enslavement under the intersecting oppressions of race, gender, sexuality and class. As is mentioned above, as a female, especially a black female, she is just white men's sex object and is extremely vulnerable to sexual violence or assault. So out of protection, Florens's mother gives Florens away to Vaark who appears to be upright. Besides, born as a black slave girl, Florens is regarded as inferior in a world of an unquestioned superiority of whiteness. This oppositional difference leads to her objectification and subsequent commodification. Valued as little more than a commodity to be traded and exploited by her owner, Florens is first bartered from D'Ortega to Vaark to settle a debt with a legal paper stating "the girl was worth twenty pieces of eight" (Morrison, 2008: 27). When her mistress Rebekka sends her on an errand to summon the blacksmith, she is given a letter which reads, "[This girl] is owned by me … " (112); such statements of ownership explicitly manifest that Florens can not claim self. Towards the end of the novel, we learn that she is about to be sold to the highest bidder. Moreover, Florens's Blackness signifies her otherness and is therefore denied full humanity by other people. When little Florens visits a native village on an errand to summon the blacksmith, she immediately alarms the brown-skinned villagers who deems her as a demon by her difference. In fact, her body is subject to a shameful examination to check whether she has the normal organs in the normal places, which alone can humiliate her humanity. Florens reports: "Naked under their examination I watch for what is in their eyes. No hate is there or scare or disgust but they are looking at me my body across distances without recognition." (113) Such an act is dehumanizing enough to rob anyone of his or her identity as a full human being.

However, enslavement means not only subordination, but also loss of the power to love anything or anyone, including love of self. Since its formation slavery has thwarted slaves' ability to have normal love, be it love of self or love between individuals. After the dehumanizing inspection of her body, the totality of Florens's self-esteem is crumbling. Morrison subtly and poignantly demonstrates this,

> Inside I am shrinking. I climb the streambed under watching trees and know I am not the same. I am losing something with every step I take. I can feel the drain. Something precious is leaving me. I am a thing apart. With the letter I belong and am lawful. Without it I am a weak calf abandon by the herd, a turtle without shell, a minion with no telltale signs but a darkness I am born with, outside, yes, but inside as well and the inside dark is small,

feathered and toothy. Is that what my mother knows? Why she chooses me
to live without? (2008: 115)

The trauma caused by her abandonment has not recovered yet, another one
is inflicted on her again. "I am losing something." and "Something precious is
leaving me. I am a thing apart." suggest the inhumane inspection of her body has
deprived Florens of her dignity and even humanity. Therefore, she slides into
an identity crisis. Florens even links this event to her abandonment—without
the accompaniment of the letter written by Rebekka she is just an outcast with
no identity marker but a darkness she is born with. What is more, Florens has
developed a "small, feathered and toothy" darkness inside, which suggests that she
has internalized racism. This can be seen in her eagerness to please others: "She
was deeply grateful for every shred of affection, any pat on the head, any smile of
approval." (Morrison, 2008: 61) Florens is even willing to "blame herself for the
meanness of others" (152). Pauli Murray claims "A system of oppression draws
much of its strength from the acquiescence of its victims, who have accepted
the dominant image of themselves and are paralyzed by a sense of helplessness"
(1987: 106). Seized by an inferiority feeling deriving from her Blackness, Florens
becomes a willing participant in the intersecting oppressions.

In brief, Florens is traumatized by her abandonment which she thinks stems from
her mother's preference for her brother. This stunts her ability to love her brother
and other baby boys. Besides, she is enslaved under the intersecting victimizations
of race, gender, sexuality, and class. What is worse, she fosters these oppressions
because she has internalized racism. By admitting her inferiority Florens can not
love herself properly. Abandoned, subordinated, and internally enslaved, Florens's
sense of self is collapsing. Consequently, she slides into an identity crisis.

5.3.3 Lina: an Exile in Her Own Land

Within binary thinking, white and black women as two groups stand for two
opposing poles, with other colored ethnicities such as Latinos, Asian-American
women, and native American women negotiating positions in between. In *A
Mercy*, as a native American, Lina's native culture is deemed by the Presbyterians
as primitive and even sinful: "bathing naked in the river was a sin," "to eat corn

mush with one's fingers was perverse," and "covering oneself in the skin of beasts offended God" (Morrison, 2008: 48), among other things. After experiencing the destruction of her family and tribe by an epidemic, Lina is adopted by Presbyterians and renamed Messalina. Scared of further abandonment, she is compelled to acknowledge she is a heathen: "Afraid of once more losing shelter, terrified of being alone in the world without family, Lina acknowledged her status as heathen and let herself be purified by these worthies." (47) Thus, ironically Lina is uprooted from her native culture in her own land that is owned and controlled by others (the whites). However, although Lina adapts herself to the ways of the Presbyterians they sell her into slavery after finding her beaten and abandoned by a man whom she once loved and briefly lived with.

As the first person to join Jacob's household, Lina dedicates herself to serving the family. Though she plays a relatively important role in running chores in the house, she remains to be a servant. Whether or not her mistress Rebekka treats her well, Lina must mutely keep serving the former; although in the very beginning, the two are wary of each other, they soon become good companions on a lonely farm; but later, after the widow Rebekka becomes a religious zealot and mistreats Lina, Lina can neither say nor do anything about it. In spite of this, she is alarmed at the possibility of losing her master because that would leave servants without a master like her the most defenseless in the world, being both "female and illegal" (56). She even compares her with a beech tree. Though both she and beech trees have lived for years on Vaark's property, she is aware that she is only an exile: "You [beech tree] and I, this land is our home … but unlike you I am exile here." (57) Lina is an exile in her home; she is homeless in her own homeland. A great injustice is perpetrated against her when she is uprooted from her native culture and transplanted into a foreign one.

5.3.4 Sorrow: a Daft Girl

Sorrow, who is "a bit mongrelized" (120), is the daughter of a captain who died with all other crew after the ship founders. Somehow Sorrow survives from the accident and is rescued by the sons of a sawyer. Since she can not remember her past at all, including her name, she is named Sorrow by the sawyer's wife.

As is mentioned above, according to binary thinking, White and Black are opposed to each other and they constitute two poles with the colored ethnicities in between. Sorrow, a "mongrelized" girl "who kept wandering off getting lost, who knew nothing and worked less, a strange melancholy girl" (Morrison, *2008*: 51) is dismissed and shunned by everyone: The sawyer's wife considers her a burden and gives her away to Vaark; Rebekka is frustrated with her slackness at work and maltreats her after becoming a religious zealot; Lina considers her the symbol of bad luck because after her arrival Mistress's children die successively. Subsequently Lina keeps first Patrician and then Florens away from Sorrow as much as possible. Few seem to notice the sorrows of Sorrow.

Besides, Sorrow suffers repetitive seduction. Being still a small girl, Sorrow is assaulted sexually by the sawyer's two young sons behind the stack of clapboards and is pregnant after she joins Vaark's household. However, being a child herself, Sorrow's birthing comes too soon for the infant to survive, which haunts her for several years. Even when Sorrow stays at Vaark's household, she remains easy prey as she, once again, becomes pregnant, although it is unclear who the father is.

Dark skinned, unable to concentrate, and an easy prey for seduction, Sorrow appears daft and disturbed to others and is ill-treated. As a result, she becomes virtually mute.

To sum up, in *A Mercy* Morrison does not confine herself to black females but goes on to focus on all colored females. Objectified as the "Other," they are subsequently commodified and exploited; being females, they all encounter sexual oppression. Under these intersecting oppressions these colored females are reduced to object. "As objects, one's reality is defined by others, one's identity created by others, one's history named only in ways that define one's relationship to those who are subject." (Hooks, 1989: 42) Besides, while formation of one's identity is closely related to one's identifications primarily with parents (especially mothers) and other individuals during one's biographical experiences, and also with groups, these colored females are all torn apart from their family and tribe, hence having difficulty developing a proper identity. Last but not least, none of these colored women except Florens have or remember a name of their own: Florens's mother only identifies herself as a "minha mae," Portuguese for "your mother"; Lina can not remember her former name after she is adopted and renamed by the Presbyterians; Sorrow, too, forgets her former name and is only named by the sawyer's wife as Sorrow because she is abandoned. Morrison once commented on the significance of losing one's name: "It is particularly problematic because it is not just your name but your family, your tribe. When you die, how can you connect with your ancestors if you have lost your name? That's a huge psychological scar." (Taylor-Guthrie, 1994: 126) Therefore, loss of names means their consequent loss of identity is complete.

5.4 Quest for Identity

As Barbara Christian maintains, "to be able to use the range of one's voice, to attempt to express the totality of self, is a recurring struggle in the tradition of [Black women] writers" (1985: 172), the tradition of women's resistance to intersecting oppressions of race, gender, sexuality and class has long existed in black women's literature. So is *A Mercy*. In the novel, such black women as Florens and her mother and colored women such as Lina and Sorrow do not give in in the face of multiple victimizations. Rather they choose to resist the controlling images applied to them and forge a self-defined identity in their own way, namely, Florens's mother by salvation, Florens by quest for romantic love, Lina by reinvention, and Sorrow by retreat into imagination. To be specific, Florens's mother strives to protect Florens, though she does so in an abnormal way, namely, giving Florens away to a stranger; craving for love desperately, Florens falls in love and tries to establish a romantic relationship with the blacksmith; Lina, a native American, converts her religious belief to Christianity and blends into nature; Sorrow retreats to an imaginary world. Though none of the attempts succeeds, they play an important role in raising the consciousness of subjectivity.

5.4.1 Florens's Mother: Salvation

Collins points out, "African American women possess a dual consciousness, one in which black women 'become familiar with the language and means of the oppressor, even sometimes adopting them for some illusion of protection' (Lorde, 1984: 114), while hiding a self-defined standpoint from the prying eyes of dominant groups." (2000: 107) As a black mother, on one hand Florens's mother has to fit Florens into sexual politics, teaching the latter about her proper place so as to ensure her physical survival. For example, when small Florens wants shoes, her mother thinks she is "dangerous" and "wild" (Morrison, 2008: 4) because such behavior is highly likely to catch Senhor's eye. On the other hand, Florens's mother needs to instill self-definition into Florens to resist the negative images imposed on black women. As is mentioned above, the fundamental mother-daughter relationship can act as a private sphere for freedom where a mother teaches her daughter the importance of resistance. Though abandoning Florens makes it virtually impossible for Florens's mother to nurture the former's psychological growth, she resorts to other method to do this.

In *A Mercy*, Florens's mother knows too well "there is no protection" for women because of her own bitter experience. Besides, Florens has drawn Senhor and his sons' attention, with the former unaware of this. However, objectified as the "Other," Florens's mother can do little to change the situation. In desperation the woman determines to distance Florens from potential threat as far as possible. Therefore she does her utmost to seize the chance when good-natured Vaark comes to Senhor's house by offering Florens instead of herself to him. By doing this, the woman hopefully ensures her daughter's complete physical survival in a hostile environment. In this sense she achieves a salvation of her daughter.

5.4.2 Florens: Quest for Romantic Love

After her mother's abandonment, lack of maternal love makes Florens desperate for love and protection. For example, she is especially enchanted by "stories of mothers fighting to save their children from wolves and natural disasters" (Morrison, 2008: 61) and "when sleep came the little girl's smile lingered" (63). When Florens grows into a teenager, she craves for romantic love. So when the blacksmith who is "too shiny, way too tall, both arrogant and skilled" (Morrison, 2008: 60) comes to Vaark's house to work on the new gate, Florens falls in love with him immediately: "Since his coming, there was an appetite in the girl [Florens] … A bleating desire beyond sense, without conscience." (60) Evidently adolescent Florens loves the blacksmith whom she perhaps deems as incarnation of protection passionately but irrationally. This is explicitly shown in her response to Lina's warning that "You are one leaf on his tree" (61) which means the blacksmith may abandon her. After hearing Lina's words, Florens "shook her head, closed her eyes and replied, 'No. I am his tree'" (61). Blinded by her baseless love, Florens cannot follow Lina's advice, let alone foresee the peril the blacksmith may bring about.

What is more, Florens is enslaved by her blind love. After the blacksmith finishes his work and leaves Vaark's house, Florens walks to search him. On the way she sees beautiful flowers and a stag. Standing between the two objects, a sense of freedom engenders in her but she does not like it: "It is as though I am loose to do what I choose, the stag, the wall of flowers. I am a little scare of this looseness. Is that how free feels? I don't like it. I don't want to be free of you because I am live only with you." (70) As a slave, Florens does not like freedom because she cannot perceive herself completely without the blacksmith. She is a slave of her irrational love.

Florens's illusion is not shattered until she arrives at the blacksmith's home. She is ordered by Rebekka who falls ill with smallpox to summon the blacksmith to cure her. Impelled more by her love than by the mandate of her mistress, she imagines a joyous reunion with her lover. But when Florens finally arrives at the blacksmith's house she is asked to stay to look after Malaik, a dark skinned boy adopted by blacksmith. On seeing the small boy, Florens is wary of him because he reminds her of her brother, the child she believes her mother loved best: "I worry as the boy steps closer to you. How you offer and he owns your forefinger. As if he is your future. Not me. I am not liking how his eyes go when you send him to play in the yard." (Morrison, 2008: 136) Out of wild passion and fear of losing her beloved, Florens can only regards the small boy as her opponent, not a helpless boy. After the blacksmith leaves for Rebekka's house, Florens lies on his cot and dreams about the recurring scene where her mother holds her brother's hand and abandons her after falling asleep. Suddenly she is woke up by Malaik's scream which she reads as "He wants my leaving" and vows "This expel can never happen again" (137). Then Florens continues to dream. In the dreams she is on grassland with perfume. To pursue the perfume she comes to the edge of a lake which she loves so much that she draws her face near the surface only to find her face lost: "Right away I take fright when I see my face is not there. Where my face should be is nothing. I put a finger in and watch the water circle. I put my mouth close enough to drink or kiss but I am not even a shadow there." (138) Absence of her face implies Florens's identity is not complete.

On the second day Malaik steals Florens's boots. In retaliation, Florens takes his doll, and as he screams, she grabs him, breaking his arm. As Malaik faints, the blacksmith enters the cabin, calling the boy's name, which makes Florens lost: "[I] know I am lost because your shout is not my name. Not me. Him. Malaik you shout. Malaik." (140) Seeing Malaik lie still with blood trickling from his mouth the blacksmith knocks Florens away, refusing to hear her explanation. Florens is confused about his decision:

Why? Why?

Because you are a slave.

What?

You heard me.

Sir makes me that.

I don't mean him.

Then who?

You.

What is your meaning? I am a slave because Sir trades for me.

No. You have become one.

How?

Your head is empty and your body is wild.

I am adoring you.

And a slave to that too.

You alone own me.

Own yourself, woman, and leave us be. You could have killed the child.

No. Wait. You put me in misery.

You are nothing but wilderness. No constraint. No mind.

You shout the word—mind, mind, mind—over and over and then you
laugh, saying as I live and breathe, a slave by choice. (Morrison, 2008: 141)

The blacksmith's declaration echoes the comments of Florens's mother
concerning how "to give dominion of yourself to another is a wicked thing" (167).
He exactly points out how Florens is enslaved: She is so obsessed with him that she
can not maintain the totality of her identity without him. To Florens, the blacksmith
is her "shaper" and her "world" (71); she even says "You alone own me." Black
feminism holds that black women's body is a source of power, a site where black
women resist the intersecting oppressions. By giving up the autonomy of her
body to the blacksmith in a craze of affection, Florens is enslaved by her singular
obsession.

Elaborating on the relationship between love and empowerment, June Jordan
(1981) claims that love begins with self-love and self-respect, which are actions
that propel African-American women toward self-definition and political activism
crucial for social change. By surrendering her sense of identity to sexual passion
and romantic love rather than fostering her self-esteem, "love-disabled" Florens's
quest for identity is destined to be a failure.

5.4.3 Lina: Reinvention

After she is adopted by the Presbyterians, Lina is introduced to a foreign
culture. Nevertheless, with a strong sense of heritage, remnants of Lina's native
American culture are embedded in her psyche and cannot be excised. As a result,

she adopts a hybrid culture that blends aspects of white culture with her own to adapt to the kind of life that has befallen her—a life in her own land amid people not her own; a life of hers owned and governed by others:

> Lonely, angry and hurting, that she decides to fortify herself by piecing together scraps of what her mother had taught her before dying in agony. Relying on memory and her own resources, she cobbled together neglected rites, merged European medicine with native, scripture with lore, and recalled or invented the hidden meaning of things. Found, in other words, a way to be in the world. (Morrison, 2008: 48)

From the description we can see Lina is a strong, self-defined woman. On the one hand, in spite of the destruction of her community and the fact that her native culture is viewed by the dominant group as primitive, she clings to her native cultural heritage. On the other hand, though she incorporates much of the teachings of her white owners, she maintains an objective judgment of their actions. For instance, although the soothsayer of her tribe once declared, "it was [the European invader's] destiny to chew up the world and spit out a horribleness that would destroy all primary peoples" (52), she believes there are exceptions. She admits that there is a superiority of morals and judgment in the Vaarks's fencing their cattle, tilling their land, or hesitating to kill pigs mindlessly. Another example is how Lina frowns upon Jacob's new house, "which distorted sunlight and required the death of fifty trees" (43). She is certain that such unnecessary destruction will lead to misfortune, and finds the workings of Jacob, like all Europeans she has encountered, mystifying.

Besides, as the first person to join Vaark's household, Lina integrates herself into nature to kill loneliness: "Solitude would have crushed her had she not fallen into hermit skills and become one more thing that moved in the natural world." (48) Therefore she takes animals as partners to whom she speaks.

In short, by adopting a hybrid culture which combines white culture with her native culture and developing a close relationship with nature Lina fits herself into the new life. Yet formation of identity occurs through identifications with others and groups, without company of other members in the house Lina can not develop a proper identity in a real sense.

5.4.4 Sorrow: Retreat into Imagination

"Morrison often uses fractured psyches to signify either resilience or stunted psychological growth." (Roye, 2012: 221) In Sorrow's case, she is resilient.

Left alone on board a ship whose crew is drown or gone, Sorrow has no one to talk to. To counter sadness and solitude she invents an identical self which she names Twin. And Twin calls her Captain. "Having two names [is] convenient since Twin [can't] be seen by anybody else." (Morrison, 2008: 114) At last the two walk to the seashore where she is rescued by a sawyer's sons. Since "before coming to the sawyer's house, Sorrow had never lived on land" (117) and lost all her kin, including her father, the Captain, Twin makes a good companion during her stay at first the sawyer's and then Vaark's house. Every time Twin calls her to play or talk, Sorrow joins her to enjoy a kind of freedom that is unknown to Lina or Florens, "Twin [is] her safety, her entertainment, her guide" (117). Because of her peculiar behaviors Sorrow is thought to be strange and consequently avoided. In turn Sorrow becomes increasingly dependent on Twin to the extent that she completely retreats into imagination.

Yet "to dismiss Sorrow as 'the odd one' ignored her quick and knowing sense of her position" (152). For example, she has different expectations when called by Twin and others respectively; when she is going to give birth to her second baby she seeks help "in exactly the right place from the right people" (152). In fact, "Her privacy protected her; her easy coupling a present to herself" (152). Sorrow's seemingly self-alienation helps her resist the social norms imposed upon her; Twin's company helps her go through hard time by giving her comfort and advice. In spite of this, Sorrow, like Lina, can not truly reconstruct her identity due to her isolation from others.

In short, Florens and her mother, Lina, and Sorrow each embark on identity negotiations in their own way. Black women who struggle to forge an identity larger than the one society would force upon them are aware and conscious, and that very consciousness is potent. Regardless of the outcome of these colored women's struggle, the act itself offers a powerful challenge to the externally defined, controlling images imposed on them. Though they fail, their consciousnesses are no longer passive since they have taken the first step of wanting to be healed, of wanting to make the journey toward personal empowerment.

5.5 Reconstruction of Identity

"U.S. black women writers not only portray the range of responses that individual African-American women express concerning their objectification as the Other; they also document the process of personal growth toward positive self-definition." (Collins, 2000: 103) In the case of *A Mercy*, a desperate Florens's mother, a disillusioned Florens, a culturally transplanted Lina, and a daft Sorrow do not constitute Morrison's final word on disrupted womanhood or girlhood. She also portrays how these colored females overcome interruptions to move ahead—Florens's mother by oral narrative, Florens by writing narrative, Lina by devotion to others, and Sorrow by claim of motherhood. Namely, Florens's mother turns to oral narrative and realizes spiritual redemption in the end; by means of writing narrative on the walls and floor of Vaark's empty new house, Florens gains independence and freedom; Lina devotes herself to Vaark's farm and Florens to assert self-realization; Sorrow becomes complete in a real sense through claim of motherhood. Though strategies employed by the females vary, they assure the latter their worth so as to enable them to (re)construct their identities.

5.5.1 Florens's Mother: Oral Narrative

According to many African-American women writers, no matter how oppressed an individual woman may be, she can achieve personal empowerment by herself. For Florens's mother, she becomes free through oral storytelling.

As is stated before, Florens's mother, a black slave woman, has dual consciousnesses. On the one hand, she fits Florens into the sexual politics to guarantee the latter's physical survival. On the other hand, it is necessary for her to teach Florens about the significance of self-definition. Though given the situation at that time she can only makes it a priority to ensure Florens's physical survival, possibility is high that Florens lives in shadows since the abandonment. Therefore Florens's mother bears a burden. To free her of the burden she chooses oral storytelling. In her short narrative Florens's mother describes how she is forced into slavery and commodified. She particularly emphasizes how black women's bodies are exploited and that is why she determines to give Florens away to Vaark, a tall white man she believes upright. With regard to this decision, she confesses that her heart will remain in dust where she knelt before Vaark forever until Florens understands "to be given dominion over another is a hard thing; to wrest dominion over another is a wrong thing; to give dominion of yourself to another is a wicked thing" (Morrison, 2008: 167). By this Florens's mother suggests that there is a key distinction between forced servitude and voluntary bondage. She claims that there is a type of slavery that is chosen, and it is this form of enslavement which proves to be most harmful to the adolescent Florens. With the narrative Florens's mother wishes her daughter to understand what she did is out of love; besides, she hopes Florens does not internalize slavery because that can definitely foster enslavement.

With the narrative which provides a detailed and penetrating analysis of the operation of oppressions Florens's mother challenges dominant discourse and finds a voice of her own. As Bell Hooks observes,

> Moving from silence into speech is for the oppressed, the colonized, the exploited, and those who stand and struggle side by side a gesture of defiance that heals, that makes new life and new growth possible. It is that act of speech, of "talking back," that is no mere gesture of empty words, that is the expression of our movement from object to subject—the liberated voice. (1989: 37)

Thus, through re-articulation, Florens's mother qualifies her status as a subject. "As subjects, people have the right to define their own reality, establish their own identities, name their history." (Hooks, 1989: 42) Therefore she can reconstruct her identity.

5.5.2 Florens: Writing Narrative

After abandoned by the blacksmith, Florens, like her mother, resorts to storytelling to reconstruct her identity.

At the beginning of the novel, Florens says, "You can think what I tell you a confession, if you like." (Morrison, 2008: 3) Here "You" refers to the blacksmith. It is the blacksmith's abandonment that propels furious and heartbroken Florens to write her story, when she actually writes it out she calms down, as "confession" suggests. Then she begins to recall her abandonment by her mother, her later life on Vaark's farm, and her encounter on her way to summon the blacksmith from an objective standpoint. Through her narration Florens comes to understand her enslavement is caused by herself, "it is the withering inside that enslaves and opens the door for what is wild. I know my withering is born in the Widow's closet. I know the claws of the feathered thing did break out on you because I can not stop them wanting to tear you the way you tear me" (Morrison, 2008: 160). By this Florens acknowledges she is enslaved by her internalized racism which leads her to surrender her sense of identity to the blacksmith. This changed consciousness is vital because it reveals Florens is no longer a passive recipient of external definition by dominant group; only with this changed consciousness can she step toward independence and freedom. Furthermore, Florens has overcome the haunting thing—her mother abandons her because dreams where her mother, holding her little brother's hand, gives her away to a stranger no longer come. This also can be seen from her confession at the end of the narrative, "I will keep one sadness. That all this time I cannot know what my mother is telling me. Nor can she know what I am wanting to tell her. Mae, you can have pleasure now because the soles of my feet are as hard as cypress" (161). Unlike before, Florens no longer calls her mother "a minha mae." Instead, she uses "my mother," implying she has emerged from the disturbing past into a mature and strong woman with the soles of her feet "as hard as cypress." Here it is noteworthy that a sharp contrast appears, "when a child I am [she is] never able to abide being barefoot and always beg for shoes, anybody's shoes, even on the hottest days" (4). This change unambiguously and powerfully reveals Florens's determination to survive despite obstacles.

Though originally Florens thinks she "cannot tell it [her story] to anyone but you [the blacksmith]" (160), at the end of her narration she thinks it is no more important whether he can read it because she suggests that she will set fire to the letters she carves on the room:

> These careful words, closed up and wide open, will talk to themselves. Round and round, side to side, bottom to top, top to bottom all across the room. Or, or perhaps no. Perhaps these words need the air that is out in the

world. Need to fly up then fall, fall like ash over acres of primrose and mallow.
(Morrison, 2008: 161)

By burning these words which embody haunting memory and bitter experineces,
Florens is trying to leap beyond the past and start a new life. Through telling stories,
Florens's psychological scars are healed and she arrives at a more coherent sense of
self. This is clearly reflected in her subsequent confession: "See? You are correct. A
minha mae too. I am become wilderness but I am also Florens. In full. Unforgiven.
Unforgiving. No truth, my love. None. Hear me? Salve. Free. I last." (161) Clearly
Florens has forgiven the blacksmith and her mother in spite of their abandonment
and reached reconciliation with past. She is reborn and "free." "In full" implies
Florens has achieved totality of her identity.

To sum, through writing narrative Florens achieves freedom and independence.
The long address not only liberates her from her destructive love to the blacksmith
but also helps her recover from the trauma caused by her mother's abandonment.
After having a better understanding of her life, as Scully observes, Florens
becomes "untouchable," meaning now Florens exerts control on her selfhood. This
establishment of subjective consciousness enables her to reconstruct identity.

5.5.3 Lina: Devotion to Others

Loss of her family and her native culture engenders a sense of commitment in
Lina. "The shame of having survived the destruction of her families shrank with
her vow never to betray or abandon anyone she cherished." (Morrison, 2008: 49)
Hence, Lina first establishes a close relationship with her master and mistress, then
with Florens.

As the first person to join Jacob's farm, Lina teaches her master, an inexperienced
farmer, some basic farming skills and accompanies him through difficulties. After
Rebekka arrives at Vaark's farm, she and Lina are initially wary of one another.
However, they soon become comrades. Lina cures Rebekka's festering mouth with
magic recipes from her native culture; together they learn how to manage the farm,
care for the infants, and survive the bleak, desperate winters. Besides, Lina always
keep Patrician, Rbekka's daughter, away from daft Sorrow because she thinks
Sorrow symbolizes bad luck.

Lina develops her closest bond with Florens, whom she "had fallen in love with right away" as "the child assuaged the tiny yet eternal yearning for the home Lina once knew" (Morrison, 2008: 60). Like Lina, Florens is an abandoned orphan. So Lina shows sympathy for the little girl and determines to protect her from corruption. First she distances Florens from Sorrow who behaves in a peculiar way, then she "determined to be the wall between Florens and the blacksmith" (60) because she is especially concerned about Florens's powerful response to the blacksmith, "since his coming, there was an appetite in the girl [Florens] that Lina recognized as once her own. A bleating desire beyond sense, without conscience" (60). As a result, Lina tells Florens how she was betrayed by her lover and warns Florens against caring for a man who will inevitably return to his home without her.

With a strong sense of loss Lina is sensitive to others' loss. So she is loyal to those who have similar experiences to her. Yet Lina's loyalty "was not submission to Mistress or Florens; it was a sign of her own self-worth" (151). "Self is not defined as the increased autonomy gained by separating oneself from others. Instead, self is found in the context of family and community." (Collins, 2000: 165) Through forming bonds with other members in Vaark's family, Lina reconstructs her identity.

5.5.4 Sorrow: Claim of Motherhood

Sorrow is pregnant twice. Though her first pregnancy makes her "flushed with pleasure, at the thought of a real person, a person of her own, growing inside her" (Morrison, 2008: 123), the infant dies of premature. However, the birth of her second baby makes a difference.

Being an orphan, ignored, and isolated, Sorrow is cheered up by the baby because she has a real company to whom she is of great importance. As a result, Sorrow changes. She no longer feels the need of Twin's company. "Twin is gone, traceless and unmissed by the only person she knew. Sorrow's wandering stopped too." (134) Besides, now she leaves all chores to attend to her baby's needs. With no kin in the world, the baby girl provides solace, and love. More importantly, motherhood makes Sorrow's life full and meaningful,

Although all her life she had been saved by men—Captain, the sawyer's sons, Sir and now Will and Scully—she was convinced that this time she had done something, something important, by herself. Twin's absence was hardly noticed as she concentrated on her daughter. Instantly, she knew what to name her. Knew also what to name herself. (Morrison, 2008: 133)

For Sorrow, the baby is hope, a base where she expresses and gets to know the significance of self-definition and a belief in their personal empowerment. In a way, the birth of Sorrow's baby heralds her rebirth. Her split self welds into a complete whole. Thus, the new name she assumes, "Complete," is most suitable. Despite all the obstacles to her healthy growth as a human, "Sorrow" decides to metamorphose into "Complete." By renaming herself, she exercises her own agency and emerges into a complete womanhood and motherhood.

Briefly, no matter how oppressed an individual woman is, she can achieve personal empowerment. And the power towards empowerment lies in herself. In *A Mercy*, though objectified as the "Other," Florens and her mother, Lina, and Sorrow manage to establish subjective consciousness in their own way. As subjects, they have the right to define their own reality and reconstruct their own identities. By depicting these colored females' struggle for identity reconstruction, Morrison gives a voice to the silenced group. What is more, she inspires all those who are marginalized to take actions and reestablish their status as a subject by pointing out strategies employed by the ethnic females.

5.6 A Voice for All the Marginal Group

In *A Mercy*, Morrison does not limit herself to black women. Instead she extends her focus to all colored women, including black (Florens and her mother), mongrelized (Sorrow), and brown (Lina) females. By bringing these ethnic females together, Morrison explores how their lives are affected by the intersecting oppressions of race, gender, sexuality, and class. Firstly, within binary thinking, these colored women are viewed as inferior and objectified as the "Other" in a society of undoubted superiority. Deprived of everything, they are relegated to object. Secondly, as women they are subject to patriarchy and regarded as secondary. Thirdly, their sexuality and fertility are controlled so as to perpetrate racial oppression. Fourthly, the objectification of these women leads to consequent commodification. Hence, they are valued no more than a commodity that can be traded and their labor and body are exploited. It should be noted these oppressions are interdependent. Therefore, the colored females experience the intersecting victimizations simultaneously. The ultimate consequence is that they lose their identity as full human being, a subject. Through the portrayal of their miserable experiences, Morrison brings them to center and protests against a highly partial social system that makes many invisible.

Yet though Morrison is critical of the Euro-American dichotomies within racial, gender, and class hierarchies, she does not aim at reversing them. She elaborates on this idea in an interview,

> In order to be as free as I possibly can, in my own imagination, I can't take positions that are closed. Everything I've ever done, in the writing world, has been to expand articulation, rather than to close it, to open doors ... I don't subscribe to patriarchy, and I don't think it should be substituted with matriarchy. I think it's a question of equitable access, and opening doors to all sorts of things. (Jaffrey, 1998)

It is obvious that what Morrison desires is an open standpoint because "exaggerated binary oppositions never capture the complexity of life" (Li, 2010: 2). So with regard to racial, gender and class relationships, she wants them to be equal and unified. Consequently, on Vaark's farm where the novel is set, not only are colored characters oppressed, white characters are also oppressed as Vaark detests slavery trade and Rebekka is left few options other than prospects as "servant, prostitute, wife" (Morrison, 2008: 77) and she has to constantly take care to "escape from the leers and rude hands of any man, drunken or sober, she might walk by" (76). Besides, black people can be free (the blacksmith) and the white can be indentured workers; men and women help each other and maintain a relatively equal relationship. For example, Sorrow gives birth to her second baby with the help of Willard and Scully and the blacksmith teaches Florens about the importance of a free mind; Master Vaark hates slave owners who maltreat slaves and treats his slaves decently and Rebekka regards Lina as good friend whose opinion she values. Adopting an open stance reveals a humanist orientation of Morrison's works; hence they are illuminating to all marginal groups.

Morrison does not stop where the colored female characters' are trapped by the intersecting oppressions; she goes on to present how they struggle for identity reconstruction. Though the forms of the ways in which Florens and her mother, Lina and Sorrow perform identity negotiation differ, actually they all point to love, whether it is self-love, love between individuals, or love of one's cultural heritage. As is stated before, love is an important source of power that propels people to resist oppression and seek justice. Given the humanist orientation of her works, Morrison attempts to propose a way out for all marginalized groups not only in America but also throughout the world by documenting her characters' journey toward identity reconstruction.

To sum up, *A Mercy* is a rich web of intertwined tales of several females from different backgrounds, unraveling their vulnerability to intersecting victimizations of race, gender, sexuality, and class. By writing about their sufferings in which nobody takes interest, Morrison is deliberately bringing marginal figures to the center of attention, thereby rescuing them and their tragic tales from a willful collective blindness and amnesia. Furthermore, she gives them a voice through portraying their journey to personal empowerment in their own way. Considering her open stance, Morrison is also seeking a voice for similarly silenced others who occupy societally denigrated categories. Besides, though the title of the novel, *A Mercy* is full of religious connotations, indeed it talks of the mercifulness inherent in and deserved by humans.

By displaying reconstruction of identity of the ethnic females in a white/male dominated world, Morrison deconstructs racial and sexual hegemony and gives a voice to the marginalized and silenced group. At the same time it should be noted that though Morrison rejects patriarchy and white cultural supremacy, she does not aim at a separatist essentialist. That is, she refuses to replace one extreme with another. What she really wants is a united and equal racial and sexual relationship based on love. Besides, Morrison's writing intention is by no means limited to empowering ethnic females in America. Rather, she is seeking a voice for all the marginal groups all over the world.

$$\mathcal{C}hapter\ 6$$

Childhood Trauma and Its Recovery in *God Help the Child*

Toni Morrison's skilled writing technique shows the charm of her unique literary style and her deep thinking to politics and culture. Her works always have their profound meanings. In most of her novels, relying on strong political sensitivity and social responsibility, she describes African-Americans' historical process and their living status, particularly their racial trauma, to show her deep concern to their living environment.

In April 2015, Morrison's 11th novel *God Help the Child* was published by Alfred A. Knopf. Writing novels over forty years, Morrison shows the world her unlimited creative tension again in the latest novel, and arouses many scholars' and readers' high interests. Unlike previous novels, Morrison turns her attention to childhood trauma in her latest novel *God Help the Child*.

6.1 Introduction to *God Help the Child*

In 2015, Morrison published her latest novel *God Help the Child* at the ripe age of 84. This novel is listed by publications such as *Publishers Weekly* and *The New York Times* as one of their most anticipated book releases of 2015. It is the first novel by Morrison to be set in modern times which weaves a story about the way the sufferings of childhood can shape, and misshape the life of an adult.

The most striking difference between *God Help the Child* and all Morrison's previous works is that she chooses current generation as the story background in this latest novel. In plot and style of *God Help the Child*, Morrison deliberately erases the barriers between lofty Afro-American literature and contemporary urban literature. Although Morrison is generally well-known for her historical writing, all her works actually comprises an unchronological journey through the whole development process of Afro-American history. For example, *Beloved* (1987) focuses on the slavery era in the mid-nineteenth century; *A Mercy* (2008) reflects the American colonial era in the seventeenth century; *Home* (2012) describes the 1950s. At 84, Morrison seems a little bit anxious to write about the current generation. She says that is "a new challenge," "I was nervous because I didn't have a handle on the contemporary," "It's very fluid." [1] (Oatman, 2015) In fact she successfully chooses childhood trauma as the handle in *God Help the Child*, and deeply reflects the changes of American social life over the past two to three decades: Innocent children are mercilessly suffering "punishments" from all sorts of personalities.

The protagonist of this novel, Lula Ann Bridewell, who calls herself "Bride," is a blue-black beauty. The story is about the devastating consequences of a light-skinned mother Sweetness who rejects her dark-skinned daughter. Bride grows up without love, tenderness, affection or apology. Although she becomes a successful career woman when she grows up, that success doesn't translate to her personal life. Her inability to heal from childhood trauma becomes a stumbling block to her growth. Luckily, where there is darkness there is light. That contrast serves to make her attempts at reshaping her life much better. This is exactly one of the most important lessons of this novel—that you shouldn't be defined by the sins of other people. What is done to children indeed matters, but how vulnerable and resilient children can overcome seemingly insurmountable obstacles matters all the more.

Morrison is good at integrating Latin-American magic-realism into her works, combining reality with myth and fantasy, and using symbolism, stream of consciousness and other modernist techniques. In *God Help the Child*, Morrison uses magic-realism to show the heroine Bride's anxiety of watching her body turns back to that of a child—her pubic hair has vanished, her earlobes are smooth, her chest has flattened.

---

[1] Quoted from website: http://www.motherjones.com/media/2015/04/toni-morrison-interview-god-help-the-child.

What's more, Morrison is also extremely skilled in using multiple narrative perspectives to make different descriptions and evaluations by different voices around the same event. By using these techniques, the openness of texts and the participation degree of readers are much increased. In *God Help the Child*, there are at least six different narrative voices. Like Gurleen Grewal writes in *Circles of Sorrow, Lines of Struggle: The Novels of Toni Morrison*: "Her novels are multivoiced, multilayered, writerly and speakerly, both popular and literary highbrow." (1998: 1) Morrison is undoubtedly one of the greatest black female writer, and the leader figure of African-American literature in modern times. Her creations reproduce the blacks' tragic fate over the past hundreds of years and push African-American literature to a new height.

In her latest novel *God Help the Child*, Toni Morrison returns to the foundation of most of her works: childhood and its traumatic influence. She takes the heroine Bride back to her childhood in order to move her forward. The length of this novel is not long which has only 178 pages. As always, this novel also has elegant style, poetic words, and simple storyline. What's more, "the marker of classic Toni Morrison" (Frykholm, 2009: 40) are here in this novel: "shifting narrators and perspectives that make it difficult to know who is talking to whom and how much they can be trusted," "a far richer and more interesting vocabulary to talk about race and racial identity than we used to," "something strange going on with the physical body of the main character." (Frykholm, 2009: 40) All of these markers add up to a rich meditation on race problem, social issues, national identity and family identity which root in the problem of childhood.

The basic meaning of trauma theory helps a lot with the interpretation of childhood trauma in *God Help the Child*. Through this novel, Morrison helps people to probe into the following questions:

(1) What are the roots of childhood trauma in this novel?

(2) What are the traumatic symptoms reflected in the thoughts and acts of the characters?

(3) What method cured the characters' childhood trauma?

Following these questions, the root causes of childhood trauma and the symptoms from cultural, social and family aspects are disclosed. Morrison shows to people the main roots of childhood trauma in the novel are colorism, child molestation and family relations. Again, Morrison's usual theme of narration functions here to display the healing power of narration, for it is through narration that the main characters Bride, Booker and other characters who suffered childhood trauma are able to recover from their traumatic experiences and access to spiritual freedom and peace of mind.

Trauma is like a polygonal mirror which reflects the long-term survival situation of the blacks from ethnic, cultural, social and many other aspects. Childhood trauma is the accumulation of social problems which reveal ethnic relations, violent culture, interpersonal barriers and other aspects of contemporary social problems that need to be addressed and envisaged. *God Help the Child* starts from the theme of childhood trauma, and reveals a variety of problems in contemporary American social life. What's more, Morrison implies attacks on American's colorism, child molestation and other social issues and her appeal for narration from traumatized people in the novel. This highlights profound sense of the era and important social significance of this novel.

6.2 Triple Roots of Childhood Trauma and the Symptoms

God Help the Child begins with the birth of midnight-black Lula Ann Bridewell whose light-skinned mother Sweetness could barely stand to touch her. Sweetness raises Lula Ann at an ashamed and bitter distance, which she thinks will toughen her up. As an adult, Lula Ann changes her name into Bride. She becomes a successful and beautiful career woman and falls in love with Booker Starbern. Like Bride, Booker also suffered terrible hurts in childhood. His beloved older brother Adam was murdered by a child molester when Booker was eight years old.

The theme of *God Help the Child* can be gleaned from its title. This is a novel about how childhood trauma influences the way adults lead their lives. It finds adults struggling to overcome childhood trauma. It is easy to see that there are many similarities between the heroine Bride's and the hero Booker's lives, such as childhood trauma, direct and indirect confrontations with accused child molesters. The root sources and symptoms of their childhood traumas are hidden in the narrative.

6.2.1 Cultural Roots and the Symptoms

According to Tao Jiajun's opinion, "The development of trauma theory can be broadly divided into four stages." (2011: 118) These four stages are Freudian psychological trauma theory, Post-Freudian psychological trauma theory, race/gender trauma theory and trauma culture theory. Trauma is originated from modern violence and characterized by three intrinsic features: intrusion, belatedness and compulsive repetition. It is the symptom of modern civilization's violent essence. Psychological trauma is the basis of traumatic study, and the traumatized people can be an individual as well as a group. The psychological distress symptoms of traumatized people simultaneously call attention to the existence of an unspeakable secret and deflect attention from it. Trauma also extends to culture field. Different from psychological trauma, cultural trauma refers to the hurts to a particular group.

Skin color has always been an important topic of racial issues which causes severe cultural trauma. Most of Morrison's previous novels involve this topic. Similarly, this topic is discussed again in the newest novel *God Help the Child*. It shows in the following two different ways.

On the one hand, because of economic and social advantages, white people spread white culture to the blacks with the help of newspapers, films, advertisements and so on. For long, black people are unconsciously influenced and internalized by white people's aesthetics. Affected by colorism, they judge the appearance of themselves and people around them according to white people's aesthetics. They despise themselves and have contempt for ugly or dark-skinned black people, especially back women. They are trying to get rid of the physical characteristics of the blacks through straightening their hair, bleaching their skin and make-up, so as to obtain recognition from white people and the society. On the other hand, because the white people are politically dominant, and they control the voice of society for a long time, so the black people's social status is lower than the whites'. They suffer severe racial discrimination from the whites.

In *God Help the Child*, the cultural roots which lead to the characters' childhood trauma are skin color discrimination (colorism) within black community, as well as racial discrimination (racism) from the white community.

6.2.1.1 Colorism Within Black Community

The famous American writer Alice Walker defines colorism in *If the Present Looks Like the Past, What Does the Future Look Like?* that it is "prejudicial or preferential treatment of same-race people based solely on their color" (2005: 290). She further points out that only the problem of colorism "is addressed in our communities and definitely in our black 'sisterhoods' we cannot, as a people, progress. For colorism, like colonialism, sexism, and racism, impedes us" (290). In the black community, light-skinned blacks may enjoy or be given a sense of superiority due to their close-to-white skin. This phenomenon leads to colorism and skin color privilege which becomes a cancer that erodes the dignity of dark-skinned black people.

In *God Help the Child*, it is colorism that results in the heroine Bride's main childhood trauma. Her mother Sweetness is at the root of her pain. Sweetness is a light-skinned black woman, and all her family members' skin are also close to white, so they are rarely discriminated against in their daily lives because of skin color. "Because of my mother's skin color, she wasn't stopped from trying on hats in the department stores or using their ladies' room. And my father could try on shoes in the front part of the shoestore, not in a back room." (Morrison, 2015: 4) Sweetness is proud of this, and she insists that this is an advantage for them as light-skinned blacks to retain their personal dignity. So they never "let themselves drink from a 'colored only' fountain even if they were dying of thirst" (4).

However, the birth of her "midnight black, Sudanese black" (3) daughter defeated her sense of superiority. Lula Ann's birth skin was pale like all babies, but when she saw that skin color turned blue-black right before her eyes, Sweetness was going crazy. It "embarrassed" (4) her. She feels perplexed and murmurs, "It's not my fault. So you can't blame me. I didn't do it and have no idea how it happened ... She was so black she scared me." (3) The birth of dark-skinned Lula Ann makes Sweetness surprised, uneasy, unacceptable, and then feel embarrassed and worried. She wishes that the baby "hadn't been born with that terrible color" (5). "I know I went crazy for a minute because once—just for a few seconds—I held a blanket over her face and pressed ... I even thought of giving her away to an orphanage someplace." (5) Lula Ann's dark skin let her self-esteem of being a light-skinned black suddenly disappeared. In order to maintain her self-esteem, she begins to treat

Lula Ann with rough and cold attitude instead of warmth and affection a mother should have.

Based on her understanding of colorism, she tries to keep distance with Lula Ann in order to "protect her" (Morrison, 2015: 41). For example, she doesn't take Lula Ann outside much. Every time she pushes her in the baby carriage, some friends or strangers "would lean down and peek in to say something nice" (6). But when they find Lula Ann's dark skin, they will "give a start or jump back before frowning" (6). This makes Sweetness feel very hurt, and more certain of what she does towards her daughter. What's more, she told Lula Ann to call her "Sweetness" instead of "Mother" or "Mama." The reason is "being that black and having what I think are too-thick lips calling me 'Mama' would confuse people" (6). Sweetness said "it was safer" (6), because she is so selfish that she only thinks for herself. It was safer for herself instead of for little Lula Ann. She doesn't want anyone know that she has a so dark-skinned baby who will make her feel embarrassed. But what a child really need is not this kind of selfish safety, but the warm care and approval from her mother. Perhaps there is a resistance psychology to call her mother "Sweetness" in her heart, Bride only called her mother "S" when she wrote a letter to her mother at the end of this novel.

It's easy to see from this novel that Sweetness spends all her life trying to explain why she was never able to love her daughter. She cannot overcome her horror at Lula Ann's dark skin, and she spends all her energy trying to justify the unjustifiable. "I had to be strict, very strict. Lula Ann needed to learn how to behave, how to keep her head down and not to make trouble … Her color is a cross she will always carry. But it's not my fault. It's not my fault. It's not my fault. It's not." (7) The dissimilation of aesthetics not only makes Sweetness lose the right judgement to beauty and ugliness, but also affects her judgment to her daughter. This results in the dissimilation of her family values which in its narrow sense embodies in her attitude towards family affairs and family members, especially in her attitude towards her daughter. Therefore, Bride lives a miserable life in her childhood under her mother and the black community's stubborn prejudice of colorism.

6.2.1.2 Racism from the Outside White Community

In addition to colorism, black people also suffer severe racial discrimination from the white community. It is another very important factor which causes the character's childhood trauma. The aesthetics the whites advocate is based on the physical characteristics of European white people: Woman who has white skin, blonde hair and blue eyes was identified as a beauty. On the contrary, woman who has black skin, curly hair was considered ugly. This long-standing aesthetics denies the black people's inherent ethnic beauty and leaves "indelible marks upon their (black women's) group consciousness, marking their memories forever and changing their future identity in fundamental and irrevocable ways" (Alexander, 2004: 1).

In fact, whether black or white, like Booker says, "it's just a color … a genetic trait—not a flaw, not a curse, not a blessing nor a sin." (Morrison, 2015: 143) This view is also implied in the answer that Evelyn gives Rain when she asks Evelyn why is Bride's skin so black: "for the same reason yours is so white," "born that way" (85). However, although the law in America was against discrimination in the nineties, it was still very hard for black people to live in the white community. In the novel, when Sweetness and Lula Ann are abandoned by Louis, Sweetness has to find another place to live with her daughter. But it is really so difficult to rent a place if a light-skinned mother has a dark-skinned child. So Sweetness leaves Lula Ann with a teenage cousin to babysit when she applies to landlords. The landlord Mr. Leigh upped the rent seven dollars from the price he advertised, but Sweetness had no other choice but only accept this unfair treatment.

> Some of you probably think it's a bad thing to group ourselves according to skin color—the lighter, the better—in social clubs, neighborhoods, churches, sororities, even colored schools. But how else can we hold on to a little dignity? How else can you avoid being spit on in a drugstore, shoving elbows at the bus stop, walking in the gutter to let whites have the whole sidewalk, charged a nickel at the grocer's for a paper bag that's free to white shoppers? Let alone all the name-calling. I heard about all of that and much, much more. (4)

From the perspective of sociology, what makes a mother treat her child in a cold way is the deep-rooted skin color consciousness and racial discrimination in the real world. Obviously, Sweetness witnesses how colorism and racism troubles and devastates the blacks' spirit in the process of her growth. It goes without saying that the discriminations her light-skinned parents have not suffered are common for dark-skinned blacks. The rules of skin privileges and racial superiority are deeply rooted in her mind.

Through the case of Bride, Morrison reveals the influence of skin color and racial differences on the blacks' family relationships and their personal life, and explores the values of beauty in the society at the same time. She is trying to let us think about the definition of beauty and ugliness, and its relation with individuals, culture and the society.

6.2.2 Social Root and the Symptoms

In addition to colorism and racism, child molestation is another big problem which causes childhood trauma. Throughout *God Help the Child*, children who have been sexually abused appear and disappear as mysterious visions. Child sexual abuse touches every person of every color in this novel and is perhaps its most important marker for the utter failure of adults to feel pain of their children. Adults are perpetrators of pain or selfish hoarders of love. "The child" of the novel's title appears already traumatized by them again and again. Through the description of these child molestation cases, Morrison exactly reflected one of the serious social problems in today's America and expressed her deep humanistic concern.

6.2.2.1 The Witness of an Incident of Sexual Abuse in Childhood

The heroine Bride saw her childhood landlord Mr. Leigh raping a little boy in a walled area led to the basement.

> He was leaning over the short, fat legs of a child between his hairy white thighs. The boy's little hands were fists, opening and closing. His crying was soft, squeaky and loaded with pain. The man's trousers were down around his ankles. I leaned over the windowsill and stared. The man had the same red hair as Mr. Leigh, the landlord. (54)

She tells her mother what she had seen, but that made Sweetness furious.

Offending Mr. Leigh means they have to look for another apartment. Sweetness knows how hard to find another place which accept dark-skinned Lula Ann, so she asked Lula Ann to keep this secret and not to say a word about it. This experience left Bride a deep childhood trauma. It was too heavy for a little child to bear this secret in mind. Although she was trying to pretend the whole thing was just silly when she told her boyfriend Booker about it, she felt so grieved that she could felt her eyes burning. Just as Booker said to Bride, "now five people know … Five is better than two but it should be five thousand" (Morrison, 2015: 55), those child molesters' evil deeds should be bravely exposed to the public because keeping silent is of no avail.

Bride's boyfriend Booker is another person who also suffers a lot from childhood trauma. Booker had been raised in a large, tight family. He had a very good relationship with his big brother Adam, "close as a twin" (114). The happiness was ended after Adam was murdered by a child molester when Booker was eight years old.

> Booker went with his father to identify the remains. Filthy, rat-gnawed, with a single open eye socket. The maggots, overfed and bursting with glee, had gone home leaving fastidiously clean bones under the strips of his mud-caked yellow T-shirt. The corpse wore no pants or shoes. (114)

In Booker's view, Adam was more than a brother to him, "more than the 'A' of parents who'd named their children alphabetically" (115). Adam was the one who knew his thinking and feeling, whose humor was both raucous and instructive but never cruel, the smartest one who loved each of his siblings, especially Booker. After Adam's death, Booker had no companion any more. He feels confused and unforgivable that his parents and siblings are trying to move on after his beloved Adam's funeral: "How could they pretend it was over? How could they forget and just go on? Who and where was the murderer?" (117) Adam's death became a nightmare for Booker and left so indelible trauma in his little heart that he cannot move forward by only himself.

Although the murderer was caught six years later, it couldn't heal Booker's trauma. "What he wanted was not the man's death; he wanted his life, and spent time inventing scenarios involving pain and despair without end." (120) Childhood trauma caused Booker's terrible revenge psychology and endless negative emotion. No one can imagine that the murderer is the one who was thought as "the nicest man in the world" (118). He was a retired easygoing auto mechanic whose smile was always welcoming, attractive. He used his little cute terrier as a lure and molested six boys. They "were kept bound while molested, tortured and there were amputations" (119). After killed those innocent boys, the devil tattooed their names across his shoulders. How cruel and mentally abnormal he was! The unwitting tattoo artist said he thought those were his children's names, not the names of other peoples. Finally, Booker found out a satisfactory and calming solution to the memory of Adam when he was sixteen. He tattooed a small rose on his left shoulder. "Was this the same chair the predator sat in, the same needle used on his paste-white skin?" (120) Those questions hanging over and over in Booker's mind when he was in the tattoo shop but he didn't ask anything.

Childhood trauma brought Booker into a painful abyss, and left a heavy imprint for his growth. Since then, he could not tolerate any abuse against children. When he saw a stranger molesting some faculty children at the edge of campus playground, his "fist was in the man's mouth before thinking about it" (109). Another time when he noticed there was a little baby screaming and crying in a car while her parents were indifferent to her and sucking on a crack pipe, "he walked over to the car, yanked open the door, dragged the man out, smashed his face and kicked away the pipe that had fallen to the ground" (128). All the three fighting adults were arrested to the police station and the little crying girl was sent to childcare services. At last Booker's girlfriend Felicity paid the fine, but unfortunately they ended their relationship after that. Booker once again became a homeless outcast.

Another very important event in this novel could also be explained by this kind of psychological resistance. At the beginning of the story, Booker abandoned Bride with only one sentence "You [are] not the woman I want" (8). No one understands what happened with these two affectionate lovers at that time, and no one can explain Booker's sudden departure, even Bride herself. At the end of the story, we finally find out that the reason is Bride told Booker she wanted to visit a child molester (Sofia Huxley) with presents and money. She tried to "help her forget and take the edge off bad luck, hopelessness and boredom" (12). Booker knows nothing about the truth, so he can't understand why Bride was set on going to help a molester. They quarreled about her promise, then he ran off and disappeared. Thus it can be seen that after childhood trauma of child molestation, Booker can't tolerate any sympathy to molesters, even if that sympathy was from his beloved girlfriend.

Several years later, Booker was invited by his mother for the celebratory family gathering after assured of his master degree. Everything was smooth and almost cheerful until he went to the room which he once shared with Adam. The room was totally different now and was occupied by his sister Carole. Everything about the wonderful memory between Adam and him was erased. What's more, he suggested to his parents to establish a modest scholarship in Adam's name as a memorial, but his father "was decidedly against it" (124). Those things made Booker feel frustrated and disheartened. What he understood as family loyalty, his siblings saw as "manipulation—as trying to control them—outfathering their father" (125). Booker has had enough of their indifferent attitude, so he quarreled with them, shut the door and stepped out into the rain. After a brief rebellious hustle and bustle, he returned to loneliness, and even despair. He became even more reticent since then and never tell anyone about his feeling of sadness, even Bride.

6.2.2.2 Personal Experiences of Sexual Abuse in Childhood

In addition to these two main characters, some other characters also suffer severe childhood trauma in this novel. The first one is Bride's closest friend Brooklyn. Child abuse shaped her and the rest of her life.

> When my uncle started thinking of putting his fingers between my legs
> again, even before he knew himself what he was planning to do, I hid or ran
> or screamed with a fake stomachache so my mother would wake from her
> drunken nap to tend to me. (139)

Brooklyn was sexually abused by her uncle when she was a little kid. Her mother didn't take care of her and was always drunk. So when the miserable event happened to her, she realized that "there was nobody but me to take care of me so I invented myself, toughened myself" (140), She escaped from home when she was only fourteen. The occurrences that children are sexually abused by their loved ones are common in this novel. Morrison also briefly describes another case about Booker's cousin, Queen's daughter, Hannah. She complained to her mother Queen that her stepfather "fondled her" (170), but Queen ignored her complaint. The consequence is "the ice between them never melted" (170). Hannah left Queen and never came back, just as Bride left Sweetness.

Rain is another important character who suffers child molestation when she was a little girl. Her mother exploited her for money. "Some guy. A regular. One of the ones she let do it to me … He stuck his pee thing in my mouth and I bit it." (101) Having suffered so many humiliations, Rain was scared by men and she confessed to Bride that men made her feel sick, so she chose to act against instead of keeping obedient to them. However, blinded by profit, her mother didn't protect her, but "apologized to him, gave back his twenty-dollar bill and made me stand outside" (101) and evicted her from home ruthlessly. "She wouldn't let me back in. I kept pounding on the door. She opened it once to throw me my sweater." (102) Such hardhearted mother left severe trauma in the girl's heart. That's why when Bride asked her what she would say to her mother if she met her again, this poor girl answered: "Nothing, I'd chop her head off." (102) It's hard to imagine what made such a little girl so revengeful to her mother. "I used to think about it a lot. How it would look—her eyes, her mouth, the blood shooting out of her neck. Made me feel good just thinking about it." (102) Maybe the fearful street life she lived after she was evicted can explain her distorted mind better. "You had to find out where the public toilets were … how to avoid children's services, police, how to escape drunks, dope heads. But knowing where to sleep was safe was the most important thing." (102) This kind of terrible life made the little girl feel despair. All in all, child sexual violence results in that child's violent tendency. Children are always weak and helpless, so the traumatic experiences they suffered will stimulate a natural rebellion within their hearts.

It can be seen from the above characters that those traumatic experiences have a profound effect on children. The sexual abuse victims in this novel include not only black children, but also white ones. Along with child molestation, some other bad phenomena such as violence and money warship were exposed to readers. It shows Morrison's deep concern to the pervasive social problems in modern

America beyond ethnic boundaries.

6.2.3 Family Root and the Symptoms

Increasing numbers of children are growing up in broken families and this has created a need for people to develop understandings about the traumatic experiences of the children who grow up in such an environment. Broken families are associated with difficulties including health and welfare related problems, such as early sexual activity, greatly increased rates of adolescent pregnancy, poor school performance, lowered self-esteem, and an increase in likelihood of demonstrating adverse behaviors compared to children who have close family relationships. Therefore, the family root which causes the characters' childhood trauma is the broken family relationships in their childhood.

6.2.3.1 Lacking of Mother's Love in Childhood

In the absence of her family's, especially her mother's, love and acceptance, Bride had a very miserable childhood. Although she is the only child of her mother, she is rarely accompanied by her mother's warmth in her growth. Her mother is always cold and harsh in her memory. Sweetness never touch her because of her skin color. "Distaste was all over her face when I was a little and she had to bathe me. Rinse me, actually, after a halfhearted rub with a soapy washcloth." (Morrison, 2015: 31) At that time, Bride was desperately for maternal love. "I used to pray she would slap my face or spank me just to feel her touch." (31) For example, she made little mistakes desperately, but Sweetness had a lot of different ways to punish her without touching her skin, such as bed without supper, locking her in the room or screaming at her.

Desperate for her mother's approval, Bride accused Sofia Huxley of child molestation that put this innocent teacher in jail for fifteen years at the age of eight. Her performance in the court not only won others' smile, but also received Sweetness's rare maternal love. As it turned out, Sweetness was indeed pleased by her "brave" and "righteous" behavior.

> The lessons I taught her paid off because in the end she made me proud
> as a peacock. It was in that case with that gang of pervert teachers—three

of them, a man and two women—that she knocked it out of the park. Young
as she was, she behaved like a grown-up on the witness stand—so calm and
sure of herself. (41)

Apparently, Sweetness was very satisfied with her daughter's performance in
the court. When they walked down the courthouse steps, Sweetness held Bride's
hand for the first time which surprised Bride as much as it pleased her. They
walked the streets hand in hand and then Sweetness bought Bride a pair of tiny
gold earrings as a gift for her. Except this special case, Sweetness didn't show her
love to Bride again. Without maternal love, Bride became hard to handle when
she turned twelve going on thirteen. "She was talking back, refusing to eat what
I cooked, primping her hair. When I braided it, she'd go to school and unbraid
it." (178) What's more, she changed her name from Lula Ann Bridewell to Bride.
The broken family engulfed the happy childhood which was supposed to belong
to Bride, and destroyed her relationship with her mother. When she grew up, she
left her mother to pursue her own life immediately. She became a beautiful and
successful regional manager in the cosmetics industry and is about to launch a new
cosmetics line called "YOU, GIRL" for "girls and women of all complexions from
ebony to lemonade to milk" (10).

The fourth edition of *The Diagnostic and Statistical Manual of Mental
Disorders* (Frances, 1994) defines PTSD (post-traumatic stress disorder) and notes
that the essential feature of PTSD is as follows:

> The development of characteristic symptoms following exposure to an
> extreme traumatic stressor involving direct personal experience of an event
> that involves actual or threatened death or serious injury," or "other threat to
> one's physical integrity; or witnessing an event that involves death, injury,"
> or "a threat to the physical integrity of another person"; or "learning about
> unexpected or violent death, serious harm," or "threat of death or injury
> experienced by a family member or other close associate." (424)

Some typical symptoms resulting from the exposure to the extreme trauma
include "persistent reexperiencing of the traumatic event, persistent avoidance of

stimuli associated with the trauma and numbing of general responsiveness, and persistent symptoms of increased arousal" (424). The individual has persistent symptoms of anxiety or increased arousal that are not present before the trauma. These symptoms may include difficulty falling or straying asleep that may be due to recurrent nightmares during which the traumatic event is relived, hypervigilance, and exaggerated startle response. Some individuals report irritability or outbursts of anger or difficulty concentrating or completing tasks.

Although the childhood lie brought Bride short-term happiness, it also gave her long-term psychological burden in the following decades. It has haunted her, so on the day Sofia was released from prison, she went to visit her with money and gifts. But her life started falling apart when she met with the just-paroled Sofia. Sofia's angry rejection of her gifts, coinciding with the inexplicable departure of her boyfriend Booker inspired such self-doubt that Bride fears regressing into little Lula Ann. Bride was anxiously watching her own body metamorphose into that of a child. First her pubic hair has vanished. Then her chest has flattened. At last her earlobes lost the piercings her mother gave her after she testified against Sofia. It was as if her body was returning to the one she had before the lie. Was this return death, disease, or redemption? As in the darkest fairy tales, there will be fire and death. Serious-minded Booker cannot leave behind a terrible family tragedy, and as Bride pursues him for answers to his abandonment, they are both transformed in more ways than one.

6.2.3.2 The Absence of Father's Company in Childhood

In addition to the cruelty of the mother, father's prolonged absence also increases strain on the mother and leads to less cohesive family function which may result in higher levels of distress in the child. From birth, Bride never felt fatherly love. Her deep black skin color caused the fights between her parents and broke their marriage to pieces. Her father treated her "like she was a stranger— more than that, an enemy" (Morrison, 2015: 5), so he never touched her and left her and her mother finally. The role of father in a family is particularly important. A lot of study of sociology and psychology shows that the absence of fatherly love will result in a child's sense of confusion, fear and abandonment that can shape their lives. "Having loving and nurturing and supportive relationships with others does not fill the void associated with the feelings of abandonment, loss, grief and unworthiness felt by children." (East & Jackson, 2007: 17) Those kind of children are much more inclined to feel angry, hurt or lonely. They tend to blame themselves for the separation of their parents. These psychological and emotional traumas seriously affect the child's physical and mental health. In other words, a complete family and intimate relationship between father and son or father and daughter will be helpful to children's physical and mental health development. On the contrary, a broken family and cold relationship between parents and children will lead to abnormal thinking and behavior in the children's growth process, and difficult-to-heal trauma. Parents are children's role models, as well as a direct source for them to get care and protection.

However, in Bride's family, her father evaded his responsibility and abandoned his wife and daughter. This resulted in the lacks of a direct male role model in Bride's life, a sense of security and the ability of self-protection. This can be proved by a study which shows that "individuals experiencing parental absence and the ensuing feelings of abandonment can also develop negative views of others" (17). These negative views includes "feelings of mistrust, lack of respect, and not being able to believe that a supportive, loving intimate relationship with a man was possible" (17). Youths of broken families experience greater difficulties in establishing intimate relationships with others than those of intact families. At the same time,

> Girls whose early family experiences are characterized by father absence tend to develop sexual psychologies that are consistent with the expectation that male parental investment is unreliable and unimportant; these girls are hypothesized to develop in a manner that accelerates onset of sexual activity and reproduction, reduces reticence in forming sexual relationships, and orients the individual toward relatively unstable pair-bonds. (817)

Bride has no certain boyfriend before she meets Booker. She never treats any relationship seriously. "Men leaped and I left myself be caught. For a while, anyway, until my sex life became sort of like Diet Coke—deceptively sweet minus nutrition. More like a PlayStation game imitating the safe glee of virtual violence and just as brief." (Morrison, 2015: 36) Fortunately, she became wholehearted after she met Booker. Although she was traumatized by Booker's sudden disappearance because of some misunderstandings, luckily they become frank to each other and finally live a happy life together.

6.3 Narration: An Effective Way to Recover from Childhood Trauma

Both Bride and Booker suffered severe childhood trauma when they were children. They listen to each other, talk to each other, and cure each other from childhood trauma. Listening and understanding to each other help the characters to relieve their trauma and release the pain. It's extremely important for victims to recover from trauma by telling trauma to others, facing trauma in the company of others, overcoming trauma-induced anxiety, fear, and restlessness. Those people who have experienced tragic events are shrouded in their growth and are in urgent need of decompression and healing. Even as adults, they cannot escape from the shadow of the past. Fortunately, main characters in this novel all found a way to narrate their traumas to others finally, and therefore recovered from childhood trauma and obtained the peace of mind.

6.3.1 Speaking Out the Ashamed Truth Loudly: Bride's Approach to Recovery

Judith Herman argues that traumatic events lead to "survivors questioning to basic interpersonal relationships, breaking down their dependence on family, friendship, love, and group, and shattering the self-construction formed and maintained in relations with others" (1992: 51). Dori Laub also shares the same view with Herman that anyone who wants to get rid of trauma, they cannot face it alone. They need to build relationships with others or the outside world and recover from the relationships. Stable social relationships can re-establish victims' sense of trust and security. Victims can build self-esteem and escape from trauma in the process of establishing relationships with others.

The process that Bride seeks to tell her childhood trauma to others is twists and turns. Because of her dark-black skin, she cannot get any dignity and love from her parents. There is no one for her to listen to her traumatic experiences, and also she feels ashamed to tell others of her sin. At her age of six, she had tried to tell her mother that the landlord Mr. Leigh raped a little child. But she was warned by Sweetness that "don't you say a word about it. Not to anybody, you hear me, Lula? Forget it. Not a single word" (Morrison, 2015: 54). What's more, the lie she said that made the innocent Sofia arrested into prison was a sore on her heart for fifteen years. She cannot face it, cannot tell others about it bravely. However, no matter how hard she tries to ignore these childhood trauma, her mind always knows the truth and wants to clarify it.

After she fell in love with Booker, she told Booker about what she saw Mr. Leigh done to the little child. Booker comforted her and told her that "correct what you can; learn from what you can't" (56) which brought her more courage. She "felt such relief" (56), "felt curried, safe, owned" (56). She even thought that she had found her guy. However, Bride ignored that the relationship between them was extremely unbalanced.

> Ispilled my heart to him; he told me nothing about himself. I talked; he listened. Then he split, left without a word. Mocking me, dumping me exactly as Sofia Huxley did. Neither of us had mentioned marriage, but I really thought I had found my guy. (62)

Overly concerned with talking, Bride ignored the fact that Booker was always played a role of listener. He suffered his childhood trauma on his own, and also accepted more negative mood from Bride. He said nothing about himself. Therefore, until he left her, she finally found that she knew nothing about the man she loved.

She thought she knew him because she knew that he had degrees from some university. She didn't know which university it exactly is, and she only guessed it from his T-shirts which were printed a university's name. "I never thought about that part of his life because what was important in our relationship, other than our lovemaking and his complete understanding of me, was the fun we had." (61) This shows Bride only cares about what Booker brings to her in their daily life. Moreover, she finds an altisonant reason for this action: "I thought he liked me especially because I never probed, nagged or asked him about his past. I left him his private life. I thought it showed how much I trusted him—that it was him I was attracted to, not what he did." (62) She said she could never have described her childhood to others as she did to Booker. Actually she indeed tells everything about herself to him, except the worst thing she had done to Sofia Huxley. That's a secret haunted in her mind but she dare not to tell anyone else including her beloved boyfriend.

She wants to make up the mistake she once made to Sofia, but the money and gifts she prepared for Sofia were rejected angrily. At the same time, Booker abandoned her without explaining anything. These two things inspired such self-doubt that Bride fears regressing into little Lula Ann. To show the fears and pains she suffered after she lost the only one who was always willing to listen to her, Morrison uses magic realism here in the novel. Bride was anxiously watching her own body metamorphose into that of a child. Firstly, her pubic hair has vanished. Then her chest has flattened. At last her earlobes lost the piercings her mother gave her after she testified against Sofia. It was as if her body was returning to the one she had before the lie. Those illusions are actually the externalization of Bride's fears in her mind. She lost the one who can tell to, just like that she cannot tell anyone about what she had seen in her childhood; she was abandoned by Booker, just as she was abandoned by her father when she was a little girl. Those encounters are extremely like what she had experienced in her childhood and enough to make her feel helpless like that little girl.

Finally, she found Booker and blurted out the hidden secret to him in a quarrel. "I lied! I lied! I lied! She was innocent. I helped convict her but she didn't do any of that. I wanted to make amends but she beat the crap out of me and I deserved it." (153) After confession to Booker, she felt more than rested and free of tension; she felt strong. "Having confessed Lula Ann's sins she felt newly born." (162) Later, her retrogressive body was also magically rejuvenated. She "touched her earlobes, felt the return of tiny holes and teared up while grinning" (169). She is more attractive than before.

6.3.2 Pouring Out the Haunted Trauma Bravely: Booker's Approach to Recovery

Literatures, especially memoir, autobiography and letter, are a form to witness trauma, because they faithfully recorded history. Felman proposes that in our generation, a new literature—testimony—was invented. She explores the significance of this growing predominance of testimony as a privileged contemporary mode of transmission and communication, and further testifies that "testimony in effect becomes at once so central and so omnipresent in our recent cultural accounts of ourselves" (Felman & Laub, 1992: 6). Since the acts of writing in literature are acts to witness traumatic events, testimony penetrates in various kinds of literature texts in different ways, to varying degrees and on different levels. "Literary readers' acts of reading are actually an indirect process to witness trauma, experience trauma, and close to true history through literary texts." (Tao, 2013: 129)

Caruth defines trauma as "an overwhelming experience of sudden or catastrophic events in which the response to the event occurs in the often delayed, uncontrolled repetitive appearance of hallucinations and other intrusive phenomena" (1996: 11). This definition reflects the causes of trauma and its continuous effects to the traumatized people. Among all the definitions of trauma, most of them generally agree that there is a response, sometimes delayed, to overwhelming events, which takes the form of repeated, intrusive hallucinations, dreams, thoughts or behaviors stemming from the events, along with numbing that may have begun during or after the experience, and possibly also increase arousal to (and avoidance of) stimuli recalling the event. These definitions belie a very peculiar fact that the pathology cannot be defined either by the event itself—which may or may not be catastrophic, and may not traumatize everyone equally—nor can it be defined in terms of distorting personal significance attached to it. The pathology consists, rather, solely in the structure of its experience or reception: The event is not assimilated or experienced fully at the time, but only belatedly, in its repeated possession of the one who experiences it.

Since experiences and understandings are often delayed, history can no longer be acquired by treating it as complete knowledge but rather be imaged as issues which we always try to avoid. In Caruth's opinion, "to be traumatized is precisely to be possessed by an image or event" (4). However, traumatic symptoms cannot be simply interpreted as a distortion of realities, the lending of unconscious meanings to realities it wishes to ignore, or the repression of what once was wished. Therefore, Caruth proposes that literature provides narrative to readers, and the narrative provides a mode which is very close to history and memory. Felman gives Caruth high affirmation for her great contribution to trauma theory. She evaluates that among all clinical, scientific and humanistic researchers who pay their attention to trauma experience, Caruth proves through her remarkable contribution that she is a real ideologist, and the most authoritative interdisciplinary theorist in this field. "She combined trauma, psychoanalysis and history into a complete, comprehensive, innovative system by extracting a brand new reading method." (Tao, 2013: 129)

Trauma therapists believes that, according to the common symptoms of trauma, trauma treatment requires a safe environment, stable interpersonal relationships and appropriate listeners. Dori Laub insists that,

> The survivors did not only need to survive so that they could tell their stories; they also needed to tell their stories in order to survive. There is, in each survivor, an imperative need to tell and thus to come to know one's story, unimpeded by ghosts from the past against which one has to protect oneself. One has to know one's buried truth in order to be able to live one's life. (1995: 63)

Narration is not only the purpose and means to support the survivors to live on the ground, but also an important way for them to successfully heal themselves. The author also believes that through narration, Bride and Booker achieve physical and mental relief, forget their childhood traumatic events, and ease their inner pains.

Booker is another one in the novel who desperately need to narrate his traumatic experience to others. People who experienced childhood trauma tend to be more sensitive and irritable. His older brother Adam's death at his age of eight is always a knot in his heart. Since then, he cannot bear any sight of child molestation. Anytime he sees child molesters, he will fight against them immediately. However, those behaviors cannot hide his inner loneliness. Although he was deeply in love with Bride, he tight-lipped on his own affairs during the six months they lived together. He left his family at first, and then he left Bride without any explanation. He prefers to write his thoughts about what he "was feeling or feared" (Morrison, 2015: 163) or most often, what he "truly believed—at the time" (163) on paper, but strangely he doesn't put any punctuation on those lines. Then he mailed these things to his aunt Queen to keep them.

However, he was utterly lacking of narration in his life. That's why his childhood trauma cannot be cured before he tells the truth to Bride. After Bride told him the ashamed secret, he finally realized that he also needs to open his heart and tell her the pains buried in his minds for many years. At last he introspected to himself that "what kind of love is it that requires an angel and only an angel for its commitment?" (Morrison, 2015: 160). "Then he offered her the hand she had craved all her life, the hand that did not need a lie to deserve it, the hand of trust and caring for—a combination that some call natural love." (175) It can be seen that narration has brought profound changes in self and interpersonal relationships.

Bakhtin believes that "any concrete utterance is a link in the chain of speech communication of a particular sphere" (1986: 91). What's more, "utterances are not different to one another, and are not self-sufficient; they are aware of and mutually reflect one another" (91). Those people who talk to others, they actually do not expect passive understanding. That is to say, they do not want to only duplicate their own ideas in someone else's mind. On contrary, they expect "response, agreement, sympathy, objection, execution, and so forth" (69). In the novel, Booker asked Bride "you never told anybody?" (Morrison, 2015: 55) and argues that it's better to let more people know about the child abuse case. This shows that narrating to others not only can decompress and cure the victims, but also can contribute to the solution of the problems.

At the end of the story, Bride and Booker got the freedom and tranquility of their mind. "Each of them began to imagine what the future would certainly be." (175) The future they imagine is: "A child. New life. Immune to evil or illness, protected from kidnap, beatings, rape, racism, insult, hurt, self-loathing, abandonment. Error-free. All goodness. Minus wrath." (175) This is indeed the hope of the society and the life that Morrison conveys to the public through *God Help the Child*.

6.4 Trauma in Common

Morrison's novels always depict the traumatic experience of the blacks, reflect the psychological pains of them, and seek for a way for them to get rid of trauma. Her works highlight the pursuit of freedom, self-searching of the blacks under the multiple oppressions of race, class, politics and culture. Using her pen, Morrison calls for attention to the bitter experience of the blacks and find a solution for them to get rid of oppression and realize freedom and equality.

The childhood traumas of the heroine Bride and the hero Booker mainly come from culture, society and family. Colorism, racism, child molestation and family relationships are big social problems which root in today's U.S. society and deserve paying much more attention. Children who suffered ethnic, cultural or emotional trauma show different traumatic symptoms in their growth. What's more, trauma has a nature of continuity. Unresolved traumatic events will haunt the victims as nightmares, hallucinations, flashbacks and some other forms. In the author's opinion, avoiding mentioning the traumatic experience, writing and some other ways which attempt to cure trauma are ineffective. Victims who want to cure trauma have to establish contact with the outside world at first. Then they need to narrate their traumatic experience to right listeners in a safe environment.

Trauma is one of the most important themes in Morrison's novels. The protagonists in many of her novels, such as Pecola Breedlove in *The Bluest Eye*, Florens in *A Mercy* and Frank Money in *Home*, were living in different eras, but they all suffered pains caused by racism because of their common black identity. Especially to those black women, racial and gender discrimination made their trip to seek self-identity extremely difficult. Through these characters, Morrison sketches out the blacks' history from the initial stage of the slavery to the present, and reveals their deep racial trauma.

Compared to Morrison's other traumatic novels, *God Help the Child* has many distinct characteristics. First of all, Morrison sets the contemporary U.S. society as the story background for the first time. Therefore, the heroine Bride in this novel no longer suffers a lot from the slavery like the heroine Pecola Breedlove in *The Bluest Eye* or the heroine Florens in *A Mercy*. What's more, the blacks and the whites in this novel are friends with each other. This enhances the novel's sense of the times, and shows the inter-ethnic inclusion and integration in today's diverse American society. Secondly, this novel is no longer a tragic story. Although this novel mainly pays attention to childhood traumatic memories of the characters, it also depicts how they all try to change their lives by their own efforts. Therefore, this novel does not bring the readers a heavy sense of oppression. Not only the end of the novel is full of optimism and happiness, but also Morrison's skillful writing adds more peaceful color to this story. Thirdly, Morrison has created the black female image Bride who is full of the characteristics of the contemporary era. This character who lives in the 21st century is in stark contrast to other female characters in Morrison's other works who are highly oppressed by racism and sexism. Bride is a beautiful, confident, and independent figure in the novel. Although suffered severe childhood trauma, she chooses to keep away from the root of her trauma and creates her own life independently instead of indulging in the distress and pains. In the help of the image designer, she tries to shape a beautiful self, pursues her own happiness desperately. Finally she achieves what she wishes, and gets ready to welcome a new life with her boyfriend Booker together.

Through this character, Morrison shows a new image that is totally different from the constant black female images in the previous novels. Moreover, this shows her strong faith in the progress of human society and good wishes for the future life without trauma.

This novel not only brings public awareness of the relationship between text and the real life, but can also remind the public to modify their existing perception of the discourse surrounding childhood trauma. The description of this novel about childhood trauma invites public dialogue about the perception of childhood trauma. Morrison accomplishes this by showing the readers a variety of individuals who suffer from childhood trauma, from dark skin to light skin to white skin, and by showing how factors outside of the individual's control coalesce to produce childhood trauma.

The study of the relationship between literature and trauma can take a step further, since literature has the ability to bring public attention to the impact of childhood trauma and to challenge the way society treats childhood trauma. The connection between literature, mental trauma and the humanities is only beginning to be acknowledged, but the initial outcomes suggest that there is great benefit to be attained. Because of the length limitation, this chapter only discussed the triple roots of childhood trauma and their symptoms and the recovery way for the main characters in this novel. A comparative study of all characters' traumatic experience in all Morrison's works is also worth conducting follow-up study. This is a direction and a key point for the author to carry out further study.

Conclusion

African-Americans have been frequently undervalued and relegated to a marginal place within American culture and the American literary tradition; writers in the dominant group have often silenced and misrepresented the subjugated group. The mainstream society has manipulated the images of African Americans in order to maintain its power structure, frequently creating non-threatening stereotypical portraits of African-Americans, which permeate the American canon, like tragic mulattos and mammies faithful to their white employers. As a late-twentieth-century black woman writer charged with the cultural and artistic representation of the life and history of her people, now finally casting off the shackles of slavery and segregation, Morrison wrote her literary works more powerfully and politically to instruct her people, to de-center the white logos and to create a universe of critical and fictional meanings where blackness will no longer connote absence, negation and evil but will come to stand instead for affirmation, presence, and good—a struggle for the right of Afro-American literature to exist. She is writing to lift the black self out of the hole, to bring black meanings out of the semantic shadows of the Master's language and to affirm these meanings in a medium which can truly be called a black text, a text whose margins are ruled by the black logos.

Morrison, acutely aware of the place historically assigned to black people and suspicious of white middle-class feminism, refuses to be influenced by stereotypes but rather attempts to depict her characters as subjects that emerge from an oppressed situation and who seek survival. African Americans must negotiate a place for themselves within a dominant culture; how they situate themselves with respect to their history and culture is a pervasive theme of Morrison's novels. In her works, Morrison offers a penetrating look at the lives of African Americans and scrutinizes the influence of the mainstream culture, especially on the lives of African-American women.

Morrison's fictions are of universal humanity and moral authority. Like an excellent singer of her people, Morrison not only makes her novel full of rhythms but also exhibits well among the lines her people's good virtues like bravery, diligence, versatility, dexterity and the deep love for life through her skillful singing. What concerns Morrison is how the black, as a marginalized member of the American society, can survive, "not to make a living—but how to survive whole in a world where we are all of us, in some measure, victims of something" (Taylor-Guthrie, 1994: 40). Morrison's fiction narrates a resurrection ritual of people called to make a home on the site of exile, called to lift themselves from the pain of loss and longing, and called to know themselves again differently. As Morrison noted: "… on the site of some information and a little bit of guesswork you journey to a site to see what remains were left behind and to reconstruct the world that these remains imply." (1987: 112)

In her novels, Toni Morrison identifies and explores the mechanisms by which black people have been able to re-make themselves again and again on the site of exile—in the American South, in the American North, and elsewhere in the "New World." Through these explorations Morrison reveals that music has functioned as a mode and institution of invention and, therefore, as a blueprint and resource for recreating a whole self.

Morrison's objective is not simply to uncover the galaxy of buried stimuli motivating the actions of a handful of black people or to reveal the means by which this "handful" reclaims and re-sounds a wholesome purpose through her writings. Rather, the most important contribution of her fiction is in providing a mechanism for uncovering the many galaxies that constitute our entire social universe, and, thereby, a blueprint for constructing more fully human relationships. Indeed, her fiction re-sounds the purpose identified by James Baldwin four and a half decades earlier, in 1962: "One is not attempting to save twenty million people. One is attempting to save an entire country and that means an entire civilization, and the price for that is high. The price for that is to understand one's self." (89)

By borrowing music aesthetic from black music, Morrison is trying to realize this goal to render people, especially black people to understand themselves, to reconstruct their ethnicity and therefore to improve themselves. Actually, she will produce not black literature but literature. By creating symphonies of passion and hatred, power and perversity, color and class, Morrison searches for the sense of the human and universal that made her great to begin with concern for the human being, evocating the pathos and tragedy of human life. She compels her readers, whatever their ethnic background, "to examine centers of the self and ... to compare those centers with the 'raceless' ones with which we are, all of us, most familiar" (Hulbert, 1992: 46) and to think about how race and class differences complicate the American ideal. Comparing to Richard Wright's *Native Son*, Morrison's works emphasize on the reconciliation and harmony with the white society. But this could not prevent her from helping Afro-Americans knowing themselves. Her readers are moved by her vivid narrative and the poetic language and they are nurtured and empowered by her trust in memory and her always masterful affirmation of that which they have forgotten or never knew about the rich cultural life of their past. She insists that in order to survive, black people should maintain their cultural independence in addition to possessing their political rights and their economic independence. Therefore, black people's cultural root is very important for their survival, independence and racial development.

The ways that are already apparent in both black music and Morrison's fiction are as follows.

Just as the literary jazz aesthetic transcends culture, race, and even language itself, Toni Morrison's fictions embody a powerful critique of dualistic thinking. In her novels, Morrison continually requires readers to confront the quite literally self-defeating and self-destructive qualities of dualistic thinking, demonstrating that half a reality is insufficient for anyone. Confronting her readers with the dangers of our customary way of perceiving the world, Morrison also suggests that transcending dualism is one ideal, imaginable route beyond our culturally ingrained and religiously sanctioned sexism, racism, and other self-narrowing dogmas. The critique of black essentialism which to some extent underpins all of Morrison's work casts light in the novels on hidden but controlling assumptions and opens up new questions about history, power, meaning, diversity and choice. She knows, however, that we are also mired in dualism that she must shake the world, mix it, and stand it on end before we can have even a glimmering of what a nondualistic existence might be. Therefore, Morrison's fictions depict a series of negotiations—between dispersion and rootedness, dislocation and relocation, trauma and triumph, South and North, village values and urban attitudes, rupture and continuity, independence and interdependence, silence and sounding—which define the experience of diaspora for African Americans. All her novels are anchored in an ever growing social complexity, the new pluralism of racial, ethnic, class and cultural forms.

Just as African American music especially jazz designates the division between the Western cultural heritage and the West African cultural heritage, Morrison's fictions also mark the distinction between the Western cultural heritage and the West African cultural heritage. However, just as the division that "jazz" calls or marks is not to be understood as a strict boundary or as a separation into clear-cut categories, Morrison's fiction lays its emphasis on the hybrid quality of the Euro-American tradition and the Western African one. Jazz signifies a demarcation, a borderline that accommodates an interpenetration of spheres, the wholeness particular to hybridity, especially given that jazz is an eclectic musical form syncretic of the Euro-American tradition and the Western African one, which is the hallmark of African American arts. Modeling her discourse on patterns of adaptation created in black music, Morrison manages to revise literary traditions from a specifically African-American perspective. Whatever one may think of Morrison's politics on race in America, their primary source and its manifestations in her work are unquestionably tied into her awareness and re-enactment of African-American cultural traditions. In her fiction, characters deeply rooted in the African American tradition have a more integrated world view. Her works, and specifically *Jazz*, are the product of a continuing process of adaptation and reinvention of literary forms based on altered content that is characteristic of African-American literature as a culturally autonomous field of aesthetic production.

From the historical point of view, being sold to America, the African lost the connection with the native culture and the support of the original society. Infiltrated by the colonial culture, their ethnic culture was completely destroyed. Meanwhile, external hegemony exerted a subtle influence on the African blacks' psychology. The distorted blacks from passively to actively accepted the identity and social position that the colonial system imposed. Facing the conflict between the two heterogeneous cultures, the black ethnic consciousness was weakened and close to be exterminated.

The ways to cure the historical trauma accumulated in the blacks' minds and to free themselves from the cognitive mistake and the exigent problems related to the black people's fate and future make Morrison deep in meditation. Through careful consideration, Morrison puts forward a good plan to cure the psychological trauma by neo-slave narrative discourse based on African traditional culture. She attempts to carefully sort out the slave history by neo-slave narrative discourse, amends the historical memories and further resists the non-mainstream marginalized social position to arouse ethnic consciousness and to reconstruct ethnic identity. Meanwhile, Morrison, based on the ancient African culture, deeply explores the modern significance of traditional culture to construct African-American ethnic culture. In the novel creation, she consciously carries on the black cultural tradition, uses abundant cream of ethnic culture, such as folk stories, mythological ceremonies and religious beliefs and makes them transformed according to the practical reality to promote the formation of the black's ethnic consciousness and culture.

However, as to the question of modern transformation, how to deal with the relationship between the ancient traditional culture and modern Western culture, Morrison makes her opinion clear "from exclusion to amalgamation" in her novel *Paradise*. While return to tradition is not the revival of oldness and backwardness, amalgamation is not equal to cater to the white's mainstream culture and to lose ethnic characteristics. What's more important is to transcend the dualistic values of center and margin, civilization and barbarism, and to meet the rich foreign culture with magnanimous, confident and open mind to accommodate to the modernized and globalized trend of the times. As for the question how Morrison amalgamates the modern and ancient culture, and Western and ethnic culture without losing the particularity of ethnic culture is pending further discussion.

Like the music she models on, Morrison's concept of narration is a confluence of separate cultural traditions; like the music, it offers a unique language for creative communication and interaction, constantly open to new influences that can be creatively and democratically incorporated into an existing structure. This concept of being open to changes and being dynamic can be found in Morrison's willingness to acknowledge the possibility of a second chance for Ruby, which is implied in the final instance, when she has Misner, who has for a long time seriously questioned his willingness to remain in the conservative community, decide to stay. Her rejection of her community's exceptionalism notwithstanding, in the final instance Morrison chooses African Americans as her focus of identification:

> Soon [Misner thinks,] Ruby will be like any other country town: the young thinking of elsewhere; the old full of regret. The sermons will be eloquent but fewer and fewer will pay attention or connect them to everyday life. How can they hold it together, he wondered, this hard-won heaven defined only by the absence of the unsaved, the unworthy and the strange? Who will protect them from their leaders? Suddenly Misner knew he would stay. Not only because Anna wanted him to ... but also because there was no better battle to fight, no better place to be than among these outrageously beautiful, flawed and proud people. (2016: 306)

Like Misner, Morrison chooses (Africa) America not because it is perfect or superior to other communities, but because it is the community that she has come to know and to love: " ... there was no better battle to fight, no better place to be." (306)

Morrison also exemplifies the traditional social tensions within America, between homogenization and the acknowledgement of hybridity, as well as America's continual attempts at regeneration and freedom through the relationship between the people in Ruby and the women in the Convent.

What Morrison tries to convey is that cultural democracy and hybridity at their core possess a positive transfiguring power for African American people and American people in general. For instance, as Convent women in *Paradise* reject the imposed definitions of their selves and share their own experiences with each other, the Convent becomes that "Third Space" of enunciation which for Bhabha allows for cultural difference. By the end of the novel, the Convent has evolved from a mixed cultural background into a projection of paradise, making the claim to a hierarchical purity of cultures untenable.

Morrison believes that good novels ought to "clarify the roles that have become obscured … and they ought to give nourishment" (LeClair, 1981: 121). Her world and characters are inescapably involved with problems of perception, definition, and meaning. The attempt to sharpen these indistinct social roles involves a cultural journey that "compels us to question Western concepts of reality and uncover perceptions of reality and ways of interpretation other than those imposed by the dominant culture" (Wilentz, 1997: 61). This visionary approach is apparent in all of Morrison's literary works, which demonstrates a deep concern for validating and enriching an African American culture that has long been under attack by both external and internal forces. Arising out of both the blues tradition and a magical African folktale, Morrison's novels illustrate with particular clarity this obligation to bear active witness to the past in order to feed the hearts of a people. Thus, Morrison's novels provide "a way of bridging gaps between the Black community's folk roots, and the Black American literary tradition" (61).

The stress on shared relationship, community, and race responsibility—the traditional African principle of collectivism—is the dominant theme of Morrison's themes. Isolation literally tears apart the family—the nuclear, the extended, and the nation. Her conscious message is that African people must neither isolate themselves, nor reject their culture. Isolation is as restrictive as being bound within a class system that is not accepting. Life is hell, but togetherness, shared experience, and brotherly/sisterly love help the characters to survive, if not to forge better lives for themselves. This emphasis on social responsibility, the unselfish devotion of Africans helping other Africans, is the essence of the collectivism as is emphasized in most of her novels.

This collectivism points to another way that is essential to the survival and identity reconstruction of the African-Americans—unity—the significant way African people can survive. It is only when the Africans, through self or forced isolation, exist outside of the collective that the struggle appears endless and the burden, unbearable. When Baby Suggs (in trying to do all the work of providing for the community by herself) and Sethe (in "trying to do it all alone with her nose in the air") and Africans in general are "resigned to life without aunts, cousins, children" (Morrison, 1981: 254, 221) —these are the times when the Africans' plight is intolerable.

Therefore, the messages conveyed in Morrison's fictions are as follows: no longer should African Americans be physically intimidated by Europeans as in *The Bluest Eye*; no longer should African American people indulge in the selfish individualism of Sula; no longer should African American people ignore their duty to pass on the knowledge of their history as in *Song of Solomon*; no longer should African American people attempt to wage struggle alone and thus, unsuccessfully as in *Tar Baby*; no longer should African American people be haunted by their past as in *Beloved*; no longer should African American people pay no attention to communication between men and women (husbands and wives), individual and community as in *Jazz*; no longer should African American people dwell on their memory of having been mistreated by others and thus find excuses to mistreat others and to practice exceptionalism as in *Paradise*; no longer should African American women deny their sisterhood between each other as in *Love*. Only in this way can black Americans remove themselves from marginalized position into the mainstream.

It is through the help of African American music that Morrison realizes her goal to convey her assertion. African American music gave the reader new insights into Morrison's fiction and prompts her to become an active listener, a participant, a co-creator, one that can join the poet in his task as an interpreter of music and the articulate decipher of hidden signs beyond the complexity of feelings in the modern American cultural experience. Such an approach to the novels reminds readers that they are all manifestations of African-American expressions while keeping the essential quality of American fiction. In this sense, Morrison conveys to the world through her fiction the clear message of what Langston Hughes entitled one of his poems: "I Too Sing America."

Then, what Morrison asserts is cultural democracy based on cultural hybridization, openness, amalgamation as well as pluralism, communication among community members, solidarity, collectivism and unity, which, as distinct characteristics of African-American music, are also solutions to African-American people's dilemma of being both Africans and Americans.

Bibliography

ACHEBE C, 1975. Morning yet on creation day: essays[M]. Garden City, N.Y.: Doubleday.

ADELL S, 2002. Literary masters: Toni Morrison[M]. Detroit: Thomson Gale.

ALEXANDER J C, 2004. Towards a theory of cultural trauma[M]. Berkeley: University of California Press.

ANDERSON B C, 1971. Adaptive aspects of culture shock[J]. American anthropologist, 73 (5): 1121–1125.

ANGELO B, 1989. The pain of being black: an interview with Toni Morrison[M]. Jackson: University Press of Mississippi.

ARHIN K, 1983. The political and military role of Akan women[G]//OPPONG C. Female and male in West Africa. London: George Allen: 92–94.

ARMES R, 1987. Third world film making and the West[M]. California: University of California Press.

ASANTE M K, 2002. 100 greatest African Americans: a biographical encyclopedia[M]. Buffalo, New York: Prometheus Books.

ATKINSON Y, PAGE P, 1998. "I been worried sick about you too, Macon": Toni Morrison, the South, and the oral tradition[J]. Studies in the literary imagination, 31(2): 95–102.

AWKWARD M, 1987. Haunted by their nightmares[J]. The New York times book review (13): 49–50.

AWKWARD M, 1989. Inspiriting influences: tradition, revision and Afro-American women's novels[M]. New York: Columbia University Press.

BABB V, 2011. E Pluribus Unum? The American origins narrative in Toni Morrison's A Mercy[J]. Multi-ethnic literature of the U.S., 36(2): 140–147.

BAKER H A, Jr. 1991. Workings of spirit: the politics of Afro-American women's writing[M]. Chicago: University of Chicago Press.

BAKER H A, Jr. 1985. Blues, ideology, and Afro-American literature: a vernacular theory[M]. Chicago: University of Chicago Press.

BAKERMAN J S, 1978. The seams cannot show: an interview with Toni Morrison[J]. Black American literature forum (12): 77–79.

BAKERMAN J S, 1981. Failure of love, female initiation in the novels of Toni Morrison[J]. American literature (52): 541–563.

BAKHTIN M M, 1986. Speech genres and other late essays[M]. Austin: University of Texas Press.

BALDWIN J, 1962. The artist's struggle for integrity[M]. New York: Jeffrey Norton Publishers, Inc.

BALDWIN J, 1963. The fire next time[M]. New York: Dial Press.

BALDWIN J, 1996. Of the sorrow songs: the cross of redemption[G]//CAMPBELL J. The picador book of blues and jazz. London: Picador: 324–331.

BALDWIN J, 2000. Many thousands gone: the first two centuries of slavery in North America[M]. Cambridge: Belknap Press.

BALDWIN J, 1955. Notes of a native son[M]. Boston: Beacon.

BALDWIN J, 1985. The price of the ticket: collected of nonfiction, 1948–1985. New York: St. Martin.

BARAKA A, 1987. Blues, poetry, and the new music[M]//BARAKA A I, BARAKA A. The music: reflections on jazz and blues. New York: Morrow.

BAST F, 2011. Reading red: the troping of trauma in Toni Morrison's Beloved[J]. Callaloo (4): 1069–1087.

BELL B W, 1987. The Afro-American novel and its tradition[M]. Amherst: University of Massachusetts Press.

BENNETT L, Jr. 1984. Before the Mayflower: a history of black America[M]. New York: Johnson Publishing Company, Inc.

JOHN B, 1972. Ways of seeing[M]. London: Penguin.

BERRET A J, 1997. Jazz: from music to literature[G]//MCKAY N Y, EARLE K.

Approaches to teaching the novels of Toni Morrison. New York: MLA.

BERRET A J, 1989. Toni Morrison's literary jazz[J]. College language association journal (32): 267–283.

BHABHA H K, 1997. The location of culture[M]. London and New York: Routledge.

BISCHOFF J, 1975. The novels of Toni Morrison: studies in thwarted sensitivity[J]. Black literature (6): 21–23.

BONE R, 1975. Down home: a history of Afro-American short fiction from its beginning to the end of the Harlem renaissance[M]. New York: Capricorn Books.

BOUSON J B, 2000. Quiet as it's kept: shame, trauma, and race in the novels of Toni Morrison[M]. Albany: State University of New York Press.

BOWERS S, 1997. Beloved and the new apocalypse[G]//MIDDLETON D L. Toni Morrison's fiction: contemporary criticism. New York: Garland Publishing, Inc.

BROWN C, 2002. Golden gray and the talking book: identity as a site of artful construction in Toni Morrison's Jazz[J]. African American review (36): 629–642.

BRYANT-BERG K A, 2009. "No longer haunted"? Cultural trauma and traumatic realism in the novels of Louise Erdrich and Toni Morrison[M]. Oregon: The University of Oregon.

BYERMAN K, 1985. Figuring the jagged grain: tradition and form in recent black tradition[M]. Athens, GA: University of Georgia Press.

CALDWELL G, 1994. Author Toni Morrison discusses her latest novel Beloved[G]// TAYLOR-GUTHRIE D. Conversations with Toni Morrison. Jackson, MS: University Press of Mississippi: 239–245.

CARABI A, 1994. Toni Morrison[J]. Belles letters (Spring): 86–90.

CARBY H, 1986. It just be's dat way sometime: the sexual politics of women's blues[J]. Radical America, 20(4): 9–24.

CARBY H, 1987. Reconstructing womanhood: the emergence of Afro-American woman novelist[M]. New York: Oxford University Press.

CARMEAN K, 1993. Toni Morrison's world of fiction[M]. Troy, New York: The Washington Publishing Company.

CARRIGAN H L, 2008. A mercy[J]. Library journal (133):17.

CARUTH C, 1995. Trauma: explorations in memory[M]. Baltimore: The Johns

Hopkins University Press.

CARUTH C, 1996. Unclaimed experience: trauma, narrative, and history[M]. Baltimore: The Johns Hopkins University Press.

CHINWEIZU O J, 1975. The west and the rest of us: white predators, black slaves and the African elite [M]. New York: Vintage.

CHINWEIZU O J, IHECHUKWU M, 1983. Toward the decolonization of African literature[M]. Washington: Howard University Press.

CHRISTIAN B, 1985. Black feminist criticism: perspectives on black women writers[M]. New York: Pergamon.

CHRISTIAN B, 1980. Black women novelists: the development of a tradition, 1892–1976[M]. Westport, Conn.: Praeger.

CHRISTIAN B, 1993. Layered rhythms: Virginia Woolf and Toni Morrison[J]. Modern Fiction Studies (39): 483–500.

COLLINS P H, 2000. Black feminist thought: knowledge, consciousness, and the politics of empowerment[M]. New York and London: Routledge.

CONE J, 1972. The spirituals and the blues[M]. New York: Seabury Press.

CONNER M C, 2000. The aesthetics of Toni Morrison: speaking the unspeakable[M]. Jackson, MS: University Press of Mississippi.

COREY S, 2000. Toward the limits of mystery: the grotesque in Toni Morrison's Beloved[G]//CONNER M C. The aesthetics of Toni Morrison: speaking the unspeakable. Jackson, MS: University Press of Mississippi.

COSER S, 1995. Bridging the Americas: the literature of Paule Marshall, Toni Morrison, and Gayl Jones[M]. Philadelphia: Temple University Press.

COTE J E, LEVINE C G, 2002. Identity formation, agency, and culture[M]. New Jersey: Lawrence Erlbaum Associates.

CULLER J, 2004. On deconstruction: theory and criticism after structuralism[M]. Beijing: Foreign Language Teaching and Research Press & Cornell University Press.

CUTTER M J, 2001. Quiet as it's kept: shame, trauma, and race in the novels of Toni Morrison[J]. African American review (4): 671–672.

DALSGARD K, 2001. The one all-black town worth the pain: (African) American exceptionalism, historical narration, and the critique of nationhood in Toni Morrison's Paradise[J]. African American review, 35 (2): 97–126.

DAVIS A, 1990. Black women and music: a historical legacy of struggle[G]//
BRAXTON J M, MCLAUGHLIN A N. Wild women in the whirlwind: Afro-
American literature and the contemporary literary renaissance. New Brunswick,
New Jersey: Rutgers University Press.

DAVIS A, 1981. The legacy of slavery: standards for a new womanhood[M]//
DAVIS A. Women, race and class. New York: Random House.

DAVIS C, 1988. Interview with Toni Morrison[J]. Présence africaine (first
quarterly): 148–149.

DAVIS C A, 1998. Self, society and myth in Toni Morrison's fiction[G]//PEACH
L. Toni Morrison. New York: St. Martin's Press: 27–42.

DEAN R T, 1992. New structures in jazz and improvisational music since 1960[M].
Philadelphia: Open UP.

DE BEAUVOIR S, 1953. The second sex[M]. PARSHLEY H M, trans.
Harmodsworth: Penguin.

DENARD C C, 2008. Toni Morrison: conversations[M]. Jackson and London:
University Press of Mississippi.

DEVAUX S, 1997. The birth of Bepop: A social and musical history[M]. Berkeley:
University of California Press.

DE WEEVER J, 1979. The inverted world of Toni Morrison's The Bluest Eye and
Sula[J]. CLA journal (22): 402–414.

DIXON M, 1987. Ride out the wilderness: geography and identity in Afro-American
literature[M]. Urbana: Illinois UP.

DOUGLASS F, 1960. Narrative of the life of Frederick Douglass[M]. Cambridge,
Mass.: Harvard University Press.

DOUGLASS F, 1994. My bondage and my freedom[M]. New York: Seabury Press.

DREIFUS C, 1994. Chloe Wofford talks about Toni Morrison[N]. New York Times,
1994–09–11(9).

DUBEY M, 1998. Narration and migration: jazz and vernacular theories of black
women's fiction[J]. American literary history (2): 291–316.

DU BOIS W, 1990. The Souls of Black Folk[M]. New York: Vintage Books.

DUCILLE A, 2006. On canons: anxious history and the rise of black feminist
literary studies[G]//ROONEY E. The cambridge companion to feminist literary
theory. New York: Cambridge University Press.

EAGLETON T, 2004. Literary theory: an introduction[M]. 2nd ed. Beijing: Foreign Language Teaching and Research Press & Blackwell Publishers.

EAST L, JACKSON D, 2007. "I don't want to hate him forever": understanding daughter's experience of father absence[J]. Australian journal of advanced nursing (4): 14–18.

ECKHARD P G, 1994. The interplay of music, literature, and narrative in Toni Morrison's Jazz[J]. CLA journal, 38(1): 11–19.

ECKSTEIN L, 2006. A love supreme: jazzthetic strategies in Toni Morrison's Beloved[J]. African American review, 40(2): 271–283.

EISENSTEIN Z R, 1979. The Combahee river collective statement[M]//Capitalist patriarchy and the case for socialist feminism. New York: Monthly Review Press.

ELLIS B J, BATES J E, DODGE K A, et al., 2003. Does father absence place daughters at special risk for early sexual activity and teenage pregnancy?[J]. Child development (3): 801–821.

ELLISON R, 1995. Shadow and Act[C]//CALLAHAN J F. The collective essays of Ralph Ellison. New York: Modern Library.

EVANS J H, 2006. Spiritual empowerment in Afro-American literature[M]. Lewiston: Edwin Mellen Press.

EVANS N M, 2000. Writing jazz: race, nationalism, and modern culture in the 1920s[M]. New York: Garland.

FEATHER L, 1965. The book of jazz: from then till now[M]. New York: Horizon.

FEATHER L, 1951. Little jazz goes color blind[J]. Down Beat: 12.

FELMAN S, LAUB D, 1992. Testimony: crises of witnessing in literature, psychoanalysis and history[M]. New York: Routledge.

FICK T H, 1989. Toni Morrison's "allegory of the cave": movies, consumption, and platonic realism in The Bluest Eye[J]. Journal of the midwest modern language association, 22 (1): 10–22.

FIELD E, 1898. Lady button eyes[M]//Love-songs of childhood. New York: Scribner's Sons.

FONER E, 1988. A short history of reconstruction, 1863—1877[M]. New York: Perennial Library-Harper & Row.

FRANGSMYR T, 1993. Nobel lectures, literature 1981—1990[M]. Singapore: World Scientific Publishing Co.

FRANCES A, 1994. Diagnostic and statistical manual of mental disorders[M]. 4th ed. Washington D.C.: American Psychiatric Association.

FREIERT W K, 1980. Classical themes in Song of Solomon[J]. Melus (7).

FREUD S, 1961. Beyond the pleasure principle[M]. New York: W. W. Norton & Company.

FRYKHOLM A, 2009. A mercy[J]. The christian century (2): 44–46.

FURMAN J, 1996. Toni Morrison's fiction[M]. Columbia: University of South Carolina Press.

FURNHAM A, BOCHNER S, 1986. Culture shock: psychological reactions to unfamiliar environments[M]. London: Mrthuen.

GATES H L, Jr, 1984. Black literature and literary theory[M]. London: Routledge.

GATES H L, Jr, 1985. "Race", writing and difference[M]. Chicago: Chicago University Press.

GATES H L, Jr, 1987. Figures in black: words, signs and the "racial" self[M]. Oxford: Oxford University Press.

GATES H L, Jr, 1990. Introduction: tell me, sir … what is "Black" literature? [J]. PMLA (1): 11–22.

GATES H L, Jr, 1991. Goodbye Columbus? Notes on the culture of criticism[J]. American literary history, 3 (4) :711–727.

GATES H L, Jr, 1988. The signifying monkey[M]. Oxford: Oxford University Press.

GATES H L, Jr. APPIAH K A, 1993. Toni Morrison: critical perspectives past and present[M]. New York: Amistad.

GATES H L, MCKAY N Y, 1996. From Phillis Wheatley to Toni Morrison: The flowering of African-American literature[J]. The journal of blacks in higher education, 30 (14) : 95–100.

GENNARI J, 1991. Jazz criticism: its development and ideologies[J]. Black American literature forum, 25(3): 449–450.

GERALD C, 1998. Jazz in black and white: race, culture, and identity in the jazz community[M]. Westport: Praeger.

GILLINGAN C, 1982. In a different voice: psychological theory and women's moral development[M]. Cambridge: Harvard UP.

GILROY P, 1993. The black Atlantic: modernity and double consciousness[M].

Cambridge: Harvard UP.

GILROY P, 1994. Living memory: a meeting with Toni Morrison[M]//Small acts: thoughts on the politics of black culture. London: Serpent's Tail.

GINSBURG M P, 1995. Fictions of authority: women writers and narrative voice[J]. Comparative literature studies (1): 68–70.

GIOIA T, 1992. West coast jazz: modern jazz in California, 1945–1960[M]. New York: Oxford UP.

GRANDT J E, 2004. Kinds of blue: Toni Morrison, Hans Janowitz, and the jazz aesthetic[J]. African American review (38): 303–322.

GREWAL G, 1998. The decolonizing vision: The Bluest Eye[M]//Circles of sorrow, lines of struggle: the novels of Toni Morrison. Baton Rouge: Louisiana State University Press.

GROGAN C L, 2011. The wound and the voiceless: the insidious trauma of father-daughter incest in six American texts[D]. Florida: The University of South Florida.

HALL C, 1994. Beyond the "literary habit": oral tradition and jazz in Beloved[J]. Melus, 19(1): 89–95.

HALL S, 1990. Cultural identity and diaspora[C]//RUTHERFORD J. Identity: community, culture, difference. London: Lawrence & Wishart.

HARDACK R, 1995. "A music seeking its words": double-timing and double-consciousness in Toni Morrison's Jazz[J]. Callaloo, 18(2): 451–471.

HARDING W, MARTIN J, 1994. A world of Ddifference: an inter-cultural study of Toni Morrison's novels[M]. Westport: Greenwood.

HARLAND R, 2005. Literary theory from Plato to Barthes: An introductory history[M]. Beijing: Foreign Language Teaching and Research Press & Palgrave Macmillan Limited.

HARRIS T, 1988. Reconnecting fragments: Afro-American folk tradition in The Bluest Eye[G]//MCKAY N. Critical essays on Toni Morrison. Boston: G. K. Hall.

HARRIS T, 1991. Fiction and folklore: the novels of Toni Morrison[M]. Knoxville: The University of Tennesse Press.

HAYES E T, 2004. The named and the nameless: Morrison's 124 and Naylor's "the other place" as semiotic chorae[J]. African American review (38): 669–681.

HEBLE A, 2000. Landing on the wrong note: jazz, dissonance, and cultural practice[M]. New York: Routledge.

HENDERSON S. 1973. Understanding the new black poetry: black speech & black music as poetic references[M]. New York: William Morrow.

HERMAN J, 1992. Trauma and recovery[M]. New York: Basic Books.

HERSKOVITS M J, 1995. The myth of the negro past[M]. Boston: Beacon.

HERNTON C, 1990. The sexual mountain and black women writers[G]//BRAXTON J M, MCLAUGHLIN A N. Wild woman in the whirlwind: Afro-American culture and the contemporary literary renaissance. New Brunswick, New Jersey: Rutgers University Press, 203–209.

HILFER A, 1991. Critical indeterminacies in Toni Morrison's fiction: an introduction[J]. Texas studies in literature and language, 33(1): 91–95.

HOLLOWAY K F C, DEMETRAKOPOULOS S A, 1987. New dimensions of spirituality: a biracial and bicultural reading of the novels of Toni Morrison[M]. Westport, Conn.: Greenwood Press.

HOOKS B, 2000. All about love: new visions[M]. New York: Morrow.

HOOKS B, 2000. Feminist theory: from margin to center[M]. Boston: South End Press.

HOOKS B, 1989. Talking back: thinking feminist, thinking black[M]. Boston: South End Press.

HOUGHS L, BONTEMPS A, 1958. The book of negro folklore[M]. New York: Dodd, Mead & Co.

HULBERT A, 1992. Romance and race[J]. New Republic,206(20): 43–48.

HUME K, 2006. American dream, American nightmare: fiction since 1960[M]. Beijing: Foreign Language Teaching and Research Press.

HUMM M, 1994. A reader's guide to contemporary feminist literary criticism[M]. New York: Harvester Wheatsheaf.

HURSTON Z N, 1983. Mules and men[M]. Berkeley: Turtle Island.

HUTCHEON L, 1988. A poetics of postmodernism: history, theory, fiction[M]. New York: Routledge.

JAFFREY Z, 1998. The salon interview with Toni Morrison [EB/OL]. (1998–02–02) [2013–04–16]. http://www.salon.com/books/int/1998/02/cov_si_02int.html.

JAMES J, SHARPLEY-WHITING T D, 2000. The black feminist reader [M].

Malden: Blackwell Publishers Ltd.

JAMESON F, 1971. Marxism and form: twentieth-century dialectical theories of literature[M]. Princeton, New Jersey: Princeton University Press.

JESSER N, 2012. Race, trauma, and home in the novels of Toni Morrison[J]. African American review (3): 469–470.

JONES B W, VINSON A L, 1985. The world of Toni Morrison: explorations in literary criticism[M]. Dubuque: Kendall/Hunt.

JONES L, 1963. Blues people: negro music in white America[M]. New York: Quill-Morrow.

JANOWITZ H, 1999. Jazz 1927. Bonn: Weidle.

KAKUTANI M, 2008. A mercy[N]. New York Times, 2008–11–05(9).

KING D K, 1988. Consciousness: the context of a black feminist ideology[J]. Signs: Journal of Women in Culture and Society (14): 45–49.

KLOTMAN P, 1979. Dick-and-Jane and the shirley temple sensibility in The Bluest Eye[J]. Black American literature forum (13): 123–125.

KOFSKY F, 1998. John Coltrane and the jazz revolution of the 1960s[M]. New York: Pathfinder.

KUBITSCHEK M D, 1998. Toni Morrison: a critical companion, westport, connecticut[M]. London: Greenwood Press.

LANSER S S, 1992. Fictions of authority: women writers and narrative voice[M]. Ithaca: Cornell University Press.

LAUB D, 1995. Truth and testimony: the process and the struggle[G]//CARUTH C. Trauma: explorations in memory. Baltimore and London: The John Hopkins University Press.

LAURENCE D, 1997. Fleshly ghosts and ghostly flesh: the word and the body in Beloved[G]//MIDDLETON D L. Toni Morrison's fiction: contemporary criticism. New York: Garland Publishing, Inc.

LECLAIR T, 1981. The Language Must Not Sweat: A Conversation with Toni Morrison[J]. New Republic,184(12): 25.

LESTER R K, 1988. An interview with Toni Morrison, hessian radio network, Frankfurt, West Germany[C]//MCKAY N Y. Critical essays on Toni Morrison. Boston: G. K. Hall.

LEVINE L W, 1980. Black consciousness: Afro-American folk thought from slavery to freedom[M]. New York: Oxford UP.

LI S, 2010. Toni Morrison: a biography[M]. Santa Barbara, California: Greenwood Press.

LOEWENBERG B J, BOGIN R, 1976. Black women in nineteenth century American life[M]. University Park: Pennsylvania State University Press.

LORDE A, 1984. Sister outsider: essays and speeches[M]. Trumansburg, New York: The Crossing Press.

LUPTON M J, 1986. Clothes and closure in three novels by black women writers[J]. Black American literature forum (20): 409–421.

MACDONALD H, 1993. The other Morrison[J]. Wall street journal (18): 24.

MACARTHUR K L, 2005. The things we carry: trauma and the aesthetic in the contemporary United States novel[D]. Washington D. C.: The George Washington University.

MALRAUX A, 1966. Behind the mask of Africa[J]. New York times magazine 35.

MATUS J, 1998. Toni Morrison[M]. Manchester and New York: Manchester University Press.

MBALIA D D, 1991. Toni Morrison's developing class consciousness[M]. Selinsgrove: Susquehanna University Press.

MCDOWELL D E, 1985. New directions for black feminist criticism[C]// SHOWALTER E. The new feminist criticism: essays on women, literature, and theory. New York: Random House.

MCDOWELL D E, 1988. "The self and the other": reading Toni Morrison's Sula and the black female text[G]// MCKAY N. Critical essays on Toni Morrison. Boston: G. K. Hall.

MCHENRY E, 2009. Into other claws[J]. The women's review of books, 26(4):16–17.

MCKAY N, 1988. Critical essays on Toni Morrison[M]. Boston: G. K. Hall.

MCKAY N, 1983. An interview with Toni Morrison[J]. Contemporary literature, 24(4): 413–429.

MCKAY N, 1994. An interview with Toni Morrison[G]//TAYLOR-GUTYRIE D. Conversations with Toni Morrison. Jackson, MS: UP of Mississippi.

MCKEOWN J, 2008. Mothers and daughters [EB/OL]. (2008–12–17)[2017–10–15]. http://www.pajiba.com/book_reviews/a-mercy-book-review.php, December 17, 2008.

MERE A, 1984. The unique role of women in nation building[M]. Dissertation. Nsukka: University of Nigeria.

MIDDLETON D L, 1997. Toni Morrison's fiction: contemporary criticism[M]. New York: Garland Publishing, Inc.

MILLER M L, 2005. Literary witnessing: working through trauma in Toni Morrison, Nuruddin Farah, Wilson Harris, and Chang-Rae Lee[M]. South Carolina: University of South Carolina.

MODLESKI T, 1986. Studies in entertainment[M]. Bloomington: Indiana University Press.

MONSON I, 1996. Saying something: jazz improvisation and interaction[M]. Chicago: University of Chicago Press.

MORI A, 1999. Toni Morrison and womanist discourse[M]. New York: Peter Lang Publishing, Inc.

MORRISON T, 1974. Behind the making of The Black Book[J]. Black world: 86–90.

MORRISON T, 2000. Beloved[M]. Beijing: Foreign Language Teaching & Research Press.

MORRISON T, 1970. The Bluest Eye[M]. New York: Washington Square Press.

MORRISON T, 1981. City limits, village values: concepts of neighborhoods in black fiction[G]// JAYE M C, WATTS A C. Literature and the urban experience: essays on the city and literature. New Brunswick: Rulgers UP.

MORRISON T, 1983. Interview with Claudia Tate[G]//TATE C. Black Women Writers at Work. New York: Continuum.

MORRISON T, 1992. Jazz[M]. New York: Plume.

MORRISON T, 2012. Home[M]. New York: Alfred A. Knopf.

MORRISON T, 2003. Love[M]. Toronto: Vintage Canada.

MORRISON T, 1984. Memory, creation, and writing[J]. Thought (59): 388.

MORRISON T, 2008. A mercy[M]. New York: Knopf.

MORRISON T, 1999. Paradise[M]. London: Vintage.

MORRISON T, 1992. Playing in the dark[M]. New York: Random.

MORRISON T, 1993. The 1993 nobel prize in literature speech[G]//HIPP J W. Dictionary of literary biography: yearbook 1993. New York: Random.

MORRISON T, 1989. The pain of being black: Interview with Bonnie Angelo[J].

Time, 133(21):120–122.

MORRISON T, 1983. Recitatif [G]//BARAKA I A, BARAKA A. Confirmation: an anthology of African American women. New York: Quill: 243–261.

MORRISON T, 2004. Remember: the journey to school integration[M]. Boston: Houghton Mifflin.

MORRISON T, 1984. Rootedness: the ancestor as foundation[G]//EVANS M. Black women writers, 1950–1980: a critical evaluation. New York: Doubleday.

MORRISON T, 2008. A slow walk of trees[G]//DENARD C C. What moves at the margin: selected nonfiction. Jackson, MS: University Press of Mississippi.

MORRISON T, 1987. The site of memory[G]//ZINSSER W. Inventing the truth: the art and craft of memoir. Boston: Houghton.

MORRISON T, 1977. Song of Solomon[M]. New York: Knopf.

MORRISON T, 1973. Sula[M]. New York: Knopf.

MORRISON T, 1981. Tar Baby[M]. New York: Plume.

MORRISON T, 1995. Toni Morrison[J]. Belle letters, 10(2): 40–43.

MORRISON T, 1971. What the black woman thinks about women's lib[J]. New York times magazine (14): 63–66.

MORRISON T, 1989. Unspeakable things unspoken: the Afro-American presence in American literature[J]. Michigan quarterly review (28): 1–34.

MORRISON T, LACOUR C B, 1997. Birth of a nationhood: gaze, script, and spectacle in the O. J. Simpson case[M]. New York: Pantheon.

MORRISON T, WEST C, 2004. Blues, love and politics[J]. Nation, 278 (20): 18–26.

MUNTON A, 1997. Misreading Morrison, misreading jazz: a response to Toni Morrison's jazz critics[J]. Journal of American studies, 31(2): 235–251.

MURRAY A, 1973. The hero and the blues[M]. Columbia: University of Missouri Press.

MURRAY A, 1976. Stomping the blues[M]. New York: McGraw-Hill.

MURRAY P, 1987. Song in a weary throat: an American pilgrimage[M]. New York City: Harper & Row.

NAYLOR G, 1985. Gloria Naylor and Toni Morrison: a conversation[J]. Southern review, 21(3): 567–593.

O'SHAUGHNESSY K, 1988. "Life Life Life Life": the community as chorus in Song of Solomon[G]//MCKAY N. Critical essays on Toni Morrison. Boston: G.

K. Hall.

OTTEN T, 1989. The crime of innocence in the fiction of Toni Morrison[M]. Columbia: University Press of Missouri.

PAGE P, 1995. Dangerous freedom: fusion and fragmentation in Toni Morrison's novels[M]. Jackson, MS: University Press of Mississipi.

PAQUET-DEYRIS A M, 2001. Toni Morrison's Jazz and the city[J]. African American review (35): 219–231.

PARKER B J, 1979. Complexity: Toni Morrison's women—an interview essay[G]// BELL R P, PARKER B J, GUY-SHEFTALL. Sturdy black bridges: visions of black women in literature. New York: Doubleday.

PATELL C R K, 2001. Negative liberties: Morrison, Pynchon, and the problem of Liberal ideology[M]. Durham and London: Duke University Press.

PATTERSON O, 1982. Slavery and social death[M]. London: Harvard UP.

PEACH L, 2000. Toni Morrison[M]. 2nd ed. New York: St. Martin's Presss.

PEREZ-TORRES R, 1997. Knitting and knotting the narrative thread—Beloved as postmodern novel[G]//PETERSON N J. Toni Morrison: critical and theoretical approaches. Baltimore and London: The Johns Hopkins University Press.

PETERSON N J, 1997. Toni Morrison: critical and theoretical approaches[M]. Baltimore and London: The Johns Hopkins University Press.

PICI N F, 1994. Hannibal ante portas: jazz in Weimar[G]//KNIERSCHE T W, BROCKMANN S. Dancing on the volcano: essays on the culture of the Weimar republic. Columbia: Camden House.

PICI N F, 1997. Trading meanings: the breath of music in Toni Morrison's Jazz[J]. Connotations (7): 372–398.

PORTER H, 1997. Jazz beginnings: Ralph Ellison and Charlie Christian in Oklahoma city[J]. Antioch review, 57(3): 275–279.

PRYSE M, HORTENSE S, 1985. Conjuring: black women writing the American experience[M]. Bloomington: Indiana University Press.

RAYNOR D J, BUTLER E J, 2007. Morrison and the critical community[G]// TALLY J. The cambridge companion to Toni Morrison. New York: Cambridge University Press, 2007.

REAGON B J, 1987. African diaspora women: the making of cultural workers[G]// TERBORG-PENN R, HARLEY S, RUSHING A B. Women in Africa and the

African Diaspora: a reader. Washington: Howard University Press.

REYES A, 1986. Ancient properties in the new world: The paradox of the "Other" in Toni Morrison's Tar Baby[J]. Black scholar (17): 21–27.

RICE A J, 1994. Jazzing up a storm: the execution and meaning of Toni Morrison's jazzy prose style[J]. Journal of American studies, 28(3): 423–432.

RICE H W, 1996. Toni Morrison and the American tradition: a rhetorical reading[M]. New York: Peter Lang.

RIGNEY B H, 1998. Hagar's mirror: self and identity in Morrison's fiction[G]// PEACH L. Toni Morrison. New York: St. Martin's Press.

RIGNEY B H, 1991. The voices of Toni Morrison[M]. Columbus: Ohio State University Press.

RODRIGUES E L, 1993. Experiencing Jazz[J]. Modern fiction studies, 39(3/4): 733–754.

ROTUNDO E A, 1993. American manhood: transformations in masculinity from the revolution to the modern era[M]. New York: Harper Collins.

ROYE S, 2012. Toni Morrison's disrupted girls and their disturbed girlhoods: The Bluest Eye and A Mercy[J]. Callaloo, 35(1): 212–227.

RUBENSTEIN R, 1998. Singing the blues/reclaiming jazz: Toni Morrison and cultural mourning[J]. Mosaic, 31(2): 147–163.

RUDINOW J, 1994. Race, ethnicity, expressive authenticity: can white people sing the blues?[J]. Journal of aesthetics and art criticism, 52(1): 127–137.

RUSHDY A H, 1999. Daughters signifying history: the example of Toni Morrison's Beloved[G]//BLOOM H. Modern critical interpretation: Beloved. Philadelphia: Chelsea House.

RUSHDY A H, 1991. "Rememory": primal scenes and constructions in Toni Morrison's novels[J]. Contemporary literature, 32(2):194–210.

RYAN J S, 1997. Morrison's Jazz: "A Knowing So Deep" [G]//MCKAY N Y, EARLE K. Approaches to teaching the novels of Toni Morrison. New York: MLA.

SAMUELS W D, HUDSON-WEEMS C, 1990. Toni Morrison[M]. Boston: Twayne.

SANDY M, 2011. "Cut by Rainbow": tales, tellers, and reimagining Wordsworth's pastoral poetics in Toni Morrison's Beloved and A Mercy[J]. Melus, 36 (2): 35–51.

SANSOM I, 2008. The divided states of America[N]. The spectator, 2008–11–05.

SARTRE J P, 1966. Being and nothingness[M]. BARNES H E, trans. New York: Washington Square Press.

SCHAPPELL E, 1998. Interview with Toni Morrison[G]//REVIEW P P. Women writers at work. New York: Modern Library.

SCHREIBER E J, 2010. Race, trauma, and home in the novels of Toni Morrison[M]. Baton Rouge: Louisiana State University Press.

SCHULLER G, 1969. Early jazz: its roots and musical development[M]. New York: Oxford UP.

SEED D, 2011. Toni Morrison: "New Directions" [J]. Melus (2): 187–190.

SELDEN R, WIDDOWSON P, BROOKER P, 2004. A reader's guide to contemporary literary theory[M]. Beijing: Foreign Language Teaching and Research Press & Pearson Education.

SHOWALTER E, 2004. A literature of their own: british women novelists from Brontë to Lessing[M]. Beijing: Foreign Language Teaching and Research Press & Princeton University Press.

SIDRAN B, 1983. Black talk[M]. New York: Da Capo.

SKERRETT J T, 1985. Recitations to the griot: storytelling and learning in Toni Morrison's Song of Solomon[G]//PRYSE M, SPILLERS, H. Conjuring: black women, fiction, and the literary tradition. Bloomington: Indiana University Press.

SMALL-MCCARTHY R, 1995. The jazz aesthetic in the novels of Toni Morrison[J]. Cultural Studies, 9(2): 293–300.

SMITH B, 1974. Beautiful, needed, mysterious[J]. Freedomways (14): 69–72.

SMITH B, 1979. Toward a black feminist criticism[J]. Women's studies international quarterly, 2(2): 180–192.

SMITH B, 1985. Toward a black feminist criticism[G]//SHOWALTER E. The new feminist criticism: essays on women, literature, and theory. New York: Random House.

SMITH B, 1987. Interview[G]//REISNER R. Bird: the legend of Charlie Parker. New York: Da Capo.

SOUTHERN E, 1983. The music of black Americans[M]. New York: W. W. Norton and Company.

SOUTHERN E, 1983. Readings in black American music[M]. New York: W. W.

W. Norton and Company.

SPACKS P M, 1975. The female imagination[M]. New York: Alfred A. Knopf.

SPELMAN E V, 1998. Inessential woman: problems of exclusion in feminist thought[M]. Boston: Beacon Press.

STEADY F C, 1981. The black woman cross-culturally[M]. Boston: Schenkman.

STEPTO R, 1979. From behind the veil: a study of Afro-American narrative[M]. Urbana: University of Illinois Press.

STORACE P, 1998. The scripture of utopia [J]. New York review of books, 45(10): 64–69.

STOVER K M, 2009. A mercy[J]. Booklist, 105(13): 70.

TAO M, 2002. A history of American literature[M]. Nanjing: Yilin Press.

TATE C, 1989. Toni Morrison[M]//Black women writers at work. New York: Continuum.

TAYLOR-GUTHRIE D, 1994. Conversations with Toni Morrison[M]. Jackson: University Press of Mississippi.

TODD A D, FISHER S, 1988. Gender and discourse: the power of talk[M]. Norwood, NJ: Alex.

PETER T, 2000. Jazz in American culture[M]. Edinburgh: Edinburgh UP.

TURNER D T, 1984. Theme, characterization, and style in the works of Toni Morrison[G]//EVANS M. Black women writers (1950—1980): a critical evaluation. New York: Doubleday.

TYSON L, 1999. Critical theory today: a use-friendly guide[M]. New York & London: Garland Publishing, Inc.

UPDIKE J, 2008. Dreamy wilderness: unmastered women in colonial Virginia[J]. The New Yorker (11): 112.

VERDELLE A J, 1998. Paradise found: a talk with Toni Morrison about her new novel—Nobel Laureates' new book, "Paradise"—Interview[J]. Essence, 28(10): 50–59.

VICKROY L, 1996. The politics of abuse: the traumatized child in Toni Morrison and Marguerie Duras[J]. Mosaic, 29(2): 90–96.

VICKROY L, 1990. Who owns Zora Neale Hurston? Critics carve up the legend[G]// WALLACE M. Invisibility blues: from pop to theory. London: Picador.

WALCOTT R, 1995. "Out of the Kumbla": Toni Morrison's Jazz and pedagogical answerability[J]. Cultural studies, 9(2): 318–337.

WALKER A, 2005. In search of our mother's gardens[M]. London: Phoenix.

WALLACE M, 1989. Michael Jackson, black modernisms and "the essay of communication"[M]// Invisibility blues. London：Picador.

WALLACE M, 1990. Black macho and the myth of the superwoman[M]. London and New York: Verso.

WAUGH P, 1989. Feminine fictions: revisiting the postmodern[M]. New York: Routledge.

DE WEEVER J, 1979. The inverted world of Toni Morrison's The Bluest Eyes and Sula[J]. CLA journal, 22(4): 402–414.

WEINREICH P, SAUNDERSON W, 2003. Analysing identity: cross-cultural, societal and clinical contexts[M]. London: Routledge.

WILENTZ G, 1997. Civilization underneath: African heritage as cultural discourse in Toni Morrison's Song of Solomon[G]//MIDDLETON D L. Toni Morrison's fiction: contemporary criticism. New York: Garland Publishing Inc.

WILLIAMSON J, 1986. Woman is an island: feminity and colonization[G]// MODLESKI T. Studies in entertainment. Bloomington: Indiana University Press.

WILLIS S, 1989. I shop therefore I am: is there a place for Afro-American culture in commodity culture?[G]//WALL C. Changing our own words: essays on criticism, theory, and writing by black women. New Brunswick, N. J.: Duke University Press.

WILLIS S, 1987. Specifying: black women writing the American experience[M]. Madison, Wis.: University of Wisconsin Press.

WILSON J, 1981. A conversation with Toni Morrison[J]. Essence (12): 82–150.

WONG S, 1990. Transgression as poses in The Bluest Eye[J]. Callaloo (13): 471–481.

WRIGHT N, Jr, 2001. The black spirituals: a testament of hope for our times?[J]. The journal of religious thought, (60): 87–100.

WRIGHT R, 1947. Twelve million black voices[M]. New York: Quill-Morrow.

贝尔, 2000. 非洲裔美国黑人小说及其传统[M]. 刘捷, 潘明元, 石发林, 等, 译. 成都: 四川人民出版社.

波伏娃, 2004. 第二性[M]. 陶铁柱, 译. 北京: 中国书籍出版社.

陈洁, 2004. 奴隶制度的"后遗症"和历史创伤的愈合：托妮·莫里森《宠儿》简析[J]. 江苏教育学院学报 (社会科学版) (6): 105–106.

陈平, 2010. 创伤性情感、历史性叙事和抒情性表现: 对于托妮·莫里森小说《娇女》的新诠释[J]. 四川师范大学学报 (社会科学版) (2): 97–104.

程锡麟, 王晓路, 2001. 当代美国小说理论[M]. 北京: 外语教学与研究出版社.

得拉诺瓦, 2005. 民族与民族主义: 理论基础与历史经验[M].郑文彬, 洪晖,译. 北京: 生活·读书·新知三联书店.

刁克利, 2005. 西方作家理论研究[M]. 北京: 外语教学与研究出版社.

杜小惠, 2007. 托妮·莫里森小说《最蓝的眼睛》的布鲁斯美学[J].电影文学 (19): 86–87.

杜志卿, 2007. 托妮·莫里森研究在中国[J]. 当代外国文学 (4): 122–129.

杜志卿, 2003.《秀拉》的死亡主题[J]. 外国文学评论 (3): 34–43.

方珊, 2001. 形式主义文论[M]. 济南: 山东教育出版社.

方生, 1999. 后结构主义文论[M]. 济南: 山东教育出版社.

福柯, 2003. 规训与惩罚: 监狱的诞生[M]. 刘北成, 杨远婴, 译. 北京: 生活·读书·新知三联书店.

福柯, 1999. 疯癫与文明: 理性时代的疯癫史[M]. 刘北成, 杨远婴, 译. 北京: 生活·读书·新知三联书店.

福柯, 1998. 知识考古学[M]. 谢强, 马月, 译.北京: 生活·读书·新知三联书店.

高春常, 2000. 文化的断裂: 美国黑人问题与南方重建[M]. 北京: 中国社会科学出版社.

格非, 2002. 小说叙事研究[M]. 北京: 清华大学出版社.

哈旭娴, 2007. 奏响灵魂深处的旋律——托妮·莫里森小说中的音乐叙事[J]. 开封教育学院学报 (3): 9–10.

郝素玲, 2016. 创伤·孩子·未来——托妮·莫里森新作《上帝帮助孩子》简论[J].外国文学动态研究 (2): 62–67.

胡俊, 2010.《一点慈悲》: 关于"家"的建构[J]. 外国文学评论 (3): 200–210.

胡妮, 2012. 托妮·莫里森小说的空间叙事研究[M]. 南昌: 江西高校出版社.

胡全声, 2002. 英美后现代主义小说叙述结构研究[M]. 上海: 复旦大学出版社.

胡全声, 1994. 难以走出的阴影: 试评托妮·莫里森《心爱的人》的主题[J]. 当代外国文学 (4): 163–168.

胡笑瑛, 2004. 不能忘记的故事: 托妮·莫里森《宠儿》的艺术世界[M]. 银川: 宁夏人民出版社.

黄丽娟, 陶家俊, 2011. 生命中不能承受之痛: 托妮·莫里森的小说《宠儿》中的黑人代际间创伤研究[J]. 外国文学研究 (2): 100–105.

柯里, 2003. 后现代叙事理论[M]. 宁一中, 译. 北京: 北京大学出版社.

兰色姆, 2006. 新批评[M]. 王腊宝, 张哲, 译. 南京: 江苏教育出版社.

李贵仓, 1994. 更为真实的再现——莫里森《心爱》的叙事冒险[J]. 西北大学学报 (哲学社会科学版) (3): 26–31.

李美芹, 2007. "伊甸园"中的"柏油娃娃"——《柏油孩》中层叠叙事原型解析[J]. 外国文学评论 (1): 77–85.

李美芹, 2002.《看不见的人》中黑人的自我异化[J]. 广西社会科学 (5): 191–192.

李美芹, 2002. 凤凰涅槃——论托尼·莫里森小说中的"自杀"主题[J]. 当代教育 (14)：45–46.

李美芹, 2004. 莫里森的民族身份认同与文化融合思想——解读《所罗门之歌》[J]. 绥化师专学报 (4)：89–91.

李美芹, 2005. 莫里森的非洲情结——试析《所罗门之歌》的黑色文化底蕴[J]. 成都教育学院学报 (3)：21–23.

李美芹, 2006. 非洲人的"天人合一"观在《所罗门之歌》中的体现[J]. 广西社会科学 (1)：132–134.

李美芹, 2006. 文化冲突中的黑色文化底蕴——莫里森与埃利森的对话[J]. 齐齐哈尔大学学报 (1)：94–96.

李美芹, 2006. 盛开在"'他者'之域"的黑白奇葩——托妮·莫里森和纳丁·戈迪默[J]. 西安外国语学院学报 (4)：73–75.

李美芹, 2009.《天堂》里的"战争"——对莫里森小说《天堂》两个书名的思考[J]. 外国文学研究 (1)：104–109.

李美芹, 2009. 托妮·莫里森小说对黑人精神生态困境出路的理性探讨[J]. 青岛农业大学学报 (2)：87–90.

李美芹, 2010. 黑皮肤，白面具——《最蓝的眼睛》中内部殖民境况下黑人文化身份探析[J]. 青岛农业大学学报 (2)：89–93.

李美芹, 2010. 主流文化祭坛上的"替罪羊"——浅析《最蓝的眼睛》中佩科拉的悲剧命运[G]//郭继德. 美国文学研究 (第五辑). 济南：山东大学出版社.

李美芹, 2010. 用文字谱写乐章——论黑人音乐对莫里森小说的影响[M]. 杭州: 浙江大学出版社.

李美芹, 2011. 从《柏油孩》看莫里森的伦理观[J]. 天津外国语大学学报 (3): 76–80.

李美芹, 2013. 文学虚构中的历史本质：论《家》的历史书写[J]. 当代外国文

学 (2)：13–20.

李美芹, 2014. 休斯诗歌的音乐性解读[G]//郭继德. 美国文学研究 (第7辑). 济南: 山东大学出版社.

李美芹, 2015. The Mammy's image in Chinese and American literary works[J]. U.S.-China foreign language (1)：68–74.

李美芹, 2015. 论埃里森 "文学爵士乐" 美学中表达的种族政治思想[J]. 国外文学 (2)：63–68.

李敏, 2007.《宠儿》美学思想评析——语言的音乐性[J]. 鞍山科技大学学报 (3): 320–322, 325.

李秀清, 2010. 女性自我书写与建构——评莫里森的最新小说《慈悲》[J]. 山东省青年管理干部学院学报 (4): 126–129.

李岩, 2012. "伊甸园" 的解构与女性的自我建构:《慈悲》的生态女性主义解析[J]. 西安电子科技大学学报 (哲学社会科学版) (4): 78–84.

刘小枫, 1997. 个体信仰与文化理论[M]. 成都: 四川人民出版社.

鲁枢元, 2000. 生态文艺学[M]. 西安: 陕西人民教育出版社.

陆扬, 2001. 精神分析文论[M]. 济南: 山东教育出版社.

孟萍, 2007. 蓝调歌者——托妮·莫里森《最蓝的眼睛》中的蓝调特征[J]. 湖南工程学院学报 (社会科学版) (2): 43–46.

尼采, 1998. 权利意志——重估一切价值的尝试[M]. 张念东, 凌素心, 译. 北京: 商务印书馆.

宁骚, 1993. 非洲黑人文化[M]. 杭州: 浙江人民出版社.

邱紫华, 2000. 悲剧精神与民族意识[M]. 2 版. 武汉: 华中师范大学出版社.

任生名, 1998. 西方现代悲剧论稿[M]. 上海: 上海外语教育出版社.

申丹, 2001. 叙事学与小说文体学研究[M]. 北京: 北京大学出版社.

盛宁, 1997. 人文困惑与反思: 西方后现代主义思潮批判[M]. 北京: 生活·读书·新知三联书店.

塔基耶夫, 2005. 种族主义源流[M]. 高凌瀚, 译. 北京: 生活·读书·新知三联书店.

谭君强, 2002. 叙事理论与审美文化[M]. 北京: 中国社会科学出版社.

陶家俊, 2011. 创伤[J]. 外国文学 (4): 117–125.

陶家俊, 2013. 耶鲁派大屠杀创伤研究论析[J]. 当代外国文学 (4): 124–131.

田亚曼, 2012. 拼贴起来的黑玻璃——弗洛伊德精神分析视阈下的莫里森小说研究[M]. 上海: 复旦大学出版社.

徐新, 2002. 西方文化史：从文明初始至启蒙运动[M]. 北京: 北京大学出版社.

徐有志, 1992. 现代英语文体学[M]. 开封: 河南大学出版社.

王逢振, 2005. 疆界2——国际文学与文化·B[M]. 北京: 人民文学出版社.

王静, 2010.《慈悲》: 距离产生悲剧美[J]. 牡丹江教育学院学报 (6): 9–10, 12.

王丽丽, 2014. 走出创伤的阴霾：托妮·莫里森小说的黑人女性创伤研究[M]. 哈尔滨: 黑龙江大学出版社.

王守仁, 吴新云, 2004. 对爱进行新的思考——评莫里森的小说《爱》[J]. 当代外国文学 (2): 43–52.

王守仁, 1994. 走出过去的阴影：读托妮·莫里森的《心爱的人》[J]. 外国文学评论 (1): 37–42.

王守仁, 吴新云, 2009. 超越种族：莫里森新作《慈悲》中的 "奴役" 解析[J]. 当代外国文学 (2): 35–44.

王守仁, 吴新云, 1999. 性别·种族·文化：托妮·莫里森与二十世纪美国黑人文学[M]. 北京: 北京大学出版社.

王守仁, 吴新云, 2016. 走出童年创伤的阴影, 获得心灵的自由和安宁——读莫里森新作《上帝救助孩子》[J]. 当代外国文学 (1): 107–113.

王湘云, 2003. 为了忘却的记忆——论《至爱》对黑人 "二次解放" 的呼唤[J]. 外国文学评论 (4): 66–72.

王玉括, 2005. 莫里森研究[M]. 北京: 人民文学出版社.

修树新, 2015. 托妮·莫里森小说的文学伦理学批评[M]. 长春: 东北师范大学出版社.

薛玉秀, 2012. 文化创伤视阈下的黑人女性主体性之构建：解读托妮·莫里森的《慈悲》[J]. 湖南科技学院学报 (11): 49–51.

杨绍梁, 2012. 象征主义手法在《慈悲》中的应用[J]. 剑南文学 (经典教苑), (6): 210–211.

杨绍梁, 刘霞敏, 2012. 创伤的记忆："他者" 的病态身份构建：浅析莫里森新作《慈悲》[J]. 天津外国语大学学报 (6): 65–71.

张静, 2012. 托妮·莫里森《慈悲》的审美召唤[J].科技信息 (1) : 452–453.

张清芳, 2007. 用语言文字弹奏爵士乐——托妮·莫里森的长篇小说《爵士乐》赏析[J]. 域外视野 (8):120–123.

章汝雯, 2004.《最蓝的眼睛》中的话语结构[J]. 外国文学研究 (4): 62–67, 172.

张岩冰, 1998. 女权主义文论[M]. 济南: 山东教育出版社.

张友伦, 肖军, 张聪, 1999. 美国社会的悖论：民主、平等与性别、种族歧视

[M]. 北京: 中国社会科学出版社.

赵莉华, 2011. 空间政治：托妮·莫里森小说研究[M]. 成都: 四川大学出版社.

赵庆玲, 2008. 托妮·莫里森作品中的创伤情节——以《宠儿》和《天堂》为例[J]. 河南广播电视大学学报 (3): 45–46.

周春生, 1999. 悲剧精神与欧洲思想文化史论[M]. 上海: 上海人民出版社.

朱光潜, 2006. 悲剧心理学[M]. 合肥: 安徽教育出版社.

朱立元, 1999. 当代西方文艺理论[M]. 上海: 华东师范大学出版社.

朱荣杰, 2004. 伤痛与弥合：托妮·莫里森小说母爱主题的文化研究[M]. 开封: 河南大学出版社.

朱小琳, 2005. 乌托邦理想与《乐园》的哀思[J]. 北京第二外国语学院学报 (4):90–94.

朱新福, 2004. 托妮·莫里森的族裔文化语境[J].外国文学研究 (3): 54–60, 171.